THE SEVEN DAYS
OF CREATION

THE SEVEN DAYS
OF CREATION

Vladimir Maximov

1 9 7 5

ALFRED · A · KNOPF

New York

THIS IS A BORZOI BOOK
PUBLISHED BY ALFRED A. KNOPF, INC.

Library of Congress Cataloging in Publication Data

Maximov, Vladimir Emel'ianovich.
The seven days of creation.

Translation of Sem' dnei tvoreniia.
I. Title.
PZ4.M2354Se3   [PG3483.2.K8]   891.7′3′44   73-20781
ISBN 0-394-48522-X

Manufactured in the United States of America

First American Edition

CONTENTS

MONDAY

A Traveler in Search of Himself

I

Pyotr Vasilievich had been having a lot of weird, mixed-up dreams just lately, but this was simply preposterous.

The Lamsky brothers, famed for thievery throughout the Sviridovo settlement, were trundling a locomotive chimney past his windows in a baby carriage; they winked at him insolently, as if to say, "Come and join us." Before he could repel them with a yell of contempt, Sanka Bayev, a ne'er-do-well neighbor of his who'd been killed in the Finnish campaign, appeared in their place, carrying a loaf of rye bread under one arm and a half of Moskovskaya in his free hand. Gripping the bottle by the neck, Bayev turned on him a drunken leer which plainly said, "Shut your trap, you old fool."

Spluttering with indignation he made a dash for the window, but at that moment a choking, hammering pain high in his chest brought him to his senses. He reached out automatically toward the bedside table and fumbled for the Valadol tablet which was always placed there each night in readiness.

The minty chill in his mouth brought an illusion of relief, and his thoughts slid into their waking routine, circling as formlessly and aimlessly as rags in a muddy millpond.

On a dull March morning roughly twenty years before, Pyotr Vasilievich had given his wife a hurried and modest funeral—even for those hungry times—and come home to a life in which the hours, like the division of a clock face, differed in conventional significance, but not in color or content.

Lying there in bed he knew that at seven sharp he would get up and knock on the wooden partition which separated him from his daughter Antonina in the best room. There would, as usual, be no answer, but he could be sure that she had heard and had risen at once and soon would begin her usual morning chore, turning on the stove and concocting his Cossack breakfast of six fried eggs. Then he would enjoy a leisurely splash at the washstand, and slowly don his normal apparel: Chinese cotton trousers, woolen socks (feet mustn't get cold!), crepe-soled shoes, a button-over blouse, a cloth waistcoat from prewar times, and a Czech jacket bought by his daughter secondhand.

Pyotr Vasilievich would eat his eggs in an impressively meditative silence, and at eight precisely, still silent, he would arm himself with hat and stick at the door, and go out into what from force of habit he called "the settlement."

For the present, until it was time to begin, the old man stared vacantly through the window flooded with the light of a July dawn. Outside there used to be a small orchard, just a couple of dozen apple and cherry trees which it had been his whim to plant alternately—he had paid tribute in his time to a certain fashionable doctrine. Now, in its place, loomed the blank red wall of a large factory. So unconscionably huge was this wall he sometimes fancied that there was nothing but empty space behind it.

The factory sprouted new buildings every year, edging closer and closer to the frail little house, squeezing it toward the road, which was itself slyly broadening. Between these two enemies, the squat cottage built by his grandfather, in which Pyotr Vasilievich still occupied one of four rooms, struggled for its independence like a little buffer wedged between giants.

Everybody or nearly everybody in the town knew him, and though you couldn't say that he was loved—he'd done nothing to deserve that— he was certainly respected; as anything (for that matter) is respected, if its mere existence preserves some vestige of the past which others are too young to remember. As a monument, or an old fort, or a famous mountain is respected.

And so, as the stick which the whole town knew so well tapped along the asphalt, almost every tap was acknowledged by a bow or a greeting.

"Hallo, Vasilich!"

Tap-tap . . .

"Good day, Comrade Lashkov!"

Tap-tap . . .

"Nice to see you."

Tap-tap . . .

"How are you, Pyotr Vasilievich?"

Tap-tap . . .

"Your humble servant . . ."

Tap-tap-tap.

So it went, all day long, from eight in the morning until eight at night, with three intermissions: to scrutinize briefly the newspaper stands, to pop into the canteen, and then between four and five to take an essential but not too protracted rest in the town square. How does the saying go? He belonged to Uzlovsk and Uzlovsk belonged to him.

Like a lot of late-nineteenth-century provincial towns in Russia, Uzlovsk had sprung up round a big station, roughly halfway from Moscow to nowhere. So the station and its various departments—the main hall, the engine sheds, the subsidiary buildings—were the focus of local economic and spiritual life.

The nearby villages, Sychevki, Sviridovo, Dubovki, instinctively turned their hungry mouths toward the town, and it owed its growth to them. They supplied the "iron road" with labor and bread. As the railway grew, they had less and less bread to give, but the labor force got tougher all the time. Women, fattened on shop-bought food, zealously ensured that the supply of reinforcements would not dry up.

Peasants with a bit more sense and schooling than the rest, fighting their way up tooth and nail, built homes nearer to the station—imperceptibly, house by house. They drew town and country closer, until the villages merged into the town and Uzlovskaya station became Uzlovsk, one more urban center for the Russian Empire.

Pyotr Vasilievich had lived in Uzlovsk for more than seventy years, but if anyone had asked him what was the most important and interesting thing about it he would have been at a loss. It would have been like answering the same question about himself, for the town and he were one and indivisible.

When little Lashkov had blown in, a mere fledgling, from Sviridovo, the town had accepted him, given him a conductor's seat in third class, and since then town and man had watched each other's lives glide by.

Uzlovsk became a district center—and railwayman Lashkov's life was embellished by a signal mark of distinction, a head-conductor's pouch. The town acquired a grain elevator—and Lashkov's cottage dazzled all Sviridovo with a cheerful galvanized roof. A spoil heap across the river marked the first coal mine—and into the young head-conductor's house, there to stay for nearly forty years, came gentle, hardworking Maria, a miner's daughter from the settlement.

Then it all happened at once—armored trains in the civil war, lifeless locomotives along the line shortly afterwards, engine drivers condemned for the first time as enemies of the people, and then in the last war, the coffins stacked beside the engine sheds, just in case . . .

Pyotr Vasilievich examined the town and from the bits and pieces which swam into his memory tried to see it whole, and as it used to be.

But the feverish sprawl of featureless glass and concrete boxes in the spaces between the old villages had not put new life into Uzlovsk proper. Another town with other songs and other ways had triumphantly refashioned it.

Tap-tap, tap-tap, went the stick on the asphalt armor of the streets. And the town's heart, suffocating down below, wheezily responded.

"I'm here!" A poplar shoot, all ready to burst into leaf, straining toward the light through the asphalt.

"I'm here!" The damp sigh of unpaved earth around a hydrant.

"I'm here!" A pool, or rather a tiny pond, flashing like a fragment of glass, powdered with lime and cement.

Tap-tap, tap-tap, tap-tap.

But the answering voices were fainter and more hopeless every day.

Every trivial detail from the past filled them with quiet joy and helped them reaffirm their vitality: "We're still alive, see?"

"Your watch still going strong, then?" said one of them happily, seeing Pyotr Vasilievich wind his "Paul Bourier." "First-class movement, that. Prewar make, anybody can tell."

Another voice joined in: "Look at the dye-works, the dye-works is still standing! Won't ever wear out!"

The town kept it up. "Why, the shirt you're wearing is one of ours, Pyotr Vasilievich! The spotted one with a button-over collar. It'll wash and wear forever!"

"And the bakery's still where it was!" The old man's heart skipped. "In ovens like these, you can make loaves out of shit! We'll show the lot of them."

Tap-tap, tap-tap . . .

Pyotr Vasilievich slumped onto a bench, blissfully easing the weight off his feet. No getting away from it, he was over seventy.

The day was at its last gasp, ebbing in a purplish yellow mist over the ridges of outlying houses. The clatter and clang of the town still reached him now and then through the empty eye-sockets of half-built blocks. It struggled desperately to give an impression of power, but a note of strain could be heard in its last labored efforts.

Pyotr Vasilievich never deviated from his established round, and if it hadn't been for the crowd around the broken window of The Paladin, a fashionable grocery, the old man wouldn't have gone out of his way even this once. What had happened proved to be utterly uninteresting and unworthy of curiosity, and Pyotr Vasilievich was not a particularly curious person anyway, but as he passed he cast a sideways glance at the broken window. One second's contact in an electric circuit is sufficient to release a flash of all-revealing light; similarly, that one glance brought instantaneous enlightenment.

His whole world collapsed. It was as though his soul, after long and hopeless struggles to escape, had at last burst free of its bonds of constraint: there beyond the broken glass, in all its bogus beauty, stood a dummy ham, on a dummy dish, surrounded by dummy sausages.

The crowd stirred excitedly, but Pyotr Vasilievich was no longer part of it, no longer heard it, was remote from its hubbub. At that moment his whole consciousness was focused elsewhere, on his youth.

A bit of trouble started in those far-off times by the workmen at the depot had trapped him unexpectedly in the market square. Things were at their hottest. The first bursts from the garrison machine-gunners had wiped the last traces of life from the square and were systematically playing over the shop windows, when little Pyotr, sheltering under one of the abandoned carts, spotted an alluring prize ahead of him. No more than fifty yards or so away, in the shattered window of Turkov's grocery, a smoked ham, golden-brown where it had been sliced, tempted and enticed him. A real smoked ham! Pyotr crawled his way across the bullet-swept square.

That forgotten morning which now suddenly came back to him had echoed to the sound of stray gunfire; at least a thousand times he had been within an inch of his life but—wonders never cease—not one of the bullets had touched him. Ignoring it all, Pyotr had crawled on till he reached his goal, but when at last he squeezed though the jagged opening in the glass his hand met the rough surface of painted cardboard.

It was only then that a dread of dangers already defied was aroused in him, and little Pyotr burst into tears, or rather a howl of horror and outrage: "Brothers! We've been had!"

II

Pyotr Vasilievich was in a hurry to get home. It was a puzzle, and all the way back he could make no sense of it. How could this old memory disturb him so much? Not just disturb him but arouse vague presentiments, new hopes, as yet elusive but unmistakable, when his life had seemed to be over. At the same time, he could not shake off that feeling of mounting anxiety which accompanied all big changes. That such changes would not be long in coming he could no longer doubt.

After a moment's hesitation at the door, Pyotr Vasilievich turned the corner to his daughter's part of the house. At once he heard the familiar whirr of her machine. Antonina took in sewing to supplement his pension. Although it displeased him, he never said a word about it, not out of tact, but simply because he was habitually silent. Without stopping to knock, he pushed the door open with his stick.

"Are you all right, Antonina?"

It was so unexpected—her father hadn't visited her room for fifteen years or so, and limited his communications to a twice-daily knock on the wall. In her surprise Antonina didn't rise to receive this guest, didn't answer, didn't even look up, just pedaled away in a hysterical frenzy. But Pyotr Vasilievich saw how the seam rushed from under her hands and zigzagged crazily over the cloth and he realized what was going on inside her. He almost had to wrench her hands away from her work.

"Have you gone mad, Antonina?"

She glanced at him briefly and quickly lowered her eyes, barely whispering.

"No, Daddy. What d'you mean . . . ?"

His heart plunged sickeningly, the ceiling lurched toward him, his daughter's bedroom spun. Antonina was drunk, so drunk that it was a wonder she could manage to work at all. The chair under Pyotr Vasilievich creaked and groaned in all its joints.

"So that's it, my dear, that's how it is, my little daughter. Where d'you think this'll get you . . . ?

But no sooner had he begun than he realized with painful clarity that his words were pointless, meaningless. Would anything that he could say be of any use? He didn't know, and could only groan.

"Oh, Antonina, my little Antonina."

At first she listened in a daze, mechanically rolling her thimble between her palms, but as soon as he fell silent, maudlin alcoholic tears began to stream unsteadily down her small, unhealthily puffy features and gather on her sharp little chin.

"Daddy!"

She spoke in a slurred and jerky mumble.

"Daddy . . . I didn't really mean . . ."

To begin with, Pyotr Vasilievich had felt injured and, of course, self-righteously angry, but as he looked at the tipsy quiver of her slack lips, the pathetic wisps of hair straggling from her bun, those weak hands, which had never known hard work, still playing with the thimble, he was pierced not by pity, not by compassion—well, he'd no time for such fine feelings—but by an as yet unaccountable sense of guilt.

"It's started then," he thought bitterly. "For good or ill it's started, all right. Deep down I knew it would."

Antonina was the youngest of the family, and the only one of his six children who had stayed with him. The daughters had made rash and unhappy marriages in their hurry to leave home, the sons had cleared off any old where, one at a time, and one at a time had disappeared from the face of the earth. They had all disowned him and left, never to cross his threshold again. Somewhere or other, far away, his children had set up homes and families, brought children into the world, and they in turn had had children of their own, but none of them ever gave him a thought. He was curtly informed when one or another of them died, but he was not invited to the funeral. That was all.

When he received these laconic messages, Pyotr Vasilievich was duly saddened but not overwhelmed with grief. Even in these moments of instinctive pain, his pigheadedness was reinforced by the comforting thought that "if he'd listened to his father he'd have been all right." As though there was nothing, not even this, that a father's authority could not put right.

Pyotr Vasilievich always thought that he was right. Right every time, absolutely right. No power on earth could make him think otherwise. Perhaps it was his job that had instilled this certainty in him. Reigning supreme for days on end over local passenger trains, he had ended by taking an official tone even in his free time with his family. The most frequently used word in his vocabulary was "don't." Don't do this, don't do that. In fact, don't do anything. But his children got bigger, and with every day that passed their world got higher and wider than his "don'ts." Away they went, and he was left with the spiteful assurance that they would soon be back, cap in hand. But his children didn't come back. His children preferred to die somewhere far away from him.

They took his oldest son, Victor, straight from the shop floor—he was a template-maker at Dynamo—noted his initials in the records and wrote him off.

Pyotr Vasilievich didn't turn a hair.

The second son, Dmitri, collided with cruel fate on the Mannerheim Line.

Pyotr Vasilievich found no difficulty in swallowing.

His daughter Barbara died giving birth to her fourth child in nearby Uglegorsk.

Once more he had no time to spare for mourning.

An antitank weapon played a cruel joke on the youngest son, Yevgeni, at Königsberg.

His father managed a sigh.

Finally, Fedosya, whose husband had left her with three youngsters on her hands, went to a pauper's grave, and her children were shoved into different orphanages.

"Well, they got the life they chose."

And that was all he thought about it.

Maria, his wife, he loved dearly after his fashion, but he did not notice her fading wordlessly away at his side. She faded and went out quietly and gratefully, on a March night of drizzle and slush. Then, at last, beside his wife's surprisingly small and skinny body, Pyotr Vasilievich had a moment of searing pain, of dismay such as he had never hitherto experienced, and was suddenly so terrified by his loneliness that everything went black before his eyes. To stand back and take a look at himself was an agonizing pleasure, but Pyotr Vasilievich would not succumb to it. He hardened his heart, and fell silent. And in his black silence he had no eyes for his daughter, no ears for the living being on the other side of his wall, the eighteen-year-old girl who after her mother's funeral stayed behind to live out her days at his side, and for nearly twenty years now had looked after him, fed him, washed his clothes, emptied his chamber pots. If she was no better-looking than most, she was no worse either. Didn't she want a husband? Didn't she just! Perhaps she had a horror of children? Ten would be fine—all boys, please. Didn't she fancy a home of her own? She'd have made a paradise of it! Antonina had wanted everything a girl or woman is supposed to have at the proper time.

Pyotr Vasilievich suddenly cut short the babble of questions which had come to mind.

He rose heavily to his feet, went over to her, and plucked at her shoulder in a clumsy attempt to console her.

"Listen, Tonya . . . You mustn't . . . It'll all work out in the end . . . So you had a few drinks . . . Nobody's perfect . . . Only you ought to give up this dressmaking nonsense and do something worthwhile . . . I can get by somehow on my own . . . It's a real treat over there in the canteen nowadays . . . Eat as much as you like for a few coppers . . . And then there are laundries . . ."

But as soon as her father showed her a little affection she began to tremble all over and broke down completely. She stroked his wrist roughly, pressing her wet cheek against his hip.

"Da-a-addy," she murmured faintly, "I'll do anything . . . Anything you tell me . . . Only don't be angry with me . . ." ("Angry," she said!) "I'll go anywhere you like . . . Only I'm better off here with you . . . If I've done something to upset you . . . You tell me . . . I'll do anything . . ."

She gradually calmed down, her breathing became quiet and even, her tears dried, soon she was dozing almost contentedly against his arm.

Pyotr Vasilievich raised his daughter carefully, led her to her bed, and put her down, limp and unresisting. Antonina fell asleep almost as soon as her head touched the pillow; he stood there holding her shoes, and, just as he remembered doing in her childhood, anxiously watched his now almost forty-year-old child pouting with each breath in her sleep. Come to think of it, wasn't she still as innocent as ever, lost in the same old childish dreams? One year or a hundred years is all the same to children.

Pyotr Vasilievich put her shoes down by the bed, took care not to bump into anything as he went, and left the room, quietly closing the door behind him.

III

Once again all hell was let loose in his dreams. Granny Natalya, a sick and rough-tongued old woman, offered him a handful of dried cherries and mumbled in his ear in a toothless slur.

"Have shome of these, Petyushka, don't be shnooty . . ."

Next comes Yegorkin, the traffic manager, long since dead, banging his fist on the table and cursing him up hill and down dale.

"Asking for a tribunal you are, Lashkov? I shan't forget it in a hurry!"

Pyotr Vasilievich began to protest loudly—What have I done, then?—but suddenly he remembered and fell silent. After Yegorkin, his own wedding floated up from oblivion, with his father-in-law Ilya Parfenich Makhotkin, a coal miner, stinking drunk, sidling up to kiss him and singing in a hoarse bellow:

"Rum tum tum tum toodle-oo,
I've a little favor to ask you:
Don't you bite and don't you bark
While I tell you kindly hark . . ."

Then a train was carrying him away through the snows in the famine years, and in the ghostly light of a smoky oil-lamp somebody was quietly crooning from the lower bunk:

"Good-bye, Marusya, sweetheart mine,
My little son, good-bye.
Never, nevermore I'll see you.
Here with shattered skull I lie."

After that he was standing on the rear platform barring the way, while crowds of faces pressed in on him from every side, faces both familiar and unfamiliar.

"Get back! Get back!" screamed Pyotr Vasilievich, but the faces pressed in closer and closer at him speechlessly.

His awakening was slow and unpleasant. Blurred nightmare visions still spun deliriously in the room, though daylight and anxious tasks ahead had already penetrated his consciousness. That very day he must wangle a job for his daughter, one in which she could do something useful, but would not feel her ties with him to be threatened.

The old man was about to reach out and knock as usual, but snatched his hand away as if the wall were red-hot, and jeered at himself.

"Losing your memory, you silly old devil! Can't manage without a servant."

The sun had barely touched the sparse outer leaves of the apple tree at his window, which were still shivering from the damp night. But the tree looked a lot more durable in its everlasting wretchedness than did the blank double wall of the factory attacking it from behind.

Over the years, Pyotr Vasilievich had got used to the furniture in his home, where things had never existed independently of one another, but had merged into one single image, and he felt a bit lost now that for some reason each object had begun speaking to him in a language of its own.

Pyotr Vasilievich examined the room, recognizing and yet not recognizing it. Something that he couldn't put his finger on had changed. He seemed to be seeing the cupboard with the dusty gramophone on top of it for the first time. Of course the cupboard and the gramophone had caught his eye countless times in the past but he had never before taken notice of them, and of each in turn. Then there was the wall-clock with the broken hand. The clock and the broken hand had been an eyesore to him for a good forty years, yet only now did the thought enter his head:

"Hm, the hand's broken off . . ."

Even in the creaking of his own bed he had never, until today, detected different tunes and timbres. If you sat down on it, it groaned aloud; if you lay down, it twanged musically; if you turned over on your side, it responded in a cracked treble.

No, the world had undoubtedly turned to Pyotr Vasilievich a face he had never seen before, shown itself in a new perspective.

He heard a rustling on the other side of the wall, then an imploring and apologetic voice . . .

"Daddy, what's the matter?"

"Nothing, my dear."

"I thought perhaps you were feeling poorly."

"Stop worrying about nothing and go to sleep."

"It's time for you to get up Daddy . . . I'm coming . . ."

"I'll pop down to the canteen, Antonina. Go to sleep."

He heard a piteous sob.

"I won't do it anymore, Daddy, I swear to God I won't . . ."

"Won't what?"

On the other side of the wall his daughter started whimpering and sniffling like a child.

"Drink . . . I won't drink . . ."

"You don't think that's bothering me, do you? I just want you to get some sleep . . . It's different for old folks like me . . . The devil won't let old men sleep, but why should you jump out of bed at this unearthly hour? Sleep in a little . . ."

Antonina's voice trembled with pain and indignation.

"I don't want . . . to sleep."

And Pyotr Vasilievich felt that if he rebuffed his daughter, even out of the best intentions in the world, he might never get her back again.

"I'm coming . . . I'll have a wash . . ."

Listening to her bustling about in the next room, he felt more sadly certain than ever that her eternal vigil at his side had become a habit and a need for her, and that there was nothing he could do to alter this.

Antonina didn't walk around the table that morning, she flew, anticipating her father's every wish, and her lightheartedness and satisfaction showed in everything she did.

So that by the time Pyotr Vasilievich left the house he had been waited upon beyond all reason, and felt, if the truth be known, that embarrassment, or perhaps malaise is the word, which usually goes with birthdays.

From a nearby field which welled up at the edge of the settlement and flowed along both sides of the road there came a scent of buckwheat in flower. Pyotr Vasilievich suddenly felt blissfully at peace, and wanted desperately to go in that direction—into that scent, into those long-forgotten boundless spaces, and without further thought he turned his back on the town for the first time in years.

An indelibly beaten track led him through a field which surrounded the nearby spoil heaps, and he walked and walked, abandoning himself to its twists and turns. Scenes from the past, confused fragments, hovered around him. He shook off those which seemed trivial and silly, and peered at the rest, trying to remember the details. But before he could bring them clearly into focus they dissolved in his memory and gave way to something new.

One thing he, for some reason, remembered vividly was a morning of searching sunshine, and Maria coming through it from the door to the table holding a plate full of thickly salted cucumbers. It was so real, so astonishingly vivid in Pyotr Vasilievich's mind, that from a distance of forty years he thought he could make out every seed and every grain of salt on it . . .

A brass band struck up somewhere back in town, and suddenly its mournful tune floated out on the almost palpable noonday silence to fill the whole neighborhood. The road to the cemetery ran through Sviridovo, and normally yet another funeral would not have attracted Pyotr Vasilievich's attention. But now that he lived a life of anticipation the music seemed to be sounding an alert, and he moved toward the band, growing more confident with every step that his expectations would not be disappointed.

From the uniforms worn by most of the procession he concluded unhesitatingly that it was a railwayman's funeral. When they drew level with him a photograph was carried past and the pallid, puffy face of Foma Leskov grinned at him quizzically.

"Still plodding along, eh, pal? I've come in first again!"

Several of the mourners bowed to Pyotr Vasilievich and quickly averted their eyes. His relations with the deceased were an old story, firmly embedded in the minds of the local railwaymen, who regarded the two of them as mortal enemies, though it was doubtful whether anybody really knew when and how their enmity had begun.

Watching the funeral procession go by, Pyotr Vasilievich was still unrepentant, but deep inside he felt a little annoyed with himself.

"Could have eased up a bit in your old age. Could have made peace with him and not waited to see him buried."

Tap-tap-tap . . .

Even the tapping of his stick held anger and regret. Snowflakes fluttered before his eyes: He was back in the first autumn of the war.

.   .   .

The head of traffic control, Yegorkin, crammed his bulk awkwardly behind the desk, making it look like dollhouse furniture, and spoke without looking at Lashkov.

"Here it is then, Lashkov . . . How shall I put it . . . ?"

With his subordinates Yegorkin invariably made his point with the help of foul language, so Pyotr Vasilievich knew from the tone of his opening remarks that he was in dead earnest.

"In short, the situation is such that Uzlovsk may have to be abandoned . . . I hope you understand that I'm speaking as one party member to another . . . In strictest secrecy . . ."

"I understand, Vaniamin Fyodorovich."

"We've had a bit of a conference here . . . You've proved yourself reliable . . . and you're an old party member . . . And, well, we know you . . . you will go with the records . . . to Penza for the time being, then we'll see . . ."

His face turned crimson, and his little eyes under their whitish brows fidgeted over the desk.

"Maybe," he said, "maybe we'll scrape through. Pick yourself a mate you can trust. Take any passenger carriage you please. You'll get all you want from Shpak, and sign for it . . . Hitch yourself to a string of engines, you'll have a quieter time of it with the drivers . . . Right, so long . . . best of luck."

Picking a mate was no problem. Pyotr Vasilievich knew without considering that he would take Foma Leskov. You couldn't imagine a better traveling companion for a journey over lines choked with special trains. At any hour and in any weather Foma could get hold of anything you cared to mention, not excluding a locomotive—in pieces, of course, for reassembly.

The string of engines, with two sleepers attached, stopping for days on end at almost every halt, rolled slowly eastward in the general swollen stream of traffic. Winter overtook them while they were still in Morshansk, tucked the first crisp snow around them, and hurried on after the trains ahead.

Leskov stole things right and left: rustled up extra rations and fuel, scorned nothing that was lying around loose, sold this and swapped that, and as a result their larder was fuller than it should have been in wartime and never looked any worse than usual. True, his mate's resourcefulness, which far exceeded their modest needs, gave Pyotr Vasilievich some qualms—he muttered and sulked occasionally, but he didn't speak up. Not until Foma started dropping hints about passengers—you could simply rake in the money from refugees, he said. Here Lashkov peremptorily refused.

"All or none. And since you can't take them all, it's nobody."

Foma knew his boss's character, and didn't try to argue.

"Up to you, Vasilich, you know best."

But the look of the man as he said it made it clear that he disapproved and that given the slightest opportunity would do things his own way.

In Rtishchev they got well and truly stuck. Foma performed his dizzy dance around traffic controllers and shunters, and Pyotr Vasilievich himself marked time before the desks of the authorities, trying to prove the almost strategic importance of his freight. They were shifted from track to track, but never got beyond the first signal.

One day, coming back from yet another campaign around the offices, right outside his carriage Pyotr Vasilievich met a short, good-looking young female with a provision sack over her shoulder, in full uniform, but without shoulder flashes or a star on her cap. She waddled up close to him and with a nod at the carriage rather rudely demanded:

"You in charge of this outfit, then?"

Neither her voice, hoarse with drink, nor her manner of speaking, nor her ducklike walk, which had a sort of sexy carelessness about it, went with her fragile face, which had not yet lost its childish bloom, or with her adolescent gawkiness. However much she strove to look grown-up and worldly-wise, however much she strained her larynx deliberately coarsening her speech, her whole appearance excited nothing but an aching pity.

"Bloody, bloody, bloody war," thought Pyotr Vasilievich.

To forestall her pleas he answered as harshly as he could:

"What about it?"

"I can see why your assistant's afraid of you," she said with a hoarse laugh. "He warned me—just try barging in when my boss gets back, he says . . . Only I don't scare easy . . . I've seen all sorts . . . Don't be frightened. I don't weigh much. I shan't be much of a burden . . ."

There was a hint of malice in her grin.

"There's no knowing when we'll get away from here . . . It may be an hour and it may be a month . . ."

"We'll be off at eighteen hundred hours . . . No need to stare like that. I've got firsthand information."

She grinned again, contemptuously this time.

"I pay in kind, old man. This war will wipe the slate clean."

He resisted as hard as he could.

"I'm carrying secret documents. I'm in no position to take unauthorized persons."

The wretched girl came closer and only then did Pyotr Vasilievich notice how her legs creaked at every step. Suddenly he understood it all— the premature hoarseness that seemed so unnatural, the deliberate roughness, that uncertain grin; swallowing the painful lump in his throat, he gasped out:

"Come on . . . I'll find a place for you."

In the compartment she lavished her gifts of rationed food on her hosts, and poured something into mugs from a flask.

"Let's get it straight: my name's Valentina. My surname needn't concern you . . . Now let's follow the good old custom and drink to our meeting . . ."

She tossed it back, and said in explanation:

"I learnt that at the front—I never drank anything stronger than lemonade before the war . . . I've got my final discharge, but there's nowhere for me to go . . . I'm from Voronezh myself and the Germans are there . . . I think I'll go to Siberia . . . Heard a lot about it in books, seen it at the movies . . . I dreamt of being a geologist. But now . . ."

Her round eyes which still looked childish went blank for a moment.

". . . let's forget our troubles. Shall we have another?"

Foma winked at his boss, rushed off to the next compartment and reappeared with a bottle of homemade liquor that he'd saved just in case. While he was pouring it out he pressed against her, trying to make it look accidental, and his free hand, quivering with desire, slid repeatedly over her back.

After the third drink Valentina brusquely pushed Leskov away, telling him with a provocative look in Pyotr Vasilievich's direction:

"You don't know the rules, mate: commanding officer first, and you get what's left."

Pyotr Vasilievich was taken aback, but Leskov, who had seen it all in his time, just let out a whistle and promptly made for the door. "Leftovers will do for poor little me."

"What about you then, commander?"

She was going to pieces fast.

"Or maybe you've got an overdose of principles, eh?"

It wasn't just malice now. She was choking with rage.

"I've seen your sort, men of principle. You know how many? They'd block the road from here to Moscow, with some to spare. Crafty, aren't you! Or maybe you don't want me? Say so, then—that pet dog of yours is sitting up and begging."

Sure enough, Foma had suddenly materialized in the compartment and hastened to his boss's rescue.

"Come on, Valentina, come on . . . Go to bed and you won't remember a thing about it . . . Pyotr Vasilievich has got enough to worry about without you . . . Documents all over the place, see . . . ?"

She resisted a while longer and kept trying to say something, but Leskov grasped her expertly round the waist and pulled her along the corridor to the other end of the carriage, where his lascivious whispers reduced her to silence.

With a sickening pang, Pyotr Vasilievich suddenly pictured one of his own daughters in Valentina's place.

"God, oh God—what does it all mean?"

Foma tried to keep out of his sight. He would dart past with a silent nod on his way to the compartment which he had chosen for his fun and games. Voices would soon be heard from it, sometimes rising almost to a shout, sometimes sinking to an intermittent whisper, until at last they died down altogether until the next morning.

As soon as Foma got bored with Valentina he started carrying her pickaback to the engine drivers in their "cattle truck." They, in turn, soon sent her back. So she was passed round, like a trophy held jointly by neighboring units.

Pyotr Vasilievich was outraged, but he put up with it because he realized that if he turned the girl out there and then, things would be still worse for her.

So when he looked out onto the rear platform one morning and no longer saw the engines next to his carriages he gave a sigh of relief.

"You can't save them all. With any luck she'll survive."

They were chased off to a remote halt out in the wilds, where there were no houses, indeed, no buildings of any sort except the station—a converted carriage without wheels. Smoke from the surrounding villages rose from deep drifts of snow so clean that they had a bluish sparkle, and the landscape might even have looked peaceful but for the black windwheels, like solitary crows frost-bound since autumn on the slopes.

Pyotr Vasilievich tugged at the rear door and it dragged open with a screech. He choked on a blast of stinging January air.

The station-hand on duty hurried over to the carriage.

"You the Uzlovsk lot?"

"What is it now? Don't tell me we're going to be held up?"

The station-hand briefed him as he came up.

"What have you fellows been up to in Rtishchev? Nasty business. Went off with a war cripple's artificial limbs. Ought to be ashamed . . . Got orders to forward 'em to address shown by first transport through."

By now Leskov was standing behind his boss, shivering and laughing uneasily.

"She left them behind herself, the whore," he said.

He dodged under Pyotr Vasilievich's arm like a mouse and lowered the two artificial legs with their felt boots straight onto the station-hand's shoulder.

"What the hell d'you think we want 'em for? Couldn't stoke up with 'em, that's for sure."

He turned towards his boss with a shifty glance. "Can't have any fun anymore!"

The station-hand, a haggard little old man wearing a threadbare great-coat on top of a winterwarmer, looked the pair of them up and down in amazement, his eyes watering from the cold. He started to say something, thought better of it, spat angrily instead, and went back to where he'd come from.

For a long time afterwards Pyotr Vasilievich had visions of that small black figure against the white snow, with two felt-booted artificial legs over one shoulder.

Slamming the door he turned on Leskov, and his face must have betrayed his feelings. Leskov went white and retreated into the carriage.

"Vasilich," he said with a catch in his voice. "You saw for yourself. She was willing . . . Nobody forced her . . . Vasilich!"

But nothing could stop the blow already aimed at him. Foma's boss crashed his fist down on his head in full fury. Never before nor after did Pyotr Vasilievich experience such desire to smash, crush, annihilate a living being. Red blots swam before his eyes, and he went on hitting, blow after blow.

"Scum, scum," were the only words he could utter.

They had a lot more traveling to do together on the Ural and Siberian Lines, and they served in the same train crew later on, but they never reminded each other of the morning they'd spent at the snowbound halt in the back of beyond.

The melody floated away over in the cemetery treetops, and Pyotr Vasilievich made an anxious mental note, as he turned for home.

"Ought to drop in someday soon, offer my sympathy. Chalked up a few miles together, we did . . . Counts for something. Yes, I ought to . . ."

IV

Pyotr Vasilievich had been in the Leskov house three or four times at most, all of them before the war. What's more, he could remember only one of them—the christening of Nikolai, their firstborn, and that simply because he had stood godfather. The train guard had lived by the old bakery, in a house erected by his grandfather, a foreman on the "iron way," with free bricks and voluntary offerings from his toiling flock; that no doubt was why it had remained standing beyond its allotted span without requiring any repairs worth mentioning.

The door was opened to Pyotr Vasilievich by a neat diminutive old woman.

"Hallo, come in . . . It's just begun," she said, with the briefest of glances at him, and vanished completely.

His eyes were still trying to adjust to the all-embracing gloom but in the next room, by the feeble light which filtered through cracks in the shutters, he could see bareheaded listeners, and a level self-confident voice came through to him.

"And there was a City. For thousands of years it stood amidst lakes and gardens, rejoicing the eyes and hearts of its inhabitants. In this City men were born praising the name of the Lord and with His name on their lips went out of the world. Here Brotherly Love and Goodness created the Law, and people did not know the meaning of crime. Every man tilled his own field and pastured his cattle, but when any had need of help, each and every one was ready to share all that he had. The City was governed by the wisest and most esteemed of its citizens . . ."

The voice seemed remarkably familiar to Pyotr Vasilievich, but though he racked his brains he could not remember the face that went with it.

"And there came a certain Some-one. And he began to trouble men's minds with foolish talk about atonement for the sake of the Kingdom to come. And the feeble in spirit believed. The feeble in spirit began to torture themselves and their children. And the word of the Stranger turned into fact and like a plague was passed from one to another. Pain became the highest criterion of human existence. And the more terrible the wounds a man inflicted on himself, the greater the respect he aroused in those about him. 'Let us cleanse ourselves,' they urged, ill-treating their own children. 'Let us cleanse ourselves,' they repeated again and again, destroying their dwelling places and the monuments to the City's former glory. Blood stained the city streets and reservoirs."

Pyotr Vasilievich was now a little more at home in the uncertain twilight. His eyes glided over the heads to the source of the voice, and the glitter of gold-framed spectacles in a shaft of light from the window enabled him to recognize a former greaser in the wagon-repair shed with the strange name of Gupak. All sorts of things had been said about him in the past. Listening to his level, unhesitating speech, Pyotr Vasilievich felt no more than a twinge of regret.

"Pity you missed your dose of lead when it was your time to go, Your Reverence."

"And peace departed from their dead hearts. They hungered and thirsted after universal pain. 'Let us exult our brothers,' cried those who were bleeding to death. 'Let us graciously bestow our truth upon them.' And only the wise remained firm in the midst of this madness. They had a means of saving the City, of uprooting the source of its misfortune —the Stranger. But this meant causing the citizens an immeasurably greater pain—that of being awakened to the ruin around them. And then the gaze of the wise men turned to Sinai. There in the midst of the sandy desert a direct descendant of the City's founder, himself a Prophet and a Luminary, was spending the remainder of his life in prayer and meditation. And the wise men came to him and told him everything. And the Prophet heard them out and said:

" 'This was ordained. Madness threatens the whole earth. The City was required to be an example, a warning sign to other cities of things to come. For the generation of the living there is no salvation. They are injured not in body but in soul and the soul cannot be made whole again. Therefore it is said unto you in the Book of Eternity that you should lead forth your children from the City. Let them return to the ancestral home healed in spirit and in body.' Thus said the Prophet."

Gupak's voice suddenly soared to its top note and he shouted his harsh command:

"Lead forth your children then, brethren! Let no one cripple their souls. Rescue your children from schools that are an abomination in the sight of God! Let no child's foot cross the threshold of their pagan temples! Lead forth the children, brethren! Save souls as yet untainted by corruption!"

The last phrase was pronounced in an imploring whisper and the room, in a surge of excitement, responded as one to his appeal.

"Amen!"

"He seeth in the darkness."

"Amen!"

"Take them to the villages, away from this pestilence . . ."

As soon as Pyotr Vasilievich stirred from his place, the same old woman bobbed up out of nowhere to bar his way.

"You leaving already, brother?" she whispered in surprise. "We haven't heard about the second coming yet."

"I'm looking for the Leskovs."

Even in the semidarkness he could see the tiny creature's face turn still whiter.

"The Leskovs haven't lived here for a long time."

"Where do they live, then?"

"Not sure . . . Ryazan Street. I think . . . Number Five, I seem to remember . . ."

The old woman pushed him gently towards the door and when he found himself at last in the hallway she solemnly warned him:

"We do have permission. We're registered."

And slammed the door behind him.

. . .

Year by year, and stone by stone, Pyotr Vasilievich had slowly and doggedly constructed a world of his own. And till now he had supposed that his work was complete. In his world, law and order reigned. Everything was regulated with the utmost precision. Life had two compartments labeled "Yes" and "No." "Yes" always somehow coincided with himself and his notion of things. "No" included "them" and everything that contradicted him. He carried this world within himself like a monolith; it could not be destroyed nor even shaken. Then all at once a bolt from the blue. Two or three trivial events, two or three chance meetings, and the world he had cherished with such loving care began to crumble, fall apart, disintegrate before his very eyes. It was clear that while his stick was tapping along from morning to night through the same familiar streets, a life of which he was totally ignorant, which could not and would not fit neatly into any subjective schemes or categories, was going on behind the walls of the houses. He crossed one threshold, and at once his own daughter showed him a side of herself that was utterly incomprehensible; he crossed another and found a greaser, whom he remembered only on account of his outlandish surname, numbered amongst the prophets. What awaited him beyond the third?

He had to ring several times. He could hear a rustling in the apartment, hasty whispers, feverish scurrying, until at last the lock clicked and the door opened to the length of its chain.

"Who d'you want?"

The next moment, however, the door was flung wide open.

"Good day, Pyotr Vasilievich!"

Nastasya Leskov, old and thick but still in good health, with a hard face that showed the strain of constant anxiety, bowed almost double to her unexpected guest.

"I'm glad you've found the way. Fomushka mentioned you before he died."

She gave a practiced sob and touched her dry eyes with the corner of a dark handkerchief.

" 'Forgotten me, Vasilich has,' he said, 'forgotten me altogether.' He died with no ill feelings for anybody. He forgave everyone . . ."

Here Nastasya sadly pursed her lips, obviously trying to indicate how much she knew of their old secret.

"He forgave everything. Come in, come in, please, you're very welcome . . . Kolya, it's your godfather! . . . My son's come home as well, you see . . ."

Her overeager show of hospitality was not altogether convincing. As though maneuvering a big fish with a net, she steered him with outspread arms into the "best room," obviously afraid that he might go through the wrong door.

"This way, Pyotr Vasilievich, this way. Sit down. Make yourself at home. I'll be back in a flash . . . Kolya, are you asleep or something? Your godfather's come!"

She disappeared into the adjoining room. Next came the sound of a muffled voice, a few sobs from the woman, and the voice again, clearer this time. Pyotr Vasilievich's godson appeared in the doorway, his mother more or less forcing him into the room.

He was a sullen, shaven-headed bulk of a man, getting on for forty, dressed in a corduroy suit and box-calf boots.

Nastasya peeped out from behind him, eyeing Pyotr Vasilievich with obsequious anxiety.

"Look what a strapping fellow he's grown up to be!"

And, turning to her son: "I can see you don't even remember your godfather . . . You just sit for a little and I'll bring you something to eat . . ."

Nastasya hurried off to the kitchen, glancing back ingratiatingly as she went; as soon as she had vanished, Nikolai put it to his godfather straight.

"Let's not kid each other. I'm living in town illegally. Been loose just a month. Got two fresh black marks already. Practically back inside, in fact . . . If Mom wants to throw caviar at you it's not because I want her to. I've got no favors to ask in that quarter." He nodded upwards. "Received in full, plus a bonus."

His hard, wind-chapped lips moved in a savage grin.

"Now I'm going to pay them back with interest."

Pyotr Vasilievich was beginning to like his godson.

"How long were you in for?"

"Five."

"What for?"

"Punched one of the bosses in the snout."

"Was he asking for it?"

"He asked for it, all right."

"Five's a bit much, all the same."

"Oh, I don't know—he's still the chemist's best customer."

"Drunk, were you?"

"No, sober. Drunk, I'd have murdered him."

"What can you do?"

"Anything. I'm a skilled man."

"Would you go to the depot?"

"That's where I was arrested."

"Would you go, I said?"

"They wouldn't have me."

"That's my problem."

"I've got two bad marks. They won't give me a residence permit."

"No need for you to think about that, either."

The bright eyes, so like his father's, which stared unblinkingly at Pyotr Vasilievich, held no hint of humor or self-pity.

"Look," he said, "it's nothing to you—you can talk and be on your way, but I'm on the rack. My next breath may be my last. Don't confuse me. Let's have a drink and call it a day, then we go our separate ways."

Pyotr Vasilievich had an answer ready for his godson—he was never at a loss for words—but at that moment Nastasya turned up.

"Don't think badly of us, dear Pyotr Vasilievich . . . It's what God has given us . . . the best I could do in a hurry."

Deftly she laid the table, with a speed surprising for her age.

"Let's drink to the memory of God's servant Foma. May he rest in peace!"

The magic tablecloth covered itself while they watched.

"Here you are, Pyotr Vasilievich, try the tomatoes, I pickled them myself . . . A bit of fish as well . . . Some sausage . . . Pour the drinks, Kolya."

Pyotr Vasilievich rarely drank, he disliked drunkenness in all its forms, and at any other time he would have refused outright. But faced with his godson's watchful eye and Nastasya's tiresome wheedling, he consented.

"Maybe just one . . . Let's drink to his memory . . ."

His hostess was keeping up her singsong for his benefit.

"I'm in my sixties, but I remember your christening as if it were today, Kolya, dear. Pyotr Vasilievich was still quite young, but he was already high up . . . Wasn't too proud though . . . Eat, Pyotr Vasilievich, eat . . . What's ours is yours, as they say . . . Now he's come back to me . . ."

She gave another dry sob and dabbed the bridge of her nose with her handkerchief.

"It can happen to anybody . . . he was only young . . . but he got his marching orders . . . Dragged off somewhere, away from his old mother. I don't call that right. You're a party person, Pyotr Vasilievich—I ask you, Is it right! . . . When poor Foma was dying . . . he kept remembering everything . . ."

Nikolai frowned and pulled her up short.

"That's enough, Mother. You should be ashamed of yourself. How could he remember anybody when he was lying there unconscious for three months . . . Let's try and behave . . ."

He knocked back his drink and planted the bottle firmly in the middle of the table.

"Right then . . . that's it . . . never overdo a good thing."

Pyotr Vasilievich made another mental note of approval, and rose to go.

"Thank you for your hospitality," he said to Nastasya, and, before she could start dissuading him, he turned to the younger Leskov.

"Fetch me whatever you've got there . . . I'll go and knock on a door or two."

His godson sprang up and dashed into the next room, while Nastasya fixed her guest with frightened, worshipful eyes; she moved her pinched lips soundlessly, trying to decide whether there was a catch in it.

Nikolai flew into the room, brushed aside the crockery, and laid out all his "credentials" for the guest to see.

"Here you are—passport, certificate, references, doctor's note for my mother . . ."

New hope had transformed him. The wolfish wariness in his eyes had melted, the jaw which had appeared set once and for all had relaxed, his movements, so slow and deliberate a minute ago, were now light and carefree—all of which made his resemblance to his father quite striking.

"All up to date . . . including a travel warrant to Uzlovsk."

Pyotr Vasilievich gathered the documents from the table and thrust them into his pocket without a glance.

"Look me up in a day or two . . . All the best."

In its first two revelations, life had done no more than surprise him with an unexpected turn of events, but once past and through the third threshold it was making demands on him, and he was in a hurry.

"I'll be off . . . Maybe I can catch somebody right now."

Nastasya silently escorted him into the corridor, handed him his stick, opened the door, and suddenly, without a trace of ill feeling or reproach, declared point-blank:

"It was after that business that Foma started coughing."

With this load on his mind Pyotr Vasilievich stepped out into the street.

V

Life in the Town Council offices was tried and true. The formula to the rhythm was: start at A and finish at B.

Anything that overstepped these bounds was considered inadmissible, and so when Pyotr Vasilievich asked the secretary whether Vorobushkin was seeing people, her painted eyes swept over him in distaste and she answered as if she were dispensing charity: "Konstantin Vasilievich is busy."

Unhurriedly the old man arranged his massive body on the chair in front of her. Her face was a victory for cosmetics over nature; looking her straight in the eye, he spoke politely but bluntly:

"First Commandment: Offer older people a seat. Second Commandment: Give a coherent answer when you're asked something. Third Commandment: If you sleep with the boss, don't make it so obvious, because bosses come and go. Now go and tell Kostya that old man Lashkov is here to see him."

After a moment's thought he added, "On business."

Next moment she had gone. She vanished through the leather-padded door, and was back again instantly, dazzling him with an obsequious, lacquered smile.

"Konstantin Vasilievich says, 'Please come in.' "

As he went past her into the office he noticed the carefully powdered wrinkles round her eyes, the telltale coarseness of the skin under its layer of cream, the chignon in her thinning hair, and thought, "She's no younger than my Antonina, and more of a fright, but who'd have thought it, somebody fancies her!"

His host was already hurrying to meet him, oozing cordiality.

"Pyotr Vasilievich! What brings you here? So long since I saw or heard of you. I began to think you were . . ."

The old man mischievously finished it for him.

"Dead."

"Pyotr Vasilievich . . . what a thing to say . . ."

His stuttering confusion made it plain that this was the very word he had bitten back.

"No. I thought, 'Maybe he's been taken ill.' I even made inquiries."

It wasn't hard for Pyotr Vasilievich to see through this either: he isn't lying, he made inquiries all right, only he wanted to know whether I was alive, not whether I was well.

"Sit down, my dear fellow . . . Some tea?"

The secretary fussed with the glasses. There was a moment's awkwardness, as there always is between people bound together by some past episode that has left one of them indebted to the other. While it lasted, Pyotr Vasilievich inspected Vorobushkin, finding him scarcely changed since their last meeting, except perhaps for a little extra fat.

It was just like that other day in '39. He sat face to face with a stocky, thickset man who looked at him from under a low forehead with the bright fixed eyes of a frozen fish. Only on that occasion they had held a look of unwavering entreaty. And they had faced each other in the reverse position: the young engine driver Vorobushkin in the dock, and Pyotr Vasilievich at the expert witnesses' desk during a railway tribunal. The outcome of the foot-plate man's trial depended on him.

Vorobushkin was on trial for malicious damage. Nobody remembers just what that meant in those days!

For no apparent reason, engines had started leaving the tracks at a bend on the Petushki-Roshcha run. The lucky survivors were put in jail, and replaced by young volunteer shock workers, but the crashes went on. At this point a commission of inquiry was set up, and Pyotr Vasilievich, among others, was on it.

They inspected the scene of the accidents, and got nowhere. The rails, buckled by enormous force and twisted under pressure into spirals, gave no clue as to what had happened. Though the commission's meetings dragged on till dawn, they still couldn't find anything like a plausible explanation.

The representative of the security branch, a towheaded boy with two pips on his tabs, called them in one by one and almost wept as he begged them to come to a verdict.

"Stop dragging it out! It's clear enough—the enemy is at work. Do you want to come to grief yourselves, and drag me down with you? Why all this talk about who's to blame or not to blame? Are engines going over the embankment? Yes. One after another? Yes. So how the hell can there be anything accidental about it! It's systematic. Systematic wrecking. And here we are playing at being objective."

Pyotr Vasilievich tried to argue with him:

"Yes, but we must get to the bottom of it, and then it'll be easier to strike back at the enemy. You don't really suppose the drivers get themselves killed deliberately?"

No sooner had he said it than he was sorry. The lieutenant's mouth, with its faint fringe of down, quivered indignantly.

"While we're here playing at Sherlock Holmes the enemy is destroying our transport. You've fooled around long enough. Finish your investigation or you'll hear from me. Damned liberal objectivists—to hell with the lot of you . . ."

The new-fledged experts were in a quandary, but they didn't give in. Railwaymen like themselves were losing their lives. There was no knowing how long it would have gone on or where it would have ended if Pyotr Vasilievich, after examining yet another engine, hadn't had a bright idea and crawled under the truck attached to the tender.

There he solved the mystery of all the crashes. One of the traction cables was too short, and uneven pressure on the brake-shoes at the turn was forcing the rails apart. And so the whole train began to describe figures of eight on the sleepers and plunged down the embankment.

Pyotr Vasilievich explained his deductions to the tribunal with a brevity and lucidity that left nothing more to be said; the prosecutor could only shake his head, and when he sat down he caught Vorobushkin gazing at him in tearful gratitude. After the acquittal Lashkov was shaken by the hand and thanked on his way out of the courtroom, but he was in a daze and took nothing in. His youngest son, Yevgeni, had left him the night before. Gone away without even leaving a note. At home, watched over by the ten-year-old Antonina, Maria lay prostrate, unable to speak or even cry.

Later on, Vorobushkin rose in the world, and took part himself in many such commissions, but—who can understand men's hearts?—his expert reports were, without exception, harsh, peremptory, and damning.

Now here he was again, face to face with a somewhat heavier Vorobushkin, who had acquired a markedly authoritative manner, who passed him tea and biscuits and said:

"Nice of you to look in."

He pressed his buzzer, and the secretary flew in, flushed with readiness for anything.

"Anna—" He checked himself and began again. "Anna Ivanovna, don't put any calls through. I'm in urgent conference. Got it?"

She did, and vanished, and he addressed himself to his guest again.

"Is there some little thing I can do for you, Pyotr Vasilievich? The Town Council will always be glad to oblige somebody like you. Don't hesitate . . ."

Pyotr Vasilievich didn't like pestering busy people, especially if it was to ask a favor. But in Nikolai's case, as he saw it, justice had been flouted, and so he saw no harm in waiving his usual rule. The old man stated his request as briefly and forcefully as he could. Vorobushkin listened, nodding sympathetically and even putting in an occasional "yes," but as soon as he realized who was under discussion he flushed with anger, jumped up, and strode from one end of the office to the other.

"Come on now, Pyotr Vasilievich, just forget it, please."

In his anger he forgot himself and began speaking with rough familiarity.

"He's a no-good! D'you know who it was he crippled?"

He came to a halt facing his guest and, obviously hoping to impress him, mentioned a name well known in the town.

"One of our best comrades, the pride of us all, you might say, and you're trying to help the scoundrel who attacked him. I'm surprised at you, Pyotr Vasilievich, old comrade!"

His guest cut him short.

"Stop bobbing about, Kostya, and sit down. Have you gone into it thoroughly? Why did he hit him?"

He set off over the carpet again.

"Why? What d'you mean, why? A man makes a mistake, does something he knows is wrong, does that mean you can take the law into your own hands? Foster anarchy? Is everybody to sit in judgment on everybody else? It won't do! We have to teach everybody respect for socialist legality."

"Maybe you've started teaching it at the wrong end."

"No, Comrade Lashkov, at the right end! We've had enough of all this demagogy. 'The masses, the masses.' Those very same masses will come and trample on you. Each side must learn from the other: the bottom from the top, and the top from the bottom."

"Well, will it be any easier for other people to handle him at the ends of the earth? Good God!"

Vorobushkin finally sat down.

"Anything you like, but not that . . . Besides, what would the victim think of me?"

Pyotr Vasilievich could see that his host wasn't used to people answering back and had grown tired of listening, that he wanted desperately to be left alone behind firmly closed doors, with the newspaper lying ready, the carpet under his feet, his tea and his utterly devoted secretary, Anna Ivanovna.

Pyotr Vasilievich rose, and decided to play the trump card which he would never have used in less serious circumstances.

"There was a time, Comrade Vorobushkin, when your name was used to scare children. On your own, you'd never have wriggled out of it as long as you lived. And whether you'd have lived at all is anybody's guess . . . You've got a short memory, Kostya."

Vorobushkin raised his hand, palm foremost, as though warding off a blow.

"Cut it out, Pyotr Vasilievich, it's not your style."

He turned abruptly towards the window. His shoulders slumped and lost their jaunty look, his round face went gray and haggard.

"Tell him to write an application to the Council commission. I'll take care of it."

He rose and, with his eyes fixed on the newspaper, stretched his hand across the desk.

"All the best, Comrade Lashkov."

His guest departed, leaving him to the peace and quiet of his imposing office, where every object knew its place and purpose, where everything spoke of order and discipline, and there could be no question of unscheduled intrusions.

VI

Strangely enough, his daytime distractions gave his dreams and mis-givings new order and coherence. He became gentler, more patient, more reasonable. He slept easily and soundly. He no longer suffered torments of anxiety at every symptom of physical failure. The knowledge that someone had need of him personally renewed him and gave his life meaning. Every morning brought a heightened expectancy, so when he was awakened one day by someone gently but persistently rattling the outside door, this early visit caused him no surprise. "So now we have a guest as well."

Pyotr Vasilievich dressed in a hurry and went out to the porch; opening the door, he caught his breath for a moment and felt faint— there stood his son Victor, Victor as a young man, looking at him tipsily and laughing, only finer-boned and more dignified than he used to be.

"Hallo, Granddad Peter!"

And only then did realization bring relief.

"It's Vadim, Victor's son Vadim!"

A woman who worked with his daughter-in-law had brought Vadim to him in a bad year for Victor. The daughter-in-law was expecting to be deported, and was farming out the children wherever she could, out of harm's way.

Pyotr Vasilievich looked on young children not with active dislike but with a sort of self-defensive disdain, and in the ordinary way he would have sent the boy back, but he was so gratified by the humiliation of his daughter-in-law who hated him that he made the best of a bad job and agreed to keep his grandson. Vadim didn't take long to make himself at home. Together with his nine-year-old aunt Antonina he explored the whole area. He soon fell in with the local ringleaders among the children, and the barefooted warrior band of which he took command had all Sviridovo moaning and groaning before long. His grandfather thawed, recognizing himself in his grandson.

As for Antonina, she was lost in worship and adoration of her nephew, while Maria went weak with happiness whenever she saw him.

In intervals between raids on neighboring orchards the boy read voraciously, and his arguments with his grandfather about politics would end in tears of rage. So that when the day of parting came in the autumn, a funereal silence reigned in the house. Antonina shut herself up in the attic and didn't make a sound, although, needless to say, she was in tears. Grandma sighed quietly as she got Vadim ready for the journey, while Pyotr Vasilievich, who was to take the boy to the capital on his normal Moscow run and hand him over to his daughter-in-law at the Paveletski station, stared gloomily into the yard, and as his bony fingers gripped the window ledge, they trembled very slightly.

For a long time afterwards Pyotr Vasilievich would hear Vadim's imperious voice in his dreams.

"Granddad . . . !"

And now, after more than twenty years, his old pain came back again, and he gasped.

"Come in, then . . ."

First of all, his grandson applied his ear to the partition—from which Pyotr Vasilievich concluded that despite his ban, his daughter and daughter-in-law had remained in touch with each other—and pretended to knock on it timidly.

"Hallo, Aunt Antonina Petrovna. Don't you want to take a good look at your little nephew Vadim Victorovich now that he's almost full-grown?"

All Antonina could do was clear her throat and gasp. She started bustling about, rattling the crockery, and muttering almost inaudibly to herself, over and over again:

"Oh, Lord! I'm coming . . . I'm coming . . . Vadim, my dear . . . I'm coming . . . Oh, Lord!"

The guest fumbled with the zipper of his smart suitcase; in between pulling out bottles of cognac he brought out an imported three-piece suit for his grandfather and two spring dresses for his aunt. Deftly uncorking a bottle of "Jubilee" with a single slap on the bottom, he put it on the table, and finally sat himself down.

"Get out the glasses, Granddad."

The more Pyotr Vasilievich looked at him, the more vividly he could imagine just what Vadim must have gone through to change his whole personality so completely. Not a trace of the Lashkov clan's sturdy solidity. All on edge, all chatter, ready to flutter off his perch at the slightest excuse, Vadim had inherited a striking superficial resemblance to his father, but none of his ways or habits.

A rush of explanations to his grandfather followed as he finished off the bottle.

"You see, Granddad, I'm just passing through . . . I'm in a concert here today . . . You wouldn't turn down the chance to hear what you might call your own flesh and blood perform. . . . Tomorrow I'm off again to Lipetsk . . . Don't look so stern . . . I live like a bird, you see, here today and gone tomorrow . . . I'll have one more if I may . . ."

Antonina came in wearing her new things and carrying a tray loaded with snacks she had made. She set plates around the table, bowed solemnly, gave her nephew a cautious peck on the head as though she were afraid of disturbing him; she sat down opposite without taking her eyes off him and drank in every word.

"We're older than we used to be, Auntie," he said, laughing drunkenly, as he filled her glass to the brim. "Soon be drawing our pensions. Drink up, Antonina Petrovna, and show the old brigade what the rising generation can do!"

She looked miserably at her father, but seeing no sign of disapproval she slowly and graciously drained the glass, wiped her lips with the edge of her handkerchief, and resumed her rapt and silent contemplation of their guest.

"That's the way," said Vadim enthusiastically. "You could go on the stage, Auntie! Who's your trainer? And more to the point, when and where does he get his funds from? You see, Granddad, you can learn how to do it . . ."

"It's too late for me."

"The classics teach us that it's never too late to learn. Maybe we could start now. Do the honors, Auntie . . ."

His grandson went on clowning for some time; he rumpled Antonina's hair from time to time when she fell into a doze, and he even tried to make them dance, but Pyotr Vasilievich was well aware that it was all forced gaiety, that he was sheltering from the inquisitive looks of his relatives behind a barrage of words, and that he was really in no mood for joking. You could sense the anxiety beneath his labored good humor. His hot eyes, damp with silent torment and desperation, had a life of their own.

Gazing into that burning despair, Pyotr Vasilievich could have sworn that he had seen eyes like that before somewhere. But where? When? Unthinkingly he turned the label of the bottle away from himself, and the idle movement jolted his memory, took him back along a chain of recollection to a March night of jagged cold on Lake Baikal during the evacuation.

It was a night of stinging, choking blizzards. The chill stabbed through their clothes. The blackness was unrelieved by the faintest glimmer of cheering light ahead. Their horse, feeble enough to begin with, lost the way and gave up altogether, pausing and panting at every little ridge in the ice before she could tackle it.

Pyotr Vasilievich's companion was the station hand Semyon Melentiev, a sour sort of creature, always looking on the dark side of things, muttering curses into his turned-up collar.

"Why the bloody hell did I get into this damn silly business! Fat lot of exchanging we're going to be able to do at this rate. Bit more of this and we'll be at rest with the blessed . . . Get on with you, you lousy mare!"

The lakeside village for which the travelers were heading, to trade old clothes for food, was ten miles from the station. They had set out immediately after the midday meal and, at worst, should have reached their goal before it got really dark, but Pyotr Vasilievich's watch showed ten o'clock, and the blackness ahead was getting deeper and more impenetrable by the minute.

The horse stopped again, snorting with apprehension. Melentiev could no longer control his rage, and tugged furiously at the reins.

"Get on with you. You rotten sod. I'll thrash the living daylights out of you."

With a great effort the horse took one step, then another, then suddenly the sledge tipped over, rear and uppermost, and she plunged headfirst into the snow between the shafts. She was caught by her forelegs, up to her neck in a deep crack. The spring thaw was already invisibly under way.

They tried and tried to help her struggle out of the trap in the ice, but to no avail. Pyotr Vasilievich dragged at the collar, while Semyon, crazy with fear, landed haphazard blows across the poor creature's convulsively shuddering rump. But with every movement the horse just sank deeper. In the end, all three of them collapsed for lack of breath and lay greedily gulping air.

And that was when Pyotr Vasilievich, squatting down in the snow by the horse's muzzle, had seen, close in front of him, eyes consumed by hope and despair like those which his drunken grandson turned on him now.

"What are you thinking about, Granddad?"

His grandson put an arm round him, drew him a little closer, and began to sing in a comic voice.

"Oh, tell us, do, the meaning of it all . . ."

"Oh, nothing," he said, taking a cautious sip from his glass. "I was just remembering . . ."

Vadim, teasing him, struck up again in an awesome bass:

"Your story, pray, my friends . . ."

But Pyotr Vasilievich didn't hear. He was still far away, in that Baikal blizzard, alone with the horse and its pleading eyes, whose unbearable sadness had suddenly forced him to his feet and inspired him to pull a plank out of the sledge which he thrust under the belly of the now utterly helpless mare. But even when they had thus managed to drag her out, she lay where she was and there was no way of making her stand. Melentiev, seasoning each blow with choice obscenities, flogged her in vain. She flinched violently, but could not get up. The station man flung his whip away and spat angrily.

"Not worth busting a gut. Let the shit-bag die . . . How about a swig? . . . never be a better time . . . Then we can think about it. This bastard isn't going to get up, anyway."

They had saved a pint of unrectified spirits, captured with a struggle from the lab assistants at the station. Melentiev drank his share and handed the bottle to his companion. Pyotr Vasilievich took a swallow, then parted the horse's unresisting jaws and poured the rest straight down her throat. They just about had time to follow the drink with a lump of frozen bread before the mare bounded to her feet and was off.

The memory of that night of blizzards suddenly filled the old man with an urgent desire to help his grandson get rid of the pain that gnawed at him.

"You ought to stay with me for a while, Vadim, and find your feet . . ."

The effects of the drink were wearing off, however, and Vadim was getting morose and restless.

"Have you forgotten what sort of world we live in, Granddad? For as long as I can remember, I've never known what it means to stop and take it easy for a while. It's not a life, it's nothing but chasing after shadows . . . I'll be forty soon, and I don't have a goddam thing: no wife, no children, no roof over my head . . . If I don't do my act today I'll starve tomorrow. How can I think about the family?"

"There's lots of jobs—you could choose something different."

"It's too late, Granddad—I'm trapped in an orbit you can't break out of. Centrifugal force. . . . It caught me when I was young, and it's still carrying me along . . . D'you know, for instance, what a Special Children's Home is? No? Or a Colony? No, again . . . And, believe me, you don't want to . . . It's where they turn your soul inside out and tan it until there's nothing human left in it . . . Granddad, Granddad, I don't know how things should be, but I do know they're all wrong. People can't go on living this way, they've no right to . . . They'd do better to take to the trees again . . . Callous, vicious, solitary, unfeeling . . . Oh well . . ."

He waved his hand and stood up.

"What's the use of talking. Auntie's asleep. Don't let's disturb her. I'll go and have a nap in her room."

"Yes, Vadim Victorovich, you've had more than your fair share," Pyotr Vasilievich said to himself as his grandson went out.

He couldn't remember when he'd last been to a concert. Must have been thirty years back, or maybe more. He disapproved of wasting time and thought theater-going a disgracefully frivolous activity for any self-respecting man. When his grandson insisted, he gave way, but it went against the grain.

An obliging attendant showed the old man to the reserved seats in the fourth row, put a program in his hand, and, with an expressive look at his unruly neighbors, said loudly for their benefit: "If anything disturbs you, Pyotr Vasilievich, I'll move you during the intermission."

The first item was an aging singer done up in velvet. She performed a few old-time love songs with more feeling than talent, and finished her act with a song about komsomols whose hearts know no rest. The applause was sparse but polite: Nobody could say she wasn't a trier.

Next, a young couple acted a sketch about life amongst Greek patriots, in which He, a general in a canvas cape, which had been crudely adapted to look like an American uniform, put the screws on Her, a valiant partisan girl wearing a large towel, evidently intended to suggest some article of national dress.

They were followed by a pair of acrobats who gave a display of tortured agility and made way in turn for a conjurer in a threadbare topper, after which at long last the master of ceremonies announced Vadim Lashkov, virtuoso of the spoken word.

Recitation was what Pyotr Vasilievich loathed most of all, and to judge by the sigh of boredom which ran through the hall there weren't many enthusiasts for oral artistry around him; the old man felt embarrassed for his grandson in advance. Indeed, Vadim himself seemed halfhearted and almost resentful when he began.

"Worn out by the heat of the day, and having had nothing to eat but undercooked and undersalted fish, Yegor the buoy-keeper is asleep in his cabin . . ."

The story really wasn't up to much. A useless clod, a buoy-keeper, or call him a ferryman if you like, lives by a river. He has a lady-friend who comes to call, and she's no great shakes either. The clod drinks himself silly, and when he's had enough he sings duets with his ladylove. What's the use of any of that to a man who wants a pleasant evening of varied entertainment for a rouble and a half of his own money?

Pyotr Vasilievich glanced at his neighbor on the right, who was yawning with boredom, and felt that he couldn't stand it much longer.

Strangely enough, however, as he listened he became more and more irresistibly involved in the fate of the God-forsaken buoy-keeper, and the words which poured from the stage aroused sadness in him. What mattered now to Pyotr Vasilievich was not the artist's performance, but the story itself. An extraordinary bond, almost of kinship, was formed between him and the obscure buoy-keeper who sang songs. The old man bled for his sorrows and relaxed in his joys. He, transport-worker Lashkov, who had given most of his life to the din and bustle of the railway, felt that the story was his own, that he was the hero's companion in his black fate and his pain.

> "Away on the sea,
> The deep blue sea . . ."

A bittersweet longing stole over Pyotr Vasilievich; he ceased to hear the hum of approval and the applause around him; he listened absorbed and trembling with agitation to the seductive echoes which filled his mind . . .

> "A swan glides by
> A swan with his mate . . ."

The artist himself seemed overcome with emotion and quiet joy as he came to the end.

"And when they are finished, worn-out, exhausted, but happy, when Yegor lies still with his head in her lap, and his breathing grows heavy, she kisses his pale cold face and whispers breathlessly: 'Yegor, my darling . . . my wonderful love, my precious love . . .'"

As he went out, the old man tried hard to remember the name of the story. "Must get hold of it and read it. Should I ask Vadim?"

In the crush at the exit his ear caught a hasty conversation above the hubbub of voices.

"Well, what did you think?"

"Something and nothing."

Pyotr Vasilievich grunted with satisfaction. That in fact was the name of the story, "Something and Nothing."

.   .   .

Vadim gazed, sad and sullen, around the station.

"Lipetsk tomorrow, Valuiki the day after, then Donetsk . . . That's how it goes for the rest of my life, Granddad . . . I'm sick and tired of it . . ."

"Yes, but even you get holidays, don't you?"

Since the concert a reflective note of deference toward his grandson was to be heard in Pyotr Vasilievich's voice.

"You ought to come and see us . . . You could go off to your great-uncle Andrei in the forest . . . he's warden in the Kurakin forestry zone these days . . . It's marvelous in the forest just now . . . the mushrooms are up . . ."

"Yes, Granddad, that's it—the forest."

Suddenly Vadim was eager and excited.

"I'll go to the forest, away from it all. That's an excellent idea of yours!"

He was obviously clutching at his grandfather's idea like a lifeline, but his anxious haste only served to emphasize the unreality of this fleeting hope.

"We'll go fishing."

But as the train pulled out and his grandson stood at the rear door of the carriage, waving a faltering and miserable good-bye, Pyotr Vasilievich realized with a searing pang that they might never see each other again.

VII

The sunlit forest floated above Pyotr Vasilievich, subtly alive, reveling in innocent secrets: pungent scents, magnified by the recent rain, lured the traveler on along countless paths all sparkling under the dew. Every new turning held the promise of a new horizon, a new discovery.

And it was a miracle. Though Pyotr Vasilievich had wandered many times about the thickets with his gun or his mushroom-gathering bag, he had never seen the forest like this before. A fir was both itself and something much more. The dew on the grass wasn't just dew—each drop demanded to be looked at separately. Each puddle on the path begged a separate identity. And this was probably why the crackle of every dry twig underfoot that morning awakened a silent but persistent ache in his heart.

He understood at last why his brother, lying shell-shocked and oblivious in the hospital, had called for one thing only in his delirium—the forest.

On that occasion an express telegram had summoned Pyotr Vasilievich to Vologda, where Andrei lay speechless and unconscious with no hope of recovery.

Vologda proved to be a cheerful little town. People and things stood out sharp and clear against a background in which everything was white, crumbly, powdery—a white kremlin, white humpbacked roofs, trees in big white winter hats. A tipsy driver, with only a patch of brick-red face and frosty mustache showing under his hood, urged on a nag which had grown gray in the frost, carrying him through that sparkling whiteness, gaily dotted with glints of red sunlight, black cars, brick-pale yellow sheepskin coats, all the way to the hospital, a squat brick building dating from Tsar Nicholas's days.

"That's it, then . . . Kuvshinovo . . . God preserve us from it . . ."

And, sure enough, viewed from inside, through the barred window of the reception room, the festive whiteness he had just seen looked ghastly, and the heavy sky no bigger than a man's hand.

It was a low-ceilinged room with two windows and a piece of ragged matting running from the entrance to an inner door; it was furnished with nothing but a battered desk and the chair wedged against it. But the main thing was the odor! None of the familiar smells which had traveled with him through his long life had any part in it. It held a whiff of something which immediately sent a feeling of silent tragedy, of agonized waiting, of utter hopelessness, through Pyotr Vasilievich, and no doubt through everyone else who entered that place.

A decrepit old man met him with a slight, apologetic smile, in which his answer to every visitor's perplexity was easily seen. "Yes, I see, I see it all, your fear and your dismay. As for that smell, I've been inhaling it for ages. But what can I do about it? Nothing, except beg forgiveness with this smile of mine. So don't take it amiss, and do please have a seat."

"Sit down—er—please sit down. We must have a talk . . . er . . . allow me to . . . I'm Professor Zholtovsky."

The old man really was very infirm, and his "erring" was obviously a senile weakness, not a sign of professorial disdain for his companion.

"As you . . . er . . . realize . . . your brother is . . . er . . . in a bad way. We've . . . er . . . done everything . . . er . . . in our . . . er . . . power. But—" he half-spread his hands, which was as broad a gesture as his strength allowed—

"Andrei . . . er . . . Vasilievich . . . isn't . . . er . . . getting any better."

Here Zholtovsky's strength failed altogether and he stopped, breathing heavily. His sagging cheeks quivered like jelly, and his rabbity eyes watered.

"Can't be less than eighty," thought Pyotr Vasilievich to himself. "It's a long row to hoe."

Zholtovsky broke off several times to get his breath before he could finish his speech. What it all came to was that Andrei was in a very bad way, indeed, that his illness was progressive and that the doctors involved had decided to try one last thing: stimulating the patient's visual memory.

"You understand . . . er . . . Pyotr . . . er . . . Vasilievich . . . yes . . . er . . . I think . . . stay here for a bit . . . we'll . . . er . . . fix you up . . . sit with him . . . er . . . as much as you . . . er . . . can . . . maybe . . . er . . . photographs . . . er . . . letters . . . signs . . . er . . . anything at all . . . you're not . . . er . . . indifferent I'm . . . er . . . sure . . . to what . . . er . . . becomes of your . . . er . . . brother."

Pyotr Vasilievich would have found it in him to do more than that for Andrei.

"Right then . . . er . . . Valentina . . . er . . . Nikolayevna!"

She had evidently been waiting at the door for the professor to call her, and came in immediately, a tall, stout woman with a massive, shapeless face in which only her eyes—small, sharp, deepset, yet at the same time full of pure good nature—attracted attention. With her arrival the gloomy room seemed to expand and become cozier and lighter.

Zholtovsky summoned up the strength for a single nod in Pyotr Vasilievich's direction, then collapsed exhausted against the back of the chair, eyes closed, like a dead man.

But the professor's help was no longer needed. The fat woman gently propelled the visitor toward the inner door, taking complete charge of him for the indefinite future, to judge from the determined look on her face.

"He's nearly as old as the hospital," she said with a sigh as they went out. "Not many last as long as him in our line of work. Wait a minute, I'll give you a gown. . . . You understood what it's all about, did you? It's against the rules, really, but we've got to try it."

With an easy stride Valentina Nikolayevna led him through the labyrinthine corridors. Everybody they met greeted her with a smile, and she beamed briefly in reply. It was obvious who brought life and light inside those pain-darkened walls.

"The main thing is that you mustn't be afraid—patients are people, too, so it's possible to live with them, though it's not a quiet life, I must admit . . . Right, we're home."

She opened one of the doors with a key like an engine driver's bar.

"Go right in."

It was a big ward with a vaulted ceiling which made it rather gloomy, and eight grated windows, four on each side. In it the now familiar smell became still more intolerable. The din of many voices, rebounding off four walls each a yard thick, only reinforced the oppressive ache in his heart.

"What have you got yourself into, Petya! Grab your legs and run!"

A youth rushed across their path, his unnaturally elongated features lighting up in an idiot smile.

"Look, Valentina Dmitrievna, did it myself . . ."

She inspected her charge's pencil drawings, not out of idle curiosity or sense of duty—Pyotr Vasilievich had landed up in the hospital once or twice, and was no novice in these things—but with unfeigned interest and even a sort of excitement.

"Well done, Pasha! Only here—I should do this."

She took the pencil from him and with a few strokes brought some semblance of order into the chaos that reigned on the paper.

"And then I should . . . Carry on with it, Pavlik!"

Under her quick caress the lad smiled still more broadly.

"Well done!"

Then, to the visitor: "Come on then . . . he's an orphan, epileptic . . . He was like a wild animal when they brought him in . . . he's thawed out a bit. You can see he's quieter now . . . Andrei Vasilievich was rather restless today; we had to fasten him down a bit."

Pyotr Vasilievich's legs were like cotton wool as he took the last few steps to the bed, not realizing that he was clinging tightly to the pocket of his companion's gown. Andrei was staring with lackluster eyes at the ceiling, sweating heavily, and struggling to free himself from his bonds. The muscles under the reddish week-old stubble were distended, as though they were trying to break through the taut, transparent skin of his face. Not a single sound escaped him, not even the mooing noises which deaf-mutes make.

Pyotr Vasilievich was filled with pain and tenderness, and tears scorched his cheeks as he stroked Andrei's convulsively clenched fist with his trembling fingers.

"What is it then, Andrei, little brother? What is it all about?"

Pyotr Vasilievich lost count of time as he sat like that, watching his brother grow less restless under his soothing touch, till at last he closed his eyes and became quiet.

The early winter twilight crept out from the corners of the ward, coaxing the inhabitants back under their blankets. The ward grew quieter and less crowded.

To one side of Pyotr Vasilievich two patients with dressing gowns over their underwear sat on their beds facing each other and exchanged confidences.

"I'm a straight sort of chap. I say what I mean and I mean what I say. 'Where's the mark?' he says. So I tell him, 'That's what we agreed, Prov Silich.' And he gives me one in the teeth. I'm a straight sort of fellow, so I say, 'What right have you got?' And he gives me another . . ."

"Quite right! After a booze-up I always drink kvass myself. Only it's got to be straight off the ice, so cold it takes your breath away."

"There's no two ways about it, I tell him, 'It's a police matter, Prov Silich.' And he fetches me such a wallop. I'm a straight sort of fellow, I am. So where do I go? I go home."

"Quite right! I remember, on the October anniversary, my father-in-law and me drank half a barrel of kvass, just the two of us, and it never touched us. That's the stuff for you, kvass."

"Well, I mean, what an attitude, but I'm a straight sort of fellow. . . ."

They talked to each other with the greatest respect and mutual understanding, and Pyotr Vasilievich, who was rather taken aback at first, realized with surprise that words are not the most important bond between human beings.

"Got anything to smoke, friend?"

A pair of crayfish eyes with a hint of condescending mockery were studying him curiously from under the blankets of the bed opposite.

"Gone to sleep, has he? He can sense a blood relation, the son of a bitch. I'd never held anything higher than ace and jack, winter or summer, and I've had enough to do with that brother of yours to last me a lifetime."

He took a light, and inhaled deeply.

"Yes, when he starts struggling you've got to hang on for dear life. So I hang on, without overtime—I'm sorry for him, he's like me, been in the trenches. I'm in Category Two as well. Let's go over to the stove while he's asleep. You've got plenty more to come."

Although his new acquaintance's sensible remarks seemed to show that he was in full possession of his faculties, Pyotr Vasilievich had already made it a rule to be ready for all sorts of antics in this place, and, to be frank, he was expecting funny business at any moment. If they were all locked up here there must be some good reason for it.

When his neighbor stood up he turned out to be a tall, bony man, with puffy reddish marks on an angular, diabolic face. A lordly dignity informed his every movement, so that even the tattered hospital dressing gown hung on him, at the very least, like the sable mantle of a tsar. He passed through the ward with the assurance and self-importance of one who always felt himself superior, whatever the circumstances.

Two orderlies were smoking silently by the purring stove. From time to time, one of them, a big, thick-lipped old man with a thin gray fuzz on his head, furiously crumbled cold cinders from the ashpan in his nicotine-stained fingers. The other, quite a young man who looked as though he'd had a shock that would last him a lifetime, looked on indifferently. They were obviously digesting a conversation just ended, and upsetting for both of them.

"Can't sleep?" said the ginger man, giving a great smirk at the younger one. "Bad sign, that. It's today, then, is it, boss?"

The boy couldn't stand the bitter mockery in the crayfish eyes. He dropped his eyes, and spoke in a scarcely audible sigh.

"Today, Ivan Sergeich."

"Right, let me warm myself one last time then, boss."

The ginger man majestically straddled the stool which the boy obligingly pulled up for him.

"Shall we roll ourselves another, pal?"

And again they all fell quiet. In the silent dusk outside the dark blue windows, snow fell in a steady stream. Light from the stove danced over faces and objects. But for the feverish muttering here and there in the ward, you might have thought that the world was by and large a warm and comfortable place: the snow might go on falling for all eternity, but for all eternity there would be a cheerful fire burning in the stove, and the three of them need fear no intrusion, need never hurry on.

Sparks from the fire flashed in crazy reflection in Ivan Sergeich's sharp eyes.

"Well, folks, I couldn't get to sleep, so I made up a story. No, by God, I didn't make it up. I lay there and lay there, and it just came to me . . ."

The orderlies didn't like his provocative tone and turned away, shuffling in disapproval, thus betraying an unease or rather an anxiety which for no obvious reason began to communicate itself with increasing insistence to Pyotr Vasilievich.

"The beginning is an old one. Once upon a time an old woman had a little gray goat. The old woman, of course, loved the little goat very much. From now on it's all mine. In good time the goat leaves the old woman, and begins twitching its horns. It's hungry, see. But winter is coming on: not a blade of grass, not a berry, to be found. He meets a fox. 'Why are you twitching your horns when you haven't got any?' asks the fox. 'I'm hungry, and there's no grass,' he says. 'You fool,' says the fox, 'what donkey eats grass nowadays? Everybody's long since been eating meat.' 'How can I eat meat,' he asks, 'when I'm a goat? It's not allowed to one of my rank.' 'Blockhead,' says the fox, 'go and work as a wolf. Everybody else does nowadays. Even hares won't go to bed without fresh-killed meat.' 'Yes, but supposing I stop somebody—who's going to be afraid of a goat like me?' 'You just use your big mouth. That's what everyone with credentials does nowadays—relies on his big mouth.' The red one fades away with a wave of the tail. The goat does what the son of a bitch told him, and starts working as a wolf. To begin with, fresh-killed meat makes him feel sick, but then he gets the habit, and even takes a liking to it. Once, in the dark, in a fight, he bites two real gray wolves. A fine life he's leading . . . only as time goes by, things get steadily worse, food begins to run out in the forest. Because the sly and artful have multiplied to such an extent, all of them gray, all of them with credentials . . . There isn't any meat, and the goat no longer fancies grass. He falls into a depression. Screw it all—might as well be dead!"

Before the lock had clicked, or so it seemed to them, all four had spun round and were straining tensely in the direction of the door, so sensitive were they to every sound. No sooner did the duty doctor appear in the doorway, with a red cap-band half visible in the brightly lit corridor behind him, than Ivan Sergeich stood up and moved towards the exit, nodding to the boy as he went:

"Lead the way."

The young man jumped up, overturning his stool with a clatter, and only then did Pyotr Vasilievich notice the military tunic under his gown, and the boots with a regulation shine you could see your face in.

The older man also rose.

"Let's go . . . Your bed's out there, anyway."

In the corridor, watched by the doctor, two soldiers from the prison escort service, and a third from the medical corps, Ivan Sergeich changed his clothes. He did it with the unhurried thoroughness of a man accustomed to long slow journeys, on which any oversight in the matter of dress may have unpleasant consequences. Only when the last button was cozily lodged in its nest did the ginger man allow himself one final bit of sarcastic bravado.

"The goat should have said to hell with it, pal. Let them die, the fucking lot of them. And started over again—at pasture . . . only it was too late."

He turned to his escort and stretched out his hands.

"Slap 'em on, boy."

The handcuffs locked on his wrists, and a moment later only the muffled slamming of doors in corridor after corridor marked his progress towards the outside.

The old orderly, avoiding Lashkov's questioning look, muttered to himself.

"Deserter. One of ours—local man. Tried to fight his way out, shot two men. Now they'll shoot him. Brought him here for medical examination. Certified normal. God have mercy on his sinful soul . . . Go to bed. If anything happens I'll wake you up . . ."

One day fell flatly into the next, as much alike as the first beads of water on the window brought by the thaw, but there was as little light or awareness as ever in Andrei's dim eyes. Just occasionally in his sleep a delirious shout would be wrenched out of him, a scarcely articulate call, a stunned word, but returning consciousness sealed his dry lips again in dumb oblivion.

They got so used to Pyotr Vasilievich's presence in the hospital that even old Zholtovsky, walking the wards with a gaggle of students, always took him for an orderly.

"My dear chap . . . er . . . see to it, will you . . . er . . . change his gown . . . er . . . Semenchuk's . . . it . . . er . . . won't do . . . er . . . won't do . . . er . . . at all . . . please."

Pyotr Vasilievich got to know the history and origins of every patient's illness as well as any staff orderly, and he became quite intimate with many of them. He found that if you listened patiently and took care to observe all that went on, you could easily discover that beneath the superficial muddle of words and actions lay an ordinary human existence with its familiar passions and purposes, each with its own internal logic. The fine points of intrigue that went on over a vacant bed by the stove might have aroused envy in the shrewdest brains of the diplomatic corps, and the contest for second helpings differed little from departmental rows over supplementary allocations. Life was the same everywhere.

His habitual silence inspired trust in minds wrestling with the insoluble, and soon he wasn't surprised when even the usually taciturn schizophrenic Mushchinsky confided in him.

"This morning, Pyotr Vasilievich, Pluto began its transit through me. It's a heavy planet, you know. Solid ammonia. I'm undergoing a most painful process. I've decided to put off dinner."

His puffy, womanish face broke into a dreamily ecstatic smile.

"Now, the day before yesterday it was Mars passing through. What a planet! Delightful! Not much oxygen, it's true, but such amazing lightness, such purity throughout! Do you know, I'm still dreaming about it."

In normal life Mushchinsky had been a successful dental assistant, without a cloud in his sky until one day a patient had died of blood poisoning after an extraction. His mind retreated from reality and the Kuvshinovo hospital gained yet another hopeless case.

At dusk, Karl Mayer appeared on the threshold of the side-ward where sick prisoners-of-war from the camps were put. He was in his underwear, and Pyotr Vasilievich, as if it were his customary duty, got up to make the hapless German a present of some Morshansky tobacco.

"Gut," he mumbled. "Danke schön. Ich bin aus Fürstenwalde. Ich habe Sohn Franz und Frau. Sie heisst Gisela. Danke schön."

He was interrupted by the irritable voice of Mokeich, a dispossessed kulak and schizoid fanatic, who suffered from senile insomnia.

" 'Ich, Ich,' you striped devil! Conquered the whole world and couldn't get the better of lousy old Russia! Just try shooting your mouth off here! Playing on most cherished hopes, that's all you're good for, sons of bitches. God forgive us, we waited for you as though you were His holy saints. They'll come and save us, we thought. You saved us all right, mangy dogs! Only hope now is the Yanks. If you can call that lot human, all wearing those hats. Feeding their fat faces like pigs in an orchard. They don't give a damn for us. Ugh, you ugly German swine, I wouldn't give you a lump of shit, let alone a smoke."

The German was dismayed by the old man's hostility; his face clouded over. He seemed to shrink, and hurriedly took refuge in the protective darkness of his cubicle while Mokeich, gratified by the effect he had produced, turned his abuse on Pyotr Vasilievich.

"You idiot, giving presents to people like that."

A few more snowstorms whirled over Kuvshinovo and then, on a March morning flooded with sunshine, Andrei opened his fever-scorched eyes at last and uttered a recognizable word.

"Pyotr?"

Consciousness returned with painful slowness; it took him many more days and nights in the hospital, and then at home in Uzlovsk, to put himself back together bit by bit, clutching at every word and every memory, until he managed to make himself a home as warden in the forest through which Pyotr Vasilievich was walking now, nearly fifteen years later.

A cart rumbled round a bend toward him, and he immediately recognized his brother by the uniform cap pulled right down over his eyes. Andrei, as soon as he clapped eyes on him, pulled the horse up short, threw down the reins, and gave a comic salute.

"Pyotr Vasilievich, sir!"

"So that's how you greet your brother."

He looked hard at Andrei, afraid that his cherished expectations might be disappointed, but the old mischievous smile reassured him and he was swept by a wave of affection.

"Hallo, you old devil!"

"The top brass came down on me this morning, and I've only just managed to get away. So I'm a bit late. Take a seat."

They rode for a while in silence. Each was searching among the tangle of words and thoughts in his mind for the most important—the most urgent. But for that very reason, what came out was an unwanted stream of irrelevant trivialities.

"Grand forest you've got here!"

"Half a loaf is better than none."

"What do you mean?"

"They're wasting it all."

"It'll last out your lifetime."

Andrei shot him a withering glance and he immediately regretted saying it. Andrei's unhappiness gave a bitter twist to his lips.

"Everybody says that—who cares whether the grass grows once we're gone? But what if people before us had thought the same? The earth would have been bare long since. There'd be neither beauty nor happiness."

His words suddenly became feverish and confused.

"It's ourselves, our very nature we're destroying . . . What's the sense of that? Locusts live like that, but we're men, given brains. I caught a man on the nursery plantation the other day. Swinging a great axe, groaning and grunting and really putting his back into it. 'What are you doing, you son of a bitch?' I say. 'It isn't yours,' he says, 'it's the government's, it won't be missed, and I need a whip.' Yes, a whip. And for the sake of one wretched whip he had destroyed twenty saplings.

He'd had it drilled into him—it's all yours, help yourself. So he helps himself. Robs nature blind. But there's a limit to the earth's endurance: It won't stand much more, it'll rebel. It'll deny us everything—bread and water. We shall be taking bites out of each other like wild animals . . . Get on, you idle creature."

The forest was thinning out as the road began to climb. On a steep rise up ahead, the dark buildings of the forestry station came into view in a clump of birches, and a bunch of people stood smoking by the veranda.

As soon as the cart passed through the gates, a squat, almost square man with a mustache waddled over to them; he was dressed in a shabby blue suit which should have been retired long ago, and waders that were far too big for him. He tried not to look at Andrei as he spoke.

"I know I'm not welcome, but here I am. My cows have counted every star in the sky by now. The big boss dropped in like a bolt from the blue and ordered me to get a roof over them. So whether you like it or not, I need forty cubic meters of timber. Here's the chit. Stake out a patch. We'll have it down right away."

His tiny eyes, hidden deep in the folds of his apoplectic face, were almost blind with hostility as they glared at Andrei.

"Well, what are you waiting for? Want me to go to jail to save your forest? Am I supposed to roof the cowshed with my prick?"

He spat angrily and turned away again.

"To hell with the whole bloody business!"

Andrei was unharnessing the horse and had his back to the man with the mustache. He listened patiently and was apparently unmoved by all that he heard. Only the tremor in the sensitive fingers plucking at the collar-strap gave him away. But when he finally turned round, his features were relaxed and expressed nothing but scorn and indifference.

"Who's arguing? Chop away, chairman! You know the copse by the gully? Go ahead and chop it down. If you take a bit extra, there's no harm done. We can settle up later."

He strode past the thunderstruck chairman to the veranda; only then did he turn and nod to his brother.

"Come on in, Pyotr Vasilievich, we'll have some tea."

Andrei spread the modest selection of food on the table with feverish haste, knocked the cardboard stopper out of a bottle of Moskovskaya with a single blow, filled the glasses to the brim, and only then sat down and said in a voice that was hollow with misery:

"Good health, Pyotr, my boy . . . The forest will last out our life-time."

"Stop. You're not a kid anymore."

"Oh, to hell with it!"

His sudden gaiety did not quite conceal his despair.

"Here's a tongue-twister for you, my dear Pyotr. 'Dry ducks drooping ducks dead ducks.' Or try this one: 'Pigeons peck seed and pashas suck pipes.' "

The blows of an axe rang out sharply in the noonday silence outside. They fell thicker and faster, echoing more and more clearly as they became harder.

"Here's another."

Andrei's frenzied eyes were swollen with tears of rage.

"Greek rides by creek,
Greek sees crab in creek,
Greek grabs crab in creek,
Crab in creek tweaks Greek."

His voice rose to a shout as he tried to drown the tattoo of axe on tree.

"This nightcap's tied too tight. Try to re-tie it."

"Andrei, man, for God's sake."

But Andrei wasn't listening.

"Try saying 'Oh what wet raw windy weather, what a dull dry dreary day.' "

He suddenly exploded.

"Chop away, chairman!"

His eyes sought Pyotr Vasilievich's and held them, full of tears. He was shaking all over as though he had a cold.

"I'll set fire to it! I will! I'd sooner see it go up in smoke! I can't stand it any more. They'll chew it all up like moths! Scavenging damn insects, they've gnawed their own souls away, now they're setting about the earth itself. Let it all go up in smoke, not into their greedy bellies. Scavengers!"

He covered his face with his hands and sat silently rocking from side to side. Pyotr Vasilievich, sharing his suffering, admitted to himself with some surprise that he had never understood this brother of his, any more than he had managed to understand the other one, Vasilii, who had got stuck in Moscow when he was demobbed after the war, working as a boilerman or a caretaker or something.

"It's high time I looked old Vasilii up as well. Maybe he's still alive. No sense in harboring grievances at our age."

VIII

Driving rain blanketed the countryside and followed Pyotr Vasilievich all the way from Uzlovsk. It was as though the train were traveling along the bottom of an enormous reservoir. Drowning in the downpour, houses, woods, and distance boards rippled brokenly in the streaming gloom and swam past the windows.

Opposite Pyotr Vasilievich, but at a respectful distance from each other, two people were suffering agonies of mutual hostility. A man and a woman. A thin scrawny old woman, and a fat man with a shaven skull, in a shabby officer's tunic with a piddling strip of ribbons on his left breast. The haughty immobility of her birdlike profile, turned resolutely away from him, left no doubt about their connection and the state of relations between them.

The fat man kept peeping at her with a piteous hunted look in his sclerotic eyes, and pleading with clockwork repetitiveness:

"We used to hold hands once . . ."

But the birdlike profile was firm and unflinching, though the sinewy hands closed tighter on a nervously clutched handkerchief to still their trembling.

"We used to hold hands . . ."

It seemed safe to assume that those halcyon days were thirty years or so behind them, but the embers of their happiness were obviously warm enough in him to awaken a feeble flicker in her chilly heart.

When she could stand it no longer she rose and sailed haughtily out of the compartment. The fat man was only awaiting her departure to pour out his sorrows to Pyotr Vasilievich.

"I drink all right, I don't deny it . . . But why do I drink? I've been demobbed for five years now, and I've got nothing to latch onto . . . They shunted me off to a House of Culture for a start . . . what way is that to treat a regular officer, making him run hobby classes? Some people couldn't feed swill to pigs but they get jobs for the asking. Me they shoved into every one-eyed place they could think of till I got sick of it and took my pension. Then there's my children. All putting on airs and not an ounce of respect for their father. They don't miss a chance to make a fool of me. They think I'm just an old blimp. It's enough to drive a saint to drink. And now, in my old age . . ." (He obviously thought that flaunting his age was the way to play on Pyotr Vasilievich's sympathies.) "A divorce. How d'you like that? Brought 'em up, fed 'em all those years, and now they want to see the back of me."

He broke off suddenly when he heard his wife's footsteps.

"That's how it is, old pal."

She came in without vouchsafing them so much as a glance, and sat down, her birdlike profile mute and still against the storm-washed window.

And in her place Pyotr Vasilievich suddenly saw another woman, a lot younger and better-looking, but in much harsher and more troubled times, sitting just as stiffly opposite him in the head-conductor's compartment of his train.

Only it was night, and summer.

He had picked Maria up at Epifanis, to oblige a railwayman he knew who was an uncle of hers. She sat wedged in the far corner, staring at him unblinkingly, almost defiantly, and didn't say a word. He was silent, too. He usually talked to such passengers rather roughly and patronizingly, and was surprised to find himself nervous and ill at ease in her presence. She wasn't much to look at, but something about this slip of a girl took his breath away whenever he tried to speak normally.

Getting his first words out was like climbing a mountain.

"You from Uzlovsk yourself, then?"

She answered briefly but without hesitation.

"No, we're from the pit."

"From Sychevka, you mean?"

"That's us."

"Been visiting?"

"No, working . . . Auntie Grusha was poorly," she hurried to explain, "and there was nobody to look after the house, but now she's up again and I'm going home . . . I've missed it terribly."

"Soon be there."

"Can't be too soon for me."

"How many of you are there at home?"

"Five, not counting me. My mother and father and three sisters."

"Can't be easy for your father."

"It isn't."

Under the banal surface of their conversation every word had a hidden meaning which only they could sense. They were seized with a presentiment that something irrevocable had happened. The lights of Uzlovsk drew nearer and ceased to dance in the blackness outside, and their voices sank to a tremulous whisper.

"I bet you have fun in Sychevka . . ."

"If you can call it fun. The lads getting drunk and throwing their weight about . . ."

"Do our lot from Uzlovsk come over?"

"No, they know what's good for them."

"What do you mean?"

"Ours don't make them welcome."

"What have they got against us?"

"You're all clean and tidy . . . And that's not all."

"What if somebody wasn't afraid?"

"You can try your luck."

Just as the conductor was savoring his victory, the first station lamp broke through the darkness ahead of them. It was probably the first time in his brief career that he regretted arriving so soon.

"So you won't chase me away?"

She coquettishly pretended not to understand.

"There's plenty of room for everybody, and our girls are just as pretty as the Uzlovsk lot."

"I'm not interested in all of them."

He would probably have let himself go there and then and revealed his sudden passion but the train gave a final shudder and stopped dead. Maria rose, rustled past him, bowed silently at the door, and instantly vanished down the corridor.

Next day, as soon as the first notes from the balalaikas on the other side of Khitrovo Pool began to cascade across the evening air, Lashkov strode toward Sychevka in a neatly pressed suit, his box-calf boots gleaming in the rosy light of the setting sun.

Before he reached the village boundary he could pick out her voice from all the others. His heart stood still and he felt a choking tightness in his throat.

> "The concertina's loud and merry.
> Let's show Mishenka the door!
> Girls who marry in a hurry
> Get more than they bargain for."

As though sensing him nearby she sent her next verse to meet him, and he felt cold and faint.

> "I'll press my dress all white and frilly,
> Down the street I'll go so gay,
> I can make the boys look silly,
> I can steal their hearts away."

He hovered around the party, too shy to butt in on the miners' jollification, until around midnight when Maria's last jingle brought her to him.

> "Down our way we're but two players,
> Balalaika and accordion.
> Stay at home and keep your prayers,
> We shall never spare you one."

She appeared so suddenly and was so close to him in the darkness that all he could say was, "I was visiting relatives . . ."

"Hallo, Pyotr Vasilievich," she answered faintly.

They said scarcely two words to each other that night by Khitrovo Pool, but on the way home he didn't walk . . . he was on air . . . alight with a joy he had never known before.

They caught him just as he was approaching the settlement, by Kimlev's orchard next door to his own ground, knocked him down, and beat him savagely, with a sort of lust. At last, when blood-red spots were floating before his eyes, a voice hoarse from this feverish exertion reached him as he was sliding into unconsciousness.

"Don't finish him off, boys, let him suffer, the bastard. He can show the others the way to Sychevka . . . ugly-looking bastards like that coming after our girls . . ."

God alone knows how he struggled home. But when he came to, he was aware simultaneously of the morning light, his pain, and a startlingly familiar voice, tinged with despair, saying:

"What have they done to you, the monsters? They're like wild animals. Dirty pit rats . . . Worse than animals, they are . . . monsters!"

"Don't go away, Masha," he managed to say as he slipped back into oblivion.

And she stayed.

Stayed until that dirty March day when four of her kin had carried her on two towels out through the door of Lashkov's cottage.

Ilya Makhotkin, her father, outlived her, and he had gone past Pyotr Vasilievich's place many a time after a night's boozing yelling drunken reproaches at the windows.

"You killed her, Pet'ka, you bloody murderer! You're all dried up, there's a smell like a mummy on you . . . Bloody vampire, you're dead but you won't lie down, there isn't a spark of life in you. Christ forgive you!"

The birdlike profile of the old woman opposite, blurred for a moment by his memories, swam into focus again. There she sat, unbending as ever, simply ignoring her pensioned-off husband's miserable pleas.

"We used to hold hands."

IX

Pyotr Vasilievich hadn't been in Moscow since the day he had handed in his conductor's pouch and his ticket-punch and gone home a humble pensioner. Now, after the comparative calm and quiet of Uzlovsk, the city seemed more rickety and uncomfortable than ever. With the help and advice of volunteers, he blundered about the spiderweb of backstreets in Sokolniki for quite a time before he found the address in his notebook. The number he wanted appeared through the leaves of a rugged poplar that grew beside a two-storied wooden house, with another house, stone-built and taller, overlooking its roof. Pyotr Vasilievich entered the yard and stood still for a while to pull himself together.

His heart was fluttering with anxiety.

"Forty years and more, it's no laughing matter!"

He fumbled awkwardly for the doorbell in a gloomy entrance hall which stank of cats and started fretting again as soon as he had rung it.

"He'll open the door and won't know me, I'm sure."

But when a sleepy face covered in gray stubble appeared in the doorway, Pyotr Vasilievich's doubts deserted him: across the threshold, like his own reflection in a mirror, shifting lazily from foot to foot, stood an old man who plainly belonged to the same Lashkov stock. He too behaved as though it was at most a day or two of separation that lay between them, instead of something like half a century, and he greeted his guest with no more than a slight whistle.

"Well, I'll be . . . Come on in . . ."

His brother's cluttered cubbyhole, more like a wild animal's den than a human dwelling, was grudgingly lit by a dim window covered from outside with a close wire mesh. The walls, pasted over with old newspapers, silently blared out prewar headlines: "Warmest Greetings to Our Heroic Arctic Explorers!" "Crush the Reptile!" "Hands off Madrid!" On a rickety table a battered alarm clock ticked off the minutes, surrounded by empty bottles of all sorts and sizes. Pyotr Vasilievich lowered himself onto the chair which his brother brought, and looked around in dismay.

"This how you live, then?"

"This is it," Vasilii answered indifferently as he took the bottles off the table and stowed them away in various nooks and crannies. "The visitors I get aren't fussy, and anybody who doesn't like it can go somewhere else . . . Come on, have something to buck you up after the journey."

With shaky hands he poured a still untouched quarter into two glasses and pushed one over to his brother.

"Here's to our reunion . . ."

In the long silence that followed, Pyotr Vasilievich studied his brother furtively, trying to fit each feature, each distinguishing mark, into the image he had formed in his mind long before this meeting. He was five years older than Vasilii, and since their boyhood he had always felt superior to his brother and patronized him. But Vasilii was as vain and stubborn as most of the Lashkovs, and as soon as he could stand on his own feet he had hastened to break away from his brother. When he came of age he went into the mine, and from there was called up into the army. The rare letters which reached his friends and contemporaries in Uzlovsk told them little except that he hadn't had an easy time of it in the army, that life had been even tougher afterwards, and that old age had found him childless and penniless in the house he had lived in all along. Ten years ago Vasilii had stopped writing altogether; memories of him in his hometown faded and then died out.

Pyotr Vasilievich looked at his blurred features, trying not to show his compassion as he noted how sallow and prematurely gray they were; it was sad to imagine what his brother had gone through during the long years of their separation.

"Maybe you'd like to come home?" he asked cautiously. "There's plenty of room. We shouldn't need much, just the two of us. Living's cheap where we are. And it'd be more cheerful if we were together."

"It's too late, Pyotr."

His eyes had clouded with the drink, and he squinted foolishly.

"Who needs me in Uzlovsk?"

Pyotr Vasilievich wouldn't give up.

"Who needs you here?"

His host's voice was tinged with unnerving sadness.

"Everything I've got is here, brother. My whole life is here. All right, it wasn't much of a life, knocked from pillar to post all the time. But however awful it was, I can't just forget it . . ."

Suddenly he stared tearfully at his guest like a rabbit and his cheek-bones stood out sharply under the week-old stubble.

"Pyotr, oh Pyotr! What a tornado hit us. I remember when I came here out of the army . . . I thought everything was before me. Just the right age, nothing but good marks on my record, take my pick of the girls. Only it didn't work out like that . . . They didn't give me a chance. They started dunning me, and I've never got straight since. Somehow or other, I was in debt all round: to God and the state and the plumber's second mate. Don't go there, don't say this, don't do that. It was like some scare story—the deeper into the wood I went the more frightening it got. And why, I ask you? What did I ever do to deserve it?"

His anger grew more emphatic with every word.

"Did I get my life on loan from somebody? You're a party man, Pyotr, how do you explain it . . .?"

As he listened, Pyotr Vasilievich's eyes were fixed on a lonely moth, near to exhaustion, convulsively wriggling and struggling in a spider's web that was slung across the upper right-hand corner of the window frame. The elastic threads swayed and quivered, wrapping their prey tighter and tighter, until at last the dusty wings in the deadly net were still.

The sympathy which Pyotr Vasilievich had felt at first for his brother's drunken misery gave way to undisguised irritation.

"Still waiting for a master, Vasilii, my lad. When master comes he'll sort it all out for us. What d'you think you were given a head for? Can't you manage without a nanny?"

Vasilii sobered up and his face grew stern; white spots stood out on his cheeks.

"We could have managed. Only you wouldn't let us. You nannied us to death, you and your bogeymen. One step to the right or left and it's desertion. That's the only tune you know. Like it or lump it, but go where you're told. And when the time comes to die a man realizes he's been going arse backwards all his life driven by the lot of you."

The conversation had taken an uphill turn, and it was against Pyotr Vasilievich's principles to back down on such occasions.

"I never made my living driving other people. I didn't get these calluses for nothing—I earned them."

Vasilii taunted him openly.

"What with, the chairman's bell at meetings? 'After hearing . . . The meeting resolved . . .' We've heard from you too often, Pyotr Vasilievich, my darling boy. Can you tell me where your children are? Can you give me any sort of address for them? I've got nothing to do in my old age, I'll go and look them up. Or maybe you'd rather tell me how you drove your wife into the grave? Can you give your old mate, Foma Leskov, his health back?"

Vasilii broke off suddenly, obviously realizing that he had shown himself to be rather too well informed.

"Let's leave it at that. The way we're squabbling, anybody would think we had a century ahead of us. I'll whip out and buy a drop more to drink, that's the best thing."

He made for the door in a hurry, to forestall any protest.

"Back in a flash."

Now that he was alone, Pyotr Vasilievich carefully inspected the room again. Everything in it bore the marks of neglect and premature decay. Things had been flung down carelessly years ago, and looked as though they had lain there ever since. Rickety furniture, rugs of every description, the odd tool stuck in a muddle of jars, flasks, and bottles cluttered the corners; everything was covered with a virgin layer of dust. In this miserable scene of neglect Pyotr Vasilievich caught an oblique reflection of his own life, so full of furious activity, yet lived so blindly, devoid of pity or purpose. Till now he had never been absorbed in the affairs and the worries of those whom fate had led across his path. He had felt sorry for them, but had erected mental barriers between them and himself. Now however, in the midst of all this decay, his eyes were suddenly opened. He, Pyotr Vasilievich Lashkov, was inescapably involved, blood brother to all of them in their common and incurable sickness. The illusory relief which he had experienced after his previous encounters, when he had given a helping hand to others and felt for a while how much they needed him, gave way to bitter depression. He was transfixed by the certainty that he could do nothing here to help either himself or his brother.

So Pyotr Vasilievich rose quietly and left, not even shutting the door behind him, never to return.

"It's better for both of us that way. Less upsetting."

X

He was still some way from the house when he saw Nikolai sitting under the window. Since Pyotr Vasilievich had managed to get him a residence permit and fix him up with a job in the engine sheds, the young man had taken to visiting his godfather regularly, but spent more and more of his time in Antonina's part of the house. At one time Pyotr Vasilievich, who was rather particular in the matter of credentials, would have sent this uninvited suitor packing, but now that he had dignified his godson with his protection he did not feel entitled to hurt his feelings.

"Let him have a little bit of womanly warmth—there's not much for him at home with his mother."

If Nikolai's vigil beneath his windows was no cause for surprise, his attitude—knees pressed together, chin resting on them, hands clasped in front of him, face gloomy and vacant—awakened a certain disquiet which grew with every step he took.

With a nod he told his guest not to get up and asked with unconcealed anxiety, "Where's Antonina?"

"Out."

The young man hemmed and hawed, looked everywhere except at him, and stammered pathetically till at last, pinned down by a direct question, he said quietly and clearly:

"She's at the Gupaks' house."

The name was a searing shock. It confirmed old suspicions which he had jealously tried to hide even from himself. It explained everything— the icon lamp which had appeared in the place of honor in his daughter's bedroom, her pious fussing over every passing beggar, the rapid old-womanish whispering on the other side of the partition.

He burned with resentment.

"Your daughter's being carried off under your very nose, and you don't lift a finger, you silly old devil."

"Sit here and wait," he said as he turned to go. "If she comes back—not a squeak about me, got it?"

His guest's only response was to hang his head still lower.

Pyotr Vasilievich dodged around outside Gupak's house till it was nearly dark, waiting for the "brothers" and "sisters" to leave after Gupak's routine sermon. When the last of them finally vanished round the corner, the old man stepped resolutely onto the porch, which was still warm from the tread of many feet. One glance from him was enough for the well-scrubbed old woman, who tried to bar his way; she vanished into the gloom of the entrance hall. The spacious parlor's only light was the lamp under an opulent icon case, so that everything in the room was blurred and vague.

"Good day, Pyotr Vasilievich! What can I do for you?"

The voice floated out of the dark space between the corner window and the stove. Now that his eyes were a bit more used to the gloom, Pyotr Vasilievich made out a chair, and the master of the house sitting in it.

"Good day. You might put a light on . . ."

Noiselessly, Gupak's wife emerged from the darkness and set another candle under the icon case. At once, Gupak's face appeared.

"I knew you'd come. I was sure you would. You couldn't help coming. It's fate, Pyotr Vasilievich. Destiny, so to speak, my dear sir . . . I've waited more than forty years and now at last you honor me with a visit . . . To tell you the truth, it's been nagging at me all day . . ."

His face, with its tough stubble of graying ginger whiskers, came closer and closer, until the bulging, bloodshot eyes were staring into those of his guest. And, simultaneously, each of them was dazzled by a vivid memory of that January morning long ago and their single, memorable, encounter.

A dim, depressingly flat light filtered through the encrusted patterns of frost on the window of the station telegraph office. A red-hot iron stove belched out fumes and a dry heat that made the temples throb and the heart miss beats.

A telegrapher with a bad chill coughed heartrendingly over his battered keys, desperately trying to contact Uzlovsk, while Pyotr Vasilievich paced round him, waiting for Mironov, the stationmaster, to arrive.

Just a week ago, when Lashkov was unexpectedly made commissar of the whole Syzran-Vyazina route, the line had been quiet. Nothing of importance ever happened on it. The operations group worked mainly on petty matters: black marketers, sabotage, requisitioning fuel supplies. But sure enough, the very day after he took up his duties, disaster struck. Two freight trains crashed head-on the last lap of the Roshcha-Dubki run. Along with the news of this event came supplementary information that Mironov, as soon as he had arranged for regional headquarters to be informed, had dropped everything and gone home to drink himself silly. This clue to the probable culprit was too blatant for the district Cheka to ignore.

Pyotr Vasilievich rushed to the scene of the collision on the handcar assigned for his use, with an operations group of three. On the way they started discussing various possible explanations for the crash.

Gudkov, a fat-faced man with a straggly, sweaty-looking beard that came nearly up to his eyes, puffed away at his cigarette ration and delivered his verdict unhesitatingly.

"It's him. Couldn't be anybody else. I know him—our little Lyova. I was a pointsman under him for ten years, more or less. The bastard! It's him. Why else would he hit the bottle?"

Vanya Krynkov was more dubious. A hard-bitten man, formerly a fitter in the repair sheds, he was always quick to prove his point with his fists, but utterly devoted to his work.

"I don't know. Why didn't he run away then? Who was stopping him?"

Luka Bondar carried scars from every front in the civil war, and one of his eyes squinted hard at the bridge of his nose. He pulled the younger man up sharply.

"Where would he run to? Tell us that. Every mouse in this place knows him. He's gone off the deep end. What officers call 'var-bank.' "

He turned away indifferently as if to dissociate himself from a conversation which he found boring and pointless.

His mood infected the others, and the operations group had passed the rest of the journey in silence, puffing at their cigarettes in the bluish gloom of the early dawn.

Pyotr Vasilievich didn't like this whole business one little bit, and now, pacing from end to end of the telegraph office, he couldn't shake off a feeling of nervousness.

"There's a catch in it somewhere, God alone knows what, though, but I'll be the one to answer for it, whatever happens. Mustn't screw it all up."

To cap it all, his teeth were aching like hell. Little red-hot hammers were tapping Morse code in his temples—dot, dash, dot—and deep inside him was a growing presentiment of some disaster which would somehow affect the case itself and him personally; it made Lashkov's condition still more unbearable.

"What am I going to do with him if Gudkov turns out to be right?" he asked himself painfully. "Seeing a hen's throat slit turns my stomach and this is a human being. I've been given full powers, but can I bring myself to do it?"

The full powers he'd been given were quite unambiguous: there was no room for pity.

Avanesyan, chairman of the district Cheka, a mournful, big-nosed Armenian who'd been in the party and done time in Siberia before the revolution, had offered the new commissar some parting advice. He had conferred those full powers of his with a single look from eyes that were yellow with congenital fever.

"Got your Smith on you?"

"Part of my job."

"The other men's rifles in order?"

"They won't let us down."

"Get on with it, then. Instructions all clear?"

"Yes."

"Right. Get going."

His orders certainly left no room for conjecture: he was to render impossible any further act of sabotage anywhere on the Syzran-Vyazina route. And the recommended means of translating these orders into action was the gun.

In Mironov he'd expected to find a bearded saboteur with a prerevolutionary technical education, and had been prepared to handle him accordingly. So Pyotr Vasilievich was a little taken aback when he saw a man of his own age or perhaps a bit younger being led into the telegraph room by Gudkov.

The bourgeois expert, wearing a nightshirt under an overcoat slung casually over his shoulders, was shivering ceaselessly like a man with a severe chill, but Pyotr Vasilievich saw at a glance that what was making the unfortunate railwayman tremble wasn't fear but a heavy hangover which was getting worse by the minute. The rabbity eyes with their fine network of red capillaries stared at him defiantly.

Pyotr Vasilievich tried to look experienced and shrewd in his unfamiliar role.

"Well, what have you got to say? Or are you going to hold out on me?"

"What about?"

"You know what. How, and with whom, did you organize the crash on the branchline?"

"What are you talking about . . .? Why don't you get on with it?"

Krynkov had been anxiously following their conversation and was obviously itching to butt in on the interrogation.

"Don't you tell us what to do," he burst out suddenly. He went up to the prisoner, eloquently fingering the wooden holster at his waist. "We'll soon cut you down to size. We haven't come here to fool around. We'll . . ."

Mironov merely frowned, lowered his eyes and retorted without thinking: "Slave."

Then he added, with rising assurance and contempt, "Slaves, all of you."

Rage at this insult, annoyance at his failure in this first job, and a humiliating awareness of the full absurdity of the situation in which he so unexpectedly found himself, swept Lashkov off balance. With considerable difficulty he suppressed an urge to settle with Mironov on the spot.

"Take him away," he said to Gudkov harshly. "Take him somewhere not too close, out in the fields. Over the level crossing somewhere . . . We don't need help, we aren't babies."

As he turned resolutely away from the doomed railwayman, Pyotr Vasilievich felt as though he had crossed some kind of a frontier, a dividing line; on the other side, all the fears and doubts, all the uncertainties which had dogged him ever since he got his orders, suddenly left him. As though he were traveling an unfamiliar route, and suddenly, round the first bend, he saw the way stretching straight ahead of him, free of obstacles as far as the eye could see. . . .

The light of that distant morning faded, giving way to the treacherous semidarkness of Gupak's home. Pyotr Vasilievich, still under the spell of his dissolving vision, could scarcely get a word out.

"Mironov? Gupak?"

His host eagerly came to his aid.

"I'm a Gupak on my dear mother's side, God rest her soul. She was from the Ukraine, my late mother. So I took the name quite honestly, exercising my right as a citizen . . ."

Pyotr Vasilievich, restored to present reality, carefully studied the familiar features, now blunted by the years.

"So my nine grammes of lead passed you by, did they, Mironov?

Obviously Gudkov reported without bothering to check up on his work . . ."

"Whatever he reported, he didn't carry out his orders."

Mironov made no attempt to conceal his triumph.

"Because he hadn't forgotten how kind the Mironovs had been to him. Who helped him bring up his barefooted horde? Who covered up for him when he hit the bottle? Who looked after his wife in all her confinements? Mironov's mother, God rest her soul, Anna Grigorievna, née Gupak, and your humble servant, Lev Lvovich. Switchman Gudkov didn't forget our kindness, you see, and didn't shoot me. 'Be off with you, Lev Lvovich,' he says, 'and good luck to you. Think of me kindly!' Evidently it's easier to whet a workingman's appetite for other people's cash than to kill the Christian soul in him . . ."

"Well, well, who'd have thought it of Gudkov?" said Pyotr Vasilievich with a rueful smile.

It was only now, as he relived Gudkov's return, that he became aware of his uncharacteristic taciturnity, his incessant smoking—he was usually so careful and economical with cigarettes—his fidgety uneasiness on the homeward journey.

"It would take more than Gudkov to prove my cause wrong, Citizen Mironov. Otherwise it would never have stood the test of time."

But Mironov went on as though he hadn't heard.

"You didn't kill it then, and now you never will. Nature played up for a bit but now it's back in the old channel. I always knew that the seed would sprout in your children, if not in you. And it has. It isn't dead. The first shoots have broken through. Through ashes and thorns, but there they are. Really and truly, it was the happiest and most beautiful day in my life when your daughter Antonina came to us, to the brotherhood. And I foresaw then that you and I were bound to meet. Saw it as plain as plain. Thank you, Pyotr Vasilievich, for doing me this good turn in my old age. What has your general rebellion done for you personally? You're all alone, without a friend in the world. I'm not out to enjoy my revenge, believe me, I just want to tell you the truth. Old scores mean nothing at our age. Repent, dear Pyotr Vasilievich, and you will find peace."

"You know as well as I do that it's all a fraud."

"What about bread, then—is that a fraud?"

"No." And, more emphatically: "No, bread is no fraud."

"Nor is faith. Any faith is good.

'Dearer to us delusions that exalt us
Than all the thronging mists of bitter truth.'

That's a saying for all time. You thought you'd discovered the light: there is no God! But your light released in mortal man his bestial nature, his animal instincts. And now you're reaping the fruits of your discovery. Everything's falling to pieces in your hands, and you can't stop it. The ocean has burst its bounds, and you want to stop it with lectures and decrees. In place of the dream of eternal life you fobbed man off with promises of universal gluttony and idleness. But what does he do? Man, I mean? As soon as he's eaten his fill he starts hankering after eternal life all over again. Try and hold him now, if you can."

And suddenly Pyotr Vasilievich caught a scorching whiff of cordite from the market square he'd crawled over, all that time ago, to the bogus ham in the shop window. "Was it really all for nothing? Has everything I've lived for been a mistake?" But his momentary doubt was followed by outrage. Bloody rubbish! Sanctimonious humbug! It'll never be the way you want it, from now till Kingdom Come.

"Gathering all the hysterical females in Uzlovsk together makes you happy, doesn't it? Makes you think you've come out on top."

As he was speaking, he recovered the strength and assurance which he had lacked at the beginning of their conversation.

"Well, you're in too much of a hurry to bury the cause I stand for. I shall be master here on earth, not you. And you'll get my nine grammes sooner or later, Mironov."

Mironov's rather red-rimmed eyes closed heavily, as though shutting himself off from his visitor once and for all. This was to indicate that the discussion was at an end.

Contrary to his custom, Pyotr Vasilievich rushed noisily into the house; not doubting that his words would reach the ears they were meant for, he said:

"No need to hide. Act your age. Move in here with us tomorrow. We'll make a go of it. The three of us together."

A single faint sigh of gratitude from the pair beyond the partition was his only answer.

XI

Pyotr Vasilievich woke up with a vague sensation of impending change, of some still mysterious turning point in his destiny.

Then he remembered that his daughter Antonina was marrying the son of his late colleague Leskov that very day.

"Getting old and past it, Pyotr, my lad," he chided himself. "Forget your own name next."

He lay in bed, surprised and proud, and he couldn't help laughing at himself. If anybody had told him a month ago, or even last week, that such a thing was possible he would have taken it as a malicious and uncalled-for joke. Could it really happen that he, Pyotr Vasilievich Lashkov, with his reputation and position in the town, could become related to the Leskovs, known to all Uzlovsk for their doubtful honesty and disorderly behavior? Anyone in Uzlovsk would have been shocked to hear it.

Well, it had happened. And what was more important, he thought of his daughter's impending marriage with profound satisfaction. What plans he had made! What blissful pictures he drew for himself! In his flights of fancy he already considered himself a grandfather.

Pyotr Vasilievich, still laughing at himself, soared even higher, dreaming to the accompaniment of two voices in harmony beyond the flimsy partition.

"Daddy isn't as bad as he seems, he's very, very kind really . . ."

"The old man's all right, he's no fool."

"He doesn't bear grudges. He's soft as wax."

"Well, the way I see it . . . he knows how to get his own way. All your family's the same—the Lashkovs have been ordering people about since they were so high."

"He's fair, though."

"I would never in my life have thought he'd let you and me . . ."

"Well, that's what I'm telling you. He's fair. Mind you don't regret it."

"Don't talk silly."

"Look at me . . ."

"I'm not blind."

"I can spend the rest of my days on my own. I'm used to it by now."

"Don't talk nonsense."

"Darling Nikolai."

"What do you know? They appreciate me!" thought Pyotr Vasilievich with enthusiastic approval. And he gave a slight cough to let them know he was awake.

The voices behind the partition ceased immediately. Then, after a minute's silence Antonina scratched cautiously on the wall.

"Daddy?"

"Time to get up."

"I'm coming."

"Don't rush—there's no great hurry."

But in the other room his daughter was already busy with the usual morning chores, with intervals for hastily whispered exchanges.

"Get up, Nikolai."

"Ugh."

"Pop out and fetch some water."

"Just getting my shoes on."

"Put your socks on, there's dew on the ground."

"I won't melt."

"No, either you put them on or I won't let you go; I'll go myself."

Everything they said was so trivial and ordinary, yet there was so much warmth and trust in each word that anyone overhearing them might have taken their conversation for an endless declaration of love. Pyotr Vasilievich listened with a smile.

"Let's hope they never get on any worse than this."

That morning the three of them sat down to their first meal together. Antonina jumped up from time to time, busily surrounding each of them with plates, dividing her favors and her gratitude evenly between the two men.

"Eat all you can, or you'll be drunk by nightfall. More, Daddy? Nikolai?"

It's no use pretending that Pyotr Vasilievich wasn't jealous of the son-in-law who had partially replaced him in his daughter's heart as soon as he set foot in the house. But Antonina's holiday mood affected him, too, making him resigned and indulgent.

· · ·

They arrived a little before time at the registry office, where the witnesses were waiting for them, all dressed up for the occasion: a sprightly
young man with a guitar over his shoulder, already a little drunk, and a
shivering girl, with questioning, permanently frightened eyes, wringing
her handkerchief in an agony of embarrassment. The young man thrust
a sweaty hand somewhat awkwardly at Pyotr Vasilievich and said with
a vacant laugh, "I'm Leonid, a cousin."

His companion blushed in confusion under Pyotr Vasilievich's specu-
lative gaze and her trembling lips barely managed to form the word,
"Lena."

Nikolai summed up these introductions: "Two of ours, Pyotr Vasilievich, from the depot."

Just before they went in, three Volgas rolled up to the entrance and
braked sharply. The party that came pouring out of the car must have
started drinking early. Conspicuous among them for his size and loudness
was Gordei Gusev, Pyotr Vasilievich's neighbor in days gone by, the
king and god of Uzlovsk fixers. A smart, well-fitting dark suit of prewar
cut hugged his body, which was remarkably athletic for his years; a gray
forelock hung jauntily over his bushy brows, and from head to foot he
exuded defiant enjoyment.

Gordei's luck had been famous from the day of his birth, when his
mother lost consciousness and half-suffocated him, but he somehow survived and shot up to become a hefty chap nearly seven feet tall with
fists like hams. All the fires and floods through which his generation
had passed in the turbulent years had somehow left him unscathed. He
had mastered a number of trades, and whenever there was a whiff of
trouble in the air, his skill at making himself indispensable proved a sure
defense.

On the day of Pyotr Vasilievich's evacuation, Gusev happened
to meet him, and explained his philosophy of life.

"I'm a man of no importance. I don't care what kind of government
we have, it's all the same to me. My job's a healthy one—I'm a craftsman. I've got no quarrel with the Germans. I worked under you a lot,
and I'll stick to my job under them. I shan't come to any harm."

Pyotr Vasilievich bitterly admitted to himself that it had all been
true.

"He stayed behind, and he came to no harm, and now he never will.
And here he is marrying his descendants off in high old style, not like
you!"

Gordei's searching eye had distinguished his old neighbor among the group by the entrance and he was already bearing down on him with open arms.

"Pyotr Vasilievich, hallo! What a long time it's been. I'm giving my granddaughter away. Soon I'll be a great-grandfather!"

There was a note of undisguised triumph in his overbearing friendliness. Compare the two of us and look who's come off best! Hurrying after the others as the door finally opened, he kept teasing Pyotr Vasilievich with his victorious smile.

"We're getting old, brother, the cemetery can't wait to see us. You might drop in occasionally, Pyotr Vasilievich. Don't look down on an old neighbor . . ."

Once again, as when he was talking to Gupak, Pyotr Vasilievich had a momentary vision of the grocer's shop on the square with its shattered window back in 1905.

"What if they win after all? What if the whole damn business was a waste of time?"

With this he stepped into the office. The woman registrar, who was rushing to receive the Gusevs, was obviously put out when she saw him. Her haggard, wedge-shaped face betrayed a titanic struggle between fear of offending a man much respected in local government circles, and her desire to oblige the omnipotent fixer. Protocol evidently prevailed. She turned to Pyotr Vasilievich and summoned him miserably.

"Comrade Lashkov, this way, please."

Now it was his turn to enjoy a malicious triumph. "There you are, Gusev. The world's a bit bigger than your back garden."

Antonina and Nikolai paraded their middle-aged dowdiness through the contemptuous ranks of the Gusev clan, past the young couple fashionably decked out in black and white. To the registrar's desk, and back again, to the welcome exit.

Neither on the way home nor at the table could the hosts or their guests shake off the tension and constraint which they brought away with them from the office. However much Antonina fussed over her friend, however often Nikolai topped up his pal's glass, they kept exchanging uncomfortable looks, and obviously found the hospitality embarrassing. When they finally said a far too hasty good-bye, Nikolai came to a decisive conclusion.

"We'll go away somewhere, Dad. There's no life here for me and Antonina."

For the first time since he'd known his son-in-law, Pyotr Vasilievich was at a loss for an answer.

XII

The night bus took them to Uglegorsk Airport. The newlyweds were flying to Moscow, and changing planes there. Antonina put a brave face on it all the way, but at Uglegorsk she broke down. She hid her head in her father's shoulder, and tearfully whispered, "Daddy, dearest Daddy . . . how will you manage without me? You should have come with us. There's nobody to do your washing or get your meals. And what if you fall ill? I'll miss you so much. Oh—Daddy."

"Now, then, Antonina, that'll do."

Pyotr Vasilievich stroked her head with an unsteady hand.

"I daresay I shan't come to any harm. How could I pull up my roots and start again at my age? Here I was born, and here I'll die. Only be sure you write, and don't forget . . ."

Nikolai stood to one side, shifting from foot to foot, looking at them like a hunted animal, and it was obvious that he too was upset. When their flight was called he rushed impulsively at Pyotr Vasilievich, gave the old man two quick rough hugs, and hoarsely blurted out, "See you one of these days . . . So long, Dad."

He grabbed the suitcases and made for the gate to the flight area. Antonina trailed after him, looking back again and again, until the steamed-over glass door swallowed her and her moaning cry, "Da-a-a-ddy."

Stunned by the onrush of loneliness, Pyotr Vasilievich wandered slowly and unthinkingly towards the bus stop. Some woman, straddling a mountain of sacks and baskets like a broody hen, called out to him cheerfully, "Sit here, Dad. Come closer, you'll be warmer! The bus won't be here for a bit yet . . ."

Pyotr Vasilievich made his way past her without answering.

The new day's light stole over the asphalt in front of him, as though in response to the tapping of his stick.

All his experiences in the few short days since his chance recollection outside the broken window of the municipal foodstore were working towards a conclusion, becoming meaningful.

Where, when, and why had he, Pyotr Vasilievich Lashkov, stopped defending his cause against the Gupaks, the Vorobushkins, and the Gusevs? What was this barbed-wire fence he had built around himself, shutting out even his own children? Where had he gone so miserably wrong?

And suddenly, out of the past, long since forgotten, his father-in-law's face, streaming with drunken tears, came floating up before him.

"You're all dried up. You stink of dry rot. There isn't a living fiber in you."

And the revelation he had been awaiting so anxiously and for so long dawned at last.

"Instead of going out to them, I always cut myself off. They got no light nor warmth from me, nor did anybody else, so they flew away like moths in the night to any lamp they could find. I must begin all over again. Better late than never."

Suddenly he felt relaxed and at peace. His mind turned to practicalities. As he walked he was thinking now about the children who would present him with grandchildren, those grandchildren's grandchildren, all those whose deeds and whose loyalty would preserve his land, his Russia, alive and indestructible down through the ages.

On he went, thinking and thinking . . .

TUESDAY

The Cattle Drive

I

After seeing his brother off, Andrei Vasilievich hurried back into his beloved forest. Between the ranger's post and his destination lay fifteen kilometers of barren hills. Andrei, who couldn't bear treeless patches, whipped his horse on unmercifully; only when he rode into the first plantation did he turn it loose to graze and take a rest himself.

It was only in communion with the forest that he felt at peace. On the rare occasions when he was called in to the district center on business he got lost, even in that far from populous place. He felt like an intruder in government offices; his tortured eyes were never still, and he didn't know what to do with his heavy hands, so out of place in such surroundings.

Now he lay face upward, gazing into a sky from which the last heat of autumn flooded down; once again he felt restored by the world he knew and loved, his life seemed full of meaning, and he knew that he was needed. Ever since he could remember, he had felt drawn to the forest, to the quiet water of brooks and pools. A soldier's dread of open spaces only reinforced this attraction. In the forest a man is invulnerable to cold and starvation. And besides, the forest makes everyone part of the mystical unity of all living things, which is something that a plain, however densely populated, cannot impart.

The death of a tree, a bush, a mere branch, especially when violent or unnatural, was taken by Andrei Vasilievich as an irreparable personal loss. Any illicit or even licit felling made him feel ill: he would mourn it for a long time afterward. And people were chopping the forest down around him ruthlessly, indeed, with a sort of drunken and savage passion. They chopped it down for good reason or for none at all, just because it was there, close at hand, full-grown but defenseless.

Not a day went by without Andrei Vasilievich drawing up reports, writing agonized appeals to the timber administration or the district center. The documents piled up, but the forest, his own forest, for which he suffered so much pain in a heart still weak from his wound, was melting away before his eyes. Nothing stronger than kvass had ever passed his lips before or during the war, but Andrei Vasilievich had gradually got into the habit of drinking on the sly. "Can't make much difference!"

Memories of the previous morning brought a painful constriction to his chest. Just before his brother's arrival, he had caught the oldest of the fatherless Agureevs in the birch plantation—there were five children in the brood, all brought up by their mother, Alexandra, a fine figure of a woman, but hot-tempered. The boy looked at the forester like a wild thing and his upturned, freckled face quivered with totally unchildlike rage: "I've got to get a whip, haven't I?"

There was such triumphant self-righteousness in his whole manner, such defiance, that Andrei Vasilievich could only spit out angrily, "You little devil, you!" and let him off scot-free.

Halfway down the slope, this scion of the Agureev clan turned round with a cheeky retort, "Devil, yourself!" And then, with pure malice, he added for precision's sake, "Crazy old devil!"

If it had been anyone else Andrei Vasilievich wouldn't have hesitated for an instant. He could impose a fine in such cases, and there had been quite a few women in the villages round about who had been forced to bring out their nest eggs and part with ten rubles. But his heart failed him at the thought that this would mean seeing Alexandra again. He sighed fatalistically.

"To hell with it. How can she manage a whole regiment of kids by herself? After all, she can't beg from door to door."

A heavy cloud crept out from behind a ragged line of luxuriant fir trees. It looked to him like a felt boot with the sole hanging loose. The leg of the boot was tinted a dull pewter, shading into a dark black patch at the heel. Andrei, half-asleep, thought to himself, "Going to rain, but it'll just miss us."

He dreamt of an empty field, raked by gunfire from all sides, with a single tree, a fir or a pine, standing out against the horizon. He was crawling toward the tree to take shelter, to hide from the deadly whine all around him; as he strained toward it, his brother's unforgettable voice followed him, calling:

"What's it all about, Andrei, little brother?"

And then, scarcely audible, Alexandra's whispered entreaty: "Be nice to me, Andrei, dearest Andrei . . ."

II

Uzlovsk reeked of charred paper. The town was ridding itself of everything that might prove a burden to its memories. Officialdom burnt such documents as it had no means of removing and ordinary people burnt the photographs and letters of friends and relations whom only yesterday they had proudly trotted out to confound their neighbors.

The occasional air-raid warnings had not as yet been capped by explosions, but the "double decker" reconnaissance planes circling in the defenseless sky announced the approach of the front line.

Andrei was hard put to find a place for his Bay at the hitching rail outside the council offices: The square in front of the building was jammed with cars and carts, people on foot and people on horseback. The human whirlpool was dotted with green—the color of war. The milling crowd in the corridor parted unbidden to let soldiers through, as though to emphasize their superior importance in the present circumstances.

The tiny cubbyhole belonging to Turkin, head of the agricultural department, was unexpectedly empty and quiet. Turkin himself, a puny, fairhaired man in an official blue suit, didn't even bother to look up from the papers on his desk, but rapped out, "Where you from?"

"Bibikovo. You sent for me."

"Oh, it's you, Lashkov."

The shortsighted, cornflower blue eyes turned to stare questioningly at Andrei. "How are things?"

He grabbed the receiver without waiting for an answer.

"Operator, Turkin here. Get me the first secretary, Vasilii Nikiforovich."

From force of habit, the head of department stood up while talking to his superior.

"Turkin here. Sorry to bother you. There's a chap here . . . Lashkov . . . no, not him . . . his younger brother, Andrei . . . warden out at

Bibikovo . . . That's the one . . . not thirty yet . . . still in Komsomol . . . single man . . . No, he's offering to go himself."

Carefully he replaced the receiver and his pasty face assumed a suitably authoritative expression.

"Right then, Lashkov, you have orders to evacuate the cattle."

Andrei had been ready for anything—a lecture on the growing losses from theft, a flea in the ear for failing to stop crop damage by animals, his call-up papers—anything, except this.

"What cattle, Vladimir Palich? Where've I got to evacuate them to?"

"What cattle?"

Turkin's voice grew sonorous and solemn.

"The herds from every kolkhoz in the district. And where to?"

His tone became still more earnestly emphatic.

"To Derbent, Lashkov, to Derbent. To the mountains. The district committee is trusting you with one thousand two hundred head of collective property. You are personally responsible for every one of them. You'll get the documents drawn up in the organization department. You'll draw weapons from military headquarters. Settle with the farm chairman who goes with you. Try and take people without big families. Live up to your name, Lashkov."

He held out a stubby, sweating hand to Andrei. In spite of his exaggerated briskness, his limp squeeze conveyed nothing but desperate tiredness.

"I wish you every success."

His new appointment took Andrei by surprise. He didn't lose his head, but he wasn't at all happy with the unexpected obligation to give orders, make demands, take responsibility. For as long as he could remember, he had always had to take orders. At home, from his father and his brother; in the army, from his section leader and all those superior to him; at work, from the chairman and numerous local officials of all ranks. Now that he had been put in sole charge of something, he couldn't picture himself at all clearly as the boss.

As always in difficult moments he felt the need of his brother. He worshipped his brother. Whenever they met, Pyotr Vasilievich tired him with his own grim determination, and with his faith in the part which the Lashkovs were called on to play in the common cause.

Andrei wandered about the corridors of the transport section in search of Pyotr Vasilievich for quite a while before a passerby put him right.

"Lashkov? In the siding past the ramp; he's taking over the records from the bookkeeper."

From a distance Andrei spotted Foma Leskov, his brother's old friend and partner, near a first-class carriage shunted onto a siding, fussing round a mountain of sacks stuffed with ledgers. When he saw the visitor, Foma grinned and shot a mischievous glance into the depths of the carriage.

"Somebody to see you, boss. Your little brother, in person."

Andrei had never found time to meet his brother in the chaotic first months of the war. He was pained to see the already pronounced stoop and the thick sprinkling of gray in the cropped hair which used to be black with bluish highlights.

"Good to see you, Andrei, lad."

His brisk friendliness obviously cost him an effort.

"I've been landed with a hell of a job here. Wouldn't wish it on anybody."

Andrei briefly informed his brother of his interview at the council offices, and made no bones of his feelings about it.

"Men my age are going off to fight, Pyotr, boy, and I'm going the other way, doing some herdsman's job."

For privacy they went into the sleeping car and Pyotr, who was usually so laconic, started lecturing Andrei at length, though without much conviction, about the need for discipline, but he suddenly changed his tune and concluded quietly and sadly:

"When all's said and done, somebody's got to do the job. We're drifting off in different directions, who knows where to. This looks to be a big war and a long one. I wonder whether we shall ever see each other again. Out of all the Lashkovs there's only two of us left. The rest are all scattered here, there, and everywhere . . . and life is going by fast."

Bitter regret showed in every phrase, and Andrei felt sure that his brother was much more in need of the comfort he had come looking for. But the words of sympathy which began to form in his mind dissolved into a short sigh. "Walk a bit of the way with me."

Their walk along the embankment to the nearest crossing was slow and silent. In those few minutes it was impressed on them as never before how much they had always meant to each other. Each of the brothers was the other's only link with all that the words "family," "clan," and "kin" convey; and without all that, each on his own, they stood for nothing.

At the crossing the brothers gingerly clapped each other on the shoulder, as though they were ashamed of their sudden impulse, and made off at once in opposite directions, without pausing or looking back.

III

Bibikovo, usually so quiet, was overwhelmed by clamoring humanity and the neighing of horses. Wagons loaded with the drovers' baggage milled around the office building. The envoys of six neighboring villages, and the cattle, hungrily bellowing in a field, were awaiting the order to set off for quiet Caucasian pastures.

Andrei had shut himself up in the chairman's quarters, and was weighing up the practical skills of each of his subordinates. Through the window he could see Prokofii Fyodorov, a drover from Kurka, carefully installing his pregnant wife Pasha in a cart, tucking fresh hay all round her, covering her legs with a quilt.

Andrei felt relieved as he watched them playfully scolding and teasing each other.

"He can be relied on. Won't let me down. Knows his job, too; wish they were all like him. His wife's very near her time, though. Never mind, there's plenty of women around, they'll deliver her."

By the kolkhoz barn, which had been fitted up as a clubroom, the lame concertina player, Sanka Sutyrin, was dejectedly rolling his drunken eyes, while he provided a farewell entertainment for the girls huddled around him.

> "These old boots may let in water,
> Those at home are shiny new.
> Kiss the mother or the daughter.
> What one's got the other's got, too."

He was the only concertina player in the district, and thoroughly spoiled by the fuss everybody made of him. His pigheadedness had brought him into conflict with Andrei more than once. "He's a show-off, of course, but he can turn his hand to anything. Jack-of-all-trades. He'll shape up."

Old Prokofich, who'd come from a family of landless peasants at Torbeevo and been christened by a shepherd's whip as soon as he could walk, was fixing the tailboard of his buggy with meditative care. His parchment face with its copper-colored beard radiated the calm efficiency of a masterhand, a worker, a craftsman, sure of his vocation in this world.

"A tower of strength. Worth his weight in gold, that old man."

As if in a dream when the mind can focus on one object to the total exclusion of everything else, Andrei's eyes and ears suddenly shut out the world around him. He had seen Alexandra. She was striding boldly across the road outside, making her way to the office. Neither the worn rubber boots, nor the coarse jacket which had been her husband's, nor the dark grandmotherly headscarf pulled down almost over her eyes could spoil the beauty of her warm eager body, or muffle the provocative sensuality of her nature.

A lot of water had passed under the bridge since that spring when she had shown Andrei's matchmakers the door and, from a host of admirers, chosen Sergei Agureev, the most hopeless layabout in Sviridovo. But even now Andrei felt hot and faint whenever he met her, and couldn't control the thumping of his heart.

Almost tumbling over himself in his hurry to unlock the door, Andrei addressed a mental rebuke to the Sychevka farm chairman.

"The old devil's twisting the knife! As though I hadn't got grief enough!"

He didn't know what to say, and she confused him further with her defiant sarcasm.

"Welcome, dear guests, how glad we are to see you, I don't think. I can't help it. Don't hold it against me, I didn't want to come."

She couldn't resist a bit of sarcastic insolence. But she checked herself and became businesslike.

"I've brought in a hundred and fifty head. The party from Sychevka will be me, and the whole Pashkov family—Pashkov's got exemption—and three Lyukovs—the old woman, her daughter, and her daughter-in-law —and daft Petya, that's our whole army . . ."

Andrei had jealously followed her fortunes from a distance, and knew nearly as much about her as did her nearest neighbors. Although no children had come along in the three years of her marriage to Sergei, they lived together amicably, contrary to the general expectation, though not altogether comfortably. Sergei volunteered on the day the war broke out, whether carried away by the general mood, or desperately to keep up appearances, and Alexandra boarded up the house in Sychevka and moved in with her mother. She could cope with any sort of job, was thorough in her work, and had a ready tongue. She soon gained respect and influence on the farm, and by the time the first scent of battle reached the district she was in charge of a livestock section. So that although he was amazed with the Sychevka chairman, Andrei couldn't help secretly approving of his choice.

"The old sod knows whom to trust with his cattle. She'll fall down on the job."

Andrei tried to master his agitation by rolling a pencil tightly between his hands.

"Not a hell of a lot, is it? A hundred and fifty head! Driving them is nothing. Petya could do it by himself. But what if there's an epidemic? Plague or something. Your old women will need nannies themselves. Some favor he's done me, your Mikhailo Porfirich."

"Well, where d'you think he can get people from?"

There was an angry spark in the depths of her blue-gray eyes, so childish still.

"All the men worth anything are over there"—she nodded at the window in the direction of the front—"and the women haven't produced a new lot yet. We'll manage the cattle somehow, provided we can have heroes like you to help us, Andrei Vasilievich."

Andrei stiffened in outrage at this blatant attack.

"You know as well as I do that I asked to go and they wouldn't have me."

"Anybody can see that strong party men are more use on the home front. To take charge of the women and kids in case they start being naughty with nobody to boss them. We couldn't get along at all without you Lashkovs, of course."

All Lashkovs were the same when the family name came up. His momentary embarrassment dissolved in blind, choking rage.

"Keep the Lashkovs out of it. The Lashkovs have never got in your way."

"No, I got in theirs."

Alexandra was openly savoring her revenge.

"The Lashkovs wanted to make little Alexandra's fortune, didn't they? Only they didn't succeed."

"You . . . why, you . . ."

He shot up like a taut spring, ready to hurl himself at her, but then sat down at the desk again, weak with shame and resentment, and turned his face to the window.

"Go away."

With a burning ache in the throat he watched her go down the office steps, and stride off toward her encampment, nodding to people she met on the way. He would have given a great deal at that moment for one of those little nods. So much had happened since he first set eyes on her and desired her, but he only had to glimpse her passing by and he was on fire again. Her figure gradually shrank into the distance, but he could not stop watching. When he came back to earth and looked round, a mournful, weary little figure of an old man was sitting in front of him, studying the opposite wall intently. He had obviously heard the whole conversation and was now silently inviting his host to admire his tact.

Andrei sullenly dropped his eyes.

"What d'you want, Dad? There's nobody in the office. I don't belong here."

"It's you yourself I want, Andrei—er—Vasilievich, if I'm not mistaken."

His voice ran the full gamut of bureaucratic emotions from respectful eagerness to condescending sympathy.

"I'm the vet from the local soviet, Grigorii Ivanovich Boboshko."

Until then, Andrei had forgotten that when Turkin had said goodbye, he had also promised to send him an experienced vet—pretty ancient, he said, but first-class at his job. This was not at all what Andrei had expected. He didn't know what to say.

"Yes, yes, of course. Think it over carefully, though. It's a long journey."

The old man evidently understood his host's feelings, and his eyes, clouded with age, lit up with good-natured irony.

"I wouldn't say no to a rest cure, of course, but, with all due respect, you can see for yourself what things have come to."

He dismissed the subject with a wave of his stumpy arms.

"So don't be too hard on me."

Andrei didn't know where to look.

"Sorry if I was talking out of turn. Let's go and look at the herds."

The cattle were bellowing on the grazing land at the end of the street. Every village wanted to keep its animals separate and this immediately gave rise to arguments and squabbles. There was a long, hard journey ahead that might hold disaster for any and all of them, but people will be people. They couldn't rise above their peacetime preoccupations, and everybody was busy grabbing for his own group whatever might come in handy on the journey. For a moment, Andrei was appalled by the burden he had shouldered.

"My God, what a rabble! How am I going to handle them? They'll tear me apart without a second thought, if it suits them."

But the habitual self-confidence of the Lashkovs came to the rescue again.

"After all, it won't take a superman. We'll survive somehow."

His momentary dismay was not lost on the vet.

"A speech might help, Andrei Vasilievich," he suggested with a quiet smile. "It's an historic moment, you might say."

Andrei scrambled onto an unhitched cart, and harangued the mob which immediately gathered around him—for he was no novice where public meetings were concerned.

"Friends and comrades, you can see that we have a tough job on our hands . . . We don't know what lies ahead, and we must all stick together. Unity is strength. Take good care of the property your farms have entrusted to you, and share everything else. A deadly force is threatening to crush us. The Fascists. You can't beat the Fascists unless you stand together. Singly they'll squash us like flies, so I shall shoot without warning if I have to."

He paused, and made it more official by adding:

"Close ranks against the enemy! Let us crush the Fascist beast! Move off!"

Bellowing and yelling, the stream of men and beasts rolled forward toward the high road; once the last calf had joined the herd, Yevse, the region's famous bull, moved to the front and led the column toward the clouds of dust on the horizon. The huge animal paced majestically along the verge, while both earth and sky and the long road ahead were clearly reflected in his deep brown eyes.

Andrei felt uneasy again.

"God knows how rough I'll have to be to get them there without losing anybody. Or, more important, any*thing!*"

IV

The night air was stuffy, and the sky, lavishly adorned with stars on the low horizon, was under the spell of Sutyrin's concertina.

> "My young man's got a party card
> And there's nothing he can't swallow.
> He drinks port wine from a samovar
> With a vodka chaser to follow."

Andrei recognized Alexandra's voice as he was making the rounds of the overnight camp.

"There she is. Let her wait and see. I'll have something to say about it. Just because there's a war on she needn't think she can get away with everything."

His face twitched with rage in the dark, but he knew that he wouldn't speak to her about it, because the only result of such a conversation would be more discomfiture. His helplessness made him even angrier.

"The rotten little bird," he thought. "She's doing it specially for my benefit. The lousy bird."

"Who d'you think you're shoving, you bastard?"

Somebody shied away from under the horse's muzzle.

"Can't you see there are people here? Oh, it's you, Andrei Vasilievich. I didn't recognize you."

Andrei identified Filya Duda, a shepherd from Torbeevo, by his manner, as ingratiating as ever. Filya had been a grandfather for some time, but he was stuck forever with his childhood nickname.

"Why aren't you asleep? Go and get some sleep. You won't get so much as a minute's pause tomorrow."

A wail came out of the darkness.

"Sleep! It only takes them half a minute to rustle a calf. The Sychevka gang have had their greedy eyes on them for ages. They'll leave us with their own scrawny specimens and drive ours away. Everybody knows they're all thieves in Sychevka. And we've got pedigree stock. The chairman will have our blood if anything happens. They're all thieves, anybody will tell you."

Andrei knew only too well that Filya could labor a subject to death without having a thing to say, so he hurried away.

"All right, then, but I still can't give you an easy time tomorrow. So long."

He felt drawn toward the sounds of Sutyrin's concertina, and turned his horse toward the Bibikovo herd. A verse came floating out to him.

> "I have loved you long, my dearest,
> I will love you evermore;
> While still the earth is turning
> And the wave beats on the shore."

Lashkov's heart went out to them.

"The women are going crazy, wondering whether they'll ever see their men again."

In the afternoon, as they were about to cross the Moscow-Kharkov Highway, the herd was halted by a long column of troops. Most of the marchers were mere boys, in brand-new uniforms. They marched with the nervous gaiety of all new recruits, whose time-honored motto is, "You only die once." There was scarcely one of them who missed the chance to show off with some suggestive crack at the women from the six Uzlovsk villages, who watched them sadly and in silence.

"Hey, you with the black hair, come for a walk with us—you won't be sorry!"

"Hallo, girls—are you two playmates?"

" 'Course they're playmates, Syoma, anybody can see that."

"I'd like to be their plaything, then."

"What, with a mug like yours, Syoma? Look at that big handsome fellow prancing round them. Isn't he a beauty, though?"

But the women stood in silence and didn't take offense. Even the most shrewish among them, who could talk the devil's hind leg off when they were in a temper, only smiled back ruefully from under their headscarves.

Have your fun, you can do what you like today.

Their indulgent silence gradually affected the marchers. The shouts grew less frequent and in some way more uncertain, until at last they ceased altogether; only the shuffling of hundreds of boots on the asphalt rose on the scorching air, to be broken occasionally by the plaintive lowing of the cattle. To the marchers, death as yet was something to be thought of, if not exactly with enthusiasm, then at least with a certain bravado. But the silence of the women watching by the roadside revealed the full price of what awaited them. What just a moment ago had been lost in a haze of heroism was now seen with soul-destroying clarity.

A little soldier, hardly more than a boy, lagged behind at the back of the column, hopping along on one leg, not wanting to stop as he struggled with an unruly puttee. When he had succeeded, he straightened up, turned his round, childishly chubby face towards the women, and wagged his finger menacingly, as if to say, "Mind what you're doing."

It was as though a gleam of sunshine had passed over their faces. Loud, uncontrollable laughter seized every female in Lashkov's tribe. They laughed till they cried.

"Hold on to me, girls, or I'll have a miscarriage!"

"I'd better run down the road for a pee!"

"Help, I just can't take it!"

"He's really scary! You could die laughing."

The herds moved across the road and resumed their journey, but the women wouldn't quiet down.

"Did you see that, Polina?"

"Better not get up to any monkey tricks!"

"We'll know what time it is when they get back!"

"Better watch out for yourselves, girls, or there'll be trouble later on."

"We'll have to be careful with wolves all round."

"Chase them off!"

"You chase them, I'm too weak."

Now, however, night had come, and their mad fit had given way to sadness and yearning.

> "A star fell from the sky above us,
>   Star like on a Christmas tree.
>   Rarely though I see my lover,
>   Seeing him's so sweet to me."

Strictly speaking, there was no need for Andrei to get up and make the rounds, and in any case he should have returned long ago to the village where he and the vet were billeted for the night. But he kept his horse Bay moving in endless circles, trying to shake off an inexplicable feeling of guilt which had given him no respite since the encounter on the highway. It wasn't his conscience troubling him because he was fit and still a civilian. That was something he no longer worried about. He had his orders, and he was carrying them out. If he was ordered to the front, he would go. No, it was simply that he suddenly saw the world divided into the driven and the drivers. The Lashkovs, for as long as Andrei could remember, had belonged to the second category. And with a painful shock he found himself wondering why, by what right? That line of thought opened onto an abyss, and to stop himself thinking he urged his horse to a gallop.

When he rode into the village, the first streak of light was already visible on the eastern horizon. Boboshko wasn't asleep. He suffered from an old man's insomnia, so that the most exhausting day's march knocked him out for two or three hours at most. He was sitting in the front garden with an old overcoat draped over his shoulders, and his birdlike eyes were sad and watery. He greeted Lashkov with affectionate reproach.

"You just can't keep still. You ought to be asleep. What d'you think is likely to happen? They're all guarding their own cattle. If anything does happen, they'll be here fast enough. Anyway, you can't have eyes for everything. This way, you'll be in a state of nervous exhaustion before you know where you are."

"You're one to talk!"

"You don't think it's worry that keeps me awake! In my case it's old age. You've got everything ahead of you, and I'm already drawing my conclusions, so to speak. I've got plenty to look back on. Have you ever heard, for instance, of the Icy March, Andrei Vasilievich? How could you, though. We were heart and soul for General Kornilov in those days. *Sans peur et sans reproche* . . . I'm not afraid to talk about it now. I've done my time! A long way off—in Pot'ma . . . There's something we overlooked, but what, I don't know . . . Perhaps I do, though. It was the psychology of the Russian peasant. We should have learned from the old risings, of course. He's an illusionist anarchist, our little Orthodox muzhik. He lives from day to day, and we offer him the Kingdom of Heaven. Why am I telling you all this? Go and get some sleep; it's only an hour or so before we start. In this heat, without sleep, you know . . ."

Andrei lay down, but he just couldn't go to sleep. He had managed to follow about half of Boboshko's ramblings, at best, but that was enough to make his muddled thoughts still harder to disentangle. Only now did he realize how completely he relied on his brother, his brother's experience, his strength, and, of course his authority. If only Pyotr were here, he'd sort it all out in a flash! Left to himself, Andrei couldn't see farther than the end of his nose. He was lost already. His life of independence, away from his brother, hadn't begun at all smoothly.

As he fell asleep, Lashkov could hear Sutyrin playing, and somebody singing.

> "See me home, my dearest love,
> By wild ways and paths apart.
> My dearest love, my only love,
> Who stole upon my heart."

"It's her, it's Alexandra."

Once more the thought of her returned to his mind as he dozed off, but this time it brought him peace.

V

For the last two days, the herds had been traveling alongside a branch line of the Rostov-Caucasus Railway, sometimes diverging from it, sometimes following it exactly in accordance with the official itinerary. A thick cloud of ash-laden dust floated in the burning air above the cattle and their drovers. It lay gritty on their teeth, stopped their breathing, penetrated into every fold of their clothing and every pore of their bodies. The flat wheatlands, stretching ahead as far as the eye could see, held promise of neither water nor shelter. All along the road, the grain was going to waste, spilling on the ground with a harsh crackle. The cattle turned greedy eyes on the fields, and the outriders posted by Andrei were stretched to the breaking point trying to check the slow but stubborn pressure of the thousand-strong herd, straining to get at the unexpected food, which could prove fatal to them.

Drawing level with the buggy in which the vet was huddled, shivering in spite of the heat, Andrei reined in.

"I think we'll stop at the first water, Grigorii Ivanovich. Everyone is dead on his feet. They're beginning to collapse."

"Just as you like, Andrei Vasilievich."

The old man had been obviously unwell lately, but he was trying to conceal it, and only the unhealthy perspiration which he kept wiping miserably from his haggard face gave him away. His inflamed eyes blinked apologetically.

"It really is rather hot . . . I don't feel too well . . . Chronic malaria . . . Get the shakes from three to five . . . You can set your watch by me . . . I shall be feverish for a week, at least . . . Never mind, it'll pass."

"Maybe you'd better rest for a bit somewhere near?" Andrei said cautiously. "You can catch up later. We shan't have gone far."

The vet was alarmed.

"What have I done to make you say that? Have I fallen down on the job? I'm coping all right, surely?"

Andrei sighed angrily and rode past.

"Can't say a word! I only wanted to help you . . . do what you like."

So many of Andrei's little clashes with Boboshko left him feeling foolish. Why was the ex-White Guardist so obstinately attached to something which did not concern him personally and which held so much hardship for him? What did he expect to get out of it? It wouldn't have been at all hard for him to get lost, to vanish in the chaos and disorder of the retreat. Yet he continued to discharge his duty scrupulously, almost pedantically, jealously resisting any encroachment on the petty prerogatives of his post. Andrei was not helped by the old family habit of dismissing the inexplicable with sweeping but handy generalizations. As a rule, he didn't trouble his head with such things but shrugged off the tiresome thought with a contemptuous catch phrase borrowed from his brother: "balls," "garbage," "nonsense." But he'd sounded the old man out once or twice now, and he realized or sensed that this was a riddle of a different order, that something much bigger than mere habit, or the bureaucrat's inveterate attention to duty, was causing the vet to be so zealous. Andrei felt that if only he could solve this riddle somehow, many things in life would become clearer to him.

"He's too tough a nut for you to crack, Comrade Lashkov!"

Far away on the horizon, a strip of water glinted like a knife-edge, and beyond it, with every step they took, the outlines of station buildings became clearer and clearer. Andrei's horse strained excitedly, tossed his head, and went into a gallop. A lake filmed with weed spread out before him, bordered at one end by a scrubby plantation and lapping at the other against the embankment, where a freight train was held up by a signal.

Andrei sighed with relief. "Just the place. We'll stop and rest for a while."

To have water and the long-awaited rest at hand made them oblivious to their surroundings. Both men and cattle let themselves go with blessed relief, heedless of anything else. When they had quenched their thirst, however, the world resumed its solid shape again and they saw the train up above, staring at them. The rough wire-covered window holes were tens of hundreds of eyes. But every single pair of eyes peering out through the barbed wire was fixed in longing not on them but on the water. The apprehensive silence which suddenly fell on the drovers reinforced their spontaneous reaction: "Prisoners!"

Andrei's heart went cold. Something elusive in the faces behind the wire singled them out from the criminals whom he had seen occasionally in the special mines at Uzlovsk. The existence of such people was no news to him. In the years just before the war, people had been picked up right and left in the towns and villages round about. He had been called on more than once to witness an arrest himself. But he had never imagined that an encounter like this, face to face on the empty steppe, would affect him so painfully.

"Why can't they leave them alone? We're all in the same mess together now."

As though to reinforce his doubts, the sun-bleached sky over the steppe was suddenly split by the hysterical whining boom of low flying Junkers. Every living thing in sight responded instantly to their menacing signal. The terrified screams of children mingled with the bellowing and neighing of fear-maddened animals; no matter how Andrei shouted and swore as he fought to improvise some sort of defense amidst the panic-stricken uproar, the confusion got worse and worse. But all the hundreds of eyes in the window slits of the carriages were unaware of the danger; they were still fixed in desperate longing on the water which lay so close and yet so inaccessible.

Andrei made his horse lie down and did the same himself. Only when he had recovered his senses a little did he spot the limping figure of Sanka Sutyrin amidst the uproar and kaleidoscopic confusion, calmly loading their reserve of bottled water into a potbellied mushrooming basket. Andrei had an awful premonition.

"What's that crazy bastard up to now! Can't he spare us his tricks for once?"

Sanka packed the bottles with the deliberate care of a man who was conscious of the implications of his action. When he had finished, he slung the basket over his arm, balanced a well-pole on his shoulder, and slowly started to move straight for the embankment, which the planes had raked with fire on their first dive. The guards and the engine crew were running in the opposite direction, but they had eyes for nothing except the shelter of the trees ahead and nobody tried to stop him or turn him back.

Limping heavily, Sanka scrambled up the embankment, and the gratitude of all those eyes behind the barbed wire seemed to protect him as he came.

He got himself as far as the track without incident, except that his cap fell off on the way. Here he set the basket down firmly at his feet, took out the first bottle, and attached it to a hook at the end of the pole. Then the boy braced himself with his good foot against the end of a sleeper and cautiously began to inch the pole upward, toward the window space; when he reached it, he deftly thrust the neck of the bottle between two strands of barbed wire. At that moment, a plane swooped, its whining scream punctuated by the harsh tattoo of machine-gun fire. Little fountains splashed up as if someone had thrown a flat stone across the surface of the water. After this round, cry after cry rang out along the train. Sanka's knees touched the chippings for a moment, he was thrown heavily on his back, and then began to slide headfirst toward the drainage ditch.

Andrei involuntarily shut his eyes.

"He's got a broken neck for his pains. That's the end of him!"

But the next minute, a dark crouching figure emerged from the belt of trees. Boboshko. Weaving like a hare, he hobbled toward the track. His rapt determination left Andrei no time for reflection. Something more powerful than fear tore him from the ground and threw him across the old man's path.

"Lie down! Lie down, or I'll shoot!"

Before the old man could heed him and lie down, Andrei dropped flat in the grass and started to crawl toward the embankment.

Several times, chattering bursts from the Junkers pinned him to the ground, his heart died within him, and he gave himself up for lost, but the flaming red of Sanka's hair, visible somewhere up in front, helped him to keep going.

Within arm's reach of Sanka, Andrei stopped to get his breath, and the almost inhuman howl that was erupting from the carriages suddenly penetrated his fevered brain. At that moment, Andrei felt real terror. His imagination supplied a vivid picture of what must be happening in those crammed and sealed carriages. "Mother, mother! Why? What in God's name is happening?"

A bullet had punched a neat hole in Sanka's ankle, but he was still alive, and even tried to make a joke as he awkwardly clambered onto Andrei's back.

"Looks as though I'm going to limp on the other one, too . . . The Lord in his mercy never forgets Sanka Sutyrin . . . sooner or later he always helps me out."

Andrei got through the return journey in a semistupor. In the midst of the deafening nightmare he felt as though he were dragging a much heavier burden than Sutyrin himself to the bushes by the roadside. A burden, Andrei knew now for certain, that he would never be rid of again.

The first thing he was really aware of, when he returned to his senses in the shelter of the trees, was Alexandra looking at him, long and anxiously, interrupted only by a Boboshko who sighed mournfully: "My God, what people, what a nation! They can endure anything, anything at all. For three hundred years they endured the Tartars. Then the Romanovs for as long again. They'll survive this too. They still have time."

Up on the embankment, the train hooted; Andrei heard it as he sank into merciful unconsciousness.

VI

From one horizon to the other, the sky was shrouded in gray cloud mottled with black. The wind drove sudden, slanting showers over the plain, and the mud squelching under foot got stickier at every step. Hour by hour, the progress of the convoy grew slower and more difficult.

In the path of the herds, a Cossack village loomed out of the rainy haze and Andrei urged his horse toward it. On the way he pulled up beside a covered cart, where Sanka Sutyrin was tossing and turning in a fever, watched over by the vet.

"How is he?"

"He'll never dance, but he'll live."

Boboshko shrugged apologetically.

"I'm not God Almighty. Or even the fellow who embalmed Lenin. Ichthyol and iodine, that's all I've got."

"Never mind about dancing, as long as he pulls through."

His tension hadn't yet subsided.

"We're near a village. There has to be a doctor."

The old man was strangely gloomy.

"Maybe. Maybe. But I doubt it. The Germans are right behind."

"So what?"

"Mark my words, Andrei Vasilievich, I'm well acquainted with the Cossacks in these parts. They've got their bread and salt tucked away, of course, but it's not for the likes of us. You won't find a decent horse-doctor, let alone the other sort. This is just what the Cossacks have been waiting for. They'll take their revenge, don't you worry. And shed blood if they have to."

"Haven't they got enough out of the Soviet government?"

"Cossacks always think that governments can and must give them more. That's why they betrayed the Tsar for Kornilov and Denikin, then replaced those two with chiefs of their own, whom they proceeded to drop in favor of the commissars, and now they won't want to be caught supporting them . . . A blend of the sergeant major's swagger and servility, aggravated by bestial cruelty, that's your Cossack, my dear Andrei Vasilievich."

Before he could answer, a bundle of damp canvas on a wretched skewbald nag emerged from the misty drizzle. It was Filya Duda, whom Andrei had sent ahead to arrange quarters for the night.

"There's nowhere to put the cattle, Vasilich. There's no pens anywhere. I rode all round, and there's nothing."

Their itinerary specified that every hamlet, village, or station on the way was required to provide an enclosure for the cattle. So far the rule had been strictly observed. So Duda's news seriously alarmed Andrei. Were the Cossacks really up to something?

Without further delay he raced past the herd toward the signs and smells of human habitation and soon Bay was pacing the village street, heading for the market place.

The kolkhoz center looked deserted. The doors of storehouses hung wide open, with their locks torn off; obscene words were scrawled over the production board by the office steps; and the glass had been knocked out of most of the front windows. Andrei passed through the dark anteroom and along a corridor, but when he pulled open the door to the chairman's office, a squat, almost square hunchback in a faded calico blouse and a skullcap with a tassel rose to meet him. He quickly weighed up his visitor with a practiced eye, and evidently finding no reason for ceremony, sat down again and muttered at the desk in front of him.

"I'm listening."

But he only listened with half an ear, staring absently out of the window, his whole attitude expressing utter boredom with his visitor's futile requests.

"An order, you say?"

The hunchback suddenly stared at him and bared his big, corn-yellow teeth in a mocking smile.

"Obliged, you say? Since when have I been under any obligation to you, you dirty Russian bastard? Hey, Tsarkov!"

A gray-headed man, all nose and no chin, popped out of the neighboring room and froze in fawning anticipation.

"D'you hear that, here's another one come to collect what we owe him . . . Maybe you'd like us to make our wives available just to complete your enjoyment? Order away, my bloody fine Russian gentleman!"

The veins in his short neck were throbbing violently.

"So you want bread—and meat, eh? Would you like some milk to drink? Maybe you'll take my hump while you're at it? A Russian pig like you gave me it to look after in 1920. Take it . . . stinking rat. Talk about bread. You won't get dogshit from me . . . I'll . . ."

Abruptly the hunchback fell silent, and shrank back, staring with eyes that suddenly turned glassy at something over Andrei's shoulder; he moved his white lips soundlessly. The head in the doorway vanished at once, and the clatter of a falling chair came from the next room. Then came the tinkle of a broken pane, and a shot. The shot was short and sharp, like the crack of a whip, and it rang out not from the street, but from behind Andrei's back. A shadow seemed to run over the hunchback's ducklike face; it went ashen and hollow. His knotty fingers crumpled the papers before him convulsively but relaxed at once and hung limp in death. The skullcap slipped off the head that rested lifelessly on the desk top and fell, exposing a naked skull furrowed with saber cuts.

"Oh dear me, Lashkov."

The voice behind Andrei's back sounded weary and indifferent.

"Not much good giving you a weapon, I can see. Waste of time talking to people like that, and you've got state business on your hands."

The man with whom Andrei found himself face to face the next moment looked at him in a bored, absentminded fashion from under faded eyebrows. The tabs on his shoulderbands—four on each—were crooked; a holster flapped against his hollow stomach; his down-at-heel boots were spattered with mud almost up to the knees.

"He won't get away," said the colonel, putting his own interpretation on Andrei's questioning silence. "My boys are outside. You're not the first they've given this sort of welcome to. Let's go."

He nodded into the corridor.

"I've been talking to your women there. They told me a few things. I'll take the wounded boy off your hands and deliver him to the nearest hospital."

His words seemed to cost him an effort, and he forced them out reluctantly.

"You'll pick out ten horses for my brave men. Ours can't carry us any further. I won't have any duds, mind . . . There he is; what a charming specimen."

They went down into the yard where the old man Andrei had seen before was squatting on his heels surrounded by three grim Red Army men.

"Come on, get up."

The man sprang up with a nimbleness remarkable for his age, and with an imploring sideways look at the new arrivals, poured out his sorrows in a breathless lisp.

"I'm not my own master . . . I've got a restricted passport . . . Been on a sort of chain all my life . . . Did whatever I was ordered . . . Got a family, there's five of us . . . Just think about it . . . Nobody will show you a thing here if I don't . . . They've hidden everything, absolutely everything . . . And driven all the cattle off, every single one . . . You know what Cossacks are."

He turned out to be the kolkhoz storeman and led them through some gardens to a deserted little brickworks by a stream, where untouched stocks had been saved for better times in the carefully camouflaged kilns.

"Right then, Lashkov," said the colonel, as they sat on the sloping bank near the kilns, from whose depths the soldiers were helping themselves to provisions with the storeman's obliging assistance.

"Take as much as you can. Pour kerosene on the rest and burn it. As for that one"—he nodded toward one of the kilns and his pale eyes suddenly lit up in avenging fury—"you can finish him off yourself."

Without warning his voice rose to a shout.

"What the bloody hell d'you think you're wearing a revolver for! Think they gave it to you to crack nuts with?"

His rage died down as quickly as it had flared.

"They have no mercy on us . . . my own children . . . in Kaunas . . . and my wife . . . buried alive . . ."

Only then did Andrei see through the colorless and effete exterior of the man sitting by him, past the layers of dust that seemed to have eaten into his face, to the marks of excruciating torment that gave him his look of doomed exhaustion. So when the four horsemen, loaded to capacity, vanished into the rainy mist, he could only say to the old man,

"Pick up your legs and walk, Dad."

They went through a maize field toward a rush-lined backwater; Andrei's heart thumped in anticipation of the final judgment he must shortly make.

Ink-black clouds ballooned and slipped raggedly toward the horizon, shedding a chilly drizzle as they went. The sweetish smell of dried dung drifted from the chimneys of neighboring farmhouses, cocks trumpeted to each other in the farmyards, announcing evening, and it was hard to believe that tragedy threatened the unruffled quietness.

Weeds squelched under the old man's knees.

"Why are you doing this to me, son! What harm have I ever done to anybody, what sort of life have I had?"

His flabby cheeks trembled, wet with rain and tears.

"I'm telling you the truth. They started running me around in 1929, and I've never stood still since. I've got three kids . . . all young . . . Where's the justice in it? Whose sins am I being punished for? I'm not asking for myself, I haven't got long to go anyway, I'm asking for my children, without me they're dead. What's life to me? It's no life, it's one long nightmare. But how will they get on without me, especially at a time like this? . . . Shoot me. I can't take any more . . ."

The old man, trembling silently, rested his close-cropped gray head on the wet ground. Something stirred and shuddered in Andrei's heart, there was a bitter lump in his throat brought on by something he had never experienced before. Tears came into his eyes, and he turned back toward the village without a word, the old man's parting words burning into his memory as he went.

"God bless and keep you, my son!"

All the way to the camp Andrei was haunted by the feeling that his life up to now had been pointless and absurd. A solid vise of doubts tightened painfully round him until he felt breathless and faint.

"How did it all come about?" he asked himself. "Why do we drive each other like cattle, some one way, some another? What's it all for, what good does it do?"

He fell asleep as soon as his head touched the jacket which the vet had thoughtfully tucked under him. And he dreamt that he was standing in swift-running water, trying to climb the bank, but the bank kept crumbling in his hands and receding farther and farther from him. Suddenly Sanka Sutyrin appeared above him with a surly rebuke: "What are you fooling around there for? You ought to be ashamed!" The water was about to sweep him away. But suddenly the old storeman materialized beside him, in uniform with a colonel's facings, and stretched out a hand.

"You help me and I'll help you, my son. We shan't come to any harm. Christ is risen."

At this point, though, some irresistible force began to drag the two of them in different directions, and he heard Boboshko's agitated whisper right above his ear: "Andrei Vasilievich, Andrei Vasilievich."

As he woke up, Andrei heard him more clearly.

"Andrei Vasilievich! Fyodorov's wife is in labor! She's about to have her child!"

VII

Prokofii Fyodorov, thin as a lath, with a handsome piratical face somewhat marred by a slight squint, was pacing frantically round the crossing-keeper's hut where his wife Pelagea was screaming in the throes of protracted labor.

"What a struggle she's having, poor thing . . . Must be a boy . . . just think what agonies women go through for us . . . There's no end to what they have to endure . . . she's not at all strong, either . . . and it's her first . . . bound to be hard on her, I suppose . . . if only it's a son, Vasilich! . . . That'd be marvelous . . . I'm more worried about her though . . . just as long as she comes through safely."

The moans in the hut suddenly stopped. Prokofii stood stock-still straining to hear, then made a movement toward the door; next moment a piercing howl, torn from the very heart of a living creature—or so it seemed—rose to meet him, and was followed after a brief silence by the triumphantly demanding yell of a hungry baby.

Prokofii shot a miserable glance at Lashkov. His strong face trembled and twisted, he gestured helplessly, squatted down on his heels, and burst into tears of dismay.

"I never thought it'd be like this, Vasilich! I thought we'd have music, do things properly. But it wasn't to be. I was born in a furrow myself, and now I'm seeing my own child for the first time in somebody else's field. I wasn't meant to be lucky, that's for sure."

Boboshko appeared in the doorway, cast them an ironic glance out of tired, watery eyes, and said with good-natured sarcasm:

"Overcome with emotion are you, you poor suffering soul? You should be dancing. Your wife's given you a boy. Come and admire the work of your flesh, you daddy."

When Andrei followed Fyodorov into the hut Pelagea was already dozing, one hand tucked uncomfortably under her head. There were dark patches on her gray, sunken cheeks but a blissful smile of utter peace softened her painfully sharp features. Fyodorov's firstborn was snuffling happily at her side, a sackcloth cocoon with a dark red blob, the color of an overripe tomato, somewhere in its depths. Things which only yesterday had seemed to Andrei awesome and mysterious—childbirth, the first cry, the first breast-feeding—now looked so ordinary and simple, and indeed somehow disgusting, that he turned away involuntarily.

"Congratulations on the addition to your family, Prokofii."

The crossing-keeper's wife, a sprightly old woman in a sun-bleached tunic, holding a wet rag, screened the new mother from them.

"You've stared enough now. They have their fun, these studs, and that's that, but the woman has to suffer. You devils, you're shameless, standing there admiring yourselves! Get out of the hut!"

Sitting in a farmyard shed, pouring out the homemade vodka saved for the occasion, Prokofii summed up his situation, not without a certain embarrassment.

"Don't be offended, Vasilich, but I shan't go any farther. You know yourself that I can't drag a woman with a little child like that to God only knows where. I'll stay somewhere near here for a bit and then we'll see."

Andrei firmly pushed his mug aside and rose.

"And the interests of the state just don't matter, is that it? I was relying on you, Prokofii, more than anybody else."

Prokofii clasped his knees and stared sullenly at the toes of his boots, obviously steeling himself.

"Isn't my child a state interest, then? Anybody can breed cattle, there's nothing to it, but this is my own flesh and blood. I may never have another. So whatever you say, I'm not going."

The vet sucked his drink slowly through his teeth, and pretended not to be listening.

"Strong, this," he said. "Haven't tasted anything like it for a long time. Undoubtedly rye. They know how to make liquor in good old Russia! May Prokofii's youngster be as strong and healthy!"

The old man's crafty intervention only aggravated the rage which had been building in Andrei all day.

"Stop it, Grigorii Ivanovich! Why play cat and mouse? We aren't children. What it comes down to is that everybody has to put himself first? And I'm the only one who's supposed to have no interest apart from the cattle? I'm supposed to carry the whole load by myself?"

The Lashkov temper broke loose and exploded.

"Perhaps you're tempted to take to the woods, Grigorii Ivanovich; you're such a worthy citizen. Well, I'm not holding you back. Be sure the Germans give you a little something for past services. But don't ask for mercy when we come back. You'll get what you deserve—you'll bite the hand that feeds you whenever you get the chance, that's plain enough."

A minute later he was whipping his horse to a gallop past the belt of trees towards the encampment, where the afternoon fires were still smoking. An angry pulse beat in his temples: "Will it all turn out to have been pointless? They don't want to take the rough with the smooth. Now's the time you really find out what it's all about."

The path, eroded by the recent rains, was sticky under his horse's hooves; a damp wind beat on his face and ruffled the spoiling fields to subtle, unhealthy colors. Andrei had never felt more lonely and despondent.

"Whom can I trust or rely on? If I can't manage on my own, nobody will help me."

He rode on oblivious to his surroundings. When the figure of a woman suddenly emerged from the bushes by the road and came toward him, his first reaction was to pull at the bridle and swing past her, but the next moment his heart stood still, then started to thump unevenly.

Alexandra came toward him, seeming to grow with each step until he could see nothing else. Her gray eyes seemed to swallow him in their gleaming depths. Under their spell he reined in, dismounted, and strode towards her.

"Well, how's Pelagea, has she had her child?"

Alexandra's deliberately defiant tone betrayed her agitation, and he sensed that her thoughts were far from what she was actually saying.

"The women are wondering whether it's a boy or a girl."

Alexandra was thoughtlessly uttering the first empty words that came into her head, but her face, her eyes, her whole body, burned, cried out, laughed up at him for reasons which had nothing to do with Pelagea's infant. Andrei looked at her speechlessly, unable to utter a sound, so taken aback by their meeting out here on the road.

Vainly she tried to hide her embarrassment in a flow of backtalk.

"What are you staring at then, don't you know me? Shouldn't wonder, all I see of the world is cows' backsides. Won't be sure of knowing myself in the mirror soon. Well, that's the way it goes."

"What do you mean?" Controlling his trembling as best he could, Andrei walked beside her, leading his horse. "I was a bit surprised, that's all. I was wondering what brought you here."

"I just came out for a breath of air." Her voice sank and faltered. "But to tell you the truth, I'm glad I met you. You're not in a hurry, are you?"

A warm glow spread inside him, making him feel weak and tipsy. The world about him was suddenly filled with sound, scent, and color. The burnt brown of withering leaves stood out boldly against a pallid sky streaked with thinning clouds, and this in turn emphasized the stubbly green of willow and hazel in the yellow ocean of the unreaped plain. From the direction of the river came a whiff of sodden wood and slimy backwaters, and the harsh clamor of hordes of birds preparing to migrate.

Still mistrustful of her invitation, he hung back and kept his voice level.

"You've got something to say to me? Then say it, if it's something sensible."

"Come over here, dear Andrei," she said, pulling him by the sleeve; the way she lingered over his name sent a warm thrill of happiness through him.

"They're all eyes here. Once our women's tongues start wagging about you, there's no knowing what they'll say. Come on. Over here."

She had evidently been lying in wait for him. A flannel blanket was spread under a gnarled apricot tree, and a calico bag with food nestled among its roots. He barely had time to observe all this before she clasped her warm hands together behind his head.

"Andrei, my darling, my dearest . . ."

The incoherent words buzzed dizzily in his ears. "I didn't refuse you out of spite, I was too proud. I thought people would hold it against me, eating commissar's bread. You were the only one I ever loved. When I used to meet you I didn't know where I was or what I was doing. I used to wonder every day how you were getting on, who you were with. My love, my precious . . . be nice to me, Andrei, my love."

He was lost for words.

"Oh . . ." and again, more bitterly, "You . . . oh, you . . ."

He almost fainted; dizziness robbed him of thought and speech. He was conscious of nothing except her eyes close to his own, shining with quiet devotion and happiness. They were like two whirlpools, lit from within by a blue spark, luring him down into their spinning depths.

Afterwards, lying beside him and stroking his hand, she spoke as though it was all settled and beyond discussion.

"Sergei and I had no luck with children, thank God, so I don't have to answer to him. I shall stay with you forever now. Where you go, I go, too."

Andrei jerked awake.

"You make it all seem very easy."

"What's the matter—are you afraid?"

He replied as though he had been expecting her challenge.

"I'm not afraid, but we've got to behave decently. No, Alexandra, my love, we can't do it. What will people say? While the men are fighting, Lashkov seduces soldiers' wives! When the war ends we'll sit down with Sergei and talk it over properly, like decent people. We Lashkovs aren't thieves, we don't go round gathering other people's property."

Alexandra shot to her feet, tossed her ruffled hair back over her shoulders, and looked down at Andrei with bitter scorn.

"Oh, you Lashkovs! If we followed your rules we couldn't go to the latrine without a permit. You won't let anything be simple. You're such a moldering, cold-blooded lot, you must have come out of some swamp. I thought you at least were a bit different. But you're the same sort of shit, only worse. If you had your way, women would have kids by rote. Thank God things haven't gone further."

She had deliberately struck where it hurt most, and he was beside himself with fury and resentment.

"And you call yourselves human beings. The Lashkovs stick in your craw because the Lashkovs want to bring some honor and justice into life. Only you prefer to live in the old swamp. You like your own mess so much, you won't even share it."

Alexandra only grew wilder.

"Why don't you organize your famous justice among yourselves first, instead of eating each other like spiders? You can't even share out the top jobs without fighting. We'll get by without you heroes to help us. That's the truth of it, my love, my dear Comrade Lashkov."

And once again his mind suppressed everything that had passed between them, except the hurts and humiliations. His throat ached with rage, and he lost control of himself.

"Go, or I'll kill you."

"It'd take more than you, Lashkov." She gave him a mocking sideways look as she went. "You're weak on your legs, and your blood is too thin. So long."

Jealous and bitter, Andrei watched her cross the unharvested field toward the encampment so quick and sure of herself, and his heart leaped and faltered with each step she took. He shuffled miserably along the road, oblivious to his surroundings.

"God, oh God, why must I be so contrary? Why do the Lashkovs always have to be different?"

Boboshko overtook him, slowed down, and rode along beside him. After a short silence the old man cleared his throat in sympathy and spoke. His voice was dull and sad.

"Oh, Andrei Vasilievich! This will get us nowhere. Shouting won't do any good. The Russian peasant is deaf from being shouted at and he doesn't hear anymore. Besides, Fyodorov is right. How can he go on with a babe in arms? It's simply impossible. We're in the middle of the worst war in history, human lives soon won't be worth a brass farthing and here we are worrying about cattle. We produce cattle and not vice versa. You and I should be rejoicing, Andrei Vasilievich; another soul has been born to be filled with God's beauty. It's no time to harbor grudges. A single human sigh is more precious than all your lands flowing with milk and honey. No earthly kingdom is worth one hair of a human head . . . Still, it's up to you, Andrei Vasilievich, you know best . . ."

How could he answer the old man? No words could fill the desolate void inside him. He kept moving out of sheer force of habit. For the time being, reality had lost all sense and meaning.

"To hell with the whole damn thing. I don't care who's right and who's wrong! What does it matter to me?"

VIII

Like a funnel, the narrow mouth of the bridge slowly but inexorably absorbed the swirling uproar of the retreat. Carts, lorries, cattle, and people hurried in an endless stream to the river bank, driven by a single urge: at all costs to reach the other side. The yells and curses bellowing and rumbling expressed one sole desire: to get across and away from the bridge, whatever the means.

The traffic controller, a lanky pockmarked major, utterly exhausted by his hectic and futile task, listened with half an ear as Andrei protested about the fatal dangers of epidemic and cattle plague, and irritably waved him away.

"Forget it. What the bloody hell's all this about sanitation and hygiene? If the Messerschmitts come over, they'll do a lovely job of disinfecting. You can just collect the horns and use the hoofs for packing."

A deathly grin twitched the sharp jaws under the pitted skin.

"Patience, man. Your turn will come. What's your hurry? To get to the front?"

The gibe was too transparent to be ignored. Andrei immediately clammed up and faded into the background.

"You're in a corner, Andrei, my lad. Anybody who feels like it can kick your arse."

As he approached the camp he was intercepted by the vet, who was being pursued and importuned by a long-armed, middle-aged gypsy, wearing a greasy velvet waistcoat over a newish officer's tunic.

Boboshko flung himself on his deliverer.

"Andrei Vasilich, my dear man! Help me out, I can't understand what he wants from me. Where can I take him? Who's going to give permission? We don't even know when we ourselves shall be on the move. But d'you think I can get any sense into him?"

Only then did Andrei take hold of himself, and notice a solitary covered wagon drawn up on the bank. Its patched and repatched canvas stood out incongruously amongst the assorted carts and buggies of Lashkov's motley outfit. He saw without having to ask that the gypsy wanted to tag along with their party and cross the bridge out of turn. He hadn't recovered yet from his exchange with the traffic controller, and rapped out rudely:

"For every clever man there's a dozen that are cunning. Don't take me for an idiot—get back in the queue."

The gypsy's moist eyes shone at him imploringly.

"Come on, boss, be human! Take me into your tribe, make me pray to God for you! We've got a man wounded, he's sick, and he's going to die. Take us. If you don't believe me, take a look yourself."

He deftly pulled the flap of the wagon aside.

"There he is, poor soul."

Surrounded by a swarm of old women and children, a young man with the look of the city about him lay there in a deep fever, covered up to his chin with a quilted winter coverlet. He was raving: "Come on, pour away—pour some more . . . I'll swim . . . I'll swim right out to the middle . . . it's cold . . . it's very cold . . ."

As Andrei turned away, a tiny gypsy boy in a tattered petticoat popped up right beside him like an imp from Hell and started drumming with his bare feet. Gazing doglike into his eyes, the boy unself-consciously performed his tap dance, and Andrei reluctantly surrendered with a helpless wave of the hand.

"All right, damn you, line up."

Their thanks pursued him: "You won't be sorry, boss!"

The gypsies soon made themselves at home. The fortune-tellers' garish headscarves bobbed about the campfires and the Uzlovsk women, yearning for consolation, filled their voluminous aprons and blouses with generous offerings. Their children wasted no time either, but circulated with them, begging and filching their share of the common booty. The camp came to life, and Andrei didn't regret his forced indulgence. "At least it'll make the women better-tempered! Doesn't take much to keep them happy!"

The herd finally got across sometime in the evening, and set up camp for the night on the fringe of the nearest farm across the river. Andrei, on his evening rounds, suddenly came face to face with the very same young man whom he had seen that morning half-dead in the gypsy wagon.

"Good evening!" There wasn't a trace of embarrassment in his voice. "I've had an idea! See how you like it!"

There was something inexplicably attractive in his speech, his looks, his movements. Every part of him seemed to have a separate existence, a life of its own: When his eyes smiled, his face was stony, and his nimble hands only emphasized the unsoldierly awkwardness of his body.

"I've arranged with the local authorities—we're putting on a one-man concert tonight. Half a ruble a head. There's a vacant barn. Oh, sorry"— dissolving into a bashful and apologetic smile—"I haven't introduced myself! Gennadii Salyuk, artist of the Kursk State Philharmonic: mime, dance, recitation. Let's be friends. How d'you like the idea?"

Andrei couldn't get over his amazement: "What a fool I made of myself! What a trick they played on me. Took me in like a baby." But the silent rage soon gave way to confusion, then to indifference. In the end the artist's irresistible smile softened him completely, and he could only manage an embarrassed grumble.

"You were pretty smart there . . ."

"What do you mean?"

"You know, in the wagon . . ."

"Oh, that!"

Salyuk's smile became still broader and more bashful.

"Please don't be angry. I've been living off these nomads for two weeks, I had to do something to help them. And you're none the poorer for it. Red Front, all men are brothers and all that. A little hoax for the common good . . . Well, what do you say to my educational enterprise?"

"Go ahead . . . I have no objection . . . Half a ruble each, is it?"

He reached for his tobacco pouch to settle down for a chat, but the young man vanished as suddenly as he had appeared. Lashkov regretfully rode on his way and, as he was finishing his rounds, met the vet with the now familiar gypsy still treading on his heels. The old man made a comical gesture of helplessness.

"He's plagued the life out of me, this son of Morocco. You just listen to him! What a mentality! He belongs to the age of primitive barter! No logic in him at all." He turned on his persecutor. "Here you are, this is the boss, he's the one to talk to, you've got me in a flat spin."

The gypsy set about Andrei immediately, apparently not even noticing that a different person now stood before him.

"I'm telling you, boss, I pay the right price. And give you some of my horses into the bargain. You got to take horses in; whether they're good or bad, it's all the bloody same to you, but I got to live, I got to carry my family and children round the wide world, over the steppes . . . You won't be sorry, boss, I pay good money . . ."

Andrei tried hard to explain the rudiments of the laws on state property, to frighten him with talk of retribution, but it was all to no avail. The round brown eyes only blinked in perplexity, and he repeated his set speech, beginning and ending with the same old refrain:

"You won't be sorry, boss, I pay good prices, good money . . . I can't give no more, 's all I got."

"Can't you get it into your thick head that my powers . . ."

He broke off in mid-sentence as Alexandra swept by among her friends from Sychevka. As she passed them, she gave him a sideways glance; her lips were pursed, but a queenly smile hovered at the corners. He drifted helplessly after her, finishing his sentence mechanically.

". . . don't go that far . . . I have no such powers."

Trying not to lose sight of her, he shook off his ineducable client somewhere along the way, and shortly reached the grain store; it had been hastily converted into a clubroom and the gala occasion promised by Salyuk was already in full swing.

An arrangement of two flour bins served the artist as a stage, and the spectator took his place where he thought fit, or where agility permitted. The fumes from a mass of oil lamps floated overhead, making the dark box of a barn still stuffier and gloomier.

". . . I must confess that I am very nervous. Never before has it been my lot to appear before such a discriminating audience. But I hope that the refined taste of my public today will be equalled by its indulgence . . . Speaking of taste, a certain citizen comes up to me on a trolley-bus, in this very place, and says, 'Aren't you,' he says, 'that Tma-Tara-kanievsky who appeared in a concert yesterday at the open air theater?' 'I am,' says I. Well, you can imagine how flattered I was: Somebody recognized me! 'You're in league with those crooks then, aren't you,' says he, 'you so-and-so and such-and-such. You distract people's attention with your patter while they rob full citizens of their wallets!' Then he turns round to the other passengers. 'Daylight robbery,' he yells. 'Yesterday at this fellow's concert'—pointing at me—'they took my wallet, and I had a three-ruble note in it and a membership card of the International Society for the Assistance of Proletarian Revolutionaries . . . Beat him up,' he yells, 'before he gets away.' Not funny? I didn't think so either . . . Right then, the finest creative talents in our country will now appear before you, masters of the vocal, and of all that accompanies it . . . To start our concert, by public acclaim, People's Artist and star of the first magnitude, Leonid Utyesov . . . Leonid Osipovich, please!"

He turned his back on the audience.

"The maestro is too shy to breathe on his public. On the occasion of his meeting with you he's got himself tight—I mean tired. The maestro will therefore sing in a rather unusual way."

He sang, and, miraculously, they heard the unmistakable Utyesov recitative.

> "In our platoon were two very good friends—
> Sing, sing, sing away.
> And whenever the one friend was sulky and sad
> That friend's friend was happy and gay."

Looking round for Alexandra, Andrei could hardly recognize his subordinates. For the first time in many days of back-breaking travel their faces were transfigured.

It was as though they were being transported body and soul to that other, half-forgotten, peacetime life. Lashkov was carried away by the prevailing mood. He completely forgave the young man for the hoax he had played, and joined in the general enthusiastic applause. Encouraged by his reception, the artist began to give everything he had.

"A concert! What enchantment, what hopes that little word contains! And what concert fails to produce its surprises? Talking of surprises . . . d'you know, the other day my neighbor knocks on my door and with a dazzling smile she says, 'I've got a surprise for you.' 'Oh,' says I, 'and just what's your prize?' 'There's a summons from the court,' she says. 'You're being sued for maintenance.' Not funny? I didn't think so either . . . Right then, second part of our gala concert . . ."

At that moment the anguished profile of Filya Duda appeared in the doorway.

"They've gone off with 'em! Driven the horses off!" His voice rose almost to a screech. "They've gone off with our horses! The gypsies! Our horses, the Torbeevo lot."

An anxious hush suddenly descended, then people were rushing and jostling for the exit, their old hostile selves once more. In the crush at the door and at close range, Andrei saw the face he would never forget, and looked into the only eyes that henceforward would matter to him; his haunting feeling of guilt turned to aching pity. He tried to elbow his way toward her, but the crowd swept him outside, where the hue and cry of the pursuers rang louder and louder in the echoing night.

Rival interests faded at once: age-old peasant instinct united neighbors who only yesterday had been at daggers drawn. Andrei rushed about for a while trying to find the main direction of the scattered pursuit, but shouts and the clatter of horses were coming from all sides, and it was impossible to say how things were going.

He could not escape a presentiment of imminent tragedy. There was not the slightest doubt that the horse thieves would get rough justice if they were caught. So when a piercing, almost animal scream rose toward the starry sky from somewhere over the river, he concluded with sickening despair that the worst had happened. Without a moment's delay he galloped toward the voices on the other side, and a light winking ahead of him soon defined the scene of battle in the darkness.

As soon as Andrei dismounted the crowd parted, and the light of somebody's torch revealed the battered body of the actor. He was still gasping and twitching, but the last spark of life in him was going out fast.

"Where to . . . where to . . . why?" his swollen lips stumbled over the words. "One of those things . . . that's the way it is, citizens."

The man who lay dying, trampled to death to ease a brief moment of other people's despair, had twice deceived Andrei, and yet his only feeling as he stood there looking down at the ground was one of burning pity.

"Oh Lord . . . you people . . . horses . . ." He was lost for words.

On the return journey a rustling in the night turned into Boboshko's voice close to his ear.

"That's the Russian peasant for you, in all his glory. He knows no bounds. They've killed a man like a fly, and now they'll start feeling sorry and moaning about it; they'll probably make it an excuse to drink themselves silly . . . There was more to that young man than met the eye . . . he could have got away quietly. But he deliberately hung back. He put himself in the way, to safeguard the gypsies' freedom. With his own life. What extraordinary muddles you do find in Russian heads!"

Only one of the vet's remarks actually penetrated. "Yes, he could have got away . . . he certainly could."

The night closed over him. And inside him, too.

IX

Early in the morning, as soon as he woke up, Andrei rode off to the pens. Heavy, wet snow was falling. Like moths against a windscreen, the flakes broke against the ground, still warm from yesterday's sun; they melted at once and gradually thickened into a squelching porridge. Big-bellied clouds were sailing over the village where Andrei's outfit was bogged down, and their leaden immensity held no promise of an early departure.

His horse carried him at a sluggish trot through the village to the herd beyond its further bounds, and the very look of the cattle told him more than any number of reports and messages. They had huddled together in a bunch, pressing against each other, trying to conserve warmth. The snow was melting slowly on their rumps and running down their hollow sides. Andrei went cold: This was certain death for the younger animals at least.

Boboshko's sharp little features appeared out of the snow in front of the horse's muzzle. With his puny figure, in a threadbare worsted overcoat fastened tightly under his chin with a safety pin, he was devotion to duty personified.

"What are we going to do, Andrei Vasilievich? We shan't get through another night without losses. And it's no good waiting for better weather."

Andrei felt a little ashamed of himself: the old man had reached the herd first at this anxious moment.

"What do you think yourself? What ought we to do?"

The vet's reply was so prompt that he had obviously had it ready, but respect for rank had prevented him from getting in first.

"We should ask the local people to billet them, or at any rate the young animals. Our people can get the heifers under cover somehow."

Andrei was moved by the old man's selfless zeal. He hadn't the heart to tell him that he had already tried all that, and had met with a flat refusal in the local kolkhoz office—they were afraid of cattle disease.

"We can't put other people's cattle at risk, Grigorii Ivanovich. But there is one way out."

His cold, faded blue eyes narrowed wickedly.

"Yes, there is a way. Drive them over there"—he pointed to a church near a graveyard—"we shall be all right . . . come on."

As he put Bay into a gallop he felt somebody's eyes drilling into him. "Alexandra," he thought at once. And once again a hot shudder of desire ran through him. As though it were somebody else's matchmakers she had turned away from her door, as though it were somebody else she had jeered at in the wood a little while back. "Oh, Alexandra, my little Alexandra, my love, you were meant to be my downfall!"

The priest had a ripe turnip face, and cornflower eyes under brows like wheat ears. Andrei didn't waste words on him.

"If I don't give you the keys you'll take them by force," the priest said with a submissive sigh. "Why should I resist? But I advise against it."

"Is that a threat? We've seen your sort before."

"It is not for me to threaten. Might is on your side. But you've got a whole life ahead of you."

"You'll never be in power again, don't rely on the Germans. We'll beat them some way or other."

"I've never been in power. And the Germans are just as much my enemies as yours. But in his dying moments a man is apt to reflect on the deeds he has done. It will go hard with you then."

"All right, let's have the keys."

"Here they are—take them."

If the priest had resisted, or put on an act, or even given him a nasty look, Andrei would have felt much better. As it was, he experienced a vague uneasiness after their conversation, an inexplicable tightness in the chest, and his steps were heavy and uncertain as he went to open up the church.

In front of it a silent band of peasants, men and women, were awaiting him. Kondrovo folk mostly, with Mark Sergeev prominent among them by reason of his size and his bearded dignity. Anxiety and apprehension could be sensed beneath their unusual stillness. As soon as Andrei set foot on the porch, Sergeev barred his way, took off his cap to him, and spoke clearly and thoughtfully.

"Andrei Vasilievich, I've drunk many a glass with your father, God rest his soul. I know your brothers as well as I know myself. God grant them good health. I've watched you since you were so high, and rejoiced to see you growing to manhood. In the name of Christ our Lord, Ruler of All, I beg you not to harm God's dwelling place; do not defile his house. Your good deed will be repaid a hundred-fold. This we beg of you one and all."

He almost choked with indignation. Whatever doubts he had had about others, he had always felt sure of the Kondrovo group: steady people who knew their jobs.

"What do you think you're doing, Sergeev? Kolkhoz cattle are perishing and you come out with this stupid nonsense. Get out of my way!"

"God's creatures are in His hands, when the hour comes; that's when they must give up their souls. But a church is for eternity, the soul of the whole nation is kept safe within it. We beg you, all of us!"

And now this refrain of his began to sound like a threat.

"Do not provoke the Lord!"

A gust of anger turning him cold to his fingertips swept over Andrei.

"Out of the way, you monster," he yelled, beside himself with rage, as red spots flared before his eyes. "All that the people own is perishing and you decide to try religious sabotage, you vermin!"

He put everything into his blow—his unhappy love, the heat and misery of the long trail, his loathing of the slush all round him, even his resentment of the weakness he was now showing. Mark rolled down the steps, the back of his head hit the ground, and a dark stain began spreading on the wet snow beneath.

Andrei no longer knew what he was doing. He undid the lock and wrenched it off.

"Drive them in! Drive them in, I say!"

The frozen calves, lowing and snuffling, began pouring through the wide-open doors. Lashkov stood at the entrance, shouting pointedly, just to stifle the doubts which were already making themselves heard.

"Get on with it! Get on! Get on!"

The dim daylight streaming through the narrow windows became still more ghostly as the steaming breath of the cattle rose to the vaulted ceiling. Icon lamps like little blue fireflies guttered and went out in various corners of the church, and only the candle before an icon of the Savior went on burning in air so thick you could cut it with a knife.

"Unless I give the order, they're not to be taken out!"

Andrei's voice echoed under the high arches—"ou-ou-ou-ou-out."

"Got it?"

Filya Duda, driving his yearling calves into the transept, cracked his whip enthusiastically, accompanying every stroke with ripe oaths or comic patter.

"Move along, you mangy bastards! There's no place warmer than the bosom of the Lord! Forgive us our trespasses, citizen saints! There's plenty of room—the more the merrier. Render unto God those things that are God's, and unto us those things that are ours. Where d'you think you're going, you stupid cunt?"

When Andrei left the church the peasants were still moving around in a tight bunch by the entrance. Only Sergeev was no longer there. It was Dmitrii Sukhov who now stepped forward to meet him, a timid little fellow, whose only previous claim to attention was precisely his timidity. He spoke briefly and quietly.

"We don't go any further with you, Andrei Vasilievich. From now on, we go our separate ways."

"Don't you know you can end up before a tribunal for sabotage?" He flushed darkly, and started tugging at the button of the back pocket in his breeches.

"Seen this before? I've got full powers . . ."

"We don't want anything to do with tribunals, you know that. Nor with guns—nobody wants to die. But we simply won't go. Don't take it amiss, our path is different from yours, and everything else about us is different. So we just won't go."

There was no hint of a challenge in his words, but something about them immediately convinced Andrei that they really wouldn't go. So he resolved on the measure which would seem to hurt them most.

"All right, have it your way. But you won't get the cattle. I have full responsibility for them. All twelve hundred head. Yours as much as the others. That clear?"

Sukhov agreed with unexpected ease.

"Quite clear. Just give us a full receipt."

"Receipt, did you say?" He thought he was gaining control of the situation. "You'll get nothing. You're under obligation to drive those cattle all the way to Derbent, so drive them. So you want to let everyone else do all the work. It won't wash. Others can sweat while you sit back with your receipt. Not on your life!"

But Sukhov wasn't a bit disconcerted. He calmly put an end to Andrei's extravagant rhetoric.

"All right, then, we'll do without the receipt. So long, Andrei Vasilievich, remember us kindly. God will be your judge."

They stood before him, his best herdsmen and drovers, unshakable in their conviction that right was on their side. Suddenly he saw himself as a small boy who had misbehaved, and wanted, oh how desperately, to throw himself at their feet and beg them not to abandon him there in the middle of all the infernal snow and slush, hundreds of miles from home. And he, Lashkov, almost humbled himself and made peace with them, but his blood-tie with the family notions of what was right and infallible triumphed.

"Good riddance to bad rubbish," he ground out menacingly.

The peasants moved off at once, walking over the mushy snow with the firm assurance of people who knew the skill of their own hands, people whose life-worth would always be recognized. A hoarse sigh from the old vet accompanied their departure.

"They've really taken offense. They won't be back."

Andrei vented his annoyance on him.

"What am I supposed to do, dance for them? They'd have let us down sooner or later anyway. The leopard can't change his spots. We know what that Kondrovo lot is like."

Later on, sitting by the fierce heat of the presbytery stove, Andrei was still seething with anger and cursing the runaway peasants for their benighted obstinacy, but however hard he tried to whip up his rage, he felt a growing conviction that he was in the wrong. His angry words rang hollow in his own ears. "More than twenty years of Soviet power and their heads are still full of incense. You hammer it into them over and over again—'There isn't any God, you're your own masters.' And still they stick to their old ideas. How long can you go on hammering? It's time people like them came to their senses. You're an educated man, Grigorii Ivanovich, you ought to be able to make those ignoramuses see sense."

The vet was staring into the glowing embers, as though they held something that he alone could see.

"It says in the Scriptures that God created man in one day. Only of course it wasn't one terrestrial day, but one terrestrial eternity. And we were conceited enough to think that we could perform the same feat in twenty fleeting mortal years. We were a bit too hasty with our damned pride, we took on something too big for us. Now we're reaping the fruits of it. But that's all by the by, just rhetoric . . . No, we shan't have an easy time of it without the Kondrovo lot, that's for sure . . ."

The old man stopped talking, and the hardships of the road ahead seemed so endless and so hopeless that Andrei saw the ludicrous insignificance of his present grievances. A chill of anxiety passed over him, and he automatically moved closer to the fire. "Perhaps winter really has set in? It'll be a poor look-out if it has."

X

A low wind bearing early snow whistled over the steppe. The droves from the different farms had long ago merged, moving through the whirling snow in a single herd. The cattle were on their last legs, and Andrei, near breaking point, was helping the herdsmen to drive them on. Their forces of men had thinned out considerably even before the departure of the Kondrovo people and now they could scarcely cope with the duty roster. Old inhabitants assured Andrei that early snows were uncommon in these parts, and that warm weather would set in before long, but he was on tenterhooks.

"We shan't last more than two days' march in a blizzard like this, for sure."

Particles of ice were stinging his face, and Andrei, hunched under the biting wind, cast a glance now and then in the direction of the vet, who was riding beside him on a cart. He wondered how the old man was getting on. Boboshko had been morose and aloof just lately, avoiding the kind of conversations they had had before. His general behavior was marked by an uncharacteristic irritability.

"The old man's just tired," thought Lashkov indulgently, but without much conviction. "When the cold goes, he'll thaw out again."

He was about to offer the vet a word of sympathy when Duda's ice-covered beard loomed dimly through the frozen mist.

"Look there, Vasilich!"

Ahead of them a train of sledges was stretched out along a cart track which joined the road. As he got closer, Andrei was able to make out more of their strange load. From each sledge several pairs of blue-black eyes peered miserably and apprehensively over the snowbound wastes. Against the dull white of the wintry plain they seemed almost unreal.

A man in a thin greatcoat with the tabs picked off and a forage cap pulled down over his ears limped heavily along the verge towards

Andrei. The whiskery face with bluish frost burns on it dissolved in a pleading smile.

"Hallo, pal. I'm evacuating these Spanish kids. I've got to load them at Halt Number Twelve, but there's a bit of trouble with one of them. He's unconscious. Must have a fever . . . I'm afraid I shan't get him that far. You're making for Borovsk, it isn't far, six or seven miles. I'll give you somebody to show you the way. There's no decent dog at Number Twelve, let alone a doctor. I'd go myself, but I haven't got a free sledge, we're packed to the limit. Help me out, brother. It's state business."

"Isn't there anything nearer?"

"Not a thing. Nothing for a hundred miles around."

"You're giving me a bit of a problem."

"You never know what's around the corner."

"As if I hadn't got enough trouble."

Andrei was torn between two feelings. On the one hand, it wasn't easy to refuse the disabled soldier, who was evidently at the end of his tether, but on the other, every fresh burden meant fresh delays, and fresh complications as a result. The bitter lessons of their recent losses had taught him caution. He couldn't make up his mind, but the imploring expectancy there in the sledge, now focused entirely on himself, grew tenser by the minute, until it became positively unbearable and he finally gave in.

"Hand the kid over."

"Thanks, pal."

The veteran's frostbitten cheeks quivered with gratitude.

"Thanks pal. Pity if the kid died . . . be back right away."

He hurried off happily, rushing back to his sledges, slipping off the verge occasionally in his haste, one leg sinking deep into the loose snow. With every step he took the children's apprehension diminished; they became calm and then hopeful.

After a brief discussion beside the leading sledge a figure in a sheepskin coat, carrying a sheepskin bundle in its arms, detached itself from the train. Seen closer, the figure turned out to be an old woman with a mustache and a hawklike nose that almost touched her lower lip. Andrei was taken aback by her unexpectedly deep voice.

"Where d'you want him? And where do I go?" she asked.

"Climb up here, mother." Boboshko, brightening up considerably, made them welcome and found room for them. "Make yourself comfortable. With a bit of luck I shan't squash you."

He helped the old woman to clamber onto the seat, and livened up so much while he was at it that he even darted a coaxing look at Andrei.

"Never mind, the more the merrier. Let's go!"

Soon afterwards the broken outlines of a Cossack farmstead took shape in the shrouding blizzard and Andrei's heart grew lighter. At last! But as the farm buildings loomed more and more distinctly through the storm, it gradually became obvious that they were silent and uninhabited. The first hut with its boarded-up windows confirmed Andrei's worst suspicions. The farmstead had been abandoned. Still, he sighed with relief. They would be able to get warm and attend to the cattle.

However, he had no chance to recuperate that day. Having made his rounds, he staggered into the hut where the vet had raised a fierce heat, and was about to lie down for a bit. But one look at the boy lying sprawled over an adult's fur-coat told him that there would be no rest for him. A feverish chill shook the little Spaniard's frail body without interruption. There was a white scum on his cracked lips, and the delirious words which he was murmuring were barely audible. The old woman who had accompanied him kept changing the wet towels on his burning forehead, sighing loudly.

"Even little children have to suffer . . . Dear God!"

Andrei suppressed his desire to sit down and at least warm his feet a bit, for fear of succumbing to his weakness and the seductive warmth.

"Wrap him up, mother." He had made up his mind, and felt better: There was no going back now even if he wanted to. "It isn't much of a trip. I'll be back in a couple of hours."

Boboshko rushed to the old woman's aid, seizing first one thing, then another, helping her to get the sick child ready. Andrei was touched by his flush of anxiety, his vexation at his own clumsiness. As Andrei put his hand on the latch, the vet commiserated with him.

"You'll always have a rough time, Andrei Vasilievich, terribly rough. Not that you've ever had it easy. God go with you. . . ."

The last thing he heard was the old woman's farewell words.

"God keep you, you dear soul"—crossing herself as she said it.

He galloped off, guessing what route he must take, keeping close to the railway track so as not to get lost. Gusts of wind brought the harsh smell of clinker to his nostrils. The storm was getting fiercer, rising at times to a howling blizzard. Bay plunged into snowdrifts and dropped back on his haunches, finding the going more and more difficult. Telegraph wires sang dismally overhead. Only the shriek of train whistles in the distance brought him some comfort in his icy solitude. He could sense the feverish heat of the delirious child strapped to his back, and felt a glow of affection and sympathy, almost of love, for his unfortunate small companion.

"Hold on a bit, my love, we'll get through somehow."

He was visited by unfamiliar doubts, and found himself puzzling over unexpected problems. Why and when had things got so disjointed, so confused, so out of whack? What force was it that hurled people this way and that, made them collide, hardened their hearts, robbed them of humanity. Who could explain why an aged veteran of Kornilov's army, who had lived through God knows what military trials and tribulations, was now dragging himself to the back of beyond to safeguard other people's property? Or why a half-dead infant from the green banks of some fairy-tale land was raving deliriously out on the steppes of Kuban, thousands of miles away from his mother. Why was all this happening? Why? Why? Why?

The dense curtain of rough swirling snow was thickening by the minute. The branch line which was his only landmark suddenly disappeared from sight. Bay was lifting his legs without making any headway, and after a while stopped dead. Andrei urged him on, whipping and coaxing him by turns, but the horse only twitched his frost-covered ears, and didn't stir. Andrei had to dismount in the snow, take him by the bridle and plod blindly onward. In the back of his mind he had long since realized that he was lost, moving with no sense of direction, but the thump of the little boy's heart at his back forbade him to stop. On he went, ignoring the promptings of despair and common sense, because he had another life, beyond his own, to answer for. When his strength had begun to fail and, for the first time in his life, he felt that the end was terrifyingly near, a thread of golden light suddenly gleamed through the snow ahead. With every step it grew clearer and brighter till at last it became the cross on the snow-framed dome of a church. Soaring upward at the door of a steep slope the cross seemed to light his way. Andrei found a second wind, and set out toward his goal. He spoke his relief out loud.

"You see, Barcelona, we've made it. It takes a lot to flatten you and me. We're tough! We'll soon be in the warm."

A delirious murmur was the only answer from behind.

XI

Next morning it was as though the snow had never been. Through the window of the hospital waiting room where he had spent the night Andrei saw the sun blazing down. The streaming gutters made it seem more like spring than autumn. Still half asleep, Andrei was flabbergasted. "What a climate—you never know whether it'll be a day for weddings or for funerals." The fine morning put him in a lighthearted, holiday mood.

"I got him here. So I've done something to earn my salt, made myself useful for once."

He relived all his wanderings on last night's journey, right up to his vision of the cross at the end:

"You probably wouldn't have pulled through, Andrei Vasilievich, without that old church there. All the same, it's ironic . . . in Uzlovsk I used to tear them down with my own hands, and here I was saved by one. You never can tell how things will turn out."

He remembered how they had demolished the church by Khitrovo pool. Priests lay buried in the churchyard there, and a brass band from the depot stood on their graves playing "Upward, Ever Upward." Seryoga Agureev, half-drunk, was throwing icons through the window as they were torn off the walls, and grinning at the gaping crowd:

"Here you are, handmaiden, these Saint Nicholases, ten kopecks the pair! Who wants the Mother of God with issue, I'm giving them away! Hey you, the little lady with the handbag, wouldn't you like to swap the brooch on your snow-white breast for a portrait of the sainted hero George the Victor? Who wants the incense-burner, do for a pisspot or for pickling cucumbers. Here you are, ladies!"

The children of Father Dimitrii, the local priest, stared at him intently from the presbytery porch, and something about their silent watchfulness damped Seryoga's spirits whenever he looked at them.

Of all that he saw that day, the unchildlike silence of the priest's children there on the presbytery porch had remained most vividly in Andrei's memory . . .

The woman from the linen room brought him back to earth as she arrived with the child's orphanage clothes and the medical superintendent's certificate that the patient had been delivered and admitted. Her puffy cheeks, sign of a recent pregnancy, sagged miserably.

"Here you are, that's the lot. He's terribly weak and thin, just skin and bones."

"Will he live?"

"I should say so!" Her smile convinced him more than words could have done that she was telling the truth. "He's lost an awful lot of weight, but never mind, he's hanging on. He's all eyes."

Embarrassed by her own loquacity, she abruptly got back to business.

"Your horse is tied up in our garage."

But she couldn't keep this up, and her face lit up again in a tender smile.

"We'll fatten him up, he'll be all right. When he gets home they won't know him."

"I can see you're fond of children."

Sadly, she relieved his curiosity.

"Can't have any of my own," she explained, "so I warm myself with other people's. Just had another miscarriage . . . I have no luck . . . There must be something wrong with my insides." Then, in a hurry, "Come on, I'll show you the way or you'll be wandering around lost again."

On the porch she held out a broad hand.

"All the best, then."

As he rode to the hospital gates Andrei could still feel her eyes on his back, and this unexpected farewell gesture stayed with him on the return journey. Birds circled in the high, newly washed sky, excited cries sounding like regretful farewells. The belt of trees by the embankment dripped melting frost, and every branch, leaf, and twig seemed to strain toward the sun, rustling in gratitude. The water in the ruts along the road steamed and evaporated before his eyes. A warm dry wind played on his face, filling him with a feeling of lightness and freedom.

The farmstead, which had been hidden by the railway track, came into view as he turned and followed the channel of a dried-up stream under the bridge near the marketplace. But as soon as the upturned shafts of his carts appeared against the sky to the left of the pond Andrei's heart fluttered in dismay. A dust cloud was billowing over the pens, and the wind brought to his ears a confused but steadily growing din. Lashkov drove his horse on, and before long he knew beyond all doubt that a savage fight was going on in grim earnest in the pens.

In his mind he feverishly ticked off all the possible reasons for a brawl. "What's it all about? Who's been getting more than his share?"

He reined in at the fence round the pens, pulled out his revolver with trembling hand, and started firing into the air, hoping to halt the bloodshed.

"Stop this brawling . . . Didn't you hear me . . . Stop it . . . I'll shoot . . . Stand still, you devils . . ."

But nobody took any notice of his shouts. Rage, some desperate blind rage, deprived them of hearing and reason. The heartrending wails of children mingled with the noisy lamentations of old women and obscenities from the fighters; all this was merged in one sustained, discordant uproar.

Klim Grishin, a squat bearded man with a neck twisted by a bad attack of chicken pox in infancy, was laying about him with a heavy pole; he spun like a top in the midst of the confusion, cursing everybody in turn in a spluttering falsetto.

"You scum! You fucking bastards! Eat yourselves sick at our expense! Gobble the lot and leave us the bones! We'll thrash you so you'll wake up without a hangover. Here, you swine. I don't want to end up owing you anything!"

Akulina Babicheva, the Torbeevo witch—a flat nose in a flat face covered with a web of fine wrinkles—leapt noiselessly behind one man after another, deftly tearing strips from their travel-worn shirts.

"You fiends, Hell wouldn't have you," she mouthed, beside herself with rage. "Where d'you think you're going without my permission? . . . Now you can go around showing your bare arse . . . ragged-arsed masters . . ."

Some way away from the free-for-all, the one-legged idiot Asya, whom the womenfolk from Dubovo had picked up out of charity somewhere along the way, was struggling in a pile of bundles and rags in a battered gig.

"Help! Murder!" she wailed. "They're killing me! Taking my life! Save me! Fire! Cock-a-doodle-doo! Cluck-cluck-cluck! Death to the German invaders! Ma-a-a-ma!"

By the time he spotted Alexandra she was surrounded by such a dense tangle of brawlers that it was quite impossible to force his way through to her. Silent and contemptuous, she had her back to a haycart, and was swinging a hefty fist, hardened by unwomanly work, down on the heads of those around her.

The vet was at her side, getting under everybody's feet, seizing people by the arm, even trying to step between them, but when somebody flung him off so that he almost hit the fence, he lost heart and subsided. His streaming eyes darted from side to side.

"Look at you, you're just as wooden-headed as you ever were. No sense of proportion and no conscience. Ready to kill one another for five kopecks. Even wild animals have more sense than to harm their own. And you're supposed to be human. Stop it, can't you? Remember God's wrath, you drunken riffraff. Calm down!"

In the hurly-burly nobody noticed the arrival of the militia patrol, who suddenly appeared on Andrei's heels. But then Grishin's pole crashed down on one of the militiamen, a puny youngster with high cheekbones and two pips on his shoulder, who collapsed soundlessly at Klim's feet with a split skull. At this the crowd instantly sobered up and began slowly drifting to the sides of the pen, leaving the murderer alone with his victim in the middle.

As the circle around Grishin widened, his ungainly but sturdy figure dropped and shrank. His weak, chinless jaw dropped in fright, and his speech became halting and disjointed.

"How could I know who he was? . . . I ask you . . . it happened by accident. . . . Why did he have to put himself right under the pole? . . . You don't think I did it on purpose, do you? . . . My hand slipped. . . ."

An elderly militiaman, built like a bull, roughly shoved his way through the crowd, marched up to Grishin and raised his hand to strike; however, one glance told him the price he might have to pay, so he merely squeezed out a few harsh words.

"Go on ahead, we have things to say to you."

A second man, in glasses, with an NCO's clipboard at his side and two fountain pens in his tunic pocket, rushed round the circle like an enraged broody hen, looking for a fight.

"Break it up. . . . Now! No backtalk! We'll run in the lot of you. You're all in it together, the whole gang of you. What are you looking at, you thug? You kill a member of the komsomol, you take the life of an outstanding comrade, and then you dare to look at me like that. Bunch of Moscow ruffians. We'll soon teach you about freedom. . . . You, the woman there, with the red hair, who's in charge here?"

He turned round sharply as Andrei made his way through the crowd and his glasses flashed hostility.

"You, eh. Where did you pick up these cons? Have you ever stood trial? Well, you will now!"

He had his clipboard at the ready, but a close look at Andrei's face stopped him short.

"Hell, where did you get frostbitten like that? All right, let's get on with making out a report on this incident. Tell the women to cover up the section leader somehow. . . . And let's have the witnesses."

Andrei wearily tried to calm the other man's aggressiveness.

"Nobody will come forward," he said. He looked round, and they all lowered their eyes as he looked at them. "You'll have to do it yourself."

The policeman was up in arms again, and his glasses glinted angrily as they caught the sun.

"What d'you mean, won't come forward? So you've got a gang of crooks here? Honor among thieves? Can't wait to go to prison, is that it? I'm warning you, don't try to take me for a ride, we've had tougher ones than you to handle."

A vague hostility towards the man in glasses was growing by the minute until it overcame any weary readiness to compromise. Another moment and he would have poured out all his seething resentment on his unwelcome guest, but Duda forestalled him. Defiantly flashing a massive, beet-root-colored bruise at the bystanders, he stepped between the two men, and tapped his chest with his fist in a gesture of disarming courtesy.

"Witnesses, did you say? I'm the chief witness of this whole bloodletting."

Before the man in glasses could gather his wits together, Filya had advanced on him.

"Honest to God, may I be frozen to the spot. I saw it all. Well, me and old Klim started arguing about some cattle, and the pole jumped out of my hand, honestly, and your lad was right there with his head in the way . . . I'm truly sorry, I couldn't be sorrier. I mean, he was only young. I got knocked about, too; look, I'm not enjoying this much either."

Such naive candor shone in his watery bloodshot eyes and his little speech was so ingenuous that the man in glasses shifted irresolutely for a moment, then spat angrily and moved off through the crowd.

"You and I will meet again in Borovsk," he threatened Andrei as he went. "When your gang of thieves gets there we'll soon bring them to their senses."

The militiamen set off on their return journey an hour later, after making out a report and placing the section leader's corpse on a cart which Andrei had harnessed for them. Klim Grishin was in front, with his hands tied behind his back and his head hung low. Before he turned onto the bridge he threw back his head, looked around and craned his neck as though to shout some farewell message, but no sound came. His shoulders hunched even more hopelessly, and he soon disappeared around a bend in the embankment.

Andrei saw them all turn to him as one, as though awaiting the answer to some all-consuming doubt.

"Those who're fed up can go. I'm not holding anybody back."

His eyes inadvertently met Alexandra's, and he began talking for her alone, as he gazed straight into their black depths.

"Another time I shan't hesitate. I've been given full powers. Only one thing matters to me—to deliver the cattle safe and sound. And I'll knock hell out of anybody who gets in my way. . . . Harness up, it's time to be off."

Silence accompanied his departure, and he concluded with satisfaction that his short speech had been taken seriously and had even met with some approval.

XII

The outfit had just settled in at one of their halting places when Duda stopped Andrei as he was beginning his evening rounds.

"There's an old chap here who insists on seeing you. Says it has to be the top man."

"Well, where is he?"

"His herd is stood over there toward the pool. He can't use his legs at all. He's got a shepherd lad with him looking after things. They've only got forty head anyway. Seems they come from somewhere round Kursk."

In a roomy cabin by a tiny pool half overgrown with reeds, a bony, bearded man lay with a quilted coverlet drawn up to his chin, staring fixedly in front of him. He merely lowered his heavy eyelids by way of greeting, then used his eyes to direct his guest to a seat on a pile of saddles in the corner.

He lay there panting anxiously, appraising his guest with sidelong glances, while slowly summoning up the strength to begin. It was obvious that what he had in mind was not going to be easy for him.

At last his thin lips, coated and cracked with fever, parted feebly and he spoke.

"I want to talk to you about a very serious matter, boy. . . . I've got thirty-eight left. Exactly. . . . When I set off there were three score. And I shan't be able to save all these either. You're driving yours to Derbent, I've heard. That's just where we want to go. Take mine in with your bunch, boy. It won't make any difference to you. Where there's a thousand another forty won't be noticed. You'd be doing a good deed. I'll hand over the documentation, so it's all fair and square. You just give me a receipt. I can't fight on any further. . . . You can see there's no strength left in my legs."

"You ought to rest for a bit, old man, and it'll pass. You'll get over it."

"You're a funny one; I'm not ill, boy, I'm too old."

"That's why I'm telling you to take it easy for a bit."

"Whether I rest or not, nobody can make me any younger."

He was suddenly agitated and his face became blotchy.

"Don't get the wrong idea. Our cattle are handpicked. There are half a dozen prizewinners, all in calf. You won't regret it. . . . Take Romashka for example, she's worth a lot. She's a Semmenthal. . . . Dorofei Karpov, a really good farmer in our parts, brought that breed all the way from Kostroma. The village packed Karpov off to Siberia, and his farm went to the kolkhoz, that's how we made a killing. . . . Now they're dying, and it's a waste. . . . Have pity. Take them."

An idea—risky but tempting—flashed into Andrei's mind. But it was still tentative, and he hedged cautiously.

"Of course I could take them. Only there's no need. Once you pull yourself together you'll be a new man. You'll probably leave us in the lurch."

"You're a funny one, boy. I'm too old, I tell you. My bones are rotten with age. Where would I find the strength?"

Deep down Andrei still felt pangs of conscience, but the temptation was too much for him, and he recklessly made up his mind.

He did some feverish arithmetic as he took the way-bill from the old man.

"Nearly forty head! I can cover all our losses, with some left over. All's fair in war. It's for the state, not myself. True, I shall have to give a receipt. Still, let's hope for the best. I'll wangle it somehow."

"Any of them sick?"

The old man was quite offended, and breathed more noisily than ever.

"Not one! I take care of them myself. I've done without quacks all my life. After all, they belong to the kolkhoz, not to strangers. Afterward we'll take them all back, just as they are. We don't want any exchanges. We know when we're well off."

"Can you manage a note of explanation?"

"I never learned to write, boy. You put what you think is needed."

It was almost too easy. Andrei's last doubts evaporated. Shivering with excitement, he was in a hurry to get it over with.

"I'll go and take a look at your animals, just to do things properly. Then we'll decide. I won't want to buy a pig in a poke."

The old man nodded his approval.

"Don't worry, the cattle are all in good shape. But check them, by all means. Things should always be done properly."

So far Duda hadn't uttered a word, but as he went with Andrei to the nearby pen he suddenly said, "You're making a mistake, Vasilich."

A minute earlier Andrei might still have thought better of it, but Duda's reproach spurred him on.

"Stop croaking, Filya. You haven't got the brains for these matters."

Filya's usually vacuous face went stony.

"It doesn't take much brains to rob a sick man. Cheat him out of what's rightfully his and go on your way, vanish into thin air."

"What are you talking about?"

Rage at such injustice made him lose control.

"Just who have I cheated? D'you think that I'm doing it for myself? That it's all self-interest? Try and work it out in that thick head of yours —what's in it for me? Why would I want to?"

"All right, maybe it's not for yourself," said Filya obstinately, "but the way it works out, your interests come first. Because what you want is to make a name for yourself, and have the benefit that way. You're all like that, you bosses. You're concerned about the public good, but you make sure not to lose out all the same."

"If anything goes wrong, you're in the clear; it's people like me who have to stick their necks out."

"Well, don't! We'd get by just fine if you'd keep your eyes and your voices to yourselves."

His voice softened as he began to wheedle:

"I trusted you completely, Vasilich. So you turned the Kondrovo lot out. That's all right. You treated Prokofii Fyodorovich badly. God will forgive you. You ordered all the cattle to be merged into one herd. Well, we thought, it must be for the best. But d'you realize what it meant to us, mixing our pedigree herds with all sorts of ragtag and bobtail? Still, we gave you the benefit of the doubt, we thought everything would be all right if you were in charge. So now you're scheming to rob somebody with our help. No, Vasilich, this time we aren't on your side. We know which cattle are ours, we can tell right away because we know whose calves they are just by the smell. But the business with that old man who'll be on your conscience; you'll answer to God for it. Don't worry, this is between the two of us. I'll explain it to the others some other way. So long."

Duda walked straight across the meadow, striding out with a firm step like someone who had suddenly discovered his own strength and value in the world. Against such calm assurance, the power which gave Andrei life and strength seemed insignificant and trivial. So when the vet overtook him, and as usual looked at him directly, full of unspoken questions, Andrei turned away morosely as he gave his orders.

"Take the cattle over from the old man. Get the receipt witnessed properly. And tell him from me not to worry, we'll get his cattle there without loss."

With that he walked away, tumbled into the nearest haycock and fell into an uneasy sleep plagued by nightmares.

He was riding through the forest toward the glare of leaping flames somewhere over the distant treetops. He urged his horse on, hurrying to reach the spot before nightfall. But suddenly Filya Duda appeared at a bend in the road and raised his hand to stop him. "It's too late, Vasilich, it's all burned to ashes." But Andrei ignored him and galloped on, with Alexandra's plaintive wail echoing behind him.

"Andrei, my love, have pity on me."

He awoke with a shiver of excitement, feeling Alexandra's breath on his face.

"You awake?"

"They'll see us!"

"What do I care?"

His teeth were chattering with suspense.

"You know what people are. That's why they have eyes—to spot things. If they catch you out one day they'll walk over you the next."

Her voice was very quiet. "Never mind about other people. Haven't we got anything better to talk about? You still angry about last time?

You don't think I really meant it all? I was only taking it out on you because you were so cold, and you decided to take offense. Come closer . . . Andrei, my dearest. . . ."

Later, after the empty lassitude that followed their lovemaking, Andrei was filled with warm contentment.

"Now I'm willing to do as you suggested, and to hell with the consequences. Why should we hide, after all? We're not children, I hope."

"No, Andrei, we mustn't. I want what's best for you. I don't want you to have a bad time on my account. When you give me the sign, I'll come, but we mustn't be seen. I'm going now. Oh, dear, I don't want to."

"Don't go, then."

"It's no good, Andrei, my dear, we decided once, and that's how it must be. Wait till tomorrow. I'll come again."

Her footsteps died away in the night and Andrei was left alone with his happiness, and the stars above his head. The moon bathed the world about him in a steady glow that cast no shadows. Andrei felt as if he had been lying there in the mound of autumn hay for an eternity, conscious of neither thought nor desire, absolved of all his cares and preoccupations, and that he would go on lying there forever: No power on earth could wrench him away from this endless peace and quiet.

It was Boboshko who broke in on his solitude, a dark silhouette against the starry sky.

"Everything's in order, Andrei Vasilievich," he reported. "Receipt duly witnessed and handed over. The old man sends his greetings. In fact, he's scrawled you a note of thanks."

"By himself?"

"Yes."

The blood rushed to Andrei's head.

"Right."

Half-choked with shame, he could scarcely force the word out.

He suddenly felt that some unknown and invisible being, somebody like that old man, was daily overseeing his every thought and action, and would someday call him to account before some peculiar tribunal of his own. For the first time in his life a thought that was frightening in its simplicity burned itself into Andrei's mind.

"Yes, you'll have to answer, Andrei Vasilievich, old friend, you'll have to answer for every bit of it."

XIII

When the sea suddenly came into view, framed between two cliffs, Andrei's astonishment took his breath away. It looked so quiet and serene. In his imagination he always saw the sea in the grip of a mighty storm, but here a smooth surface, touched with blue and flat as a table, stretched away as far as the eye could see, its boundless desolation un-relieved by a single sail or the smoke of a lone steamer. In the face of this unbroken expanse Andrei felt like some poor whelp cast out by fate into an alien and incomprehensible world.

The road which the herd was following to the farm specified in the itinerary shortly swung away into the mountains, and the guide who had been attached to Andrei back in Makhachkala—an elderly Circassian with little bright blue eyes in a face burned almost black by wind and sun—gestured with his whip toward the depths of a gorge and clicked his tongue reassuringly.

"One pass to cross. After that, road's good . . ."

The herd was strung out in a long chain on the narrow, stony road, and as he stood aside to let them pass Andrei was forced to inspect each animal individually.

Previously they had all merged in a multicolored but indistinguish-able blur, hovering like a mirage before his eyes, giving him no peace or rest, but now each of them revealed its distinctive markings and char-acter. There were beige ones dappled with chalky patches, their big lustrous eyes moist and hypnotic; brown ones, their short horns briskly probing the air in front of them; red ones, their high, arching necks glinting with black lights. And every single one of them had her own particular habits and appearance. He warmed to them. "There you are, even cattle are all quite different from one another."

As soon as the herd penetrated the mountains a group of riders appeared around the first bend; one of them immediately detached himself from the others and hurried to meet them. He reined in a few steps from Andrei, pressed his only hand to his breast, and bowed his head in its lambskin cap.

"Greetings, friend." He spoke Russian without the slightest accent, and only his excessively careful pronunciation gave him away. "Welcome to my home."

He turned his horse skillfully and rode at Andrei's side.

"How many have you brought?"

"One thousand, two hundred head minus a few." Andrei found himself inadvertently making excuses; he had heard from the guide about the one-armed state farm manager and his stern temper. "Parted with some—got receipt for them. And some died, of course."

"People I mean, how many people, friend?"

"Five, counting me."

"That's all?"

"It's a long journey, all sorts of things happened."

"Without people your cattle are no use to me. I've got cattle. What I lack is manpower."

All brightness and eagerness left his face, which was as chiseled as the profile on a coin. He seemed to lose interest in the conversation.

"It's a bad business, my dear chap. You've kept the cattle together but the people have run away. All right, get yourself fixed up. We'll talk later."

He put his horse into a gallop to join his waiting companions, to whom he said something. They turned as one man and the whole group soon disappeared around the bend.

Boboshko rode up, and Andrei didn't trouble to conceal his bitter resentment.

"What a welcome. Might as well turn around and go home."

"What d'you expect, Andrei Vasilievich. He's the boss here and he really does need people more than cattle." There was an undisguised note of weariness in the vet's conciliatory words. "Unfortunately, cattle reproduce much faster."

"He ought to try doing my job for a bit."

"It probably wouldn't make any difference. People like you, Andrei Vasilievich, are all the same. You want to do the best for everybody, so you're bound to come to grief. The dark masses you have undertaken to enlighten are utterly unreceptive to the light. They don't care how bad things are as long as everybody suffers equally. However hard you try, those whom you want to overwhelm with kindness won't understand your motives and will run from you sooner or later. Forgive an old man's bluntness, but it's better for you to hear it now from me, before it's too late. You deserve to know. I've got to know you during our time together. You won't be able to carry the burden you've taken up, Andrei Vasilievich. Anyway, you took it on out of family pride rather than conviction. You really are very pure. In fact, I'm inclined to think that you'll end up believing in God . . . Excuse me, I must go and look at the bull, Yevsei, er, he's out of sorts today, and mean. Been on his feet too long, I daresay."

It was only perhaps now, at the very end of the journey, that Andrei really sensed the full weight of the load he had shouldered in Uzlovsk. Longing for affection and soothing, simple words drove him in search of Alexandra. She saw him coming from a distance, but instead of hurrying to meet him as usual she turned aside as though to avoid a conversation.

He rode right up to her, sensing that something was wrong.

"What's the matter with you?" he asked anxiously.

"It's all a mess, Andrei," she almost groaned, avoiding his eyes. "When I saw that one-armed man just now, it turned me cold. What if something awful happens to my Sergei? I had a bad dream as well. What's between you and me is a sin, I know it. I'll have to pay for it one day."

"Come on, Alexandra. Whatever's got into you? You're worn out with all this commotion, that's what it is. We shall be back down in the valley tomorrow, and everything will be all right. I'm not enjoying it either."

"Please forgive me, my love, but I can't stay now, I'm too upset. Give me a little time to calm down, or I don't know what will happen."

"Spare a thought for me, love!"

"It's all very well for us, cuddling each other here, but what's it like for him? This manager isn't a local man at all, that Circassian was telling me. He came here from the front, he didn't fancy going home, given the shape he's in now, so he settled here. Maybe my Sergei is pining away somewhere, with no arms or legs. I'm sorry."

He gave way completely in a great sigh of despair.

"Alexandra, darling!"

"No. It's no good right now." She turned away abruptly and urged her horse on. "I'll come tomorrow. There's nowhere to hide from you. . . . Forgive me, Andrei, dear."

By midday, the herd was over the brow of the pass. A spacious valley came into view, and the central buildings of the state farm stood out in a neat rectangle. Just outside the settlement a hitherto unused pen had been made ready, along with two freshly whitewashed temporary sheds behind a sturdy fence.

As soon as the herds were installed in their new home the manager sent for Andrei. While saddling Bay, he caught Alexandra looking at him strangely. His world collapsed and he felt sordid, and utterly alone.

XIV

When he came back, toward evening, she wasn't there. "Must have got bored by herself," he decided indulgently, "went looking for company, that's it."

But time went by, the sun sank gradually over the ragged wall of snowy mountains, the first dim stars appeared in the high, cold sky, and still she hadn't come. Corrosive doubts began to eat away at him, growing by the minute. Could she have left? When he could stand it no longer, he returned to the settlement; he looked in at the shop, and not finding her there either decided to go down to the railway. There was nowhere else she could have gone—the only road ran beside the branch line.

Andrei tried to keep his hopes up, to relieve his anxiety with comforting thoughts, but as he approached his goal the appalling certainty that she had gone grew steadily harder to withstand. Anger and despair drove him on to where the trains were hooting in chorus at the foot of the hill.

He walked faster and faster, although by now he had lost all hope. Pebbles shot from under his feet and rolled, endlessly rattling, down the precipitous slope to the stream running somewhere in the depths. The darkness all around seemed mysterious and awesome under the sharp southern starlight. When the slope was behind him, and the bluish lanterns of the freight inspectors began to twinkle ahead, he came to his senses, with an agonized recognition that there was no point in going any further, that he would never get Alexandra back.

He almost ran back the way he had come. The starry heavens enfolded him and seemed to move with him, step by step. At times it was as if he could reach out, if he wished, and touch every star. The sound of the stream died down to a mutter, and the stones rolling from under his feet into the gorge sent no echo back. He was moving too high.

At last, returning painfully to his senses, he fell his length on a patch of prickly grass by the roadside, full of bitterness, his heart beating furiously, and wept. Wept like a woman, loudly, with no attempt at concealment or restraint. Why should he care about anybody now? Who was going to tell him what to do when life had suddenly lost all meaning? There had been one brief glimmer of hope in his short lifetime. But the Fates had merely beckoned enticingly, only to pull this happily found support right out from under him. He suddenly saw himself as a dumb animal, driven Heaven knows where or by whom, not allowed to take a step without permission. The realization of his impotence made everything still more unendurable. "Where am I going, and why? I want to stop. I want everybody to stop."

Through his fevered state Andrei became aware of light, unhurried footsteps on the road, then a slight tactful cough and a lengthy rustling in the dry grass. From his habitual shuffle he guessed with some exasperation that it was the vet. "What the devil brings you here?" he thought sullenly. "Your attentiveness is just about the last thing I need." Out loud he said, "Can't you sleep or something?"

"Sorry, Andrei Vasilievich."

"It's a bit late for me to be needing a nanny. And it wouldn't do any good."

"You mustn't carry on like this. You can't let yourself go, you simply can't. This is no time to go to pieces. You've got a lot of living to do yet. You'll need strong nerves—oh, how you'll need them."

"Right now I don't give a damn. It's all a mess anyway."

"Oh, Andrei Vasilievich, you'll burn like this a hundred times without dying of it. It isn't you that's weeping, it's your youth. You ought to be glad. It means your soul hasn't dried up yet."

"Just now, I'd sooner not live at all. It's agony."

Boboshko heaved a sigh of sympathy.

"Life is like a three-field farm, Andrei Vasilievich. While one field is in flower, another lies bare and the third runs wild. On the whole, though, it's beautifully organized . . . There's a parable, or a sort of fairy tale, rather. D'you want to hear it?" His voice grew richer. "Once upon a time, long, long ago, on a distant and beautiful planet there lived some wonderful people. They had made for themselves a life that was unique: a life without war, without disease, without death. They were all equal in the sight of what we may call intellect. And the only thing they lacked was neighbors for spiritual stimulation. The most advanced flying machines sped to neighboring worlds in search of kindred beings. But none of these journeys was successful. The planets round about, even the most distant, were uninhabited, or else populated by terrifying monsters. So, like it or not, thousands of years went by. The civilization of the beautiful planet was growing old in boring isolation. Then one day a space ship returned from the remotest corner of the galaxy and brought good tidings. It turned out that the tiniest little planet, somewhere in the furthest reaches of the universe, was inhabited. It was, unfortunately, true that the creatures who peopled this little planet were at the very lowest stage of development: War and pillage, fraud and violence reigned amongst them. Then the Supreme Intelligences on the wondrous planet summoned the Best of the Best. And the supreme Supreme Intelligence said to them: 'Only one of you is needed, one who is willing to go out to them and proclaim the Truth to them. Which of you is willing to do this?' And each of those invited bowed his head in token of consent. And one of them was chosen. Then the most enormous spaceship they owned set out for the other end of the heavens to leave that bold spirit there. At long last the bold spirit found himself alone with his likenesses, with human beings that is to say, Andrei Vasilievich. He healed the sick, raised the dead, comforted those in travail. In a word, he proclaimed the Truth to them. But they, can you imagine it, crucified him. For the Truth meant nothing to them. He died in torment such as he had never imagined on his own beautiful planet. But the Intelligences did not leave his body to be profaned by earthlings. It was brought back, and resurrected. In the high council of the Intelligences it was decided to stop all attempts at intercourse with savage and inhospitable neighbors. But the Resurrected One, strange as it seems, protested. The Intelligences, naturally, were not a little surprised. 'Surely,' they said, 'you don't want to try again?' and he replied, 'I do.' Then they asked him, 'Surely their life was not to your liking?' And he replied, 'It is almost unbearable, but it is beautiful. . . .' It may sound silly, Andrei Vasilievich, but I swear it's so."

A fierce anger, which he couldn't have explained to himself, took hold of Andrei. "Why is he telling me all this? What does he want from me? What right has he got to come prying into my feelings?" He forced himself to reply, scarcely containing his fury.

"What's it to me? What's it got to do with me?"

"Think it over."

"I don't want to. I've had enough. I've thought until my head's fit to explode."

"That too will pass, Andrei Vasilievich."

"What will?"

"Everything."

He was choking with blind rage.

"Listen, Grandpa, why don't you go to bloody hell. I'm fed up to the teeth with your bedtime stories. I'm sick of the lot of you, you're less than shit to me. I hate you all more than I've ever hated anybody. Goddamn the lot of you! Don't push me too far; pick up your feet and get the hell out of here or I won't be answerable . . ."

Deafened by his own shouting, he didn't hear Boboshko shuffle off toward the road and melt silently into the night, leaving him alone with the darkness and the sound of his own voice.

XV

What most astonished Andrei about Derbent was the extraordinary variety of languages. As he jostled his way round the bazaar his keen ear caught the sound of Russian now and then, but it faded as quickly as it had come, blotted out by foreign tongues. Even when he chanced upon a compatriot with whom he could exchange a word or two, he failed to discover anything about Alexandra. Nobody had seen or heard anything of her.

As he passed a beer stall, a legless veteran, with pockmarked, powder-burned cheeks, winked lazily and nodded toward the upturned cap in front of him.

"Come on, pal, help a cripple."

Andrei shrugged helplessly in reply.

"God knows, I haven't got a kopeck, friend."

"Sit down here and you soon will have," said the cripple invitingly.

Andrei was often to remember that legless ex-soldier and his spine-chillingly cheery hospitality.

After long and fruitless searches Andrei wandered into an eating house in the market and there, in the noisy crush at the counter, he bumped into someone from his own past, belonging what is more to a distant and long forgotten branch of his own family. His name was

Lyovka, and he had come originally from Torbeevo, but had worked for as long as anyone could remember at the depot, which was where Andrei sometimes met him while visiting his brother. In Uzlovsk Andrei couldn't have been bothered to pass the time of day with him, but here he shook the young man by the shoulders, childishly delighted by this unexpected meeting.

"What brings you here, you curly-headed devil? Am I glad to see you! Let's sink a few!"

Obviously flattered by his distinguished kinsman's attention, Lyovka nodded excitedly.

"Just a minute, Andrei Vasilievich . . . I'll give you a full report. . . . I heard some time back that you'd been driving cows to Derbent. . . . Right away now . . . it's our turn."

Lyovka drained the warm, flat beer in big gulps, chuckling happily, and a flush of animation darkened his pallid face from time to time.

"Metal workers like me can get any price we ask nowadays. When the evacuation started we were all sent off to one place or another, and I got sent here, see. Piss off and reinforce the gates of the Caspian they said. So here I am, reinforcing."

"Haven't they got enough of their own people?"

"Everybody's at the front," said Lyovka haltingly, "and I've got flat feet. And I've got a deferment, of course—highly skilled worker."

He brightened up again, fidgeted on his chair and crossed his legs under the table. "I saw a girl from our way down here. . . ."

It took Andrei's breath away. "Who?" he gasped. "Maybe you made a mistake?"

Lyovka triumphantly came out with his trump card.

"Not likely! Mistake Alexandra Agureev, when all the boys back home were crazy about her? And so were you!" He broke off, avoiding Andrei's eyes, which suddenly became vicious. "No mistake. No way."

"Where?"

"Where what?"

"Where did you see her, I mean?"

"I just happened to meet her. I was coming from the depot. On the platform. She was off to Baku or somewhere in that direction."

"Talk to her?"

"No, I didn't know her at all in Uzlovsk. I just gaped at her from a distance."

He suddenly had no further desire to talk to Lyovka. The beer seemed flatter than ever, the heat and the stench of the market more stifling, and his companion's homely features, perfectly welcome a minute ago, were making him feel sick. He jumped up in a hurry.

"So long, curly."

Lyovka's drunken voice came whining after him. "Where you off to, for God's sake? We've hardly started talking! And after you said you wanted to have a few!"

He seemed to shrink with distress.

"I've got some women, first-class, evacuees who are working with the track-laying crews. What d'you say?"

Andrei gave him a twisted grin from the doorway.

"Right now I'd as soon be buggered myself. So long."

He happened to pass a recruiting office and went in.

A harassed captain wearing a medal looked up with hostile eyes that were yellow with jaundice, and rudely asked what he wanted. Hastily running through the documents Andrei gave him, he brightened up and shouted over his shoulder to somebody in the next room.

"Mukhin! There's a man here for enlistment! Go and fight, my boy!"

And the captain bent over his papers once more.

XVI

When Andrei Vasilievich awoke, the whole sky above him was filled with rain clouds, not very heavy ones, but obviously there to stay. As always in such weather the smells became more pungent and distinct, and the hidden life of the forest started to make itself heard. "It's the wrong time for such weather," he decided, "bad for the hay."

He rose, his mind reverting to his usual everyday concerns: the allocation of haymaking rights in the forest, permits for felling, the forthcoming repairs to his office. Strangely enough, while he was absorbed in these and a multitude of other petty concerns, he was also aware that today, or rather, just now, he had crossed some momentous dividing line, some mysterious frontier, and that henceforward life would be clearer, simpler, less constricted.

With a sense of relief, he harnessed his horse, moved off, and rode into the warden's compound.

WEDNESDAY

*The Yard at the Midpoint
of Heaven*

I

Life for Vasilii Vasilievich went on as usual. His brother's unexpected arrival and equally abrupt disappearance did not disturb its blank monotony. From morning to night he sat hunched up by the staircase window on the second floor of the outbuilding, where he had a sad and sober bird's-eye view of the yard. Except for one week of oblivious drinking each month he sat there daily, summer and winter. He was totaling up his balance sheet, in the knowledge that he hadn't long to live.

He could probably have dismantled the house opposite, and re-assembled it brick by brick, every biscuit tile in the cornices, every window frame and pane, without a single mistake. He knew the business of every inhabitant as well as he knew his own. He had taken part in their moving in, their christenings, their funerals. Rivers of drink had been consumed and diluted in oceans of drunken tears, and now there was nobody to buy him one, let alone say a friendly word. So it was no longer death that Lashkov feared—he had got used to the idea of it—but this oppressive alienation from everyone and everything, this utter silence and isolation. It was as though some sinister force were tearing people apart one from another, and he, Lashkov, in obedience to it withdrew farther every day into himself and his unhappiness. At times a savage, almost animal desire welled up in his throat, a desire to resist the inevitable, to scream blue murder, throw a fit, bite the ground, but a paralyzing weariness fell upon him, and his poor inflamed throat could produce no more than a painful croak. "Let's have three rubles worth, right?"

Vodka seemed to seep into every corner of his soul, filling it with warm, boisterous happiness, and everything around him was suddenly good and interesting. On days like this Lashkov would drag himself down to the yard, and there, sitting on a bench he had fixed in the ground, he would find that peace, that sense of continuity with the past which he missed more and more each day, coming back to him. At such times his pension turned into a fortune, and the retired yardman shelled out ruble after ruble with sober generosity to help his boon companions with their hangovers.

But even on days wrested from his normal unhappiness, the rainbow curtain of drink would part now and then to reveal the frail figure of the old woman Shokolinist like an apparition, a black omen in the blue landscape of the past. Spry as ever, in a dark panama tilted down almost over her eyes, she hurried past with her ducklike walk, muttering incessantly to herself. She collected overdue books for the local library. She'd been collecting them for twenty years now. She scurried from house to house, apartment to apartment, darting like a mouse, and every time they bumped into each other, some string in him vibrated briefly, painfully, and left him ill at ease.

As the years went by, he had a growing presentiment of some imminent discovery, some revelation; but above all else Vasilii Vasilievich had the growing conviction that this was all tied up with old lady Shokolinist.

How could any of those living in the house thirty years ago have imagined that its founder and mistress, more of a ghost than a living person even then, would outlive so many of them? Moreover, Vasilii Vasilievich knew for sure that she was destined to outlive him, too, and perhaps the house itself. All this held some almost supernatural significance for the old man.

Lately he was forever thinking, trying to find the thread which would help him unravel the tangled skein of events.

He went back to the very first day.

II

The first to move into Number Five on the first floor was Ivan Lyovushkin, quite a young man, with a leathery-cheeked face, from Ryazan, with his wife, Lyuba, who was already pregnant. Slightly tipsy, with his shirt unbuttoned on his sweaty chest, he twinkled mischievously at the Jewish dentist Meckler, who had been ordered to make room for him, and trod all over his personal belongings.

"It's God's will. Some can't have everything while others go without, can they? My wife here is near her time. I mean to say, she can't bring a proletarian kid into the world in some moldering old barracks, can she? It isn't because the government says so, it's God's will. Don't worry, we'll get on all right, I'm a peaceful chap, and my wife, well, you'll hardly know she's here at all . . . . And she's clean. . . ."

Meckler, wearing just his jacket over a string vest, stood at the door of the room assigned to him, with his hands clasped behind his back, swaying tensely from side to side. When he spoke, his low voice trembled slightly.

"It's quite all right. I'm not arguing, am I, especially as it's God's will?"

The Jew pronounced "God" with bated breath so that it came out as "Ghod."

"Your children are my children. Rather like the Red Front."

Several pairs of absolutely identical eyes—brown, with lighter-flecked pupils—watched the strange newcomers peeking around from behind the dentist's back. Each time Meckler swayed, all the eyes swiveled, too, and the carefree Lyovushkin had probably never aroused so much personal hostility before at any one time.

"I'm a dentist, dentist, d'you understand?" said Meckler, and the light flecks suddenly disappeared in the dark fury of his brown eyes. The way he pulled in his suddenly trembling chin so tensely, the muscles twitching under his swarthy skin, showed that it afforded him some satisfaction to utter a word which his new neighbor could not know.

"But I don't think that you will have any use for me for a long time yet, young man."

Several pairs of eyes turned slightly, enveloping them all in a blanket of hostility, then the door slammed, and Lyovushkin's smile faded.

"We're among the swells here," he sighed vaguely.

Lashkov, helping Ivan Lyovushkin to drag his few belongings into the vacated corner room, which looked onto the yard, had already noticed that there was something about him that was lacking. His brashness, his shouts of unrestrained laughter, all his cheerful dashing about, gave no impression of self-assurance or enjoyment, there was no heartfelt pleasure in it.

Every now and then, a hint of unease or, rather, discontent, of which he himself seemed scarcely aware betrayed itself in his movements, his words, his laughter.

Later on, when they were sharing half a bottle, Ivan, suddenly sober, said sadly, "I suppose I ought to be happy, but there's no enjoyment in anything. I just can't. It's enough to drive you crazy."

"Putting it on a bit," thought Lashkov, "he's showing off." But out loud he said, "You'll settle down, pal. It's always the same in a new place."

Ivan sighed and thoughtfully crunched a gherkin.

"Even your own wife seems more tempting in somebody else's barn, but still . . . ."

While they were talking, Lyuba glided, silently smiling, from table to sideboard and back again, spicing her cookery with her singsong Moscow accent.

"Go on, eat, don't be shy . . . ."

There was something catlike and restful about her. Ivan pulled his wife to him and lovingly stroked her firmly rounded belly.

"My Lyuba's going to bear me a girl. I like girls. Easier to handle. One girl, two girls, three girls." Here he suddenly clenched his teeth and looked grim, unmistakably a peasant. "But I want a son as well. So he can study to be a dentist. A son, Lyuba, d'you hear?"

He stopped talking and knocked back his drink in one gulp.

"Come on, old pal, let's have a song—what about 'Khazbulat'?"

It was after midnight when they went out to the yard. Big summer stars flickered and twinkled, growing brighter until they danced. From the earth they looked like nervously roosting birds. Every now and then one or another of them would flutter in fright from its perch, streak the slaty darkness with a blazing wing and vanish behind the nearby house-tops. In the next yard a Gramophone was furiously scratching out "The Gypsy's Farewell," while a drunken tenor tried in vain to pick up the tune: "La-a-asts so-o-ong I sss-ing."

The friends sat down on the bench in the yard. Suddenly Ivan's head jerked in the darkness, and he groaned with nostalgia.

"The buckwheat will be flowering just now back home in Lebedyana."

Lashkov had never in his life seen buckwheat in flower, and probably wouldn't have known it from millet, but the sensuality of Lyovushkin's homesickness affected him, and he gave something like a lover's sigh himself, echoing his friend.

"It'll be flowering."

"And the concertina. . . ."

"The concertina . . . ."

"And the grass smelling like new milk."

"That's just how it smells . . . ."

As they talked, the stars flickered and fell behind the housetops, scorching the darkness. Flickered and fell.

On the face of it nothing they said was of the slightest importance—they talked about the weather, about daily routines, about all sorts of trivialities—but they both sensed a deep affinity, and Lashkov suddenly felt as though Ivan and he had been sitting there like that for years and years: Stars fluttered from their perches, burned up as they traveled, fell to earth, and still they sat; the buckwheat flowered and shed its flowers, and still they sat; Lyuba, and Lyuba's daughters, and Lyuba's daughters' daughters bore yet more daughters, and still they sat under the very midpoint of the dome of heaven.

"It's lonely here in the city."

"You'll get used to it."

"And the crowds . . ."

"You'll soon fit in . . ."

"The tobacco plants are up by now—and the best . . ."

"Yes."

A ray of moonlight split the outbuilding in two and crept along the wall. As if waiting for its touch, an icon-lamp flared in the far corner window, conjuring up the almost disembodied silhouette of old lady Shokolinist out of the darkness. From below she could be seen in the cruelest detail: the toothless, mumbling mouth, the frantically clenched hands, even her timid eyes, now glazed with ecstasy.

"Who's that old witch?" asked Lyovushkin in a muffled voice. He crossed himself and flinched a step to the side. "Lord, what a spectacle . . . I'm off . . . Lyuba's waiting for me."

"Former mistress of the house," said Lashkov, also rising. "Praying for her sins. Well, so long. I've got to be up bright and early."

As he walked home through the entrance of the outbuildings, he became aware for the first time of a tight ache in his chest, as though he were stifling. A silent anxiety took hold of him and became part of him forever.

III

Old Khramova in Number Eleven refused to give up any room voluntarily. She stood in the kitchen doorway, a big heavy woman in a soiled housecoat, watching Lashkov and Stabel, the plumber, lugging furniture from the dining room to her daughter's bedroom, and resentfully bewailed her lot.

"My papa"—from her it sounded comic and pathetic all at once—"my papa, as everybody knows, was under arrest many times . . . yes, yes, for his political beliefs. How can *they* have forgotten?"—stabbing at the ceiling with a sclerotic finger. "Is it right that the family of a celebrated artist should be robbed? What about Lyova, where's he going to rehearse? I ask you, where? And my little girl? My little girl has such talent . . . such fingers . . . aren't they needed any more?" She rushed at Kalinin, the block sergeant, who was standing stock-still on the landing. "Has nobody any use for fingers? Where is she going to practice, I ask you? Of course, silence is neither here nor there in a beerhouse or in a brothel, if you'll pardon the word . . ."

Kalinin only frowned painfully and the bones in his consumptive face stood out more sharply. It was obvious that he was long since sick and tired of the whole business, that he wanted no part of it, and was in a hurry to wash his hands of it and go home.

The two Gorev women stood behind him, propping up a mountain of bundles and packages: the wife, quiet and colorless, in a baggy gray suit and canvas shoes but no stockings, and her sister-in-law, a stoutly built girl, who looked out at the world with mischievous, smoldering eyes.

Alexei Gorev himself, a pockmarked fellow of thirty, in his squeaky Sunday shoes, hovered helplessly around the sergeant and for some reason kept shoving the housing order into his reluctant hand.

"I'm not here because I want to be. I don't care where I live as long as there's a roof over me. I've done everything in the proper legal way."

When Kalinin gloomily waved him away, Gorev rushed at his wife.

"What does she think she's doing, Fenya? We've got an order!"

Fenya gave him a miserable look and said nothing, so he turned for sympathy to his sister.

"Grusha, try and calm her down! What a housewarming. My dear woman, we've got the law on our side . . . Look, here's the stamp."

But the old woman had other things on her mind. She was parting with something without which life would no longer hold any meaning or value for her. One minute she was aloof and rigid by the kitchen window, staring into the courtyard with lackluster eyes; the next she was wandering around the apartment, fetching bits and pieces from the dining room and piling them up on the kitchen stove—glassholders, little china ornaments, family albums; or she would suddenly forget this and start appealing to her son. He was standing with his back to her, frowning in distress and rubbing his temples. She tugged at the edge of his jacket.

"Lyovushka! You're an artist, after all! You must go and tell them everything, you know where!" Once more her finger shot towards the ceiling. "For your grandfather's sake! He treasured every little thing here. They have no right! Think of Olga! What will become of her! With her fingers! Remember what Taneev said about her!"

She tried to make him look at her, but his eyes eluded her, and stared upward, through the wall, across the yard, at something far, far away. He loosened her grip, and tried to reason with her in a low voice, as though anxious not to be overheard.

"Mama, think what you're saying. What's happened, after all? Nothing. Anyway, I'm willing to sleep in the corridor. Olga can have my room. She'll get more peace there. Mama, what are you doing to yourself? That's enough now, Mama!"

Khramova subsided, but a minute later she was clinging to her daughter, cautiously stroking her almost ethereal hands.

"Just look at these fingers. No, just look at them! Taneev himself admired her fingers. Olga, my darling, don't smile like that! I beg you not to smile like that."

Olga didn't hear. She was leaning against the doorpost, rocking slowly from side to side, with a quiet, solemn smile. She was facing Kalinin. The block sergeant frowned and his wasted cheeks twitched, and the girl smiled. Of course she saw neither Kalinin nor what stood behind him. She was quite simply living in some other world, where it was still possible to smile quietly and in bliss. All the same, it made Lashkov uncomfortable to look at the two of them. There was an almost frightening resemblance between them in their desperate intensity. His anger and her beatific happiness were twin poles of the same affliction and there was no escape from their cruel affinity. Thrown together by chance, they stood facing each other on the landing, each locked in a private world with its own secret truths.

Stabel worked with a purely German respect for the things he handled. He cautiously assessed the solidity of each object before laying hands on it, then lifted it solicitously, and, feeling his footing as though walking on ice, carried it to the bedroom, where he was arranging everything according to the strictest rules of symmetry. But even this painstaking care of his exasperated old Khramova.

"Whoever puts chairs on a table, Stabel? Who puts chairs on tables, I say? Does your German mama do it? Or your German papa? Maybe your German uncle does? That furniture came from Hamburg, let me tell you! Your life's wages wouldn't pay for a table like that! Nor twice as much! Nor three times as much! And you put chairs on it."

She trod on his heels, gray-faced with impotent rage, shaking all over, trying to hit on the best way to humiliate him.

"Other people's belongings mean nothing to you, naturally. You have neither house nor home, nor country of your own. You'll live down there in the boiler room on a heap of rags, till the day you die. Oh, dear, and I used to think you were a decent person, Stabel. You're German, after all."

Stabel kept quiet. He was good at keeping quiet. How could this shabby Moscow gentlewoman with the cheeks seamed into a patchwork know what road had brought him here from his homeland? He meticulously adjusted another chair, pulled a handkerchief from his trouser pocket, and pensively wiped his hands. He did not speak until he had folded the handkerchief in four, reinserted it in his pocket, taken the old woman by the shoulders, turned her around almost effortlessly, and begun gently but firmly pushing her towards her son's room.

"I am Austrian, Madame. I have listened to you, now you listen to me. I do not know what your government wants, but I am used to respecting all governments. When they say to me, 'Stabel, it must be done,' I am doing it. But I do not want workers dying in the boiler room. Forgive me, Madame."

He led her to the table, turned her around to face him again, and sat her down with a gentle pressure on her shoulders. Once seated, she calmed down at once, sagging like soft dough. The plumber came back and touched Lyova on the shoulder.

"Lyova, take your sister to your room. It's bad for her to stay here. Very, very bad."

Lyova gave a frightened start and came to life. He seized his sister's hand, and began coaxing her in the quiet voice he had used with his mother.

"Come on, Olga, my dear, you must come with me. It's time for you to rest. We're only in the way here."

She turned a surprised smile on him.

"Why, Lyova, dear. It's early yet, and there's so much sun here. Just look at it. It's ringing. Listen to it ringing. And we've got all these curtains up. These awful curtains. And there are so many people here. Will they be living with us? Why does Mama rant at them like that? Oh, these curtains. Couldn't we take them down?"

"I'll take them down. I'll throw them out. And open the windows wide. Come on, Olga, dear. That's the way."

Her brother drew her after him, and she yielded limply, still smiling and looking around eagerly for somebody, anybody, to talk to. The corridor was empty, and the Gorevs silently started to move in. Alexei and Fenya shifted their belongings on tiptoes as though someone were lying dead in the apartment. They seemed ashamed of their own success, but Grusha at once established herself as the mistress of this new home, her whole manner declaring that all this was rightfully hers as of old, and that there would be only a slight further delay before justice finally triumphed.

She moved about with noisy self-assurance, issuing peremptory orders to her wordless sister-in-law and her brother.

"Just push those people's table over to the other corner, Fenya. We'll put our own by the window. Stop looking like something the cat dragged in, Alexei, and help her to move the damned thing. Look at them standing there . . ."

Vasilii took an immediate liking to this big-bosomed, rough-looking girl with the strong, mannish hands. She had a housewifely smell of fresh sweat and laundry. When he tried to embrace her in the passage between the kitchen and the attic, she only shrugged her shoulders, but gave him such a look that he flushed to the roots of his hair and didn't know where to put himself. Nonetheless, something stirred inside him and when Gorev was treating them all—Lashkov, Stabel, and the sergeant—to warm, flattish beer in the nearest bar, he couldn't restrain himself.

"That sister of yours is really something, Alexei Mikhailich, I must say. Extra-special. What they call dee-lux!"

Gorev beat a little tattoo with his imported shoes and muttered into his beer mug. "She's a Gorev through and through."

Stabel concurred after a little thought. "With a woman like that in the house"—he raised his index finger portentously—"ah!"

Kalinin remained silent. In his condition he couldn't be bothered with girls. He was bored and depressed by the unseasonable and unbroken heat, the warm flat beer, the tedious conversation which didn't seem as if it would ever end. He was concentrating stubbornly on his own thoughts, or, rather, on his disease. He felt it growing inside him, conquering him pore by pore, surrounding one nerve after another, and he sometimes fancied that he could even hear its movements—the stealthy, rustling music of gradual disintegration. By comparison, everything else in the world aroused in him a boredom that was as sluggish and sticky as tar. Wearily he tore off a bit of dried fish with his almost black teeth, chewed it, drained his mug, and curtly ended the gathering.

"Time to go home."

Lashkov, slightly drunk, had a dream that night. He and Grusha were walking arm in arm through Sokolniki Park. All dressed in good worsted and crêpe de chine. The trees, shot through with lights, murmured overhead as though they were about to fly away, and all the people looked around and smiled after them. What a fine couple! Suddenly he felt a shock: All those faces were as alike as peas in a pod, and all like poor crazy Olga Khramova from Number Eleven. Lashkov wanted to shout at them in anger and defiance . . . but this dream grew confused.

The yardman awoke, irritable and perplexed. What did it mean? Then he put the most flattering interpretation he could on it. Maybe it was prophetic? Vasilii, my boy, he commiserated with himself coyly, it looks as though your bachelor days are nearly over.

IV

Sima Tsygankova was racing about the labyrinth of washing on the lines, like a mouse in an egg box. Her two brothers were pursuing her. Both of them had low foreheads and black locks falling over bushy eyebrows. They chased her with drunken inefficiency, and although more than half the washing lay trampled in the mud, Sima still contrived to escape their clutches, occasionally making a break for the gate. But one of her brothers always intercepted her, and it began all over again. The brothers closed in on her relentlessly, in perfect silence, as though she were a wild animal. The only sound was their hoarse panting and the echoing twang of snapping clotheslines.

Vasilii knew from experience that it was best not to get involved with the Tsygankovs single-handed. They had moved into Number Nine not long ago and their first day in the yard had been marked by one of those brawling fistfights for which Volugda is famous, with the militia and the ambulance by way of finale. The family had disfigured Valov, the elderly teacher of literature, who lived next door to them, and Ivan Lyovushkin, self-appointed champion of all the wronged, while they were at it. Next day the elder Tsygankov took all the blame on himself and went off to prison for the year prescribed by law. The teacher of literature applied for a change of residence and slept at the Mecklers', while Ivan went proudly about the yard with his broken skull, which had been hastily bandaged up in the emergency ward, and complained indignantly to everyone who crossed his path.

"Is it God's will, knocking an old man about in broad daylight? It simply can't be allowed. Where are their consciences? We're all answerable to God, and they never seem to remember that fact."

Sima was the odd one out among the Tsygankovs. Thin, fragile, almost childlike, in her washed-out blue cotton dress with white spots, she tiptoed about the yard with downcast eyes, walking on tenterhooks, as if apologizing for her good-for-nothing family. But it had to be seen to be believed, the way the bachelors in the house looked at her, and the married men, too, if it comes to that. Sima was a prostitute, with the face of an angel in an icon.

While Lashkov was still pulling on his coat to go and fetch the block sergeant he heard somebody shouting from above.

"Monsters! Get those ugly great boots off my tablecloth. Why were you sent to plague us? Bastards! You're on my tablecloth. Are you deaf?"

Lashkov reached the yard in time for the kill. Tikhon had finally driven his sister into the corner between the boiler room and the outbuilding. Sima fell down and rolled into a ball, covering her head with both arms. A mud-caked sole was about to descend on her bespattered frock when Lyova Khramov suddenly appeared out of nowhere between her and her brother.

"Don't you dare touch her! You should be ashamed to strike a woman!" He waved his pale, thin fist under Tsygankov's nose.

It looked silly, of course. The ferocious Tikhon wouldn't have needed to hit the skinny actor, he could just have given him a push, and an ambulance would have been required. For a moment Tikhon stared at him dumbfounded like an elephant at a rabbit, wondering whether to squash him or ignore him. He decided to squash him, and his terrifying bulk was bearing down on Lyova when Stabel's heavy hand fell on his shoulder.

"Listen to me, boy. You see?" Otto held up the piece of lead pipe he was gripping in his free hand. "You want your pension now, hit him; if you don't, go home."

Tikhon sullenly looked him up and down, calculating how much a fight with the sturdy Austrian might cost him, then exchanged a brief glance with his brother, who nodded equally sullenly. They moved away, and had reached the front door before Tikhon uttered his drunken threat.

"I'll settle your hash, you ugly German bastard!"

Stabel smiled, but only with his eyes, put one arm around Sima and the other around the actor, and pushed them toward the boiler room.

"Come sit down in my place. You have plenty to talk about. We'll have a little smoke here," pointing to Lashkov. "We have plenty to think about," nodding at Lashkov again. "And to discuss."

Lashkov waited in patient silence while his friend puffed a clay pipe and studied the darkening sky. Vasilii knew Otto Stabel: The longer he thought, the more serious his pronouncement would be.

The yardman had met the Austrian by chance at the labor exchange, where he had gone at the house administrator's request to find an efficient boilerman and plumber. Stabel caught his fancy immediately. He looked sensible—he thought ten times before speaking—and it was this thoughtfulness that won the yardman over. If a man goes to the labor exchange it's hardly likely that he can afford to be choosy, but before agreeing, Otto interrogated him exhaustively, sprinkling his Russian with German words, about the locality (What was transport like?), the conditions of employment (What about days off?), overalls (How often were new ones issued?), even the tenants (What sort of people were they?).

Lashkov, defying the customs of a period which did not believe in pampering workers, performed prodigies of salesmanship.

He knew that the administrator would buy him more than one drink for finding a plumber like that. Transport, right under your nose. Wages? We shan't do you down. Overalls? We won't be mean. Tenants? Angels was the word, not tenants.

The new boilerman shortly took over Lashkov's cubbyhole in the boiler room, and the yardman moved into a spare bedroom on the second floor of the outbuilding, which Nizovtseva the dressmaker had been forced to give up.

The first uncertain star of evening hung over the housetops. The star grew, filled with twinkling blue light, and two voices from the depths of the boiler room merged with the rustling of poplars beyond the gates.

"Mother's never sober. Nor those two either. It's money all the time. I give them all I get as it is. Why did we have to come here to this hellhole. So they took the forge away from us. Is there nothing in the world besides forges? We would have survived. We're all healthy. It's nice, where we lived on the Volga. Plenty of room. They kept on talking about going to the factory. Some factory it turned out to be!"

"How horrible! How horrible! My poor dear little girl . . . it's horrible! Why have all these dreadful things happened to us! Go on talking . . ."

"You say it's horrible, but we've got to live somehow. The old folks say we're doing it for our sins."

"What sin did any of us ever commit to deserve something like this?"

"They say it's inherited in the blood."

"Good God, whose blood, and in what century? How can I get through to you? Believe me, there was no such race or tribe, and no such century. And even if we had sinned dreadfully, monstrously down all the ages, our punishment at most should be death. But this is horrible!"

"You mustn't," she said quietly. And again, still more quietly, "You mustn't. You can't be sorry for everybody. Me, for instance, why did you stand up for me? They might have beaten you. Beaten you to death even. What has it to do with you?"

"A lot."

"Because you're kind. That's why you're so weak . . . and gentle . . . it's out of kindness. Kind people are always weak."

"That isn't true, my dear. You just think it is. I will always protect you."

"Some protector." Very very quietly.

"And be your servant. We'll live together. I don't mean anything wrong. Like brother and sister."

"If that's what you want I will be your slave . . . and it doesn't have to be like a sister."

"My little girl, my dear little girl."

"You've got hair like flax, so soft and nice to touch."

The poplars rustled beyond the gates, and above the world there floated a blue star and those two voices.

V

Sima was sitting on the bench swinging her leg and eating bread and mustard, thickly sprinkled with salt. She must have found that it tasted a lot better than the cakes people used to buy her in restaurants, or she wouldn't have been swinging her leg as she sat there on the bench in the yard, and laughing thoughtlessly in that particular way: raising her face to the sun, and almost choking on her food.

Otto Stabel had not kept silent for longer than usual without good reason the previous evening. He didn't like idle and unnecessary words, so it was only when they were parting that he had spoken to Lashkov.

"You listen here, Vasilii, my friend. Your dressmaker, she has a storeroom. Tell me, Vasilii, why should she need a storeroom? One storeroom—that means two people. Good. Anyway, Khramova won't allow them in her place."

He disappeared downstairs, and his voice echoed out of the darkness. Lashkov merely shook his head. What a queer man he was! They had been discussing that storeroom on and off since winter. The yardman had spotted it and thought of his friend. It wasn't much of a storeroom, nine feet by six, more or less, but it had one great advantage. Nearly one-third of one side of the stove which heated the apartment abutted onto it. It would be child's play to turn the storeroom into living quarters. They had only been waiting for summer. Now Stabel had gone and decided otherwise. And Lashkov, in the end, agreed.

This was why Sima was now sitting on the bench, eating bread and mustard thickly sprinkled with salt, and laughing carefree, lifting her face to the sun and almost choking on her food. Sima was going to have a room.

You couldn't make much of a home out of an old storeroom, true enough, but who wanted a mansion? Especially when so many people immediately began working their magic on it? Three Gorevs, two

Lyovushkins, Stabel, and Lashkov, and her own husband, now that she was married, Lev Arnoldovich Khramov. True, he only fussed about in a bewildered and ineffectual way, wondering where to start, but what did that matter to Sima? She was going to have a room.

Ivan Lyovushkin rigged up a workbench in the corner of the yard right outside his window, and a pungent smell of resin arose as the shavings hissed and streamed from under his plane.

As he worked he smiled at some secret thought of his own. The wood seemed to be telling the carpenter strange and funny stories. One by one, yellowish slats of wood were arrayed along the wall, all intended to make Sima happy. And from the Lyovushkins' room a smell of baking floated out over the neighborhood, and Lyuba, flushed from the heat, and almost pretty, darted between the house and the outbuilding exchanging a look with her husband whenever she passed him; he would wink at her, and they'd smile at each other naughtily.

Alexei Gorev was skillfully covering the former storeroom with a light blue, springlike wallpaper, and his speechless Fenya looked up at her magician of a husband almost with reverence, while the paste brush in her hand described weird arabesques.

Grusha with her skirt hitched high, country-fashion, was clearing away the last of the rubbish, and when she bent over too far her firm calves quivered almost imperceptibly, and Lashkov's heart raced, then came to a stop somewhere in his throat.

He and the plumber laboriously dragged disused furniture down from the attic, and put it in Lyovushkin's capable hands for repairs. Lashkov kept close to Grusha. She pretended not to notice him, let him see that as far as she was concerned he was on the same footing as the others, but she could not help favoring him from time to time with a quick look or a slight smile. He was in seventh heaven. The sun flooded the yard with all the intensity of June light, and Vasilii, blissfully light-hearted, felt that everything about him was imbued with some deep purpose.

"Mother, dear mother, what does a man need in this life? So very little; almost nothing! Yet what happiness that nothing contains! When you have it, you have everything! You can live!"

Well-bred courtesy reigned at the table that evening. Each guest tried to show that he was not uncouth, that he was conversant with the rules of etiquette, that though denied education himself he knew how to behave in the company of cultivated people.

They drank red wine, not quite filling the glasses; they dabbed at their lips with clean handkerchiefs; and when they ate they left a little on the plate: It's not the first time we've seen food, you know! To crown it all, they contrived to dance, in an indescribable crush, to "The Waves of the Amur." Before the party broke up, Ivan Lyovushkin made a short speech.

"This is what it should always be like, friends." His voice shook. "We live as if we were animals. But we're all human. I used to think my neighbor wasn't. But I know now that dentists are human as well."

As they said goodbye the guests exchanged significant looks and solemnly shook hands with the newlyweds. Lyova Khramov was moved to tears, and stood outside the door calling into the darkness after them: "Please call on us, we shall be very, very glad to see you. Just drop in, anytime. All we have is yours!"

Lashkov asked Grusha to go for a walk. She accepted and took his arm before he offered it. It was all exactly like his dream: the trees of Sokolniki, shot through with lights, murmured overhead, and people often turned around to look at them.

They sat on a bench in a dark avenue, and he put his arm round Grusha and kissed her. She didn't resist.

"Only let's do things properly," she said calmly, when she had straightened her hair a bit. "It has to be legal first."

"Of course! What else?"

And the trees up above were floating away. Perhaps it wasn't the trees, but Lashkov and Grusha themselves who were floating. That was it.

VI

Late on the eve of the anniversary of the Revolution, Nikishkin was moving into Number Seven on the second floor, to share the place with Kozlov, an ex-colonel, and subsequently a military expert in the Red Army. The new tenant was small and delicately built, but he turned out to be a caustic man with a vitriolic temper. As he came up the stairs he was already snorting like an irate bull, and rubbing his hands in pleasurable anticipation of a row.

"We'll have you by the short hairs, Mr. General."

Nikishkin was evidently conferring this promotion on his new neighbor to make himself feel more important.

"Yes, my white blackbird, we'll have you singing like a canary. Your time's up, you've sucked the blood of the workers for long enough." He tugged at Kalinin's sleeve. "You, comrade, will be my witness, in case anything happens. He can't wriggle out of it, this isn't the old regime."

The block sergeant ignored him. He merely gave him an odd look, and the muscles tensed, then relaxed again under his gray skin.

The door was opened by the occupant himself. In spite of the late hour Kozlov was not in his dressing gown to receive them, but in a neatly pressed "military expert's" suit, and his chalk-white mustaches, cultivated according to the best Guards traditions, were defiantly waxed.

"Please come in, gentl . . ." He broke off, but recovered immediately: "mm—so very pleased to see you. I know," he said, before Kalinin could get his notebook out, "you've brought me a neighbor." He bowed politely in Nikishkin's direction. "Very pleased to meet you, young man. The administrator has already informed me. So you, Vasilii"—turning to Lashkov with a shrug of his narrow shoulders—"have been troubled quite needlessly, my friend."

It would have taken a shrewder connoisseur than Nikishkin to detect a single false note in this utterly impeccable behavior. But in the emphatic politeness with which he rounded every phrase, the exaggerated courtesy which informed his every gesture, there was a hint of such contempt, if not disgust, for his new neighbor that even the usually apathetic Kalinin permitted himself an approving grin.

The nonplussed Nikishkin had just decided to take offense, when the old man wearily allowed his pale eyelids to droop, and cut that ground from under him.

"I was required to vacate the dining room—but I'm an old man, and an old man only needs a bare minimum of space in which to end his days. Moreover, I have dismissed my cleaner. With the permission of the authorities, therefore . . ."—he bowed solemnly to the block sergeant—"I shall retain only my study. The rest is all yours, including the furniture. At my age the only timber a man needs is for his burial." Here Kozlov turned to Nikishkin, and for the first time sparks of mockery danced in his pale eyes. "Am I right, young man?"

Nikishkin seemed to sense an insult, but the prospect of acquiring extra living space, fully furnished into the bargain, was enough to mollify him.

"I've left my family behind for the time being, just making a reconnaissance, you might say." He shot a glance at his neighbor, to see what impression his knowledge of military terminology had produced. Then, satisfied that he had been understood correctly, he continued in a voice that was now all gentleness and conciliation. "Here you are, you can check, it's all fair and above board. No, please be so good as to look."

Kozlov languidly pushed away the documents which his guest was holding out.

"Come, come, young man. You are welcome. Make yourself at home—it's your home now."

He pronounced the word "your" with a particular emphasis that made them all suddenly feel uncomfortable, and Vasilii thought that Nikishkin would do well not to meet the ex-colonel under different circumstances.

Kozlov hospitably opened the dining-room door, switched on the light and asked them in.

The new tenant was about to roll himself up into a spiky ball again, but at the sight of the carved dining suite and the practically untrodden carpet on the parquet floor, he recovered his equilibrium and was even inspired to reciprocal magnanimity.

He held out his hand in a token of class reconciliation.

"Right then, citizen military expert. Best wishes for the holiday."

This time the old man insulted him openly by hiding his hands behind his back.

"My young friend, I am a deeply religious man, I observe only the holidays of the Christian Church and the birthday of the heir to the throne, Alexei Nikolaevich Romanov. Please forgive me."

With a soldierly, left-about turn, Kozlov showed his back to his guests, vanished into his study, and with two turns of the key shut himself off once and for all from his future neighbor.

After a moment's paralysis Nikishkin flew into a passion again, and looked as though he were about to rush after the old man.

"Pompous old devil. I can see you need a swift kick up the backside, Mister General . . ."

The block sergeant wearily interrupted him without further ceremony. "That'll do. Stop jigging about. Let's go."

The yard, framed in stars and autumn snow, looked tiny and forsaken. Only the colorful rectangles of the windows warmed the chilly darkness and gave it shape. Every window had its own special silence.

The new tenant was still at the boiling point when they got down there.

"We simply have to report him, comrade officer. A self-confessed enemy is at large. What he says to me today he'll say in public tomorrow."

Kalinin lit a cigarette and inhaled furiously.

"I shouldn't be a bit surprised if he did—in public . . . now get the hell out of here."

Nikishkin took a step backwards, as though preparing to strike.

"I don't understand . . . you represent authority, and yet . . ."

"Out, I said . . . and take care not to be so obvious."

"I . . ."

"Get the hell out of here."

He spoke softly, laconically, through his teeth, but even Vasilii, who was used to the block sergeant's occasional outbursts, had a sinking feeling in the pit of his stomach, and finally realized why Kalinin was so reluctant to reminisce about his work in an army security section during the Civil War.

Nikishkin didn't dare answer back. There was an unspoken threat and warning in the way he walked off, as if he were driving nails into the snow with his heels.

Lashkov sighed vaguely.

"The old man's put a rope around his own neck. That one won't let him get away with it."

The red eye of a cigarette stub described an arc in the darkness, fell into the snow and went out.

"I could finish him off myself for talking like that, of course," declared Kalinin, his voice still trembling with anger. "But people like that at least know how to die decently. You wouldn't be ashamed to shake them by the hand. Well, so long."

He strode off into the night, tall and bent, the snow crunching loudly under his boots. And Lashkov was stung, perhaps for the first time in his life, by a frighteningly simple thought: "Why is it all like this? Why, oh why?"

VII

Around about the New Year, Kalinin knocked at the yardman's door again. He came in, took off his cap, leaned his chest against the Dutch stove, and was racked by a long spasm of coughing. Then he spoke without turning around.

"Got a drop to drink anywhere?"

He emptied the cut glass tumbler at a single gulp, looked askance at the pickle he was offered to go with it, and sat down, his head bowed. The frost made his consumptive flush deeper than usual.

"Right, then, Lashkov. We've got to arrest Tsygankova. I've got a warrant. Her family have turned her in."

Lashkov had been expecting some dirty trick from the Tsygankovs. They weren't the sort of people to give up a source of easy money just like that, and he had been aware more than once of the malicious looks which passed between the brothers when they bumped into Khramov and their sister. But he hadn't foreseen anything like this.

"What for?" he almost shouted. "What for?"

"Article one hundred and fifty-five of the Criminal Procedural Code, subsection A. And the worst of it is"—the militiaman banged the table with his fist—"the dirty bastards have found witnesses! Witnesses, can you believe it? The sons of bitches took advantage of her, and now they're rushing to dig her grave."

"But she's married!"

"That's just it, it isn't on the register."

"Maybe she could go away for a bit?"

"Onto the streets, d'you mean?" He raised his eyes and dropped them immediately. "She could, of course, there's a demand in every town."

"Well, then . . ."

The conversation petered out. Vasilii poured one for himself and drank it. An intolerable weight was pressing on him and he couldn't and wouldn't be the first to get up and go to Khramov's storeroom. It was only a few steps away, but the distance suddenly seemed insuperable. Lashkov would have given anything not to have to see them that day, to look them in the eye, and talk to them. And the inevitability of what lay ahead made his distress still more intolerable.

Kalinin raised a sinewy fist once more and banged it down heavily on the oilcloth.

"Let's go."

It was Sima who answered their knock.

"Who is it?"

The block sergeant answered in a muffled voice.

"Open up, Tsygankova. Got to talk to you. It's me, Kalinin."

They heard a hasty, anxious whispering, on shifting notes, then a broken moaning cry, "Coming."

The latch clicked and Sima Tsygankova, wrapped in Khramov's overcoat, stood motionless in the doorway, sadly and silently interrogating her untimely guests. She didn't need to be told that block sergeants don't pay early morning visits out of excessive courtesy.

"Yes?" she breathed, and then, in an echo, "Yes?"

Kalinin for some reason removed his cap and stood with downcast eyes, smoothing his hair.

"Well, it's like this, Serafima Tsygankova, you'll have to come with me to the station. I've got a warrant. That's all."

"Yes?" Her heart missed a beat and she repeated, affirmatively this time, "Yes."

"What's it all about, Alexandr Petrovich?" Khramov looked out over Sima's shoulder, feverishly pulling on his shirt. "What's it all about?"

Sima turned to him, took his hand in both of hers, and started stroking it, as though soothing a sick man.

"I'll be back soon, Lyova." Her voice was very quiet, and but for the quivering of her chin you might have thought that she was perfectly calm. "You'll see, I'll be back soon. You go to bed, you've got a rehearsal. Only don't forget to fetch the loaf. Don't worry, Lyova, my love, I'm only going there and back."

Sima tried to smile, but only managed a pitiful grimace.

But Lyova was beside himself.

"Can't you explain, Alexandr Petrovich? What's it about?" he groaned, clutching at the lapels of Kalinin's greatcoat. "Whose toes has she trodden on this time? Surely you can't arrest somebody without giving a reason?"

Kalinin was staring stubbornly at his toe-caps.

"I know the reason. But I shan't explain it to you, Khramov. Go to the prosecutor's office and find out yourself. My job is to take her in."

"Then I won't let you have her!" Lyova flung out his trembling arms to shield Sima. "You can't have her, and that's final, d'you hear, Alexandr Petrovich? Good God, what is all this? Look, give me a day or two. I'll go and see somebody about it. I'll get it sorted out."

The sergeant put his cap on, moved away from Khramov's door, and spoke to the yardman in a hoarse, tired voice.

"Go and call two men off the beat. I can't be expected to fight them."

Lashkov dithered. He didn't want to disobey the block sergeant, but he wasn't going to hurry. Maybe everything would turn out all right after all!

The policeman repeated his order more harshly and insistently.

"Go on! I didn't sign the warrant. It's no good, Khramov," he barked over his shoulder, "it's the law."

Khramov's frenzied cry followed him out to the yard. "Damn all laws! Damn the people who made them! Damn, damn, damn!"

When Lashkov returned, a semicircle of tenants had formed around the doorway of the outbuilding. The light morning snow crunched under dozens of feet, and a flurry of agitated whispers hovered about them.

"Oh dear, oh dear, what a dreadful life . . . Who'd have thought? The poor girl was just beginning to lead a decent life."

"Aie-ai-ai! We've all got to answer for our sins. If not to God, then to the People's Court."

"It's a present from her family, they say!"

"Monsters, there's no other word for them."

"What a business."

Ivan Lyovushkin was wandering around among the tenants, with nothing but galoshes on his feet, and an overcoat draped over his undershirt. The tapes of his underpants were sticking out from his trouser legs and trailing in the snow.

"What d'you call this, citizens? What sort of murderous business is this? Is this God's will? We can stand up for her if we all stick together. We can go to higher authority. There they were, living all quiet and peaceful, not bothering anybody . . . What is all this, friends?"

Lyuba pulled at his sleeve to take him home, but he wrenched his arm free in vexation, began looking for support again from his neighbors, and buttonholed Gorev.

"Lyosha, you were at their wedding party. Did they ever do anybody any harm? You'd hardly know they're in the house. You're a party member, you know how to go about things, stand up for her. Do the right thing, Lyosha, stand up for her."

But Gorev shrank, looked timidly away, and mumbled half-audibly: "They'll sort it all out, Vanya, we're not in the jungle. You'd better go home and get dressed . . . You'll catch a cold."

Lyovushkin waved him away in bitter despair and rushed over to Stabel.

"Why don't you say something, Stabel? You can twist a piece of pipe into a corkscrew, but now you're not doing a thing—what does it all mean, Stabel? They just want to live, and look how they're being treated. Is it right?"

But Stabel said nothing. Stabel could twist a pipe into a corkscrew, but the powers-that-be could twist him, Stabel, into a corkscrew, too.

The Tsygankovs huddled together, apart from the rest, darting triumphant, gloating looks at the outbuilding while waiting for the climax. Their mother, a thin, stringy woman, combed the crowd with her dull eyes, looking for sympathy, and screaming out from time to time in a drink-sodden voice: "She'll find out how the other half lives, the dirty bitch. It won't be like it is in rest-ahr-ants with them sugar daddies of hers."

Nikishkin was hanging about right outside the entrance hall. Talking to no one in particular, but obviously eager to remain as long as possible at the center of attention, he started to gabble loudly: "Have to stop that kind of thing. Give them an inch and they'll be hanging red lamps on every house."

Shouts and screams came pouring from the outbuilding. While Sima was getting ready, Lyova, on his knees, clung to the hem of her dress, convulsively stroking her legs. He pressed his cheek against her hand, and talked, talked, talked.

"They're all against us, little girl. But I'll go. I'll go whatever happens . . . I'll tell them . . . I'll tell them everything . . . I don't give a damn for their barbarous laws . . . you'll see, they won't dare . . . they won't dare . . ."

She ruffled his hair with her free hand, while minute tears ran down her cheeks one after another and gathered on her chin.

A militiaman pulled cautiously at her sleeve. "That'll do now."

Sima shuddered, and went rigid, as though trying to remember something very important to her, something essential, and then found the words which she forced out of blue, faltering lips.

"Forgive me for everything, Lev Arnoldovich. Nothing will ever make me dirty now that I've known you. I'm clean now. Clean, and that's all there is to it. But some people . . ."—her face became remote and hostile—"people are going to pay for these tears of mine."

Khramov plunged toward her, but the block sergeant got a neckhold

on him, and he thrashed about, gasping, like a fish on a hook. The militiamen grasped Sima's arms, but she slipped out of their hands and grappled
with Kalinin.

"Don't you dare touch him, you ugly servile bastard. Take me, beat
me, knock me about as much as you like, but don't touch him. He's a
sick man. He's weak."

They dragged her to the door. She dug her heels in, and they had a
struggle to tear her away from doorposts and window ledges before they
could finally push her into a car drawn up right in front of the door, and
even then she continued to resist.

The crowd let the car through, and as it went out of the gate the
semicircle closed round Khramov who lay there on the ground. He
rubbed his head in the snow and wept, and his streaming tears sank into
the snow without a trace.

"Sima, Sima, little girl, what will they do to you? . . . I love you,
little girl! I love you! I love her, love her, love her!"

He gave one last convulsive sob, and lay still, with his arms twisted
awkwardly behind his back. Stabel silently swept Lyova into his arms
and the crowd let him through as he headed toward his boiler room. A
minute later there was no one in the yard except the yardman, the block
sergeant, and Lyovushkin.

Kalinin undid his clipboard, took out a note, and held it out to
Lyovushkin. "Here, send your woman out for a liter, and we'll sit and
warm up with Lashkov while we're waiting."

VIII

That spring struck Vasilii as having a scent, a lightness, a color all its
own. Everything around him seemed to quiver, free from the laws of
gravity. And he saw himself as younger than ever before, and amazingly
buoyant. If he had been reminded, hour after hour, minute by minute, of
what lay behind him, he wouldn't have believed a word of it, and in any

case would have tried to forget it at once. He was acutely aware of the novelty of all that was happening to him. What was all that about coal mines? What desert? Famine, what famine? He must have dreamed it all on a stuffy night. And if it was no dream he would gladly have gone through it all again, three times over, for the sake of one such spring, one such day.

Grusha and he faced each other across a little table in the open air café at Sokolniki, drinking beer and smiling at each other in silence. The birch trees were splashed with the new green. Somewhere beyond them a band was pining for the little hills of Manchuria, and its mournful harmonies sent birds soaring noisily skyward to vanish instantly in the intense blue.

There was a sparkling foam on the beer, and through it, right before his eyes, Lashkov saw Grusha's hands floating toward him like two big white fishes. He tried to touch them, but they slipped away, supple and endlessly elusive. Her slanting eyes twinkled invitingly, and seen through the bubbling foam they became scattered drops of blue light.

"Stop fooling about, silly," she scolded.

Lashkov only laughed in reply and said nothing. In fact, there was nothing to say. However hard he tried he could never put into words all that he was feeling for the first time. Thirty-three wasn't exactly his first youth, but still she wasn't eighteen, either, and, anyway, when it's the first time it always seems as though all eternity is ahead. His past was not without its little episodes, nor probably was hers. But all that was irrelevant now. Casually satisfied desires, more smoke than fire, had touched each of them, but neither had been really burned. Perhaps that was why they had saved themselves for each other.

Then he took her through the wood, and the trees hemmed them in closer and closer, till at last a thicket of birch saplings barred their way, and Lashkov spoke his first words, which he had thought up in readiness.

"Let's go over there"—he waved vaguely toward a narrow cutting among the birches—"all the way to heaven."

"There isn't any heaven, stupid."

"What if we go anyway?"

"You've had too much to drink, silly."

"I'm not the least bit drunk. I just want to go there. With you."

"Come on then, stupid."

"We'll walk and walk and the woods will never end. We'll walk all the hundred versts to heaven, and it'll be through woods all the way . . ."

"There you are, there's no woods left, stupid."

They had come out at a little hollow, with the park fence beyond it. Vasilii took off his new light overcoat and spread it out on the grass.

"Let's stay here till night, Grusha, or till morning if you like."

"We shall catch cold, stupid."

She sat down all the same, and he lay at her side and put his head in her lap and looked up. Suddenly he imagined that the sky had come so close that he could touch it and write on it with his finger, any word he pleased, the way you can on a misted windowpane. He touched it and wrote, and what came out was, "Grusha."

"Your knees are so warm. And I can hear your heart beating."

"Stupid."

"No, honestly."

"Stupid."

"Why wait till we get a room, Grusha? We can manage with my twenty-four square feet for the time being, we'll make room."

"What about children?"

"Good Lord, that's a long way off."

"Might only be a year."

"Grusha . . ."

"What, stupid?"

She bent over him. The sky vanished. They drowned in each other's eyes and their bodies melted into one another. The world about them ceased to exist.

When she got up she said with tolerant affection, "What was that you said about children?" She paused for a moment, and added sternly, "Don't try to make a fool out of me though, I can be nasty!"

"Grusha! Don't be silly."

"You're all the same at first."

"Don't be silly!"

"Get up, stupid, it's time to go home."

"To my place?"

"Yes."

"Honest?"

"Honest."

Grusha had never been in Lashkov's room before. She cast a house-wifely eye around it as she entered, and immediately rolled up her sleeves.

"Sychevka bachelors, good lord! Up to your knees in dirt, and heads in the air."

She set to work, skillfully and quickly, but at the same time without unnecessary fuss, and under her light touch the room gradually became a plausible home. As she worked, Grusha seemed to be observing herself admiringly, as though she realized how Vasilii must enjoy watching the regal perfection of her every movement. Vasilii indeed looked on with the tactful timidity of a bridegroom, smiling happily and apologetically.

A beam of moonlight stole across the room, from door to stove, and music flowed through the open air vent. It was the music that Vasilii always heard when the Khramovs left their windows open. In the past, it had always sounded wild and incomprehensible, had always annoyed and irritated him, but now, for no reason at all, it moved him to tears.

Grusha left toward dawn, leaving behind an ineluctable smell of clean washing, and the lingering echoes of night music.

IX

They came at the end of May, in the middle of the night. There were three of them. A shaven-headed one in plain clothes, a silent nondescript major, and a Red Army man with a blurred, permanently sleepy face. The shaven-headed one cast a cursory glance at Lashkov's room, and gave his orders without preliminaries.

"First we'll go to Number Seven, Kozlov's place. You are required as a witness. Can we find one up there?"

The house had had its share of arrests in the past, but it was usually the militia, and more often than not Kalinin in person, who carried them out. This one carried a whiff of the Lubyanka. The plainclothesman stared unblinkingly at his host. Lashkov caught something in his ironic, yet not exactly unfriendly gaze, something that made him feel small, insignificant, terribly vulnerable, as though he were in a shallow trench with shells whistling overhead.

Nikishkin needed no explanations. As soon as he saw his visitors he became somber and intense, and hastily tidied himself up, making it clear that he fully associated himself with what was to come. He nodded toward the end of the corridor.

"This way. The dear man's asleep."

He squinted conspiratorially at the shaven-headed one, who passed him without sparing a glance. But before the visitor had taken three steps, the door to Kozlov's study opened wide, and its occupant came out to meet him, tightly buttoned up in his usual dress uniform, breeches tucked in and boots polished like mirrors.

"Come in, gentlemen!" This time the old man didn't stumble over the word, but rapped out every syllable, "gen-tle-men," clearly, leaving no doubt that he was fully aware of what awaited him, and that for that very reason he would make no concessions. "I'm ready!"

His voice, his bitter arrogance, his ironical resignation set the tone of the arrest. The visitors became quieter, more economical in word and gesture, working quickly and efficiently. Whenever the need arose, the plainclothesman addressed his host by his name and patronymic, which in itself was a reminder to those present that a former colonel and military advisor was different from ordinary mortals. Nikishkin took out a book, examined its spine with a sardonic sneer, and was about to make a pronouncement when the plainclothesman went over, silently took the book from him, restored it to its place, and drove him with one quick, burning glance to the door, where he made himself inconspicuous.

While the inventory was being drawn up in case of confiscation and the major was familiarizing the witnesses with the rules of evidence, an abrupt conversation, sharp as an exchange of gunfire, took place between the colonel and the shaven-headed one.

"What am I to take with me?"

"A change of linen."

"That's all?"

"Why take more?"

"Are you that quick on the trigger?"

"We're short of time, Prov Aristarkhovich, short of time."

"Toilet accessories?"

"Please yourself."

"Undercollars?"

His guest grinned unpleasantly.

"You know better than that, Prov Aristarkhovich. Does a priest need a concertina?"

"You, young man, cannot be expected to understand because you are a materialist. But Russian Guards officers always try to die in clean undercollars."

It was all over within the hour. Before he left, Kozlov looked slowly around the room, object by object, and as he did so his prominent Adam's apple bobbed repeatedly, as though he were having difficulty in swallowing something.

On the landing the plainclothesman nodded to the major. "Take him away. I can manage up there by myself." His eyes indicated the ceiling. Then he turned at once to the witnesses. "You follow me to Number Eleven."

The blood rushed to Lashkov's head and hammered in his temples. Surely they couldn't be after the half-witted Khramov girl!

They went up two flights. Exactly twenty-four steps. A minute's walk. But during that minute, like a thread through the eye of a needle, a wild chain of agonized thoughts was drawn through Vasilii's mind— enough to last him for many a sleepless night.

He was sorry for the military advisor, of course. A harmless, slightly eccentric old man. The yardman could sympathize with him to some extent, admire his self-possession, even feel a measure of concern for him, but the fate of the ex-colonel could not touch him as closely as that of a workingman like Alexei Gorev. They both had calluses with the same smell and the same color. They had spent a lot of time together, drunk the required amount of vodka with beer chasers and dried fish to follow— in short, they had become friends. What was more, they were about to become in-laws. So when the plainclothesman negligently tapped on the door of Number Eleven with the toe of his shoe, Lashkov became aware for the first time of a wave of suffocating rage which threatened to choke him. He was seized by an almost uncontrollable desire to hurl himself on the shaven-headed man, to trample him down along with his self-assurance and his wildcat's grin of triumph. He turned away and gripped the banisters in order to subdue the temptation.

The plainclothesman by now was face to face with Gorev.

"Get ready, Gorev. We want a talk with you—a long one."

He was much more offhand than he had been with Kozlov. He rooted around noisily in drawers, casually leafed through volumes from the bookcase and tossed them on the floor, glanced briefly, and with contemptuous carelessness, into a cupboard. Then he sat down facing the master of the house and began to harry him.

"Hurry up, Gorev, we haven't got all night!"

But, try as he might, Gorev couldn't get his shoe on. It persisted in slipping off his foot.

Fenya pressed herself against the wall space between the windows, trembling all over, and Grusha looked at her brother sternly from under a blanket pulled right up to her eyes, as though passing sentence on him.

Occasionally passing his tongue over his dry lips, Alexei tried to reassure his wife.

"They'll sort it out, Fenya, they'll sort it out. Hold on, that's the main thing. I'll be back soon—you'll see—they'll sort it out."

The elaborate care with which Gorev fastened the buttons of his blouse, while avoiding his sister's eyes, showed that he was trying to reassure himself rather than his wife, and that he had little faith in his speedy return.

Little Sergei, Gorev's first-born, woke up. He didn't cry, but merely stared at each of the nocturnal visitors in childish perplexity, resentfully wrinkling his nose. His father went up to him and tousled his hair. "Go to sleep now, Sergei. We'll go to the zoo on Sunday."

His son's eyes followed him to the door, dark with doubt and apprehension. Children look at dead people that way, not realizing what has happened, but instinctively sensing some fearful mystery.

Gorev turned to his friend as they were going downstairs. "Look after them for me, Vasilii, my friend. I'll make it up to you. We're bound to meet one of these days."

"Forget it. You don't owe me anything."

"They'll sort it out."

"Yes, they'll sort it out," said Lashkov, and, catching an ironic look from the shaven-headed one, added without much conviction, "of course they will."

The night smelled of stoves gone cold and poplars blowing in the breeze. Engines whistled to each other shrilly in the freight yard a few streets away. The lamp over the gate picked out a little island of freshly rain-streaked pavement in the darkness, and the whole street was dotted from end to end with similar islands, receding into the distance. Shadows trembled and broke on their shimmering surfaces. A night like any other, like last night or the night before, or this time five or ten years ago, but when the fitfully winking rear light of the car finally dissolved in the darkness, Vasilii's soul was filled with a sense of loss much greater and more irreparable than that of Alexei Gorev.

Nikishkin, still excited by what had happened, came within earshot and murmured: "Exterminate them all. Root and branch, all of them. We fought, we shed our blood, and they reject the results. If they don't like it, they can have nine grams of lead instead."

Vasilii found himself breathing with difficulty. If Nikishkin had said one more word the yardman would probably have stomped him in another fit of rage. But Nikishkin, sensing trouble ahead, fell silent, and Lashkov disappeared into the night. As he went, Nikishkin's invitation reached him from one of the little islands of light, sounding through the furious buzzing in his ears.

"Listen, Lashkov, why don't you drop in for a cup of tea sometime! We'll have a chat, play some lotto."

"Snake," thought Vasilii, and made no reply.

X

As Vasilii pulled open the door to the visiting room of Butyrki Prison the discordant racket of a multitude of voices bounded off the vaulted ceiling in staccato bursts. Some mysterious force spun the colored whirlpool of humanity within the four filthy gray walls of the semisubterranean hall, so that it was virtually impossible to catch an intelligible sound or an individual face. Every word was strung on the same single note, like leaves on a stalk. All the faces were of a piece. It was as though misery itself lived here, within a kingdom of iron grids and thick brick walls.

By vigorous use of his elbows, Lashkov cleared a path for Grusha and Fenya to the window they wanted where they took a place in the queue. It was perhaps only now, lost in the frantic roar, that the two women fully realized what had happened to them. Yesterday, or even an hour ago, they still had a glimmer of hope: but not now. They saw that their loss was so small and insignificant that nobody other than themselves would ever give it a thought. The life suddenly went out of Fenya altogether; she became more silent and colorless than ever, while Grusha was withdrawn, listless, subdued.

Standing in front of Vasilii was a woman wearing a beret and a dark silk dress trimmed at the collar with fine lace: a lonely island of austerity and silence in a sea of chaotic misery. There was something of the icon about her in her simple, majestic self-sufficiency. She gazed calmly around the room with great prominent eyes but there was a hint of something in their quiet imperturbability to discourage almost any attempt at conversation.

The woman next to her in the queue, a haggard, scarecrow figure in a man's jacket, darted furious little glances to either side and chirped away beside her.

"Got caught, the miserable devil, and left me with three on my hands, and all they can yell about is food. Where'm I supposed to get it from? They've tortured the life out of me, and I'm no age at all yet."

Her mean, sad little face stiffened until the veins on her hen-like neck stood out; it was easy to believe that she had indeed been on the rack for some time.

The woman in the beret spoke in a low voice. "Why do you talk like that? You mustn't. It makes it harder for them in there."

A reply was all she needed to vent the spite which was eating into her the way rust eats into scrap iron.

"Oh, it doesn't mean much to you, of course. Things aren't all that desperate if you can go round weaving silk. Look at your hands, never been used. You put yourself in my shoes and you'd sing a different tune. Anyway, it's not so hard on your kind, being in jail—you're fighting for what's yours—but why did mine have to stick his neck out? What was he after—a life of luxury? They don't make that any more."

Her neighbor interrupted briefly but sternly.

"My apartment is sealed—I spend the night with friends. So the dress I'm wearing is my only one. Anyway, even in this calamity can't you stop thinking about who has more and who has less? If we can't, then life just isn't worth living."

"If you've got capital . . ."

"I have no capital," said the woman in the beret emphatically. "I am a poet."

The other woman looked her up and down in bewilderment. "Eh? What? How d'you mean?"

"I make up verses," she explained. Her weariness showed in her eyes. "Excuse me, please."

"Oh," said the gawky woman in what sounded like a disappointed sigh, but when the meaning of what had been said finally reached her, she pulled herself together. Suddenly bleak, she asked simply with none of her former asperity, "Can you make up anything about this?"

The woman in the beret slowly passed her hand over her face. It was as if she had removed an invisible veil. Only then did she answer, simply and quietly, "I can."

And there was such assurance, such deep certainty in her voice, that it was as if she were shutting out all the noise and confusion around her. All those nearby fell silent, looking at her as though a river ran between them.

Vasilii found a note waiting for him at home. "Come over. Must talk to you. Kalinin."

The block sergeant lived opposite, in an old wooden house with stanchions all along the street side. When Lashkov came in he was walking around the room in breeches and slippers, occasionally taking swigs from a quart-sized enamel jug. He pulled up a chair for his guest.

"Sit down. Look, my dad's sent me some dog fat from the country. I'm swallowing it. They say it helps . . . Filthy stuff, and I wouldn't wish it on my worst enemy."

It wasn't like Kalinin to be so long in coming to the point. Vasilii expected the worst, but he suddenly plucked up his courage and took the plunge.

"All right, Alexandr Petrovich, why drag things out; let's have it, we aren't children."

Laboring for breath, Kalinin sat down at the table, put his jug aside and spoke hesitantly, as though he could not find the words.

"Well, it's like this, Lashkov, see . . . how can I put it?"

"Don't keep me on tenterhooks, Alexandr Petrovich."

"Well, then, a man called on me, wanted to know about you, who you were, what you were like . . . What are this Lashkov's relations with the Gorev family? he asks me. So I explain how things are, but you know how it is, you can't really talk to these people . . ."

"I'm my own man. I brought two bullet wounds back from Chardzhou. Surely you know me well enough, Alexandr Petrovich!"

Kalinin breathed heavily down his nose.

"Get it into your head, Lashkov, they're putting better men than you up against the wall nowadays. They don't bother to ask how many bullet holes and how many shrapnel wounds you've got. What they ask is where and when did you join the conspiracy. And d'you know how they ask . . . ? Well, think about it."

Vasilii suddenly recalled that unforgettable night in May and the shaven-headed man in plainclothes, with his blood-curdling ironical friendliness. A shudder of terror ran down his spine. He swallowed the bitter lump in his throat, and hoarsely said, as much to himself as to the sergeant, "But what about her? What about her?"

"Tell her it's till everything's cleared up. It won't make it any better for her if they really do take you away, will it? She's a sensible woman, she'll understand."

"Maybe nothing will happen in any case."

Kalinin spat angrily, and stood up.

"All right, so long. I can't give you any more advice. Only when you're begging them for Christ's sake to put a bullet in you, remember what I told you. That's all."

The policeman started pacing the room again as thin and ruffled as a woodpecker in spring, but, although he was obviously vexed, he could not help shouting after Lashkov.

"Use your brains, Vasilii, I'm not your enemy."

Vasilii sat on his bed till late evening, clutching his head. "Mother, oh, mother! What have I done to deserve all this? Haven't I had enough already? Haven't I suffered enough to earn an ounce of happiness? Whom have I ever upset?"

He remembered old lady Shokolinist's nocturnal vigils, and the Khramov business, and Gorev's arrest, and many things besides. And he was overpowered by the cruel conviction that Someone existed with a will for vengeance that destroyed any semblance of peace. And Lashkov was unbearably afraid of Him, because of his own impotence. Painful exhaustion overcame him. He fell into a troubled sleep.

"Sitting in the dark?"

Grusha came in, switched on the light, and filled the room with her presence, her sure movements, and the smell of washing.

"You ill or something?" She sat down and put an arm round him. "Come on, what's up?"

He put his head on her warm knees and wept like a child. She ruffled his hair. "What is it then, stupid? People always get maudlin when they've had too much." Grusha spoke these last words without her former assurance, as though she saw something bad ahead. "You ought to drink less."

His words came out in a gasp, as though he had been holding his breath.

"We've got to take our time . . . Stay apart for a bit."

"Why? What d'you mean, apart?"

Angry and confused, Lashkov poured out the gist of his conversation with the sergeant. She listened in silence without interrupting. She stared with unseeing eyes into the night, apparently not taking in what he was saying, but as soon as he had finished she rose abruptly.

"All right, Lashkov, all right, Vasilii," she said slowly and distinctly. "Right. So you're worried about your own skin, are you? And what about me?" Without realizing it she was repeating his question to Kalinin. "What about me? You've had your fun, and now it's good-bye and good luck? Thanks, Vasilii, but I won't be hanging around to wait for you . . . You can live in a burrow somewhere but I'll look after myself."

As Grusha reached the doorway, Vasilii made as if to run after her, but she turned sharply and stopped him with a look of burning scorn.

"Don't come after me, Lashkov. You can sweep the yard on your belly and I won't come back now. My Red hero!" When the door slammed he felt rather that it was some part of himself closing off . . . tight shut . . . never to open again.

XI

Lyovushkin staggered in; his tottering rush carried him straight from the door to fall on the yardman's neck.

"Vasilii, old pal . . . at least there's one living soul in this whole box. I'm sorry, my dear old friend . . . Khramov and me made ourselves a bit the worse for wear . . . They've given poor Sima five years . . . Well, that's how it goes . . . I can't stand any more; I can't, it hurts inside . . ." —he banged himself on the chest—"just there . . . I'm longing to get away from here . . . There's a work gang that wants me to go somewhere down the Volga . . . I'm going . . . I'm sick and tired of it all here . . . I'd sooner live among wolves. I'm sorry, old friend . . . Come on, we've rustled up a bottle, Khramov and me."

The carpenter's eyelids were as heavy as lead; his eyes were dull, muddy and bloodshot, his disheveled head nodded, and he was swaying limply on his feet as though his backbone had been removed.

Vasilii gave a sign of distress. "Why carry on like this, Vanya?"

"I'm sick and tired of it all, old pal, that's why."

"What about the rest of us?"

"Well, I'm sorry for everybody . . . People are getting as tough as hide . . . Is it God's will? Where's the escape?"

"They've asked you to go off down the Volga, so why don't you go? Maybe things will be easier. You'll end up with d.t.'s if you go on like this."

Lyovushkin placed a finger on his lips. "Sh-sh-sh, Vasilii, boy, I'm scared of that myself . . . Still, we only live once! Come on, Vasilii, be a pal, keep us company."

"Come on, then . . ." All hell was let loose in Khramov's attic. Lyova was enthroned at a table loaded with bottles of all descriptions and improvised snacks. He had his chin propped on his hand and was drunkenly commiserating with himself.

"That's the way of it, Lev Khramov. Their blueprints for love aren't taken from Shakespeare but the Criminal Code. They haven't got time, they're in a hurry. There's still a great deal in the world they don't like. What do they care about you, Lev Khramov, let alone Shakespeare! You can't render Shakespeare down for shoe polish, or stitch a pair of shoes out of him. Anyway, they only want what they can eat. So let them have your heart, Lev Khramov! Or your soul, maybe . . ." He started drunkenly as he noticed his guest. "Ah, Vasilii, come in, my friend, don't be shy. . . . Ivan Nikitich and I are holding a solemn requiem mass for Russia . . . It's self-service today, pour yourself one . . ."

When the three of them had emptied the bottle in two rounds, Khramov fished a ten out of his jacket and held it out to Lyovushkin. "Ivan Nikitich, you know what they say—you're not obliged to but I'd be much obliged if you did . . . I'd go myself only I'm afraid I'd never make it. . . . This empty bottle has begun to depress me."

While Lyovushkin was away with his ten rubles the actor gazed at the yardman with half-closed eyes, like a roosting hen, and clarified his relations with the human race.

"You see, Lashkov, how shall I put it, life's a great flowing current, but you and me, we live in a stagnant backwater. We are part of its general process, an inalienable part of it, but the stream itself keeps flowing and flowing, while we stand still all the time and . . . decompose. You understand, Lashkov?"

Lashkov gave an affirmative sigh, although he didn't understand a word.

"Why are we condemned to rot away? Sima says it's for our sins. But every punishment begets a new sin. And so on to infinity. The simplest of geometric progressions. You understand, Lashkov?"

"Yes," he sighed again, making no effort to follow Khramov's disquisition. He was trying to catch a fly under a glass, and was completely absorbed in his task. "Of course."

The fly was finally caught, and buzzed furiously as it stormed against its cut glass prison. Vasilii felt mean, vengefully sadistic. "Go on, drive yourself around, you shit." The fly fell down, near exhaustion, but flew off again immediately to resume its vain search for a way out. Vasilii jeered again morosely, out loud this time.

"Round and round!"

"What?" asked Khramov, puzzled.

"Just talking to myself."

"Oh . . . Well, Lashkov . . . Wait a bit, where was I? Oh yes . . . Anyway, all this philosophy isn't worth a damn . . . I used to have Sima, and now she's gone, that's where philosophy begins and ends for me . . . Even if another million Shakespeares are born, the men who make the laws will still be in the right, instead of poets. And laws are made by useless little nonentities who have dirty little urges instead of great passions and who substitute the 'family cell' for love. What an expression to think up—'family cell'—as if we were bugs. Just think who makes the laws! Failed priests, half-fledged attorneys, crackbrained discoverers of perpetual motion . . . Ask any one of them what he can do and he won't know what to say! No, he won't! They're no good at anything. They've never in their miserable lives used their own hands. They pander to the worst instincts of the mob and its animal roar soothes their unsatisfied ambitions . . . these . . . barren fig trees. They say: Take from the well-fed and feed yourselves, take from him that hath, and clothe yourselves, take from the rulers and rule . . . And the crowd takes. The crowd is blind and greedy and does not know that there will be no more bread in the world than there was, that clothes don't grow on trees, that being ruled won't become any more enjoyable. The spirit of Smerdyakov has conquered Russia. Make way for His Majesty, Mr. Smerdyakov! All things are possible, nothing is forbidden. The Foma Fomiches have gone into politics. They'll send the world up in flames before they're finished, you'll see, Lashkov. And when they make their laws they go by their own narrow rules of thumb. They don't give a damn for the lessons of history. Their laws are about as rational as the reflexive kicking of an urban child. If one of them happens to have piles, he's sure to introduce preferential treatment for people with piles. If he has only one wife, monogamy is made law. If he has a weakness for children, women are told to go ahead and have as many as they like. If he has none, we must practice abortion. If he drinks—enjoy yourselves, you only live once. If he's a teetotaler, you get prohibition! In fact if a eunuch turns up in high government they'll castrate the nation . . . castrate the lot! What does one little Sima Tsygankova matter to them! They can only count in millions."

Khramov was gradually sobering up. He brought out the last few words firmly and distinctly, with his eyes wide open, as though all his prophecies were coming to pass before his eyes. Vasilii, who until now had been stupidly staring at the doomed fly, suddenly shuddered as Khramov's bitterness struck home. Not that the yardman understood the actor—unfamiliar words swirled above him like dead leaves in the air, but he was affected by his companion's tone and mood and abruptly began to talk.

"I spent two years chasing the Basmachi around the Kara Kum Desert." He tore open the neck of his shirt, exposing two lumpy scars just above his collarbone. "Look at those. They didn't come from a shop. And now it looks like I won't be allowed to breathe without permission. Is that right and proper?"

The friends talked on, each about his own troubles. They couldn't hope to understand each other, their lives were too different, but they shared a pain and a doubt, and without thinking obeyed the healing instinct to share what they had. Each listened to the other without interruption.

When Lyovushkin got back the actor was rapping the table with his knuckles, leaning toward Vasilii, and declaring, "The nation is doomed!" while Vasilii kept stubbornly repeating, "Nobody can know how I feel till he's been through it all himself."

After the first round, the carpenter was too drunk to sit up. His head sank onto the table. Sobbing like a child, he struck up, "Remember how you used to speed the plow . . ."

He couldn't get the second line out. He trembled silently for a while, then repeated, ". . . used to speed the plow . . ."

Khramov stroked his head affectionately, trying to comfort him.

"What are you crying for, Ivan Nikitich? What are you crying for? You are a member of the ruling class. It all belongs to you, and here you are crying. You ought to be dancing for joy and singing aloud. The earth is yours, the sky is yours. And St. Isaac's Cathedral is yours, too. Yet you sit and cry, Ivan Nikitich. Isn't it enough for you? Isn't St. Isaac's enough? Take the Metro as well then. Crying, eh? The ordinary Russian is always crying. In the old days because he was thrashed, and now because he's sick at heart. What's happened to us, Ivan Nikitich?

Vasilii poured down glass after glass. He got no kick out of it and felt no drunker. But his heart was a swollen lump of lead, and a dull ache of thought stirred sluggishly in his heavy brain: "That's right, what *has* happened to us? Why do we keep on crying?"

The fly under the glass fell down for the last time, turned on its back, and was still.

Lyuba scratched at the door, like a cat begging to be let in.

"Ivan, my love, come on home, dear. You know you'll feel awful tomorrow. Come and sleep it off, I'll bring you some myself in the morning . . . You've got children to think of . . ."

Ivan's only reply was an incoherent bellow, but Khramov, who still had the use of his tongue, came to his defense.

"What is all this about, Lyubov Trofimovna? Isn't Ivan Nikitich Lyovushkin allowed to commemorate the death of his country? In fact, it's his duty to be present at the funeral of the old lady he has murdered. You would do better to come inside and adorn the gathering, Lyubov Trofimovna. It's boring without a woman . . . Boring without a woman . . . boring and miserable."

Vasilii suddenly needed air, and got up and went out. By accident he bumped into Lyuba in the dark and instinctively put an arm around her. He was about to release her after this momentary confusion, but she had interpreted his movement in her own way. She pressed herself against him and whispered submissively, "Make it quick."

There was something repellent in such submissiveness, and when his lust was spent, all he could say was, "Right, go on home. When he collapses I'll bring him over."

Lyuba went away, and he dragged himself into the little garden in front of the outbuilding and lay right there among the flowers, wet with the first dew.

Dozing feverishly, he could still hear the carpenter crawling on all fours in front of his window and groaning, "Lyuba, some pickle brine."

Khramov came in with his old refrain: "The nation is doomed!"

"Lyubushka, do me a favor."

"The nation . . . dying."

"Bring . . ."

It was the last word to reach Vasilii before he lost consciousness.

XII

The heavy sky was full of migrating birds, threading their way low over the rooftops of the town in unbroken lines from morning to night. The day was choked by their guttural cries. Lashkov looked through the window, listening to September's stealthy encroachments, and a blurred indifference to the world in general soaked into his soul like water into cotton wool. The days dragged by slowly and monotonously. Whenever he was off duty he killed time with Stabel in apathetic games of "odd man out." The world gradually grew hazy, objects lost their individual identity, and everything about him merged into shimmering chaos, in which Stabel started looking like a king of diamonds, and a poplar leaf like an ace of hearts. Or vice versa.

The plumber grumbled as he shuffled the pack. "I don't understand what sort of people the Russians are! Yesterday she says where is my little girl going to practice her music? Today she drags the piano away and sells it."

"Got to fill our bellies. Can't live on music," Vasilii remarked dully, just to keep the conversation going.

"She has hands? And a brain?"

"She's never used those hands, summer or winter. She'd be some worker."

"Selling something is no way out. The thing is sold, and then what?"

"We've still got plenty of porches, thank God."

"Porches?"

"Church porches, you know."

Otto clucked reproachfully. "Ach, that's not nice, what you say. Daughter of a great maestro . . . begging. That is not nice at all. She gave me a ten—help the men move the piano, Stabel—I refused. I could not. I looked at the girl's eyes and I couldn't. The old woman locked the girl in her room but I still said no."

"She sold it just the same, and a ten wouldn't have hurt you. You're a sucker, Stabel."

The plumber's protuberant eyes blinked angrily and he flung down the pack.

"You Russians! What do I want a ten for? I don't need a ten! Depriving a girl of her music for ten rubles? It's not nice, Vasilii. You are kindhearted, Vasilii, why do you talk like that? Did you hear how she screamed?"

"I heard."

"My ears are still ringing with it. That poor girl."

Yes, Vasilii had heard Olga Khramova screaming after her mother had locked her up and the piano was carried out of the apartment. But somebody else's suffering, and especially what he regarded as the silliness of a spoiled upper-class girl, could evoke no response in him now: he was too numbed by his own pain. He was answering his friend so as not to offend him, but the meaning of what was being said hardly sank in.

He was mechanically dealing the cards into two piles for another game when a brand new Molotov slid like a black beetle into the yard.

With a grin, Lashkov watched the car's labored efforts to turn and drive right up to the front door. The yard was too small for the car's wide body and it spluttered to a standstill with its front wheel embedded in the garden strip in front of the outbuilding, immediately outside Lashkov's windows. The yardman rushed to open them and curse the driver but was brought up short with his hand on the latch: Grusha Goreva was struggling out of the "M," supported under the elbow by a moderately bald and immoderately drunken major-general.

Outrageously drunk herself, wearing a dark crêpe de chine dress and high-heeled shoes, she took a tottering step towards the door but suddenly turned around and clung to the fence that surrounded the little garden. Her blazing eyes nailed Vasilii to the spot.

"Have a good look, Vasilii, love, look till your eyeballs pop out. You thought I'd come to grief without you, didn't you? Well, I didn't. I ride around in a car, and I eat chocolates, and wash 'em down with fancy liqueurs. Who did you think you were foisting yourself on? I've got officers sniffing around now, different sort of stuff from you! I'll really show you what I think of you before I'm through. I'll have you cleaning up my shit." She had begun in a drunken singsong, but after a while her voice cracked with self-pity and rose to a scream. "So you dreamed about a girl like me, you mangy bastard! Dreams are all you'll get. So near and yet so far! You can gnaw your own flesh instead."

The major-general, visibly sobering up during all this, was trying to pull her away from the fence, and looking round apprehensively.

"Agrafena Mikhailovna! This won't do at all. Such a respectful woman, and suddenly you start behaving like this. You invited me here, and now . . . Agrafena Mikhailovna, I beg you . . ."

The tubby little general bobbed around her helplessly, but she roughly shook him off. He retreated and stood gazing about wild-eyed like an animal at bay, trapped in the crossfire of windows and shutters opening with a bang on every side.

Fenya ran out, unkempt and pathetic. She paused at Grusha's back, pleading with her in a tearful babble.

"What are you doing to yourself, Grusha? What a disgrace. Hold onto me, Grusha, dear, and let's go home . . . I'll give you some tea . . . People are looking at you, Grusha!"

"What do I care about people?" she snarled without even looking at her sister-in-law. "Do I owe them anything?" She stared defiantly around the yard with a glazed, blank look. "What are you staring at like owls? Spit on me, then—if you're such saints. What about you, Nikishkin? How many lives have you sold lately? Or you, Tsygankova? Are you wearing your daughter's cast-offs now that she's in jail? Are you still using the church as a Poor-Relief Office? And what are you mouthing and mumbling about, you old bag? Waiting for the Tsar to came back so you can put us in the gutter again? Go fuck yourself! Drop dead!"

Shutters slammed, like punctuation marks, after each sally. Where personal morality was concerned there were not too many publicity lovers living around the yard.

Vasilii stood numbly at the window. He was unable to move, to flee from Grusha's words or her eyes. He was filled with a burning shame that threatened to choke him and right then he would have been happy to sink into the earth or die on the spot.

Stabel touched his shoulder. "Don't upset yourself. I'll go. I'll tell her . . ."

A minute later, Lashkov saw the plumber go out into the yard, walk up to the soldier, and take hold of a button on his tunic, which he twisted as he patiently tried to get something across to him. The soldier indignantly pulled away, waved his hands, and even tried to protest the ruling of this self-appointed referee, but his elbow was gripped in Stabel's deadlock, and he sagged and moved unsteadily toward the car. Otto wove some magic spell at the driver's window, and the next moment the car started up and glided out of the yard, enveloping him in a cloud of blue fumes.

The plumber gently nudged Fenya in the direction of home, and she went without protest. Then he carefully took the suddenly silent Grusha by the shoulders, led her to the bench, and sat her down at his side. At first she listened to him with sullen indifference, then she began answering with apparent reluctance, but gradually she became more animated, and in the end they were getting on like a house afire.

Dusk was falling on Lashkov's window from every corner of the yard when the plumber rose and took Grusha by the hand, and she obediently followed him to the boiler room. The yardman watched in suspense, still hoping in the depths of his heart that Grusha would change her mind at the last minute, turn back and go home. But she didn't change her mind and she didn't turn back, and Stabel's broad back shut her off from Lashkov's gaze. For good, this time.

The pain in his heart made him shut his eyes; he backed away from the window and fell as if pole-axed onto the bed. From the next yard, as if from another planet, somebody sobbed out in a reedy tenor:

> "Vanya's sitting on the stove,
> And smoking felt boots instead of baccy."

XIII

"Vasilii, Vasilii, open up, my dear man! Vasilii!"

Old woman Khramova was drumming desperately on Lashkov's window, where the groundwind had piled up a snowdrift. He wrenched open the ventilation pane and his neighbor's watery-hued face quivered in front of him like jelly.

"Help me, my dear man, I'll pay you. Pay you well. I can't manage her. She has to go to the hospital. They're coming for her right away. I've rung up. She's shouting and throwing herself about . . . Fenya's children are there . . . they're screaming too . . . and I'm all alone. Be good enough to help me. I'll pay you."

All hell was let loose in Number Eleven. Olga Khramova was circling round the room with her arms outspread, uttering high-pitched cries.

"I'm a bird, I'm flying. How high I'm flying! Don't get in my way! Everybody move, I'm flying away." She kept bumping into things as though she were blind, and everything crashed down and rolled about the floor wherever she turned.

"I'm flying away! Don't hammer nails into my head! It hurts!"

From behind the door of the Gorevs' room, Fenya's two children were howling their heartfelt accompaniment to their neighbor's screams.

Without a single glance at the new arrivals, she vanished into her brother's old room, then reappeared in the kitchen.

"Give me back my sky, I want to fly away. Oh God, why have you taken the sky away from me!" Then, suddenly, without any transition, "Why is everything so silent? Why has everyone gone dumb?" She put her ear to the old cupboard, then to the wall, the stove, the door, repeating in anxious bewilderment, "There's no sound! No sound! No sound!"

Her mother trailed after her, trying to catch her arm, and pleading with her pitifully.

"Olga, my little girl, my flower, my dearest, you can have anything,

anything at all you want. Only I implore you to come into your own room. If you like, I'll sing you to sleep. You always used to like me to sing to you. Olga, dearest, look at your mama. I'm here with you . . . Come on, darling, to your own room."

Whenever Olga slipped away from her, the old woman glanced anxiously at Vasilii, still hesitating to resort to his help, and began to moan all over again:

"Olga, dearest, my little daughter, have pity on your mama, listen to me! If you like we'll go to the forest tomorrow. You like it in the forest. Don't break my heart, Olga, come to your room. Be a good girl. You always were a good girl. Being a good girl suits you . . ."

The bawling behind the Gorevs' door reached its climax.

The mad girl resisted with frenzied desperation. Before Vasilii could get her hands behind her back, she contrived to scratch his cheek, pull the buttons off his jacket, even bite him twice on the shoulder, but, once she was tied hand and foot with towels, Olga soon quieted down, her face smoothed out, and there was nothing but a bluish white foam at the corners of her lips to recall the fit just past. He looked at her exhausted face, at the eyes sunk deep in their sockets, and he felt an unaccountable pain, which grew stronger from moment to moment, until it finally articulated itself in a prophetic insight. "Oh Mother, everybody's got one little thing that means everything to him. Take that away and all that's left is a feeble, foolish shell." And Vasilii painfully understood at last what creeping numbness was making a desert of his heart.

Back in the kitchen the old woman held out a greasy five-ruble note.

"Thank you, my dear man . . . Oh God, what have I done to be punished with such children? How have I angered thee, O Lord?"

"To hell with your five," thought Vasilii, but to his own surprise he took the money and even thanked her politely. "If you need me for anything just shout."

In the yard he bumped into Lyova, who gripped his lapels, eyes shining feverishly.

"How are things there, Vasilii Vasilievich? Better?"

"She's quieted down. They'll come and fetch her shortly."

They sat on the bench. Rubbing his temples in desperation, and staring at the ground, Lyova lacerated himself.

"I'll go up there right away . . . She can't eat me! I'm her son, after all! I'll go on my knees to her and beg forgiveness. Oh, Olga, my little sister, what is happening to you?" He started up. Lashkov silently took him by the shoulders and pushed him back into his seat. "It's all my fault, the whole thing! It's because of me that Mother sold the piano. D'you think I didn't know they had nothing to live on, d'you think I couldn't have given them something? True, I had supposed that Mother still had something left . . . but what was the good of supposing? I'm an egoistic monster."

"You can hardly make ends meet yourself."

"Yes, but I'm alone, and I'm a man. It's all horrible."

A car blew its horn outside.

"They're here," said Lashkov, rising, and went to open the gate. "Coming," he shouted. Then, turning to Khramov again, "You sit here, mate, and not a squeak out of you, or else I can see us having to call another ambulance."

The yard came to life. There was a staccato rattle of windows and shutters, as though the tenants were answering a roll call, and raucous remarks chased each other around the echoing box.

"Who've they come for?"

"Mad Olga's having a screaming fit."

"About time they took her. She's nearly driven me crazy with that piano of hers. Enough to make you move somewhere else."

"She's usually quiet, though!"

"Quiet! Our ceiling's been jumping nonstop for two days now."

"She's still only a girl."

"Bad blood. The upper classes . . . Even being young doesn't help."

"It's all that champagne in the bloodstream."

"God have mercy on her! Oh what miserable sinners we are."

"Clear the kids out of the yard. She might bite, you never know!"

Lyova hid his head in his lap, stopped his ears, and sat like that for some time, rocking rhythmically. Then he sprang up and ran out into the middle of the yard.

"Be quiet, all of you," he screamed in a fury. "D'you hear, be quiet! Or I'll smash your pigs' snouts for you. Just let me hear one sound out of any of you! Animals! Dungbeetles!"

Vasilii sat him down again. He was about to start shouting something, but just then they carried Olga out of the main door, covered with a stenciled hospital sheet, as though she were dead. When the stretcher drew level with the bench, Lyova became oblivious of everything else and drifted after his sister, shaking convulsively.

"Olga, little sister, what is happening to you? Olga, my love, we were going to give concerts together." He dragged along behind the stretcher. "It's all my fault! It's all my fault! Olg-a-a-a!"

When they got to the car a tall blond man with a slab of a face, a doctor to judge by his double-breasted smock, stepped between Lyova and the stretcher. His fleshy lips made deprecating little chewing movements, and he took hold of the actor by a button on his raincoat.

"You shouldn't be here, my dear man. You're on the verge yourself. Maximum of quiet, minimum of excitement . . ."

Khramov seized him by the hand.

"Tell me, Doctor, will she come home again soon? I am so terribly to blame for what has happened to her."

"Who knows, my dear man?" said the doctor in a flat voice, "who knows? Miracles are not as uncommon as all that." Then, as he was slamming the car door, he added, "Keep calm, though. Don't make me have to pay you a second visit. You've got the best part of your life in front of you, my lad . . . Let's go."

Lyova took a few steps after the receding ambulance, then turned round to trudge back the way he had come, but as he did so he bumped into his mother, who had been standing right behind him all the time; quite spontaneously, he let his heavy head fall onto her shoulder, and both of them found relief in quiet tears.

Lashkov, watching the Khramovs cross the yard arm in arm, and vanish through the main entrance of the house, did a little calculation: should he fit up the attic for storing logs, or what?

XIV

Stabel came in, banged a half-bottle down on the table, and sat down without waiting for an invitation.

"Vasya"—his voice was firm—"I said, no hard feelings. You didn't want Grusha, you were afraid. I'm not afraid. I have said to Grusha, 'Be my wife.' She has agreed. Now you have hard feelings." He shook his head reproachfully. "Not nice. You are my friend. Not nice."

Lashkov, trimming a herring, muttered sourly.

"There's nothing to discuss anymore . . . nothing at all."

The plumber's hand covered his.

"Listen here, Vasya, be friends, help me build a house. A wife in the boiler room—not nice."

Lashkov had known what was coming. For a week past, Otto had been bringing visitors to the yard, obviously on business. First an expert from the housing association, then the fire inspector, then various jobbers. The visitors conscientiously measured up the corner of the yard between the boiler house and the wall of the nearest building, then descended to the plumber's hospitable boiler room, and shortly reemerged, visibly the better for drink. Then, the day before yesterday, the yardman had received precise news from the block sergeant. Stabel had been given permission to build.

"There you are, Vasilii Vasilievich," thought Lashkov to himself, "you're in a real mess. Now you can knock another nail into your own coffin. And, of course, you will."

Out loud he said: "It isn't you I should have hard feelings about, it's myself. I won't try to fool you, it nags at me all the time . . . but let's forget it. When d'you think of starting?"

"My day off. Your good health."

Lashkov emptied his glass in two gulps, without tasting the vodka or getting any kick out of it, and said curtly, quietly, "I'll come."

Never before had Vasilii seen Lyovushkin so solemn and serious. You'd have thought he wasn't digging a foundation trench, but setting off on a very long and uncertain journey, from which he hoped of course to return, but couldn't be sure. He drank from the christening cup as though taking holy communion. Before he began digging he looked around them all with stern affection and said quietly:

"What we're starting on is a work of God, brothers: a house. There mustn't be any nonsense and fooling around. Not to finish such a work is a sin. And a mortal one." He crossed himself. "God bless our handiwork."

He labored in silence, his teeth tight clenched, never a spade's load behind the powerful plumber, who in turn wheezed and grunted in his efforts to keep ahead of the conscientious carpenter. Grusha sat facing him, peeling potatoes on the doorstep of the boiler room. She was squatting on her heels to peel them, and Otto, as he swung his spade, ran his eyes carelessly over her firm calves with a look that glowed with love and satisfaction. Every now and then Grusha cooled him off with a glance of mock reproach, but did not change position and was obviously enjoying their wordless game. Otto Stabel, at thirty-eight, was enjoying those happy years when a man, especially a strong, good-natured man like himself, is attractive to all women, be they fifteen or a hundred.

Vasilii looked on without jealousy. Indeed, his resentment had burned out, but all the same he couldn't escape a feeling of loss, of major, irreparable loss. It was as though he had suddenly found himself deprived of something which he needed in order to feel equal to the others. His depression stayed with him all day.

When the time came to stop, Ivan scrambled out of the trench in a flash, fetched a huge log from the fuel bunker, hunted for a couple of spare planks in the shed, trimmed a bit here, planed a bit there . . . and with three strokes of the hammer—it was a joy to watch—a table appeared in front of the bench in the yard. Grusha was amazed.

"If only you had some brains to go with those hands, Ivan, darling. I was just wondering where we were going to sit. I could make a man out of you, my love."

Ivan guffawed good-naturedly.

"The Lord didn't forget me when brains were being given out. And, anyway, there's different sorts of brains, Grusha, dear. There's brains for doing things and brains for explaining things, and one's as good as the other. Some do things, and others explain what's what. And I don't need you to make me a man, because I've got two legs already. So don't let it upset you, but you're wrong all down the line."

The last flashes of sunlight slid from the rooftops as they started to cool. And evening, as tranquil as one in June, filled the yard and deepened to a rich, inky blackness. Faces became more and more blurred. Such evenings put people in the mood for abstract conversations that avoid any mention of current problems and cares.

Inhaling a cigarette he had rolled himself after the meal, Lyovushkin sighed dreamily.

"It's a great thing—a house of your own."

"Yes," said the plumber in solemn agreement.

Lashkov stayed silent, but Grusha pensively took up the refrain. "What could be better? Your own roof over your head. Not somebody else's. Not one you got as a present."

"I can't promise a palace," added Lyovushkin, "but I'm ready to bet it'll stand a hundred years. You didn't have one like it back home in Vienna."

Stabel didn't answer immediately, but when he did his voice stayed on its deadest note.

"In *Wien* I had nothing. I had the front. I had prison camp. I had the Civil War. But in Vienna I had nothing."

"And you don't feel homesick?"

"No," said Otto firmly. "No."

Grusha shivered a little, and laughed.

"Funny way to talk."

"Well, I can't stand it here," said Lyovushkin sorrowfully. "When I think about it, I want to howl like a wolf . . . People here are always yelling at each other, and dithering around without doing anything . . . Pointless fuss, that's all it is. But back home there's peace and quiet. And work isn't just work, it's pleasure. Here even the soil smells like a moldering doormat—I sniffed it just now . . . Oh dear God! I have to get away."

Lashkov couldn't resist a little sarcasm.

"What about your son? You wanted him to become a dentist, like Meckler. . . ."

"What Meckler does is all right for Meckler. Poking about in other people's mouths is his business but my little Boris will be trained in my own line of work."

"Funny way to talk," said Grusha, shivering again, but not smiling this time.

Stabel covered her shoulders with his coat and rose.

"We're going to bed."

The two dark silhouettes merged into one and dissolved in the darkness.

"Makes you sick." The carpenter spat his cigarette end into the fire.

"Makes you sick all right," said Lashkov sympathetically.

"I'll go away somewhere. Only not to the country. There's no life there for me. Soon as Stabel's gets built I'll go. I'll get seasonal work. In the Crimea. There's sea there . . . Have you ever seen the sea?"

"No, I haven't."

"I haven't either. It'd be interesting."

"What's interesting? Just water, that's all."

"You're a bore nowadays, Vasya; it's miserable sitting here with you. I can't see why you go on living! So long."

The yardman lowered his head onto the table and sat thinking. Everything came back to Lyovushkin's "Why?" The mainstream of his memories became hopelessly fragmented into a network of tributary thoughts, which were lost to sight somewhere at the headwaters of his childhood.

How and why had he lived his thirty-nine years? Where had he been going? What had he been looking for? Had he ever once in his life tried to swim against the current? Yes, just once—in his youth, when he had left home and gone to the mine. He had given up every-thing—a comfortable home, his brother's powerful protection, quiet Maria's gentle care. He became a mechanic. When he picked up a tool his heart sang. He went into the army as if to a birthday party. They sent him to the desert to chase Basmachi. The Basmach is an enemy, so hit him, crush him, give him no quarter. Only once did he see this enemy of his, face to face. His enemy was at the very most seventeen. His enemy lay at his, Vasilii's, feet, and a bullet from his, Vasilii's, carbine had passed right through him. And something in him turned to ashes.

He looked stupidly at the drops of sweat still glistening on the Turkmen's unbearded lip, and, try as he might, he could not take his eyes off them. For a long time after, they haunted him. He was finally demobilized, with a mutilated forearm and a dislocated knee. And a sort of anguished restlessness began gnawing at his insides. At twenty-three he got his job as yardman. Was there no real work to be had? There was, but he just happened to fall prey to a smart operator from the housing association: here you are—catch hold of this broom and pin a badge on your apron. Enjoy your stroll around the yard. And stay cheerful. He had nothing to dream about, no personal attachments. One stroke of luck had brightened his life—and he had rejected it, afraid of the trouble it might bring. Trouble that didn't amount to a row of beans.

There was a rustling in the darkness near Lashkov's ear. Somebody was wandering about the yard. The dark shape came straight toward him, and old lady Shokolinist's unmistakable mutter made itself more and more audible.

"One little nail, just one little plank . . . The devils! I'll get it all back again, shaving by shaving, pebble by pebble . . ."

Vasilii had known for some time that she had a weakness for gathering and hoarding all sorts of rubbish, but only now did he understand the passionate greed that dominated the old woman. For some reason he remembered the drops of sweat on the lip of the youthful Turkmen in the dirty fur hat. Again, the anguished question: "Why couldn't we all live in peace together?"

XV

Lashkov loved that part of the morning when the world was full of light although the sun was not yet high. The shrill hoots of shunting engines, the chatter of birds, the clip-clop of hooves on the roadway—at that time of the day the yardman heard them all with unmuffled clarity. The world was talking to him alone. He had only a small section of street to clean— ninety feet of pavement and the same of cobbled road. He could manage the lot in half an hour. Then he would sit on his bench as if immersed in silence itself, while a deceptive feeling of peace came over him. It was as though nothing had ever existed or ever would exist, except—since the beginning of time—this long silence before sunrise, and himself in it.

But today, just as Vasilii had put his broom away, a tall, round-shouldered man with a beard, who looked as though he had traveled a long way, and on foot, to judge by his ill-assorted and bedraggled clothes, came into the yard, and looked around as though he belonged there. He stood for a moment leaning on his stick, took in the scene at a glance, and nodded to Lashkov.

"How are you, Vasilii Vasilievich! Forgotten me, I daresay?"

Surprise lifted Lashkov half out of his seat: a priest in sackcloth is still a priest—it was Stepan Tsygankov all right. Stepan had vanished after the Valov business and there had been no sign of him for eight years. True, Kalinin had once casually remarked that old man Tsygankov had done another spell in jail—and a long one—but hadn't explained properly what it was all about, and they had soon forgotten Stepan. The yardman held out his hand uncertainly.

"Hallo. Sorry, Stepan Trofimovich, but you've been given up for dead a hundred times over! Your wife is having masses said for you."

He recognized, yet didn't recognize, his neighbor. There was no mistaking the Tsygankov breed: the bearlike strength, the roughly but boldly hewn face, the hand as big and strong as a spade. But Stepan now spoke thoughtfully with assurance, and his eyes shone with a gentle, steady light.

"I'll sit with you for a little bit, Vasilii," he announced, settling his sack between his legs, "and then I'm away. Moscow is forbidden ground to people like me."

"What d'you mean?"

"Wrong passport. Got an endorsement."

"You ought to go and see your family. Just for a day. I'll fix it with the precinct office."

"What for? They've buried me once, it's better that way. Are they all alive?"

"Alive, yes . . . Only your youngest is . . ."

"What?"

"Inside."

Stepan received the news with the usual calm resignation, as though he had known it all in advance, foreseen that it was bound to happen eventually, and so did not take it too seriously. He merely gripped his stick with both hands and rested his chin on it.

"Have they quieted down?"

"Time they did. Tikhon's brought a wife home. Expecting an addition."

Stepan screwed up his eyes in a grin.

"So I'm going to have a grandson, then. Well, he'll get by without a grandfather like me."

"Maybe I could call your old lady down, at least?"

"How is she?"

"Started running to church all the time."

"What's that palace on three legs over there?"

Stepan nodded towards Stabel's structure, already a quarter-built.

"The plumber's building a house . . . He's got married."

"There you are, you see, Vasilii Vasilievich, we all get shaken up, so we don't know whether we're on our head or our heels, and we go wild and rush about like madmen. God knows where we think we're rushing to, nor the devil either. Then before you know it, everything's settling down again, back in the old rut. People have kids, sing in church, put up houses . . . everybody gets what's coming to him. It's like a holy procession from the pub to the police station. The old ones say it was always like that in Russia: the ones on top minding their own business, and the others underneath minding theirs. After the big shakeup everything is a shambles at first. Then some other crazy man gets on top and thinks he can knock the guts out of Mother Russia. But

Russia, God bless her, is like a stream that gets churned up and muddied for a while, then flows on just as it did a hundred years before."

"What can we do, though?"

"You ought to think less and stop sitting around in one place. You've got so much of life in front of you! You ought to get up, cut yourself a strong stick, and head for the Urals, or into the steppes."

It suddenly seemed to Vasilii that it would be so easy to do just that, so simple that his breath was taken away by this revelation. "Just get up and go somewhere. By yourself maybe, or else with Lyovushkin. Nobody's stopping you, you son of a bitch!" But then a doubt caught up with him, and then another, then a third, and his inspiration of a minute ago seemed fatuous.

"Where would I go? There's nowhere to go. It's the same everywhere. Anyway, you can't get far nowadays—they soon find a place to put you."

"People can live in those places, too, and learn something. Only little kids are frightened of the 'place.' Look at me—I'm still all in one piece; they didn't eat me."

Lashkov, deliberately sliding away from an awkward topic, seized on Tsygankov's last phrase.

"Where've you been then, Stepan Trofimovich? I can see you've taken a beating!"

"Here and there. And I certainly did take a beating," Stepan replied vaguely, shutting his eyes and nodding as though he were falling asleep. "All sorts of things happened to me." He raised his head again, looked hard into his companion's face, and said in a dry, unemotional voice: "I murdered a human being out there, Vasilii Vasilievich."

Tsygankov's blunt candor was a kind of declaration that he had nothing to hide, and that his companion could please himself as to what attitude he took.

All that Vasilii could feel at that moment was expressed in a single question.

"Where to now, Stepan?"

"Summer will soon be over. I'll make my way to somewhere warm. Spend the winter in Kutaisi or Batumi."

"Why don't you come in and have a bite? There'll be a drop of something as well."

"I've never had a drink since . . ."

Stepan's "since" was heavy with sadness and regret, and Lashkov was overwhelmed once more at the thought of the burden that this man, who meant nothing to him a little while ago, must carry about the world. "I always have food. I usually stick to the villages and it's impossible to go hungry there with hands like mine . . . Don't take it amiss, I'd like to accept, you know that, only I'm afraid . . . They're living in peace and quiet. Thank God for that. At times I can't believe myself that I used to live here, that I've got a wife and kids, that I used to have a forge. It's as if none of that ever happened, as if I've been wandering the country, begging in the name of God, since the world began. Seems queer!"

A force much stronger than mere fellow-feeling drew them together and they embraced. Like children who have been terribly hurt, they found some comfort in it—for a moment, the world was a warmer and better place.

Stepan, tall and rangy, stepped out onto the pavement, and sunlight came spilling over the housetops to spread at his feet as though it had been lying in wait for him.

XVI

The plumber's house was growing by leaps and bounds: row by row, it rose, each row two-and-a-half thicknesses of the best firebrick.

Ivan Lyovushkin went over to a nearby building site once or twice, had a quick word with the bricklayers, did a bit of laboring for one or another, and Otto Stabel was the beneficiary—his home rose steadily under Lyovushkin's clever hands. The plumber, acting as bricklayer's mate, could only smile and shake his head in wonderment. Vasilii was mixing mortar down below, and when Lyovushkin looked down and winked at him, his facility for mastering each new task was transmitted to his aide.

Lyova Khramov, who had volunteered to carry water, sat on the bench hugging his knees, watching Ivan in amazement, and swaying in time to his movements.

"Ivan Kirillich," he said suddenly, and his voice was full of wondering admiration, "Ivan Kirillich, it's not just work, it's a symphony! A monument should be put up to your hands! I'm not joking, Ivan Kirillich, truly I'm not. You seem to have magic tools of some sort instead of hands. They do whatever you want them to."

The flattered carpenter gave a complacent grunt.

"Well, they'll do it if I tell them."

"There's probably a Michelangelo or a Cellini languishing inside you, Ivan Kirillich!"

Lyovushkin didn't understand, but sensed that he was being praised again, and his movements became still more precise and skilled.

"We can't measure up to those foreigners, of course," he said mock-modestly, between two sweeps of the trowel, "us in our clogs and them in their galoshes! We'll be satisfied as long as it doesn't tumble down."

He grinned at Grusha, who was busy laying the table, and sprang nimbly down from the scaffolding.

"A smoke and a nap!"

But before they could take their places, Nikishkin appeared in the yard, accompanied by the block sergeant and a fireman with a briefcase. He walked straight up to the new building, like a general reviewing his troops, one pace ahead of his retinue, bringing his heels down like rubber stamps on the yard. Every step he took prepared them for a threat and a challenge, and his angry eyes were full of determination.

"What's this bird want?" thought Lashkov, scratching his head in dismay.

Stabel rose and went to meet the visitors, standing between them and the house

"I am listening."

Lyovushkin carefully pushed past Grusha, who was stiff with anxiety and also left the table.

"What's the vulture dreamed up now? It's all according to the book. Nobody can cause any trouble here."

Nikishkin surveyed the plumber out of the corner of his eye, then addressed himself by turning to the fireman and the block sergeant, as though they were the only people present worth talking to.

"I measured it myself last night—exactly eighteen feet. A whole three feet bigger than in the permit. Culpable negligence. They're always out to grab more than their share, and damn everybody else. And if I want to erect some kind of shed to put stuff in, where am I supposed to put it—next to the cesspool?"

He stated his complaint in a single breath, and only then did he bestow a defiant and triumphant glance on Stabel's troops.

In a graveyard hush, the gaunt fireman, his unsteady legs swimming in boots that were far too big for him, like pestles in two mortars, opened his pancake of a briefcase, took out a tape measure, and carefully ran it over the front sill of the basewall.

"Eighteen feet," he pronounced in an unexpected bass voice, "eighteen exactly."

Vasilii saw the plumber's bull neck flush darkly and his huge tawny fists bunch and swell. The yardman started to restrain his friend, but Otto's shoulders suddenly slumped, and his whole body went slack; he bowed his head low, turned awkwardly, and dragged himself off to the boiler room.

Ivan groaned aloud, swung his head angrily and advanced on Nikishkin. He was choking on his words, and the tears left clean furrows down his dusty cheeks.

"You're like a blight eating away at our lives; goddamn you to hell . . . What sort of wild bitch and mangy hound were you born from? I want to spit on you. I hope you die like the dog you are. Why should you live to torment us all our lives?"

The carpenter seized him by the chest and Nikishkin waved his arms helplessly, trying to pull away. There was no knowing how it would have ended if Kalinin hadn't thrust an arm in and parted them.

"That's enough. You, Lyovushkin, sit down and cool off. And you"—he turned to face Nikishkin—"go home. We can carry on without you now. I'm not responsible for your health."

Nikishkin hung around a bit longer to save face, his eyes fidgeting angrily about the yard, but the memory of Kalinin's quick temper obviously lingered, and he took care not to cross him. He still felt bound to have the last word.

"Got an appetite for jail soup, Lyovushkin? I've got witnesses. I've performed some services to the state. We can't let the primitive masses run wild. You there"—pointing his finger at the fireman—"you will be my witness. He had his claws in my chest!"

The fireman blinked his rabbity eyes disconsolately, and kept turning for support to the block sergeant, hissing over and over again: "Alexandr Petrovich . . . please, Alexandr Petrovich . . . oh, dear, Alexandr Petrovich."

The block sergeant merely frowned by way of reply, and turned his back on Nikishkin, thus finally excluding him from the general discussion. He threw his clipboard on the table and sat down.

"Well, boys, here it is. You'll have to pull some of it down in any case. Fire regulations. No need to make a fuss, it's fresh laid brick, taking one wall down is a day's work. As for that bird, I'll stick a lighted fuse where it'll do him most good before I'm done."

Ivan was up in arms. "It isn't just taking it down, Alexandr Petrovich. The heart's gone out of it. He might just as well have sprayed it with shit!"

He flung up his arms in desperation and went over to Lashkov.

"Be a pal, Vasya, give us a five."

Vasilii fumbled in his pockets and scraped together about three rubles, copper and silver included.

"Here, that's all there is . . . Maybe you shouldn't, Ivan, eh? You'll be having the blue devils again . . . and you're our only hope."

"No, I'm going to get drunk. And have the blue devils." Ivan raked up the money and rose. "D'you think a louse like that will ever let Stabel live in peace? Maybe tomorrow he'll want a shithouse put up out here in the yard, and we'll have to pull a bit more down? When it comes to that sort of thing, count me out."

"Wait a minute." The block sergeant stopped the carpenter, undid his clipboard, took out a five-ruble note and laid it in front of him. "You'll only tickle your appetite with three rubles' worth, then you'll be hawking your underwear. Here, you don't owe me anything. Only take my advice, carry it home. It'll be safer."

Lyovushkin made an indeterminate gesture—something between "Teach your grandmother" and "What the hell do I care?"—and vanished though the gate.

The block sergeant looked after him with a grin of sardonic pity, and suddenly became brisk.

"Right, Lashkov, you start before Stabel comes to his senses. I'll come around later and help you. In a day or two the wall will be better than new. Come on, Konstantin Ivanovich"—he nodded to the speechless fireman—"inform your superiors that everything is in order."

In the evening Lyuba ran into Vasilii's room.

"Come on, he's calling for you. I can't think what I'm going to do with him. He's got it firmly fixed in his stupid head that he's going away. He's packed all his things in a box. Oh, God! He'll be done for. He'll drink himself to death. How am I going to manage with two kids? And little Boris has got to start school. It's torture, sheer torture living with him. Vasya, do what you can with him. He's fond of you, he always listens to you. 'There's only one human being around,' he says, 'and that's Vasya.' "

He found the carpenter dressed for the road, sitting on his traveling chest with a knapsack and a toolbox between his legs.

"Sit down, Vasilii Vasilich." His formal invitation was accompanied by a nod at the nearly full quarter-liter on the table. "What I've got to say won't take long." It was clear enough that Ivan had been drinking, but only in moderation, and that his intentions were serious. "Come on, just one little drop before I set out, and no more. The road favors sober men, they say."

"Vanechka! Think what you're doing. Think of the children. How can I manage them by myself? What's got into you? What could I have done to please you that I didn't do? Vanechka!"

Lyovushkin seemed not to hear his wife. She might not have been in the room at all. Carefully sniffing at the bulb of a scallion, he gave his friend a detailed briefing.

"I'm worried about my boy, about Boris, Vasilii Vasilich. He's got to go to school. I don't want him to fall in with roughnecks. Maybe you'd take care of him a little. Keep an eye on him, set him right? If anything happens, a thrashing wouldn't do any harm, eh? Because you know Fenya's lad has run off, the son of a bitch, and never been heard of since. Be a friend, eh?"

Vasilii tried to calm the carpenter down.

"I'll do everything I can, of course, only perhaps all this is unnecessary. Why don't you lie down instead? Things will look better tomorrow."

The carpenter stood up, shying like an angry horse, and spoke sternly.

"Vasilii Vasilich! I'm talking to you as my best friend, I'm pouring my heart out to you, and you shove a teat in my mouth as if I was a calf. Is that God's way?"

Obviously Lyovushkin wasn't going to go back on his decision. Doing his best to ignore Lyuba's agonized pleading, Vasilii said, "I'll put him with Stabel, to keep an eye on him. Stabel could teach a cock to play a concertina, you know that. And I won't lose sight of him."

"Right, then," said the carpenter with satisfaction, taking hold of his sack. "I feel easier now. Walk as far as the gate with me, brother. So long then, wife! Don't give me up for dead too soon! I won't die till my time's up. I'll be back soon. With presents."

Lyuba set up a wail. "Vanechka, my dearest, don't abandon us, don't leave us without a pay packet . . ."

Ivan quickly cut her short. "That's enough. Don't come trailing after me. We'll say good-bye in the house." He embraced her perfunctorily and pushed her away. "That's it then." He went up to the curtain behind which the children were sleeping, pulled it aside, glanced in, and closed it again. "Don't spoil them with too much sugar. They're just the age to get rashes. Come on, Vasilii Vasilievich."

At the gate Lyovushkin slung his sack over his shoulder and held out his hand to the yardman.

"Look after yourself, Vasilii Vasilievich, and tell Stabel I hadn't got the guts for it, so I went away. He'd do better to hang up his hook and go home as well. This paradise of ours won't amount to a . . ." He used a foul word, and vanished into the night. But as Vasilii turned to go home, the darkness found its voice and yelled at him in Lyovushkin's tones: "And I know all about you and Lyuba, mate, don't think I don't!"

XVII

The early days of the war had nothing special about them, no smell of their own. There was no apparent disturbance in the regular rhythm of things. The only difference was that people's gestures were more economical, their words quieter, their clothes darker. Toward the end of the week, however, the silence in the yard was shattered by the howls of old Tsygankova in Number Nine: both her sons had been called up, Tikhon and Semyon.

Doors and windows burst open with loud bangs, like firecrackers going off.

"Are they taking them, then?"

"Yes."

"The married one as well?"

"Both of 'em."

"Women will have a rough time of it."

"We've all got it coming."

"They say we'll soon finish them off."

"They say! We've surrendered Polotsk!"

"For strategic reasons."

"They'll strategically reason themselves all the way back to Moscow."

"She's screeching as though they were being buried."

"When they take yours, you'll howl worse than that."

"Mine's exempt. He's got a blank card."

"Why, won't the camera take his photo?"

"He's got sclerosis."

"Ha, ha, how did he get that, then?"

"Caught a draft after he'd been to the baths, maybe?"

"Shut up, you bitches. You ought to be ashamed of yourselves. People have got trouble at home and you turn the place into a bazaar."

"You used to curse 'em yourself."

"What's it matter now who used to curse who?"

Call-up papers seldom set dates far in the future. Within an hour, the Tsygankov family rolled noisily, tearfully, and in full force into the yard. The brothers were obviously drunk, and in an ugly mood. As soon as Tikhon came through the main door he pointed himself in the direction of Stabel's house and advanced toward it, the full width of the yard, stepping as carefully as if he were walking on crumbling sand. He stopped in front of the door, his legs wide apart, and after a torrent of hair-raising obscenities, began his speech.

"So you've lived to see the day, you German swine? To shed the blood of folks like us after eating our bread, eh? You'll see, we'll shed so much of yours, you'll be able to start a dye-works. The men'll be wearing red pants for the next hundred years. Come on, open your dirty great gullet just once, I want to count your fangs!"

Stabel's door opened, and the master of the house appeared on the threshold, pipe in mouth as always. He stood before Tikhon with his hands thrust deep in his trouser pockets, puffing away.

"I am listening to you. Speak."

Tsygankov was momentarily taken aback, but he felt his brother's breath on his neck and lashed himself into a fury again.

"I just wanted to know how you're getting on, Mr. Hitler, and what price you're asking for Russia today? A ruble a ton maybe? Or more? I must have the final reckoning with you now—in full."

His great bulk almost dropped onto the plumber, but he was suddenly awkwardly doubled up and found himself hanging by his wrists from Stabel's arms.

They were looking each other in the eye now, and the plumber spat his hatred right into Tikhon's face.

"Listen to me, Tsygankov. You had a forge, I had nothing. You were murdering people with a sawed-off gun, I was fighting for Russia. You are a parasite. I am a worker. Who is Hitler? Am I Hitler? No, you are Hitler."

He released Tsygankov, thrust his hands deep in his pockets again, and went on puffing rapidly at his extinguished pipe.

"Leave me in peace."

Tikhon's wife, still covered with yellowish blotches after her confinement, hung on her husband's sleeve. "Leave it, Tishenka, come away. The bastards are all staring at us, every one of them, as if they'd like to see us wiped off the face of the earth. Look at them all standing around and gaping."

She darted a look of hatred at Grusha, who was standing behind the plumber's back, and didn't bat an eyelid: she knew that her Otto could stand up for himself.

The Tsygankov brood set up a wild, unearthly howl, and Tikhon, with the two women hanging from him like two little dogs from an elephant, headed for the gates, still raging and cursing. They erupted out of the yard in a great tangle of yells and oaths.

The day when the first strips of newspaper were pasted crisscross on the windowpanes, Meckler's oldest son, Misha, knocked at Vasilii's door.

"Papa asks you to come and see him." The lad's golden eyes gazed at the yardman with unchildlike sadness and seriousness. "Papa's leaving for the front."

The Mecklers were sitting round a table laid with odds and ends, saying nothing. Nobody was eating anything, everybody was looking at the head of the family, who was looking back at all of them. There was something oppressive, yet ritual, in this eloquent silence. A few brief words, the bare bones of a thought, were exchanged from time to time. Then silence fell again.

Someone gave up a chair to Vasilii, and he sat down. The master of the house in person poured him a glass of vodka and pushed over the food.

"As you see, Vasilii, I'm not going to be making your denture for you. I've got to go and do the opposite right now. What a lot of work there'll be afterwards, though." This was Meckler's attempt at a joke: it had a graveyard ring from a mile off. "Such a lot of work! Misha will finally get his bicycle. And Maya a doll that shuts its eyes."

Words of sympathy would have been wasted, even superfluous in this room, but etiquette obliged him to try.

"They say our troops have crossed the Romanian border. Shouldn't be surprised if you never even get to the war, Osip Ilyich."

Meckler's eyes lit up in mockery and turned completely yellow.

"May your children be no farther from a fortune, Vasilii."

Another drink was poured, but for Lashkov alone this time, and the yardman understood that he had no real business here, in this silence, that he was merely a tolerated guest, that he had better go away and leave them alone with their misery. He was suddenly in a hurry.

"Thank you for your hospitality, Osip Ilyich. If you want anything done at all, I'll always be glad. Rakhil Grigorievna only has to give me a shout."

"Look after yourself, Vasilii," said Meckler, and several pairs of absolutely identical eyes were lowered in agreement.

Vasilii went to the door, trailed by a long, re-echoing silence.

Lashkov was awakened that night by the block sergeant. Kalinin was in a state of agitation, which was quite unusual for him.

"Get up. Stabel's place, and be quick about it."

"What's up now?" the yardman wondered as he dressed. "Have they been robbed? Or has Grusha done something? She's liable to. Hanging round the flea market from morning to night. You can get it in the neck for that sort of thing nowadays!"

The door of Stabel's home was wide open, and the yellow rectangle of light revealed the front of a battered Gazik. A soldier was dozing at the wheel.

Stabel, his face puffy and creased with sleep, was laboriously poring over a scrap of paper, while a boyish little lieutenant, who obviously hadn't started shaving yet, was hovering impatiently on the doorstep.

"We've still got two places to go to, Citizen Stabel," said the little lieutenant in an imposing bass voice. He kept checking a wristwatch on a metal band against Stabel's grandfather clock, and coughing importantly into his hand. In short, he was doing his best to look as businesslike as possible.

"A decree is a decree. You and I can only obey. This is a temporary measure, and does not affect your rights as a citizen."

The plumber didn't hear him. His brow was furrowed by the effort to make sense of what lay before him, and he was mumbling half to himself:

"I fought for Soviet power . . . I have been wounded . . . I have fought at Kherson . . . I have fought at Uralsk . . . Why am I to blame for Hitler? Why must I leave my wife, my home?"

The lieutenant tried to get through to him. "Your wife can choose to go with you or wait here for you. You can contact her about this from the place of residence assigned to you."

Stabel jumped at this mention of his wife.

"No! She is in the country to have her child. No need to disturb her. What for? I want a healthy child." He sprang up and feverishly began to get ready. "What can I take for the journey?"

"Only the bare essentials. This is a temporary measure. To ensure your own safety. You will soon be back."

"Yes, yes," the plumber answered mechanically, as though trying to remember where on earth the bare essentials could have got to, and what was meant by them anyway. He blundered about the room, picking up and dropping one thing after another. Then suddenly he threw up his arms in despair. "I take nothing. I go like this."

The lieutenant brightened, and made way for Stabel with alacrity.

"As you wish. It is only a temporary wartime measure."

As he was getting into the car, Otto spoke to Lashkov. "Vasya, tell Grusha, I will be home soon, very soon. Grusha must not have any excitement. I will be writing soon."

The little lieutenant cast a suspicious eye over the speechless yardman, and gave a piece of confidential advice to the block sergeant, who, of those present, was the only other person initiated into the ultimate mysteries of governmental policy, and therefore capable of understanding him.

"If there is any talk, make appropriate explanations to the population."

"Rubbish," said Kalinin, with a vague gesture.

The little lieutenant's astonished eyes floated off into the night, and the Gazik carrying Otto Stabel the plumber was shortly to be heard honking at the next corner.

"Alexandr Petrovich . . .?" The yardman was too flabbergasted to complete his question. The policeman's reply was terse.

"A decree. Persons of German origin to be resettled in specified places of residence."

"He's Austrian, Alexandr Petrovich, and he's down as an Austrian in his passport."

"That's the same thing, Lashkov. Hitler is also Austrian. Still, it's really all effing nonsense, of course."

It was difficult to make out Kalinin's face in the darkness, but his loud, uneven breathing betrayed his bitter indignation.

"Here you are, give them to Grusha. Nothing's been touched in there."

He prodded Vasilii with the keys of Stabel's house and the night closed in between them once more.

XVIII

The block sergeant sat by the white-hot, portable stove in the yardman's room, trying to warm his blue hands and hoarsely thinking aloud.

"You won't catch that devil bare-handed. Anyway, maybe Fenya only imagined that she saw him. You start imagining stranger things than that if you're hungry enough. Maybe we ought to call the Criminal Investigation Squad? But what if it wasn't Tsygankov at all, or maybe he was there but won't come to the same place twice? We'd look pretty stupid, Lashkov. That's it, then. Dead loss, however you look at it . . . Still, we shall have to give it a try, the pair of us. Can you handle a weapon?"

"I didn't earn my Group Two with a wooden pop-gun."

"I'll give you a pistol. A spare. That's just in case, though—we've got to take him alive. Otherwise it's good-bye to the ration cards. And you can forget about catching his partners. So there you are."

Kalinin was trying hard to whip up his courage, fidgeting on his stool with feigned excitement. But his underlying anxiety was not lost on Vasilii. The policeman was coughing more than usual, loudly, nervously cracking his finger joints, gradually lengthening the meditative pauses between his sentences. The yardman could see that some morbid anxiety was gnawing away at him. The policeman wasn't talking to Vasilii, but interrogating himself.

Yet it all seemed simple enough. The day before yesterday, the house administrator's office had been robbed, and about three hundred ration cards stolen. Strictly speaking, it was up to the Criminal Investigation Squad to do something about it, and Kalinin could have sat back with a clear conscience. But that morning Fenya Goreva had sworn by all that's holy that she had seen Semyon Tsygankov in the Preobrazhenskii Market, and about a week before that, when she was going up to hang out some washing, she had bumped into old mother Tsygankova on the attic landing, carrying what looked like a parcel of laundry, only with a kettle handle sticking out of it. Then again, Khlebnikova, the school teacher who had recently moved in next to the Tsygankovs, had remarked at some point that her neighbors lived pretty well considering there was a war on.

The block sergeant had been notified back in autumn of the search for the deserter Semyon Tsygankov. Now, by calculations known to him alone, he had taken it upon himself to establish a link between these apparently quite unconnected facts and prepared to give battle. Long ago he had vowed, after Sima's arrest, to drive the family out of his precinct, but now that he had one of the Tsygankovs in his sights—and of that he was absolutely sure—he was frowning with vexation and his pauses for thought between sentences grew longer all the time.

"I've given all my usual mob a going-over and a taste of what they can expect . . . Fish Face, the Dragon, Boxer, Mercury, the Lone Wolf . . . I know them: If they weren't all clean, one of them would have ratted by now . . . So there's nobody else, it must be him . . . Still, I want to look him in the eye myself . . . and I will . . . Only we must take him alive."

He stood up and reached for his greatcoat, but he went on debating with himself while he dressed, and stood stock-still for a moment with his coat half on. Then his jaw clenched resolutely, and he took hold of the door handle.

"Right, then, Lashkov, you block off the roof of Number Twenty-seven, and I'll start driving him toward you from here." Even now, Kalinin turned around irresolutely in the doorway. "Maybe we should say to hell with it, Lashkov? Let the CI boys sort it out? Why should we hunt him down like an animal?"

But these last words came from the hallway. Kalinin had lost his struggle with temptation, and was not going to stop now.

In the yard they separated, and Vasilii made for the house next door, shivering at the cold feel of the pistol handle in the pocket of his quilted jacket. The roofs of the two houses touched, so that they formed a highly convenient refuge for anyone temporarily at odds with the law.

Lashkov scrambled into the loft and settled down to wait. Through the left window he could look down on the city spread out under the low January sky. It was difficult to believe that life lurked behind that dark, chaotic jumble of corrugated roofs. And it occurred to Lashkov that here he had been living all these years in his yard, never going anywhere, yet somehow he had managed to learn so much that was new to him. People were born and died, people were taken away somewhere or other by people just like themselves, people fell in love or went mad. All this had happened in his presence, before his eyes. But there was a lot that he hadn't seen, too. People tried to live as much of their lives as possible on their own or with their families. So he, Vasilii Lashkov, would have needed more than five lifetimes to learn all there was to know about this one yard. And how many such yards there were in Moscow, in Russia, in the world!

For all those yards, there was only one sky. Perhaps it could happen, just once anyway, that all the people in all those yards would look upward at once, all at the same moment feel the painful longing for a kind word, for a kindred soul, that he felt now.

A sharp cry interrupted his thoughts. "Stop!"

There was a thundering of hobnailed boots on the roof of the neighboring house. Lashkov released the safety catch, jumped out onto the roof, braced himself against the gutter with his foot, and fired a warning shot. It had been so long since he had used a gun that his shoulder ached from the recoil and he had pins and needles in his arm. The roof was silent for a moment, no more, then the stillness was broken again by the clatter of feet, and a blurred silhouette moved slowly nearer. Lashkov fired another shot. Where the hell did he think he was going?

Kalinin's shout was a hoarse rattle in the frosty air. "Stop, or I'll shoot."

The confused clatter stopped, and the fugitive's steps became short and precise: one-two-three-four. Suddenly, a shrill cry burst over the roof ridge and ended in a groan as though a man's breath had been snatched away in fear. Then, from below came a heavy smack, like a resounding slap in the face.

Vasilii felt a sickening emptiness. He realized at once what had happened. The gutter of a third house, which fronted on a parallel street, was quite close at one point. There was a gap of about five feet, maybe a little more. Children sometimes jumped across it on a dare, but only in summer. If anybody tried to perform this trick in winter it would certainly be his last. Lashkov and the block sergeant both knew about it, but hadn't allowed for this possibility. Only somebody as desperate as Tsygankov would have clutched at such a straw. It had failed him, as such straws generally do. When they met at the junction of the two roofs there was no need for explanations.

Back in the yard again, Kalinin spoke to the yardman with no trace of emotion.

"Run down to the station, tell them to send the police surgeon and an ambulance. I'll go to your place and warm up while I'm waiting. I feel a bit chilly."

He walked away. There was something strange about his walk: a sort of jerky undulation, like the movement of a shadow.

Vasilii was back in fifteen minutes. As he entered the room, the word he had ready died on his lips, and he froze in his tracks. He felt his fingertips go cold and nausea rose in his throat.

The block sergeant might have been asleep or listening hard to something with his ear to the table. But the arms dangling helplessly by the knees, the slackness of the mouth, the unmistakable hush that goes with death, left no doubt as to what had happened. A fine crimson trickle running under his temple had gathered in a little pool where his cap had rolled off, and was beginning to tinge the fabric.

The expression on Kalinin's face was relaxed, and perhaps a little puzzled, as though in the moment which separated him from life forever he had had time to feel surprised that it was all so easy and so simple.

XIX

Lyova Khramov was lying surrounded by pillows and from the downy depths, for the yardman's benefit, he observed:

"We are weak in our desires. We want everything at once, immediately, while we are still alive. And when we are denied this, sooner or later we try to gratify our passions by force. And so there is bloodshed from generation to generation, and from age to age, but the ideals for which this blood is supposedly shed, alas, remain no more than ideals. It is much easier, of course, to redistribute the bounty than to add to it: That requires patience and work. But we have no patience, and we don't want to work. So the cry goes—'Beat them, smash them; we only live once.' You understand me, Lashkov?"

The yardman hastened to agree. It was all the same to him. He listened to the actor because he was sorry for him, because it was the only thing he could do to make his existence a little easier. Khramov's body no longer responded to morphine, and he struggled desperately to find relief from his pain in endless talk. His cancer daily accelerated his journey toward death. Lashkov sat by his couch for hours on end, and the sick man could not have wished for a better audience for his lengthy monologues.

The old woman and her son had moved into the outbuilding some time ago. Nizovtseva, the dressmaker, had changed apartments with them —for a consideration, of course. Khramova had not exactly let things slide, but circumstances had compelled her to take a simpler and more realistic view of things. After her daughter's funeral, she had gone to work in a hospital as a ward maid, and since then the yardman had started dropping in on them like an old and welcome acquaintance.

He and Lyova were tied together by a nagging feeling of doom, an awareness that the end was near. They heard each other's voices without listening to what was said, but loneliness retreated under the flood of words, and they enjoyed the brief illusion of a full existence. Each needed the other, could not do without him, and who could say whose need was the greater.

The actor's thin, bluish fingers plucked nervously at the fringe of the coverlet. When he was excited, he turned pale, his eyes sank ever deeper, and a fine mist of sweat appeared on his upper lip.

"We must begin all over again, Lashkov, do you understand? Otherwise there will be no end to the bloodletting, and we shall take to the trees again. We must learn to think in millennia, not just in terms of a human lifetime. We must teach ourselves to rejoice in the happiness and well-being of our descendants, train ourselves to work for it. Work, Lashkov, work! And we don't want any more idiot orators getting it into their heads that they are mighty men of action. When a man starts out in life, he must be asked what he can make by himself, unaided, with his own hands or talents. Bread, houses, books, art? We must work, work, work! And beauty will triumph! It will! You understand, Lashkov?"

Lashkov said yes, but he was thinking of something else, and at the same time straining to catch the quiet conversation in the kitchen, where Khramova was saying good-bye to the doctor.

"Perhaps he'd better go into hospital, after all?"

"Up to you, dear lady, up to you, but I don't advise it."

"Is there no point even in hoping?"

"You and I both have one foot in the grave ourselves, dear lady, so why delude ourselves with pious frauds?"

"I'd go instead of him this very minute . . ."

"Oh, those beautiful gestures you and I were trained to make in our time! You mustn't, dear lady. Times have changed. As for the hospital, he could go there, but our state hospitals are no place for anybody with his nervous system . . . It's heredity, as you know yourself . . . No, don't ask me to do it, my dear, it's quite pointless . . . yes . . . good-bye."

The front door banged, and Vasilii heard the old woman collapse heavily into a chair. She sat there without a sound while Lyova, who was growing more and more excited, tried to shout down his pain.

"Before we can begin, we have to have an artist, an artist, not someone like us pygmies. It needs a giant to come and say: You are all human, all brothers. But it's the way he will say it that matters. Christ has said it, and so have many, many others. But not as it should be said! It needs saying simply and comprehensibly. It must be said so that it will strike home to everyone . . . Everybody must be made gravely ill by it, and fight to recover his health . . . Yes, yes, it must be like an infection . . . Suddenly, and all at the same time, men must see themselves as they are . . . see themselves, and weep, and embrace . . . and say, 'Let's begin all over again.' It needs an artist. Only an artist can create harmony. With a single word . . . a single word . . . he will find it . . . It will be as simple as breathing . . . You understand me, Lashkov?"

The actor was out of breath. As he uttered these last words he jerked his head from the pillow, and tried to sit up, but immediately fell back again and closed his eyes. In a minute, his breathing became regular, and his face, which had turned white with excitement, took on its usual earthy tint. Lyova was asleep.

Vasilii straightened the coverlet and went out to the kitchen. Old Khramova was sitting by the stove, staring apathetically in front of her. She didn't stir or even notice him.

"He's gone to sleep."

"Oh," she said with a start.

"He's gone to sleep, I said."

"Oh."

Khramova froze again in her former position, and Vasilii thought as he went through the entrance hall that it couldn't be easy, outliving your own children.

XX

Lashkov was sitting under the shelter in Lyovushkin's little garden, listening to the carpenter droning out the same old tune over and over again:

> "I'm a girl in the bloom of youth still,
> Yet my heart is a million years old."

He held the accordion on the edge of his knee, as though it didn't belong to him, fixed the rainy sky with eyes that were dulled by drink, and obstinately insisted:

> "I'm a girl in the bloom of youth still,
> Yet my heart is a million years old."

The shelter leaked. Sleety March snow dripped and splashed on the carpenter's brow and the bridge of his nose, and ran down his cheeks until it looked as though he were crying. But it only looked that way. In reality he was simply drunk, dead to the world. He and Vasilii didn't talk as a rule. In the twenty years they had known each other, they had said everything there was to say. Shared all their thoughts. They communicated in sign language. The carpenter, for example, would stick his little finger out to the side, raise his thumb vertically, and look questioningly at his friend. Vasilii would nod silently, and both would begin turning out their pockets. After two or three such sessions they would have drunk themselves into a total stupor, and Lyovushkin would lay hold of his battered squeezebox. He played all sorts of tunes, but never more than two lines of anything. Ivan had acquired this accordion ten years before, when he was continually on the road, trying to earn some easy money, and had never been parted from it since. Lyuba wouldn't let them into the room as a rule, so they sang out there under the shelter, while the dirty March snow dripped down. Everything was behind them: their youth, their hopes, their lives—if that succession of agonized and despairing moments could be called living. No, Ivan's heart no longer ached and even his habit of mentioning "God's way" was long forgotten. He seemed to have grown impenetrably thick-skinned and indifferent; nothing could now succeed in disturbing his lifeless equilibrium.

The sky above, weighed down with humid air, seemed to flatten everything around them, pressing it into the ground. Up there, Lashkov imagined there was nothing beyond that thickness of gray, no sun, no stars, no sky even, only empty space, but an emptiness as dirty and viscous as the rain now falling on them.

Lyuba's dull eyes squinted at them through the window. She was as hoary-skinned as an old pike. Her head was like a melon with oakum gummed onto it. Her furious muttering rose through the ventilation pane into the yard. But neither she nor her hellcat temper could strike a spark in the ashes of Ivan's soul.

The carpenter had started executing his dizziest fingering passage for the third time when Nikishkin came into the yard, his head bent and his "little woman" hurrying along wailing beside him. He was walking more slowly than usual, his steps heavy and uncertain. He had got much bigger over the years, and run to fat. A captain's epaulettes nestled snugly against his plump shoulders. When he reached the little garden, Nikishkin suddenly flew into a rage. His pendulous cheeks turned blue and wobbled.

"What's all this, then, eh? What do you think you're doing? On a day like this you sit here swilling vodka. You sons of bitches you, I'll . . ." He was panting with rage. He rushed at Lashkov, grabbed him by the shoulder, and began to shake him furiously. "Where's the flag? Where's the flag? You filthy traitor! Answer me when I'm talking to you."

He suddenly released the yardman, started to tremble all over, and burst into tears.

"Sons of bitches! Sons of bitches! Masha! Masha!" Nikishkin clung to his wife. "What sufferings *he* took on himself for this scum. What sufferings and sacrifices! He dragged them out of the mud, out of the dung, and here they sit swilling vodka . . . wallowing in it." Nikishkin shook himself and rushed at Lashkov again. "You louse! I'm going to finish you off right now!" His twitching fingers were already fumbling with the button on the back pocket of his breeches. "You filth! See how you like this!"

Drunk as he was, Vasilii felt the tickle of death in his nostrils. All the crooks in Sokolniki trembled at the very name of Nikishkin, chief officer in Butyrki Prison. But the carpenter suddenly pushed the yardman aside with his limp hand, and stepped forward to shield him, flinging his accordion to the ground, where it collapsed with a stifled moan.

"Come on, shoot me with your little popgun," Ivan began quietly, as though asking a favor. But gradually the blood mounted to his face, and soon he was almost shouting at the thunderstruck Nikishkin. "Come on, shoot me! I've had no life and I never shall have now. So why should I go on? You've gobbled up my life along with all your government canteen dinners. I wanted to train my son to be a dentist, but where is he now, where's my son now, eh? I owe it all to you. I've spent my days sweating and slaving round all the godforsaken holes in Russia. All because of you, you dog. So come on, shoot!" He tore open the collar of his blouse. "What are you waiting for?"

The chief prison officer wasn't tough enough to withstand this kind of pressure. He began to sing a different tune.

"Now, now, don't get smart with me. If necessary I can find a spare cell for you, too, my fine friend. I'll have something to say to you later." As he walked away, he called to Lashkov over his shoulder. "We're in mourning, you bastard, in mourning. Get the flag up this instant—I'll be back to check. Traitorous scum." And off he went.

Lyovushkin snatched up the accordion from the ground and bawled after him in blatant mockery:

> "Down our way we may seem queer,
> We don't do what others do.
> Folks as well brought up as we are,
> Gobble shit and never spew.
> Up yours, you bastard!"

XXI

Before his illness, Vasilii Vasilievich had had no eyes for many things that were quite fascinating. The sun, for instance; it merged into his usual humdrum surroundings, as familiar as the rain, the wind, the air. But just recently it had begun living a life of its own, separate from his. He could hear the sun now, smell it, even feel it with his hands. The sun did its work and got tired. The sun moved from place to place in a remarkably purposeful fashion. The sun knew joy and indignation. The sun had friends and enemies. And Vasilii Vasilievich had no share in it all, separated as he was from all this happiness by the deadly frontier of his disease.

He felt as though he were discovering the world again. You would have thought that there wasn't a single spot in the yard that he didn't know, in the minutest detail. Yet now that objects had begun to exist for themselves, and outside of him, they began to seem as enigmatic as they had in his infancy. For instance, he had spent something like a quarter of his life in the boiler room, and the smells of rust and warm cinders had become part of him, yet there it stood now outside his window, its dark presence as mysterious and alluring as the entrance to the nether world. Strange as it may seem, again and again the old man pondered over concepts which he had mastered hundreds and thousands of times before—"fence," "tree," "ball." And each of them for the first time gave up its amazingly simple secrets.

"Yet it was always there, always the same," he reflected. "Do you have to be dying before you notice all this or feel any of it?" The thought disturbed him, and as usual in such cases he dragged himself down to the yard for a walk or a casual chat to muffle, smother, the dread which suddenly came over him. A bulldozer stood shuddering and rumbling by the hydrant. The operator, a lanky young fellow in a beret and a tarpaulin cape, was washing a rubber boot under the tap. The floating sky was mirrored in its gleaming leg.

"More digging?" asked Lashkov, lowering himself onto the bench, right next to the young man. He wasn't really curious, he just wanted to start a conversation of some sort. "It's the fifth time . . ."

The bulldozer operator wasn't to be interrupted, and didn't so much as glance at Lashkov. He merely jerked his head toward the corner of the yard, where Stabel's abandoned shack still clung to the boiler room and explained succinctly.

"I'm knocking down that Colosseum over there. The firm needs bricks. That's all, Granddad."

Lashkov immediately lost all desire for further conversation. He regarded that little two-windowed house as part of himself. Together with Stabel and Vanya Lyovushkin, Vasilii Vasilievich had invested in it not just his labor, but a particle of that which is left to a man after all his labor is done, after his cares and anxieties, his workdays and holidays, his wars and his armistices are past history. And now here was this businesslike, pimpled brat in a tarpaulin cape who didn't give a damn about Stabel the plumber and his shack. Nor did he care whether the gaunt old man on the bench left anything behind him or not. The firm needed bricks, and there was no time to be wasted in meaningless chat.

"Come on, Daddy." The boy was at the wheel in one bound. "Sit back a bit, or I may knock you accidentally."

The machine shuddered, turned slowly, and advanced straight on its goal with the leading edge of the grab. The front of the bulldozer sailed past Lashkov, then the wide-open cab, with a rubber boot framed in the doorway, and the sky going dull in its steaming mirror.

The house was dying like any living being. When the razor-sharp bottom edge of the grab bit into the basewall, the house rocked, barely perceptibly, but stood fast. But then the operator pulled a lever toward him a little, the steel blade cut deeper, and the house crumpled and collapsed, dragging the roof down with it . . . Dirty white dust billowed over it like smoke from a bonfire, rising toward a high, cloudless June sky, just like that of thirty years ago.

XXII

Vasilii Vasilievich left the beerhall in the blissful state which always comes over a heavy drinker in the first stages of intoxication. Everything seemed ridiculously simple and extremely clear—the past and the future, good and evil. On the corner of Rybinsky Passage a wiry, strong-looking old man in a canvas cap was buttonholing passersby, and Vasilii watched him for some time with drunken sympathy. The old man clutched elbow after elbow with his gnarled, tenacious fingers, and began with the same stereotyped phrase.

"Back home in Cherepovets . . ."

Everyone backed away in fright, obviously taking him for a drunken madman. Anyway, who wants to know about other people's troubles when he's up to his neck in his own? One or two, though, gave him a word of advice: "Why don't you go and get an hour's sleep or two, Daddy?"

The old man just waved them away and resumed his feverish quest. "Back home in Cherepovets . . ."

And so it went on. The militiaman on duty by the foodstore watched the old man's maneuvers for a while, and was beginning to look just a little bit restive, when Lashkov decided to save the unfortunate native of Cherepovets from what was a certain stretch in the cooler.

"Nothing to it," he reassured himself, "I'll give him a ruble or two, the old boy will have a drink, it'll clear his head a bit, and he'll be on his way."

But Vasilii Vasilievich evidently was not exactly what he was looking for. The old man's shiny, round eyes slid over his face, and he went on past him. Lashkov called good-naturedly after him, "Come on, then, let's have it. What happened back home in Cherepovets?"

The old man turned around and looked sternly at the yardman with angry eyes. Then, all at once, the harsh lines in his face softened a little, he waved his hand as much as to say what the hell, and seized Lashkov by the elbow.

"Back home in Cherepovets, dear comrade, there is no justice. See . . ."

And the old man began telling Lashkov the old, old story, more or less as he expected.

"My brother-in-law, he's a shoemaker, he was sent to jail for nothing at all, he's disabled, wounded in the war, got six kids in the bargain, all young. They said they were after the leather, but there wasn't enough leather to make toe-caps for a man with no legs." And so on in the same vein. The old man told his story with a wealth of details, all backed up by the appropriate documentary evidence. Then he chattered on for nearly an hour about his own services to the community, as for instance: "I came down with typhus in the Civil War, and, well, you know, I fought . . ."

In conclusion, the old man put the question to him point-blank.

"So, come on, you live in the capital, tell me, is there any justice back home where I live in Cherepovets, or isn't there?"

The strength of his conviction was such that Vasilii had to agree, although he hadn't understood a word of the story.

The old man sighed with relief, gave a gap-toothed grin, and rose.

"Forgive me, dear comrade, at first you looked as if . . . as if . . . as if there wasn't much iron in you, let's say. Well, you don't look very per-severing. But I can see now that I was wrong. You've given it your intelligent consideration, and I'm grateful to you, dear comrade. If you're ever in Cherepovets ask for Fyodor Terentievich Mikheev. Every dog in the place knows me. We'll drink some tea, and chase it with the hard stuff."

Lashkov chuckled to himself. "Come on then, ask me," he thought. "I won't refuse." Out loud he tried to encourage the old man.

"You must have had a lot of expenses, it's a long journey."

To the yardman's surprise the old man turned cold and lectured him severely.

"I'm a skilled craftsman, comrade, and skilled craftsmen are never short of money. I've got money enough and I can lend you some if you like, without repayment."

Lashkov was taken aback, but tried to keep his end up. "I don't suppose you know your way around at all. You've got to be sharp to survive in Moscow, pal."

The old man pulled a wad of City Information Bureau slips out of his pocket, rifled them under Lashkov's nose, and said, "I've got all Moscow here in my pocket, and anybody who tries to take me for a ride will find I'm sharp enough. Anyhow, so long, and thanks for letting me take you into my confidence."

The old man marched off along the pavement towards Sokolniki. His stride was steady and purposeful. And Vasilii Vasilievich suddenly thought what a good idea it would be to run after the old man and tell him all about himself, about his yard, about Stabel, about old lady Shokolinist, and a lot more besides. He also thought that if it had been so easy for him, Lashkov, to bring relief to this old man, then perhaps the right word that Khramov used to talk about, the Word that would make all things new, was abroad in the world inside every human being. This flash of insight disturbed him so much that he couldn't help turning into a nearby secondhand shop, taking off his jacket, and throwing it down on the counter.

"What can you spare me for this?"

XXIII

One stuffy July night, Lashkov was awakened by a knock on the window. He pressed his face to the pane, and couldn't believe his eyes. His heart began to pound and he felt hot and short of breath. It was Stabel.

Before embracing, the two friends ran their hands over each other dubiously, as though each needed to make sure that the other was real. Then they were locked in a hug which they could scarcely break.

"Yes," said Lashkov.

"Yes," said Stabel.

And then again, "yes," "yes."

Each "yes" carried a burden of days and years, rain and sunshine, common joys and common grievances, and much more that can never be put into words.

Then they sat down at the table and Stabel spoke, thoughtfully rubbing an ink stain on the oilcloth while he looked hard at Lashkov with eyes that were as calm as ever, but rather less bright.

"There is government and there is law and order. I have always respected government and order. But twelve years is not law and order. I have left Taiga, I left the family. Yes, yes, I married. Taiga is difficult without a family. I have come to tell the government: twelve years is not law and order. I believe in government. I believe in all governments. Government is law and order. My children in Taiga is not law and order."

Lashkov was surprised to see how well, on the surface, his friend seemed to have survived. The plumber didn't seem to have changed at all except that the skin of his neck was slacker and his shoulders, though as burly as ever, had the stoop of age. But his thick fingers trembled as they gripped his wine glass, showing that the years had not left him unscathed.

The yardman felt that he should have such a lot to tell Stabel, yet after all those years his news wouldn't have covered the back of a postage stamp.

Grusha? There's not much to say about Grusha. She had a miscarriage after that business, she grieved for a time, then calmed down, and moved in with Fenya. She's still alive, but she's often ill. Ivan? Not much to report. Drinks. Goes off on contract jobs. Son in a camp for juvenile delinquents since he was quite little. The actor? The actor's dead, pal, long ago. Kalinin? Well, Kalinin's dead, too. Meckler? Meckler's alive. Fitting people with crowns. And making dentures.

Vasilii Vasilievich broke off as the room filled with the familiar sound of Nikishkin in full flight. His words streamed across the yard from an upper story of the house.

"What is labor? I am asking you, you sons of bitches—what is labor? What is labor a matter of, eh? I am asking you—labor is a matter of what, you horde of parasites? A matter of honor. And what else? Have you nothing to say, you criminal degenerates? A matter of valor and of heroism. He who does not work shall not—what? You there, you red-haired swine. I'm asking you. He shall not eat. And what d'you think you're doing? D'you think you're exempt? Dumb idiots. I'll soon teach you—scum. I've got punishment cells for the lot of you. I'll teach you all . . ."

Echoing on the calm and empty morning air, the voice seemed absurd beyond belief.

"What is that?" asked Stabel in alarm.

Lashkov grinned sardonically.

"Your godfather's acting up. He's a bit mad. He was one of the bosses, and now he's . . . you know . . . He practices at the window first thing every morning. He varies it a bit sometimes, but mostly it's like that. The yardmen from other streets come to listen . . . He has a fan club."

"Yes," was all Stabel said, but once more it spoke volumes for both of them.

Nikishkin was still pontificating from on high.

"What sort of songs do you sing, you degenerate mongrel? I'm asking you, what do you sing? You sing 'Murka,' don't you? And 'The Rolling Stream'? And 'I've Got a Nice Fur Coat.' And that other one— 'Behind the Walls of Brick'? After all my efforts, you sing crap like that, you scoundrel. You get your rations, you've got a mattress. Get taken to the baths, eh? Well! And then want five days' solitary? I'll stick you in with Lebedev-Kumach. And you'll learn all his songs by heart, d'you hear?"

Stabel rose.

"I must go now."

"I'll see you off."

"It's not necessary, Vasya, it's not at all necessary."

They haggled for a bit, although they both knew to begin with that they would go together. As the friends walked through the dawn streets towards the center, Vasilii gave the plumber his earnest advice.

"Stick to one point, that's the main thing. Tell them you won't have it, and that's the end of it. There's no such law. The war's over and done with. The worms have eaten Hitler long since, yet people with children are still being detained. It's the local authorities being a pain in the neck, that's all."

But when Stabel vanished through the doors of the oppressive building that sat like a massive lump of stone by the roadside, Vasilii's heart gave a painful lurch.

They had arranged to meet where they had parted, on the corner by a cigarette kiosk. Lashkov wandered aimlessly around the streets, came back, wandered off again, came back again. No Stabel. Vasilii Vasilievich had a chat with the man in the kiosk and even bought five packets of Belomor cigarettes, one by one, to encourage business. Still no Stabel. No Stabel an hour later, nor two hours later.

The kiosk salesman, shutting up shop, gave him a suspicious look, and spent a remarkably long time fiddling with the locks.

Gradually, the windows of the big building went blind . . . one, two, three . . . Lashkov, observing them, tried to reassure himself. "Here we are, that's the one . . . he'll be on his way now." But still Stabel didn't come. Then the very last square of light, right up in the roof somewhere, vanished, and there was nothing left for Vasilii to think, except, "That's it, then."

XXIV

One day toward the end of summer Vasilii Vasilievich had a guest whom he had never expected to see again. "It's Dad!" was the first thought that flashed through his fuddled brain when he opened the door. The likeness was so striking. But in a moment he had sorted things out. "It's old Pyotr!" One couldn't say that his forgotten brother's sudden visit was a surprise: Vasilii Vasilievich had long ceased to be surprised at anything. But it made him wonder. "What brings him here? Does he think he's going to die soon, or what?" But then from the depths of the past, through the drowsy twilight into which he was sinking deeper every year, his old affection came welling up in a hot spasm that threatened to choke him. As he helped his brother to slip off his raincoat he searched in vain for something sensible to say, but could only feebly repeat the same words over and over again.

"Sit down, Pyotr, my boy, sit down . . . We'll soon get something organized. There's something left over from yesterday—must have known you were coming. Come on, sit down."

While he was fussing with the table, Vasilii Vasilievich watched his guest out of the corner of his eye, noting with jealous concern every little line, every mark which had been missing in the Pyotr of his youth and earned or added since. Somehow Vasilii Vasilievich had never realized as keenly as he did now, after so many years of separation, how much the loss of home and family had meant to him. What had turned out to be his last day under his father's roof came back to him with almost three-dimensional clarity.

He had gone down to Uzlovsk immediately after his discharge from the army, though without any intention of staying. He only wanted to take a last look at the home he had loved before setting off to seek his fortune.

Vasilii had sat in the place of honor, with nephews and nieces hanging around his neck, while Maria made a special fuss over him, setting before him the best of everything she had to offer. Watching his sister-in-law's quick hands darting silently about the table, Vasilii Vasilievich could tell from their work-worn roughness what a price she had had to pay for the prosperity and hospitality of her husband's home. "You earn your keep all right, Maria Ilyinichna," he thought.

After the third round, Pyotr's father-in-law, Ilya Parfenich Makhotkin, who was beginning to show the effects of drink, engaged the guest in conversation.

"So you fought in the desert? How come you were shunted off out there? Or perhaps you'd left something behind? And now, you feel hard done by because you were put on the spot when you least expected it. And what if that Asiatic barbarian had come up here trying to lay down the law to us? You'd have offered him bread and salt, I daresay, instead of a bullet? It's always the same. You Lashkovs are missing a screw up there and a mighty important one at that. You're always scheming to make the whole world a beautiful place, and your own back garden is nothing but weeds. Why don't you start your beautifying in your own back yard? As it is, you're over-reaching yourselves; your arms aren't long enough . . ."

"Daddy . . ." Maria addressed him piteously, clasping her hands in entreaty. "Please don't, Daddy . . . He's had a hard journey. And he's been wounded. Please don't, Daddy."

Makhotkin suddenly softened, and smiled affectionately at his daughter. "All right, all right. Can't a workingman even have a joke anymore? You're like the Mother of God, always interceding. All right, all right. I won't say another word. Pour us another and let's make peace."

"Wait a minute, my dear father-in-law." Pyotr's long-fingered hand clamped down over the glass in front of him. "We can't make peace just yet. Let's get it clear first what you're driving at, and what program you stand for. According to you, the world revolution ought to ask your permission to go forward or stand still. Is that right?" Makhotkin was tense and angry again.

"Well, who should be asked? If it was made for me, I have to be asked. And so here's my reply—that's enough, cool off for a bit. Things haven't worked out. I don't want any more. It's done no good. Just a change of overseers, that's all. The last overseer, God rest him, at least knew his business. Now they're all like you, hoping to get by with a loud mouth. And they've found all these clever names for themselves. What used to be called a meddler is a Marxist nowadays. People who had their nostrils pulled out for armed robbery are now 'expropriators.' Any marketplace layabout is now one of the top dogs in the revolution. Me, I was squatting at the coalface before and that's where I am now, only I get paid three times less. There's such a plague of parasites like that that a man can't move."

He rose clumsily, and spoke more gently to his daughter. "I'm sorry for you, madam, you'll shrivel up, living with this old bastard, shrivel up and never once get a thank-you. None of my business though, you made your own choice. Good-bye then, you super-comrade commissars."

An uneasy silence set in after Makhotkin's departure and was broken only by Maria's sobs. It helped Vasilii understand exactly what had happened much more clearly than all that Pyotr proceeded to say in a bid for sympathy. He lectured him, rapidly and exhaustively, about the class struggle, proletarian solidarity, and revolutionary legality, but his brother's words touched no chord in Vasilii, awakened no response of any kind; the questions which Makhotkin had flung at him were those he had already asked himself out in the desert, with the youthful Turkmen's body sprawled on the ground in front of him. It was his turn to get up and make for the door.

"Maybe you're right, Pyotr. But we all have the same blood. It doesn't matter how much you shed, no good can come of it. Nothing but chaos and misery, misery it'll take us a thousand years to get over. Don't be angry with me, I want to go on my own way, like everyone else. I, for one, have had my fill of fighting."

Pyotr turned away sharply, indicating that he had no intention of pursuing the conversation. The world was henceforth to be divided into two halves—his own and his brother's.

Looking at his brother now, Vasilii Vasilievich felt neither malicious satisfaction nor resentment. If anything, he felt sorry for him, and sad himself. But the ruthless force now personified by Pyotr had trampled his life too painfully for him to muster any genuine feeling of connection to his guest. "You started the fight, pal, but we were the ones who got hit." Before he could stop himself, he was reproaching Pyotr with his own wretched and pointless existence, but, sensing no response, he subsided. "No good bringing up old scores. Anyhow, why blame him? In fact there's nobody to blame. The same madness got hold of us all."

To try and make up for his blunder, Vasilii Vasilievich suggested another drink, dashed off to the shop without waiting for an answer, and came back shortly with a bottle of red wine, to find his brother gone. The world went cold and dreary. "We weren't meant to come together, then. Have to put up with it, that's all. You'll die alone, Vasilii, my boy, all alone."

XXV

Grusha was buried in late autumn, when the first frost whitened the rooftops and the ground. The yard, hemmed in on all sides by the chilly sky, looked to Lashkov like a stone sack, with the coffin lid burning inside it like a yellow candle. It burnt softly, but proudly, and no power on earth could extinguish it.

Then, from the front door of the house, shadows floated out past the coffin lid like silent fishes. They floated over the yard in an endless unbroken stream. After the shadows, voices began to emerge from the entrance hall, but not even they could warm the cold well of the yard.

Grusha was carried out, and came to a standstill on the shoulders of the faceless bearers, right beside the coffin lid. From his window above them, Vasilii Vasilievich could see all of her, from head to foot; now she belonged to no one but herself. A ring of faces closed in on her. He recognized all of them. The old women, Tsygankova and Khramova, Ivan Lyovushkin and his Lyuba, Nikishkin with all his family, Meckler, and Fenya Goreva. They stood around her in silence and she seemed to rise above them and forgive them.

The silence grew tenser, stretching the nerves beyond endurance, until at last the string snapped. The Nikishkins' youngest daughter, Svetlana, burst into tears. This spark ignited the whole yard. Their heads rocked as they wept. But their weeping was not for her, for Grusha. People weep like that for the living, not for the dead. Lashkov felt— he knew—that they were finding a way to cry for their own pain, the same pain that he felt when he thought about his impending death, the pain of a soul in torment.

He found himself sharing their thoughts. "What have we found since we came here? Happiness? Hope? Faith? You there, Tsygankova, who lost everything? You, Lyovushkin? Where's your dentist son? You, mad Nikishkin? What did we bring here with us? Kindness? Warmth? Light? For whom? For Meckler? For Khramova? For Kozlov? No, we brought nothing, but we have lost everything. Why? Why? Every one of us had some good in him, and probably still has. Lyova knew what he was talking about. 'Weep, mankind, weep: There is great power contained in a tear.' "

Vasilii Vasilievich leaned out as far as he could, and suddenly caught sight of old Shokolinist in the depths of the yard, where Stabel's house had once been. There she stood, a tiny black figure moving her lips without a sound; gradually she began to grow larger and larger until she filled his whole field of vision and shut out the sky. He collapsed on the window ledge, and it is likely that the earth alone heard his dying gasp:

"Lo-o-o-o-ord . . ."

THURSDAY

Late Light

I

Vadim was taking a last look at the snow-sprinkled streets of Moscow and could not imagine himself ever coming back. He thought of his present progress to the Troitskaya Hospital, which all Muscovites know so well, as the last journey he would ever make. From this distance, the ill-famed Stolbovaya appeared to him to be a sort of dungeon from which there was no deliverance. "Oh, Lord," he thought miserably, "what have I done to deserve this?"

Out of town, the minibus twisted off the main road, and the cozy little houses of the Moscow dacha belt, with a crisscross of dirt roads between them, flashed past the window. The young man on the floor, a violent case bound hand and foot, was gradually coming round from his dose of drugs. He groaned painfully and started twitching all over. Foam appeared on his badly chewed lips, and his haunted, bloodshot eyes looked ready to jump out of their sockets.

Their escort was a little fellow in a leather jerkin that had seen better days. Life, and heavy smoking, had worn him to a frazzle. He spat lazily in front of his feet and spoke in a croaking voice.

"Look at him trying to turn himself inside out! Haven't had one like him to move for quite some time. Can't be long for this world if he's going to the Troitskaya."

These remarks confirmed Vadim's bitter supposition. "It's the end for you, Vadim Viktorovich, no two ways about it." His heart contracted in icy dread. Something gave way inside him and he felt faint. He felt rather than heard himself speaking.

"It's all up with me, is it, Pop?"

"What d'you expect?" No, this vicious slob in the leather jacket would give him nothing, not even a glimmer of hope.

"Just think where you're going. To Stolbovaya." He lingered over the name as though he enjoyed the taste of it.

Vadim made no further effort at conversation. What sense was there in torturing himself, in playing on his horror of the future? By way of self-punishment for his momentary weakness, he reeled off a silent string of obscenities, adding in conclusion, "Dirty filthy son of a bitch."

But his companion couldn't sit still and keep quiet; he was bursting with every vicious slob's sadistic longing to torment a fellow creature, to put the boot in.

"When medicines aren't any use, that's where they send them." He lingered over the name even more lovingly than before. "To Stolbovaya, I mean. There are heaps of them like that there. Stuffing themselves full, drinking, having all the women they want. Quite a party!"

He was a vicious, gloating husk of a man with nothing inside. The smell of his rotten teeth hovered in the back of the freezing minibus. "I know how I'd deal with them. Why should they clutter up the earth, when they're no use to anybody? There's a technique for that sort of thing nowadays—know what it is? They rock you to sleep as sweet as you please. One little prick—and that's the end of you."

Any more of that and Vadim would probably have assaulted him. The orderly, however, chose that moment to make an unexpected gesture of generosity and tossed down an almost full packet of cigarettes. "Have a smoke, pal, or you'll freeze completely."

"I don't smoke." Vadim's rage ebbed immediately. "Never caught the habit."

"You weren't in the war, of course, you're too young." The haggard face of the sadist in the leather jacket softened. "Sometimes when you're lying in a trench, the lice are giving you hell, you want a woman, and your knees are aching fit to crack, then you take a couple of drags and things don't seem so bad; you can carry on. What were you before?"

"Actor."

The leather jerkin creaked respectfully.

"You don't say! First time I've transferred an actor. Family turned you over to us, I suppose."

Vadim held his tongue, but the orderly saw from signs known only to himself that he had hit the mark, and he was so pleased with his own perspicacity that he became cheerfulness itself. "Got their greedy eyes on your property, I expect; so the snakes had you certified."

"I haven't any property, not a thing!"

"Well, someone's playing intrigues then," the orderly declared triumphantly and squinted slyly at Vadim to see what effect he had produced. "That's it, intrigues! So you'll be stuck into the Troitskaya, and there you'll stay. And the doctors in there are bribed, true as I'm telling you . . . "

He was obviously getting ready for a long speech, no less vicious than the first, but at that moment the minibus went over a bump and from then on it was one jolt after another. They had reached the end of the asphalt road, and a cart track was now visible outside the windows. The villas gave way to sturdy cottages with television aerials on their galvanized iron roofs. A halfhearted ground wind was slowly sweeping the snow into bellying drifts as they passed.

The long-haired young man began moaning and twitching again, and lurid spots appeared on his exhausted face. Vadim turned cold, and saw more clearly than ever what desperate straits he was in. "Might as well hang myself now as end up among people like that."

To his surprise, the escort also looked depressed; he quickly shifted his eyes to something outside the windows and quietly began to whistle "Russians Don't Want War" with startling virtuosity. Vadim realized at once that his viciousness sprang from stupidity and mental laziness rather than congenital malice, that life had gutted him long ago and turned him inside out, which was why he looked so tortured and empty now.

Vadim's fear was lessening, or, rather, was becoming part of his permanent condition, so that he almost ceased to be aware of it, and now that he was finally capable of ordinary everyday thought, all the events of the last few days began to form a single logical chain, an interlocking sequence.

On the night of his departure from Uzlovsk, when he had watched from his carriage window as the last light disappeared and the damp darkness pressed in against the glass, he had felt that the ground was giving way beneath his feet. His visit to his relatives, as he pictured it in his imagination, was to have released him from the isolation and spiritual loneliness in which he had felt trapped by fate almost from infancy. He had thought that through his grandfather and his aunt he would establish a direct, intimate contact with some part of the world outside himself, such as he had lacked all these years.

Even while he was wondering whether or not to turn up at Pyotr Vasilievich's house, Vadim had foreseen and indeed prepared himself for a letdown.

That in fact was the explanation of all his efforts, though he could scarcely stand upright, to make his grandfather happy, of his nervousness and his showing off at the table. It was all because he saw, sensed, that there was no real mutual affection, that the feeling of oneness with his family which had sprung up so suddenly would last only as far as the door. It was as though they were doomed to live on opposite sides of a triangle, and, when they met at its apex, to have neither the strength nor the will to stay there. He could, of course, make yet another attempt to tie up the loose ends, but the mere thought of anything so patently futile sickened him and provoked him to weary revulsion.

Vadim had been surrounded by strangers for almost as long as he could remember: friends who were strangers, girlfriends who were strangers, then a stranger-wife and her stranger-relatives. Whatever his connection or relationship with them, however vital their common concerns, none had ever become more than merely a friend, companion, wife, wife's relation. Their lives followed their own course, and were not inseparably harnessed to his.

Amid the excitement and distractions of a struggling actor's career, Vadim hadn't even given it a thought until he was thirty. But one evening in a dingy hotel room in Kazan he woke up with a heavy hangover and suddenly saw himself from outside: a small, lost, pathetic creature, of no concern to anybody in the whole world. He had curled up under the blankets, as he used to do in the orphanage, and wept—no, not wept, but howled like an unwanted and abandoned dog. The dread left in him after that night in Kazan was what had driven Vadim to the home he had almost forgotten, where for so many years no one had expected ever to see him, and where after all he found no solace. A note was waiting for him back home in Moscow: "I am at Mother's. Give me a call when you get in." There was a time when every new lie she told had brought on an attack of impotent rage, but now he could think over the naive system of mutual protection used by his wife and his mother-in-law with no more than a grimace of contempt. What fools!

Vadim had married casually, and to his own surprise. He was racketing around with a very mixed bag of people and somewhere in the crush, through a drunken haze, he had become vividly aware of two moist, almond-colored eyes, the only ones in the world for him, or so it seemed for the moment. In the morning she had buried her head on his shoulder and implored him, sobbing convulsively, not to abandon her for a while at least, so that it would be easier to explain to her mother why she had stayed out for the first time in her life. He had put up only a brief resistance. "After all, why not?" he thought. Since then, tears had been her weapon against him. With tears she had forced him to marry her, with tears she did penance for her somewhat more than fleeting infidelities, tears were her solvent for their frequent quarrels and sulks. Sometimes Vadim couldn't take any more, and started packing the bare essentials for a bachelor existence. But as soon as he took hold of the doorknob an outburst of tearful hysterics would fill him with contemptuous pity, reducing him to helplessness and weary surrender.

Vadim could not be jealous of his wife because he had never loved her. But he was maddened by the triumphant little smiles of their friends and acquaintances with whom she flirted. They were usually trivial, trashy people. The more of a nonentity his latest rival was, the more ruthlessly did Vadim curse his own weakness. But this would be followed by a tempestuous scene and it would all begin again.

This time, as he carelessly pushed his wife's note aside with the edge of his hand, Vadim didn't even bother to ask himself why she had left it. By now, any explanation seemed to him so trifling, so insignificant that, remembering his attacks of suffocating rage on other similar occasions, he was amazed to think that he had once been so acutely sensitive.

"My God, how idiotic the whole thing is, after all!"

At that moment he was aware only of a dizzying emptiness, an unbearable burning nausea, which rendered everything else tedious, fatuous, pointless. He felt like a man who has struggled to the middle of a narrow pole stretched over an abyss and has neither the breath nor the will to go on. Nothing that was happening on either side of him could possibly interest him at that moment. To perish, he had only to look down, into himself, that is. He could not resist the temptation. He looked.

The key to his private heaven turned so easily, so unresistingly . . .

Vadim lay on a couch, put his hands behind his head, and blissfully let his eyes close. He didn't fall suddenly, but rather almost seemed to hover. At first there was a faint, perhaps slightly sickly odor of gas, then a delicious dizziness, like being on the merry-go-round at Sokolniki when he was a boy, and finally blissful oblivion, like when he was drunk, only more complete and surprising.

The first thing he felt when he realized that he was looking at a hospital ceiling overhead was shame. A numbing, stifling shame that almost made him vomit. He tried to struggle out of his bonds, but he was so firmly bound to his bed that he cried out in an agony of humiliated helplessness, and he was never silent again. He yelled incessantly for days and nights on end, yelled to deafen his self-loathing, and by the time he fell silent his fate had been decided. He featured in reports and records as a serious case.

Now he was being taken by ambulance to an out-of-town hospital, and a sour-tempered orderly in a leather jacket was whistling "Russians Don't Want War" to himself. Whistling it with extraordinary vehemence as though he really wanted to convince some invisible listener that Russians wanted no such thing. The minibus slowly mounted a hill and made a sharp turn. Through the curtain of snow which was now falling much more heavily, Vadim made out a squat barracks-like block with many auxiliary buildings and outhouses dimly discernible around it. Windows barred with gratings like sightless eyes absorbed in the diffuse light of a snowy day without releasing a sound or a glimmer to the world outside. The orderly came to life at once and busied himself.

"Right, boy, you're home. Out you get. I'll turn you over officially and then you go to your ward and get your head down. Eat and sleep, that's the only work you have to do here. I'm really jealous." You could see he wasn't lying. He really was envious, and he flushed with emotion at the thought of Vadim's bright future. "As God is my judge, I am. Come on, walk in front. They'll pick him up"—he nodded briefly over his shoulder—"later on."

In the reception hall the orderly's manner showed that he was quite at home here. He went around from room to room, opening and shutting the doors with his own key and pestering everybody loudly; when he finally got his receipt he said a sentimental good-bye to Vadim.

"It's a strange life, pal. A soldier dies, but the fight goes on . . . What does it matter where you live, as long as you eat? You're young yet." He bit his already puffy lips in sympathy, and generously delivered himself of a few more pearls of wisdom. "You know what they say—no money, no misery. Don't give up! You can live and learn, and still die a fool. We all have our day. The higher you climb, the harder you fall. Like the song says—'Come, golden freedom, come to me, find shelter in my welcoming heart.' "

He started pulling his cigarettes out of his pocket, but obviously remembering that Vadim did not smoke, he stuffed them back in again, made a gesture of defeat, whisked gaily to the exit and was gone. The felt-lined door closed with a gentle thud behind him. The last thread connecting Vadim, however tenuously, with that other world had snapped and he was alone in a new one.

When they took Vadim into the house physician's room the doctor was busy studying his case notes. He did not even look around, but nodded silently at a chair somewhere near the desk and went on with what he was doing. This beaky profile of his swarthy face stood out sharply against the whiteness outside the window and made the snowy January day seem all the more unfriendly.

Reading somebody else's life history evidently gave him considerable pleasure. He kept returning to pages he had already scanned, occasionally using his fountain pen to scribble something in a notebook which lay open at his elbow, and making a succession of reflective and portentous little coughing noises. He finally snapped the looseleaf binder shut, having carefully smoothed out its pages, pushed the dossier aside, and turned to Vadim, introducing himself in a friendly voice.

"My name is Pyotr Petrovich."

"Lashkov." Vadim choked on his words. The doctor's face was even stranger than he had thought, narrow, all nose, with slant eyes so wide apart that he could observe the person he was talking to without turning his head. "Vadim Viktorich."

"Yes, Vadim Viktorovich, yes." He spoke gently, insinuatingly, as though he assumed his patient to be seriously ill and dangerous, and was letting it be known that he, Pyotr Petrovich, was personally ready for any surprise. "I am most pleased to meet you, Vadim Viktorovich."

But as he realized in the course of conversation that the person in front of him was of sound mind, and had no problem with his memory, the doctor's birdlike eye dimmed, his comments became perfunctory, and his movements slack, almost mechanical. His sharp face began to look more and more injured. He seemed to be sincerely grieving for the whole panel of Moscow psychiatrists, who, instead of a full-blown schizophrenic with aggressive tendencies, had sent him some common, ordinary idiot without a delirious dream or deviation to his name.

In the end, the doctor, frankly ignoring his patient's account of what had happened, called plaintively in the direction of the door: "Nyura!"

A tall, bony old woman in embroidered felt boots appeared immediately in the doorway, bore down on Vadim, brought him to his feet with an imperious jerk of the head, opened a door for him with her own key, and propelled him gently into the ward.

II

It was only on the following day, with all the upset of admission and a half-feverish night in an unfamiliar place behind him, that Vadim took a proper look around. This section consisted of a broad corridor with low vaulted wards to either side. The corridor ran down the middle of an enormous square hall with pillars, so that communication between wards was easy and continuous. One ward was fitted up as a dining room, and served between meals as a somewhat rowdy club. In it, inmates furiously played all known table games, discussed their chances of being discharged, and, in passing, debated problems both of national and of global dimensions.

Vadim tried to join in the general hubbub, but he was obviously not fully accepted as yet, and could find nobody to talk to. He went back to his own ward after a minute, without any feeling of hurt or resentment. The patient in the next bed—a dark man with a shaven head, and a massive, jutting chin—raised damp eyes the color of pine tar to look at him, smiled in a friendly way, and buried himself again in the shiny exercise book which he was filling with his small, rapid writing.

As soon as Vadim lay down, troubled scenes from his recent past crowded in on him. First he dreamed that he was assembling a team from the Yakutsk Philharmonic and Vlasov was withholding his approval; then his mother-in-law, Alexandra Yakovlevna, appeared, accusing him of all the mortal sins, and harping endlessly on her daughter's ruined life; then his grandfather was sitting at his feet, wagging his head in silent reproof as he looked at his ne'er-do-well grandson . . .

Somebody was shaking him roughly.

"Come on, now, boy. Wake up, pal!"

A blurred face appeared before Vadim's sleepy eyes. It became clearer and clearer until at last it was one big incredulous smile: don't you recognize me, pal? The whole appearance of the man sitting opposite Vadim was that of someone who had knocked about the world and learned its tricks. Wherever you met him, on board ship, at a bus station, or on some railway platform, you would immediately have identified him as one of the restless, anarchic breed of incurable wanderers. Their most obvious symptom is a suppressed agitation, a fitful excitability, which makes them seem insecure and reckless all at once. It is as if they are sliding down a mountain; the descent may be thrilling, but it ends in a dense fog which hides all the trails; not even the devil who gave them the first push can see what lies beyond. With the frenzied look of a gambler who will stake everything on the next card, they roam the endless roads of this enormous country. Relegate any one of them to any godforsaken hole, to the back of beyond, to a desert which would offend even a camel, and the poor devil will sweat blood until he wins himself a place in the sun. And as soon as he wins it he will leave it to go somewhere else. Because he is already obsessed with the idea that there are better places, where he knows for certain that a life really worthy of his talents is awaiting him. Such people drift from one end of our great country to the other, always searching for a better existence, and a better one after that. And suddenly they are old. And God alone knows where that better existence is to be found.

As Vadim now gazed at his unexpected companion, the broad,

shaggy-browed face began to detach itself in his memory from all the intervening faces and voices, and the first words the man spoke suddenly fixed his recollection.

When Vadim got back to the hostel after an hour's pushing and shoving in the payroll line there was pandemonium. The plasterers and painters were drinking their advance pay. Mityai Telegin, a gap-toothed man in a dark blue satin shirt open at the neck, was glaring around from under his ferocious eyebrows, and struggling to make himself heard above the drunken hubbub.

"I come in and I tell him: I'll use any shade you like. You can have it just sized, or gloss paint, or if you want I'll give you oak graining like your mother never saw. I'm no slouch at plastering, either. I'll produce something that'll make your mouth water. 'So why d'you give me nothing but digging, you son of a bitch,' I ask him, 'instead of giving me a chance to show what I can do?' You know what he says to me? 'You got a hundred and fifty rubles' travel money, didn't you?' 'Yes,' says I. 'Right,' he says. 'Work it off on the job you were told to do. Talk about fulfilling the plan,' he says, 'if you all start kicking over the traces I'll be in the gutter.' "

His miserable eyes searched the faces around him for sympathy, but they were all busy with their own conversations and only listening with half an ear. The painter waved his hand helplessly—what's the good of talking to you birds—and passed between the rows of beds on his way to the door, yelling at the top of his voice as he went.

"That rat of an agent promised us a gold mine, and it works out at seventy rubles per head, and that's it. Just try eliminating eighteen cubic feet, it'll break your heart! That's what you get when you try to earn a bit! And the folks back on the farm write and say the roof's leaking. What am I supposed to mend it with? My pants? I've never known such a hopeless mess . . ."

As Mityai wended his way to the door from the other end of the barracks, where several ex-convicts had set their beds apart from the rest, a raucous choir bawled out its own words to the tune of "Two guitars beyond the wall, dolefully complaining."

> "Uncle Vanya grabbed his wheezing
>   Accordion in a merry mood,
>   Struck up in the prison precinct,
>   And they shot him where he stood."

There was no hope of rest that night. Vadim went out, paused at the door, looked around, then made resolutely for the open field. The site of the new gas works, with the barracks huts sticking out like advance posts, bordered on kolkhoz land; the scent of drying hay and wormwood reached him. The smells of earth as yet untouched by earth-moving machines competed with the hot reek of tar and the harsh tang of lime on the site.

Vadim lay face down in the first haystack he came to, and was plunged into a different world, like that which he had so recently lost. He had grown up in remote and inhospitable southern Bashkir, and the congestion of roads, buildings, and people in these parts depressed him, provoking an irritation and a bitterness which he did not understand himself. In the orphanage, and later on in the factory school, he had imagined his future adult life as something quite different from this. In the stories of his more experienced contemporaries this part of the world was portrayed as a promised land, where the visitor from beyond the Urals would find a million opportunities to shake off the wearisome monotony of the steppes as if it were a bad dream. But reality dispelled his illusions. When he was sent to the gas works site he found himself among people who had come together from all ends of the country, and who had but one thing in common—a desire to earn their fare home. Nobody's trade was mentioned in his employment agreement: the recruit might demand work that corresponded to his qualifications, and that wouldn't suit the hiring agency. So Vadim, with his Grade Five rating, had to consider himself lucky when he was signed up as a plasterer's assistant. Even though he didn't drink, it was a rare week when he made ends meet. But it wasn't really the shortage of money that oppressed him—he hadn't spent his young life in the lap of luxury—so much as the soul-destroying unrest which subjected him daily to the pull of utter chaos, never giving him a chance to draw breath or to find his feet in his new surroudings. Now, as he lay in the mound of July hay, Vadim recalled with bitter-sweet longing the cold Bashkir steppe, with its faded colors and its short summer, which he had once abandoned without regret. All the things which up until then had seemed boring and dreary—the long winter nights, the chilly winds in autumn, the emptiness—now began to seem awesome, mysterious, significant.

There was a rustling in the grass nearby.

"Somebody catching up on his sleep here?" Vadim recognized Telegin's voice without having to turn around. "Mind if I join you? It's you, Vadka, isn't it?"

Vadim didn't answer. He would have preferred solitude just then, but Telegin sat down beside him all the same, struck a match, and inhaled.

"Look around—there's everything the heart could desire." His words came out in a stream, but were quite lucid, even gentle. "The crops rustling, all sorts of creatures chirring and chirruping. The earth resting. And in the middle of it all, drunken men farting about, fouling the place up like so much shit. It's enough to make you retch. It's so bad you can't even cuss about it. Wish I were back in my village now. Get up before it's even light, clear my head with a drink of kvass, put my scythe on my shoulder . . ."

"Well, what's the problem?"

"What's the problem? Only a little mark in my passport to say I'm contracted to do this job. Can't very well barge in on the chairman with that stamped in my book. He'd send me straight off to district head-quarters."

"Shouldn't have got yourself into it." Vadim was deliberately rough, hoping to get rid of him. "You're always looking for a bigger ruble."

Telegin squirmed indignantly. "Listen, pal, it'd take a ruble a mile long to patch up half the holes I have to worry about. They haven't printed one big enough yet. What's the sense of sitting at home, though? All you earn on the kolkhoz is fair words and fat promises. You've only got your own plot of land to live on. How long d'you think you can live on that? So of course a man wanders off elsewhere trying to earn a bit of money, even if it's not much . . . In fact, it's so little you're ashamed to mention it."

"You never stop drinking."

"All right, you don't drink, so how much do you have put away in the savings bank? You see? Whether you drink or not, you don't have a damn thing in your pocket. So you might as well try and enjoy life."

"Some enjoyment. Three went off in the ambulance last payday"

"They're pretty backward," said Mityai with a deprecating sigh. "When they drink, all their bad feelings come out. So they start knifing each other. It's a bit of a shock till you get used to it, of course . . . Where d'you come from yourself?"

"Bashkir."

"Oh, you're a long way from home! It's all sort of steppes out there, isn't it?"

"Yes, sort of," Vadim echoed, and repeated more gently—"sort of."

"Long nights, from what they say."

"Long nights and long days."

"Lots of cattle . . . and oil as well."

"No shortage of either."

"Marvelous, isn't it?"

"What is?"

"What a damn great place Russia is. In Tula province, where I come from, you'll hardly ever come across a hare . . . All the fish gone as well . . . exterminated . . . The lot. Well, you might catch a baby occasionally, but nothing worthwhile; not on your life."

"If you're fed up, buy a ticket and head for my part of the country. There's no end of that sort of thing out there."

"Costs so much just to get there, though. You can spend all you've got and it's still not enough . . . I've got kids . . . six of 'em . . . But it would be nice," he admitted dreamily.

Telegin's wistful words were an echo of Vadim's own nostalgia and drew a sympathetic reply.

"We've got wide open spaces out there. One hundred miles there is like a single train stop here."

"You mean it?"

"The people are open as well—good people."

"Really?"

"And it's quiet everywhere."

"You don't mean it!"

And here was Mityai today, still solemnly shaking his head as though he were continuing that previous conversation.

"You don't mean it! . . . I was looking at you, and I was sure I knew you . . . All these years, but I recognized you just the same!" He was childishly delighted at their meeting and fidgeted excitedly on the next bed, nudging Vadim from time to time, inviting him to join in his exultation. "I haven't drunk myself into a total stupor; I've still got a bit of memory left! How time flies . . . I've had a few knocks, I can tell you . . . Ever since I left the village I've been measuring the length and breadth of the Union on foot . . . The old lady died before the money reform, and the kids gradually got married and went off; there's no knowing where they are now . . . Nor worth knowing either, they've forgotten me anyway . . . I just sign up for job after job, it's like selling myself into slavery over and over again . . . I ended up in here because of something I did when I'd had a drink." His embarrassment was so acute that sweat appeared on his forehead. "I picked up a good deal of money, in Tyumen, on the oilfield, and I drank a lot of it in the station bar on the way through. . . . So I hit a man, without thinking. . . ." Telegin carefully steered the conversation into a different channel. "Ever heard about Tyumen? You can earn three hundred there, just doing manual labor. . . ."

Two years ago, seduced by the crazy money he had been offered, along with star billing, Vadim had joined a scratch troupe and toured the marshes beyond the Irtysh, by the light of the well-head flares. The workers' clubs were little wooden boxes bursting with earsplitting obscenities and alcoholic fumes. Each day in the filthy, unheated hotels was twenty-four hours of bedlam. The roads were forever under repair. Later on, when he was resting in the Crimea, the mere mention of that tour was enough to send a piercing chill through him. So while he listened to Telegin's tales of a land flowing with milk and honey, Vadim could imagine precisely what had reduced him to alcoholic savagery. "It's a wonder he didn't turn into an animal in that hellhole and lose all power of speech!"

They went on talking till dinnertime, or, rather, Telegin talked and Vadim just listened, but he found Mityai's monologue so absorbing that he ended up feeling as if he too had been reminiscing uninterruptedly.

When Telegin went away, the man in the next bed, who had been silently occupied until then, tore himself away from his exercise book, pushed it under his pillow, rose, and held out a skinny, hairy hand to Vadim.

"I'm Mark. Kreps. Producer. Let's go and eat."

His neighbor's cheerful, laconic friendliness was disarming, and Vadim felt a corresponding glow of trust and liking for this new acquaintance. "Seems a bit odd, but a nice guy, and his smile is dazzling."

III

Heavy clouds of tobacco smoke hung one above the other in the entrance to the lavatories, turning faces into a blur. Vadim was surprised to realize that he had started smoking. One day he had mechanically accepted the cigarette which Mark offered him, inhaled uncertainly, then, when he realized what he was doing, decided to brazen it out and finish the thing. Since then he had become an habitué of the hall outside the latrines. He smoked almost incessantly, with a sort of manic enjoyment, as though he were anxious to make up for all the cigarettes he had missed in the preceding thirty years. Tobacco smoke gave him a feeling of wry fatalism, and reality looked less empty and hopeless each time he inhaled.

Two old men next to him were slowly stupefying themselves with stale "Ocean Breakers," and haggling about an overcoat. The overcoat existed somewhere out there, in the other world, and it looked very much as though neither of them would ever wear it, but each was confident that he would shortly be discharged and defended his interests with absolute passion.

"It's got a padded lining, prewar quality." The bristling gray brows met over the faded eyes in an imposing frown. "You'd have another twenty years' wear out of it. Just get on a Number Eleven, go straight to Cherkizov Street and ask for Gavrik's Passage. House Number Four. Everybody on the yard knows me. To you I'll let it go at sixty-five. Dirt cheap. You can't lose."

"Have to think about that for a bit. Six-and-a-half bills is a lot of money! For six-and-a-half you can buy a new one nowadays, nice as you like. Six-and-a-half is sheer robbery. Take six and don't complain. I'll have to waste at least a ruble getting to your place. . . ."

Kreps's gentle face suddenly appeared facing Vadim against the whitened window.

"Smoking?"

"Can't sleep."

During his few weeks here Vadim had learned all or nearly all there was to know about Kreps. From the theater where he had unsuccessfully tried to put on the plays he wanted to produce, and in the style he thought best, and where he had had one scene too many in the Repertory Administration, he had been committed for psychiatric examination, and had never returned. The melancholy incomprehension with which the ex-producer reacted to everything that had happened to him—incomprehension in the face of invincible ignorance—awakened solicitous, protective feelings in Vadim.

He smiled into Kreps's sad eyes, dimly visible through the smoke. "Still thinking? Feeling haunted again?"

Kreps's angular profile stood out sharply against the dead glare coming through the window. "We are so constructed, Vadya, that we dare not stop thinking. The conscious layer that surrounds our brains is very thin, and beneath it lies the abyss. A man has only to stop for a single moment, to interrupt his train of thought, however trivial, and his consciousness will storm the breach and be lost in the abyss. That's how madness begins. But it doesn't happen very often. Our instinct for self-preservation does not permit it. So we keep on thinking. It doesn't matter about what. It can be about the theory of relativity, or about bonuses. The main thing is to avoid a breach. Our safety lies in continuity."

"What are you writing about all the time, Mark? That's to say, if it isn't a secret."

"About why man suffers innate feelings of guilt."

"Can you make it a bit clearer?"

"How can I explain it, Vadya . . . In my childhood, the first time I was taken for a Jew I went home and asked my father, 'Am I really a Jew?' 'Yes, my boy,' he answered, 'you're a Jew.' Now I was perfectly well aware that my father was a pure-blooded German and my mother Armenian. When I asked him many years later what he had meant by it, he said something like this: 'That was something you had to go through to become a human being. A human being, understand?' And I understood, once and for all, that for as long as you are capable of feeling personal guilt toward other people, no one can turn you into a pig . . . Well, that's roughly what I'm working on in my notes. Putting it in a simplified way. Let's try and get to sleep, Vadya, maybe we'll be lucky this time."

"I'll smoke for a bit longer."

"Be careful . . ."

Vadim envied Kreps and people like him. Envied, whenever he met them, their belief in a rational universe, their wisdom and sense of purpose, in fact, envied them all that they had and that he himself had been aware for some time that he lacked. The drunken chaos of his youth had been followed the morning after by the pains of maturity and Vadim had stood back and seen himself as he really was: a casually employed variety artist, thirty-five years old, prematurely aged by debauchery. His fellow students at the Theatrical Training School already had positions in famous companies, were dazzlingly accomplished and successful, while he was still rushing around the country with scratch troupes, chasing the big money, postponing his serious work for the future. Vadim knew for sure by now that "the future" had already passed him by, that he could do nothing to alter his destiny, and, worst of all, that he had been engaged all this time in something that meant nothing to him.

"Can't you sleep?" Vadim knew that persistent insomnia was reducing Kreps to total exhaustion, and, as always, offered to share his suffering.

"Have a smoke. Maybe you'll drop off afterwards."

"It's no use."

"Have you tried?"

"It doesn't help."

Mark's equable friendliness tempted Vadim to speak his mind.

"I keep wanting to ask you something, only promise you'll give it to me straight."

"I'll try."

"If you got a theater would you take me on?"

"You want the truth?"

"Let's have it."

"Well, I wouldn't."

"Thank you for being frank . . . Now we understand each other."

"It's like this, you see." Kreps gently touched him on the shoulder with the tips of his fingers, as though apologizing for his enforced candor. "You're too sorry for yourself. In my theater"—he placed a heavy emphasis on the "my"— "the actor must be sensitive to the sorrows of others, and think of himself last . . . or, rather, not at all . . . The aim of art, it seems to me, is to give yourself, not to assert yourself . . . You, Vadya, are probably a first-class actor in the ordinary sense . . . but what I shall be needing is not so much actors as thinkers, sufferers even . . ."

"Teach me, then!"

"It can't be taught, it either comes by itself or it doesn't come at all."

"What must I do to make it come?"

"You must achieve peace of mind."

"I haven't the time."

"Time is neither here nor there."

"What is here or there, then?"

"The heart, probably."

"The heart hasn't time, either."

"So stop complaining."

"Go to hell . . ."

"Everything has to be paid for, Vadya. You want to have your revelations for nothing, but they have to be paid for, often with everything you have. It's a choice—either the magic crystal, or savings in the bank. Any combination of the two is out of the question. I'm sorry, but you yourself . . ."

"Carry on, carry on."

Vadim wagged his head magnanimously, though he felt his patronizing indifference give way to a keen distress, which he couldn't yet explain.

"There's quite a touch of the beautiful savage in you. And that's what will save you in the last resort."

"It's too late. I'm thirty-five now."

"Savages like you are children all their lives. Just think, at any moment you can start all over again."

"Start my life over again as well?"

"Of course! You can exist for a lifetime without adding a year to your age, and you can live through a year which contains the experiences of a lifetime. You just have to shake off petty preoccupations and spiritual laziness."

"How?"

"On that point, no advice is worth anything. Everybody finds himself in his own way."

"How did you do it, for instance?"

"Look, Vadya, there's a little parable that goes like this. Two men were walking through a wood. They'd been walking for a long time. At last, one of them couldn't stand it anymore. 'We're lost,' he shouted. The other calmed him down. 'Let's go on. I know the way; I'll bring you out.' The first man believed him and went with him. They walked and walked, and in the end they did get out . . . Then the first one thought to ask: 'If you knew the way, why were we wandering about for such a time?' and the second one answered, 'It's less important to know the way than to keep going.' "

"In short, you don't know yourself?"

When he was embarrassed, Kreps's smile seemed more guilty and pleading than ever.

"No, Vadya, I don't know . . . Keep going, that's all the advice I can give you."

"There's no way out of my wood."

"It's best to keep going all the same."

"If only there were somewhere to go . . ."

Two silent figures, their silhouettes blurred by the dim ceiling light in the corridor, were mirrored briefly in the window. Then one of them vanished into the smoke. Vadim, left alone, summed up his feelings sadly but without rancor.

"There's nowhere to go, Mark, my old buddy, and nothing to go for."

IV

Saturday was visiting day. A nervous expectancy dominated the wards from early morning on. The remains of last week's parcels were tipped out of provision sacks, the week's growth of beard was shaved off under the supervision of ward orderlies, soiled pajamas were freshened up as much as possible. Everybody, even those who never had visitors, wanted to look smart and alert on this one day.

The ward sister, Nyura (or "The Doormat," as the old hands called her), plodded around the department in her famous outsized felt boots, while her slack jaw shook and she urged them on with little cries.

"Move, boys, move! Straighten up those beds. Let's make it look more like a sanatorium! Everthing out of your lockers! Take a little walk to the latrines, then off to see your visitors! And no more talking."

To begin with, Vadim had secret hopes that the duty orderly would call his name someday, but one Saturday after another went by and none of his friends put in an appearance. After a while he stopped expecting anyone. Life was giving him an illustration of the precariousness of drinking friendships. As for his wife, the last ties between them had been broken long ago. By refusing to take Vadim home from the hospital she had put an end to their brief and—for both of them—incomprehensible liaison.

So when he heard his name one day echoing loudly through the wards Vadim's heart sank. "Who the devil can it be? Why can't they leave me alone once and for all?"

Along with the others he was conducted through the long corridors to a dimly lit, vaulted room where the first visitors had already taken their places at the square tables, each of which could accommodate four people.

Before Vadim had time to look around, somebody at a table in the far corner rose and came to meet him, swaying slightly as he walked. It was his old friend and drinking companion, Fedya Moroz.

"Hallo, old friend!" The bulging eyes with their drunken squint were moist with affection. He lolled awkwardly against Vadim. "What d'you think you're doing, Vadya, eh? Didn't even let me know. Did you lose faith in me as well? I'm your friend, aren't I?"

Although Vadim could recognize Fedya's drunken effusions as such, his heart beat more easily and the world became a larger place. Not everyone had forgotten him, then; some of them remembered.

He and Fedya Moroz had met by chance at a soirée given by the Theater School for students of the Literary Institute. Moroz, along with others in his class, had recited his own poetry. Vadim had not found it especially attractive—it was just verses, neither good nor bad, passable run-of-the-mill stuff—but there was something reassuring and appealing about the big-browed young man with the clean-shaven skull, about the way he held himself, with his fists clenched in the pockets of his antiquated jacket, and his legs wide apart, his head thrust forward like a boxer.

They had spent the rest of the night roaming side streets around the Arbat, while Fedya, between poems, told Vadim the brief but colorful story of his life.

He had been orphaned as a child and enrolled in a Seaman's School, from which he went off on his round-the-world voyage. He sailed in tramp steamers for two years, seeing the continents and their peoples. Smitten by literature when he was still a child, the boy had spent the hours between watches filling notebooks with crabbed rehashes of Kipling and Bagritsky. Without any real hope he had enclosed them with an application to the Literary Institute, and to his own surprise was accepted.

"So you see, I let myself in for it!" Fyodor had said, finishing his confession with a sideways glance out of round eyes that shone with innocent high spirits. And he went on to declaim:

> "We defy the gales that rage around us.
> Clench our fists and brave the storm again.
> Rats may rush to leave the ship that founders.
> But those are rats, and not seafaring men!"

To begin with, they met only casually, but each time they became a little closer, and soon it was difficult for them to live without each other.

Success came to Fyodor quickly, but not permanently. His verses were much sought after by publishers. He was besieged with offers of the most flattering kind. But as he became more popular and better known, as his name appeared more and more frequently on the mastheads, his face, once so round and good-natured, became sharp and peaky and dark circles formed under his eyes. He drank himself into a stupor with increasing frequency until it became a disease and ruined him. His friends and companions gradually fell away. One by one, they all deserted him, and Fyodor found himself alone.

For weeks on end he sprawled on his camp bed, inert, expressionless, getting up only to drink and then lie down again. He was delirious, but occasionally his agony would break through his ravings in some less incoherent form.

"It's all wrong, Vadya, the words are wrong . . . I didn't have the talisman after all . . . You know . . . the one that makes you get up one day and announce quite simply, 'Evil at last had palled on him.' Palled on him! What d'you think of that, eh? Those little ensigns could express themselves! No, it's not all nonsense. Pour me one, old friend, and don't lecture me. I'm not one of those specimens at the club . . ."

Gradually his flow of work dried up, and he ended up by writing nothing. He translated a few things, published some of his old cast-offs, earned a bit extra on the quiet by writing material for variety performers and doing advertising copy. They had met infrequently in the last few years. When they did meet they had nothing to say, and each of them, preoccupied with his own affairs, promptly forgot the other. So Vadim, as he listened to his visitor now, was embarrassed, and blamed himself that they had become such strangers lately.

Meanwhile Moroz was visibly sobering up and pulling himself together.

"You see, Vadya," he said, "we are being made to pay for something. For some grave sin. Inside us there is a vacuum. One that neither drink nor anger can fill. We are being stifled inside. That's why nothing we do turns out right. One or another of us manages to utter a cry occasionally, but nothing that will echo down the ages. So we all have our ways of sublimating—women, being a busybody, denunciations . . ."

Vadim, while listening to him with half an ear, kept glancing at the next table. There sat a neat little old man, with a sparse and apparently radiant halo of fluffy gray hair round his pink dome; he had noticed him fleetingly in the labyrinth of the neighboring wards. With him was a girl of twenty or twenty-two, wearing a greenish lightweight autumn coat. The girl was holding the old man's swollen hand between her thin fingers and their conversation was obviously intimate and affectionate. She had a fresh face, unmarked as yet by lines of care, but when sometimes he made her smile, her narrow, rather close-set eyes sparkled mischievously and her face revealed her inner calm and strength. Once or twice the girl caught Vadim staring at her, froze for a moment, then set her chin stubbornly, shook off the spell, and looked away.

Vadim nodded mechanically in time to Fedya's words but scarcely heard him; he was terrified lest he let slip, lest he destroy his tremulous, mounting presentiment of some wonderful change that was soon to come in his life.

"No, I didn't have the magic talisman after all, Vadya." Moroz by now was oblivious to his surroundings, and talking to himself rather than to Vadim.

"And why dirty paper needlessly? There are plenty doing that already . . . I'm better off writing one-liners for comedy teams. At least my conscience doesn't trouble me." He grinned mirthlessly into space. "Shall I tell you a little story?" He glanced absently around the room, and didn't wait for an answer. "In the hungriest year of them all, an important member of the literary élite met an old poetess in a state of absolute penury. So out of the goodness of his heart, he made a gesture in keeping with his lofty position, by giving her his personal permit that granted admittance to a canteen of the very highest quality. Take it, make good use of it, and bless me till the day I die! Of course, he obtained another for himself. After a suitable interval the benefactor met the old woman again. 'Ksyusha,' he said, 'what d'you mean by it? I haven't seen you once in our canteen!' 'My dear,' she answered, 'the ceilings there are so vulgar!' That was in forty-two, Vadya, forty-two, mind you . . . I suppose that's why she was able to write like that . . . She lived with inner calm, in harmony with herself. Hers was the world of light, and we all dwell in darkness. Our own darkness is consuming us. Hey—why do I keep telling you all these fairy stories?" he said, suddenly livening up and smiling apologetically. It obviously gave him enormous satisfaction to lay his modest gifts before Vadim. "Don't turn your nose up, pal, I've been round these establishments in my time. You don't need delicacies—what you want is sausage, sugar, something to smoke, and plenty of it—that's the main thing. And here"—with a conspiratorial wink—"are some biscuits to go with your tea. Mind you don't drop them, or they'll run out."

The biscuit box, as Vadim immediately ascertained, held two full bottles. Showing a proper appreciation of his friend's selflessness, he gasped in surprise.

"You're too generous!"

Praise to Fyodor was sweeter than manna from heaven. "We have to live somehow, Vadya! In a dog's life like this, if you don't drink you'll worry yourself to death. Vadya, Vadya, life's getting worse all the time.

Can't alter it now." He rose suddenly and was in a hurry to be off. "I'll stop somewhere along the road and have a couple. So long, Vadya, look after yourself. Hope I haven't upset you in any way!"

They gave each other a slight hug for convention's sake, then Fedya disengaged himself limply from Vadim's embrace and moved toward the exit. Relief, as well as fatigue, was to be read in his suddenly hunched shoulders, his walk, the droop of his head. He appeared again, his slouched back dimly visible in the corridor, until it was blotted out by the light. Vadim, touched with gratitude, said a regretful and compassionate farewell. "He's breaking down, breaking down fast."

As he went past the next table Vadim darted a quick look at the girl; his heart thumped as he noticed that his attention was returned, and, even when he followed the orderly out into the corridor, he could not suppress the flush of nervous excitement which swept over him.

Later on, when he was sitting with Kreps and Telegin in the space between two corner beds, finishing off the liquor Fedya had brought, the mere thought of her sent him into a joyful reverie, through which drunken Mityai's unsteady voice somehow penetrated his consciousness.

"You call this frost? It's just a joke. The frosts in Igarka are really something, I can tell you. Forty-five below zero. It cuts you to the quick. But I was strong then, and I could take it . . . Nowadays I can freeze just sitting by a ventilator . . . My engine's dying. I shan't keep going much longer. The earth's calling. One thing vexes me: I'll be buried in a strange place. No cross on my grave, nobody to remember me . . . I've got nobody and nothing . . . no kennel and no chain . . . and my ruble a mile long is still up in the clouds somewhere. Who are these creditors whom I never seem to finish paying? Lord, my poor heart's jumping! Like a sheep's tail." He thrust his hand under his shirt and started carefully massaging the left side of his chest. "I'll go and lie down . . . *Merci* for the hospitality . . . I don't feel too well . . ."

Mityai walked unsteadily away, scarcely able to drag one foot after the other. His bloodless face, with its gray stubble, was wasted by disease. It was obvious that he was near the end of his strength, and that for him the only way out of this place led to the hospital cemetery.

"There you are, you see, Vadya." Mark's hairy hands shook very slightly as he poured the last drops into their mugs. "They removed the Russian peasant's soul and offered him nothing in its place except drink. So there he is, the Russian peasant, burning inside with a blue flame. All our crackpot Russian reformers, like Peter and his Marxist admirers, have died with a sense of duty well done, died respecting themselves enormously, and we're the ones who get hurt when their bright ideas misfire.

We, who have no connection at all with them, not even indirectly. What law says that a whole nation must pay for the murderous foibles of a few paranoiacs? And go on paying for centuries! And what a price!" Other effects of the drink were hardly noticeable; only his bitter vehemence, so unlike his normal self, gave him away. "What's more, everyone is free to curse us. The whole world curses us! Yet the world ought to bless Russia from now till doomsday, because with her own experience of Hell she's shown all the rest what not to do!"

Kreps's last words reached Vadim as he was dropping off to sleep. He seemed to see the girl in the greenish lightweight autumn coat floating across the morning snows to meet him. Then the storm blotted her out, and Telegin's voice began to aggravate his own secret hurts. "I've got nobody and nothing . . . there'll be no cross on my grave and nobody to remember me." Then, as though he were wide awake, the old man immediately appeared before him, with his bulging, almost unwrinkled forehead, and the crown of white fluff round his pink dome, and whispered gently in his ear. "As I see it, Mark Frantsevich, you are wrong in this particular instance . . ."

The old man became clearer, more substantial . . . and there he was, no dream, but sitting on the edge of Kreps's bed facing Vadim, who was now wide awake, and putting words together into measured, sonorous, and unhurried speech.

"Yes, you're wrong. The Savior did not ask his Father to have pity on him but love for those who crucified him . . . He was terrified that he might come to hate them. He was afraid that he might not bear the cross of atonement to the end."

"I believe, Father Georgii, I believe!" Vadim had never seen Kreps like this before: He was white, his lips trembled, he was clutching convulsively at the lapels of the old man's dressing gown. "Only why did the Creator allow one particular people to become the sacrificial victim in an act of atonement? How much longer can it be crucified? We can endure our sufferings. We do not lack endurance. But love is draining away. Rage is stifling Russia. If it ever breaks its bonds, blood will be held cheaper than water. What atonement will ever pay for that?"

Silent tears of rage welled up in his bulging eyes, collected in the corners, and ran slowly down toward his chin. Mark did not notice them, but sat there gripping the lapels of the dressing gown draped over the old man's shoulders, until his companion took hold of his hands and spoke to him calmly.

"Every people must bear its share of the burden. It is for us to bear it worthily, to help the Savior in His divine purpose. If we murmur against Him, we do not go forward, but mark time. We have work on our hands, Mark Frantsevich, holy work, necessary work, work that is pleasing in the sight of the Lord. It will be our salvation and that of many others, too. All we have to do is to cast off our fear of the world's vileness, and take as our starting point not the things around us but ourselves, our own immediate tasks . . ."

As though spellbound by his unhurried speech, Mark grew calm; his face brightened and he recovered his customary unruffled serenity. As he finally fell asleep, Vadim found himself wondering about the old man. "Why ever did they put that old fuzzy-head in here?"

V

The daily round in the exercise yard was, as usual, silent and unhurried. Inside their stone box, words were all they had to relieve the boredom of existence for one another, so, once outside, everyone was intent on absorbing his full share of quiet and solitude.

Kreps, a short, stocky figure, with his head set firmly and gracefully on his broad shoulders, paced out the yard with the sure and steady stride of a man who doesn't believe in wasting a step or a breath, and has no time for doubts and worries. Vadim, trying to walk in step with him, could hardly keep up. The snow crunched quietly underfoot. The air was still frosty, and held a pungent whiff of damp straw burning in the villages nearby. Overhead, on the hard, frozen branches of snow-laden poplars, rooks seemed to be jeering at each other with their lazy cawing.

"Look over there. Interesting old man," Kreps hissed, without turning his head.

They were approaching a bench; on it sat an erect, carefully shaven old man with a drooping white mustache who was shivering and hugging a dressing gown to himself over a skimpy jerkin. From a distance he looked like a frozen condor, condemned to winter under an alien sky.

Kreps bowed respectfully as he passed the old man, who glanced at the place next to him by way of reply. Mark nodded to Vadim and they sat down, whereupon the man with the mustache searched his jerkin and produced a sheet of glossy paper folded in four which he silently handed to Kreps.

Kreps held the document away a little so that Vadim, too, could glimpse the gist of it. The French Embassy informed Monsieur Tkachenko, Valerian Semyonovich, that at the request of his wife, domiciled in Paris, it was prepared to facilitate the exit of the above-mentioned to take up permanent residence in France.

"And what have you decided, Valerian Semyonich?" Kreps looked straight ahead as he returned the paper. "Will you go?"

A vague smile framed a set of regular, perfectly preserved teeth. "Probably not. I'm getting on for eighty. Every day I live is a bonus. I've spent more than half my life wandering in foreign countries. Now I want to die here, in my homeland. If I had to choose, I'd sooner be in a madhouse in Russia than in any European almshouse . . . I'm sorry for Annette, of course, we went through a lot together, but I daresay she'll understand."

"Perhaps at least you'll apply for your discharge?" Mark had put his hand over the old man's. "You shouldn't be ending your days living off the hospital."

"Yes, but where can I go, Mark Frantsevich?" Even an expression of helplessness could not blunt the sculptured precision of his features. He nodded toward the fence. "I've got nobody out there. And, anyway, what is there for me to do? Everything has changed in these forty years. I couldn't get used to a free life now. At least I have a roof over my head and eat regularly in here. No, Mark Frantsevich, it's too late now for me to start all over again."

Kreps frowned wearily and stood up. "Well, it's up to you, Valerian Semyonovich. Come on, Vadya."

After his talk with the old man Mark moved much more slowly. He looked dejected, and kept hunching his shoulders as if feeling the cold. He was obviously longing to say something, but put a respectable distance between himself and the man with the mustache before he burst out in a feverish whisper:

"Whatever is happening to people, Vadya? A full general, the first man to command the Russian Air Force, won the George Cross three times, and thinks himself lucky to be whiling away his last days in a lunatic asylum. The world has gone crazy. Just look at him—he's contented. Yes, contented! This awful Russian nostalgia! He doesn't mind what he is—slave, or beggar, or homeless dog—as long as it's in his homeland. 'The homeland,' he calls it! The fact that this very same homeland has first disowned him, then made him run the gauntlet of its prison camps from Kolyma to Pot'ma, and finally, as a special favor, graciously permitted him to draw rations in a madhouse till his grave is dug—none of that counts. It suits our rulers. In fact, they cultivate this kind of debasement in people. Well, it's patriotism, isn't it? No, it isn't: Patriotism should create heroes, not lackeys. What will become of us, Vadya? We're degenerating fast!"

Vadim didn't know quite what to think. "What brought him back here?" he asked.

"They caught him in 'forty-five, in Yugoslavia. He was teaching Latin in a Russian high school there."

"And afterward?"

"Afterward? Afterward—the prison camp. When he was released he had nowhere to go. He started trying to get permission to emigrate, so they shut him up here. Now he himself doesn't want to go, as you can see. Twelve years in this bear-garden is enough to get anybody down, of course, but I still can't take it in."

"But perhaps he's right, Mark. If you and I couldn't adjust, it would obviously be still harder for him. We at least were born and brought up in this shit-hole."

"Yes, but unlike us, he now has freedom of choice."

"You have to be able to earn your living over there, Mark, my boy, and just remember how old he is."

"You're just as bad!"

"Yes, but it's the truth."

Mark merely waved his hand as much as to say "Go to hell," and made for the building. Vadim couldn't resist the temptation to look back before he followed his friend. The old man was still sitting on his bench, with his head hunched into his shoulders, so that he looked even more than ever like a sick and stranded bird.

VI

They had no sooner undressed than a visitor from the next ward arrived. He beamed all around with protuberant, cement-gray eyes, swung his brick-red wedge of beard triumphantly from side to side, and flourished an open newspaper in absolute ecstasy.

"I congratulate you, comrades!" He was bursting with joy. "The Bratsk Hydroelectric Station has begun operations. Just think, comrades, what a blow this will be for our ill-wishers abroad!"

The visitor's name was Bochkarev, and he was regarded as one of the aboriginal inhabitants. He had been put inside, to use his own terminology, for his active struggle against religious survivals. This struggle had taken the form of confiscating an icon of John the Baptist from the woman next door, and contriving to burn it on a gas ring. Inside, Bochkarev had remained faithful to his beliefs. He had the right to come and go at will, and first thing in the morning he went down to the village for the papers. Next, he read them through from end to end, carefully underlining what he considered to be the most significant passages, and after that sat down to write approving communiqués to the highest authorities. In his missives Bochkarev always "warmly approved," "enthusiastically supported," and "unreservedly welcomed" the latest measures and decisions of the powers-that-be. His letters began with a conventional "in our healthy collective of invalids," and ended with the traditional "communist greetings." The periodicals and the postal expenses completely swallowed up Bochkarev's allowance, but this only inspired him to further selfless activity. When he received polite replies in envelopes bearing official stamps he would cast proud and secretive glances at those around him. Nothing on earth, it seemed, could jolt Bochkarev out of his chosen rut.

"But that is not all, comrades!" His radiant happiness was becoming almost intolerable. "The oilmen in Tyumen's province have struck another gusher! Scientists claim that our reserves of black gold in that region are practically inexhaustible!"

This was too much for Kreps. The blood drained from his face and he bared his white teeth in a crooked snarl. Gripping the edge of the bed, he trembled violently like a roped horse.

"Listen, you little swine, if you don't get out of here right now, I'll knock your face in. Move!"

Bochkarev didn't need to be told twice. A decade and a half spent in the section for violently antisocial patients had taught him a salutary caution. He retreated instantly, but wouldn't be deprived of his soapbox oration in the corridor.

"You are losing your class feeling, Comrade Kreps! You do not rejoice in your country's successes! You are slipping back into revisionism! Fouling your nest. Anyway, I have a message for Comrade Lashkov! Comrade Telegin asks him to drop in! Comrade Telegin is seriously ill!"

The news of Mityai's illness was a fresh reminder to Vadim that his friend, usually so boisterous and sociable, had not been seen recently either in the dining room or in the exercise yard. He was full of reproaches as he rushed off to Telegin's ward. "Call yourself a friend. Ought to be ashamed."

Mityai was sinking fast. His thin face was sharper than ever, the skin under his week-old stubble was puffy and shiny, his short, skinny body twitched convulsively from time to time under the blanket which covered him up to his chin. The head nurse sat by his bed, her heavy hands folded in her lap, and now she didn't look in the least like "The Doormat," whose appearance in the yard filled everyone with melancholy and dismay. Her whole ungainly body was wracked with grief; even her ugly face was transfused with a semblance of womanly kindness. She tried not to look at him as she rose.

"Sit with him for a while, dear, till he goes to sleep. When I've done my chores I'll come and take over."

Nyura's heavy steps died away in the corridor, and Vadim, as he sat down on the stool she had warmed, was surprised to find himself perceiving her in a new light. You never knew whether people would turn out to be devils or angels!

Mityai's breathing was shallow and uneven, but he managed a painful smile from under half-closed lids.

"She's taken it hard. A woman is always a woman. They all want someone to be sorry for. Thanks for coming . . . I'm shattered, it's terrible . . . I've drunk myself to a standstill . . . Engine's died."

Vadim had a sinking feeling in the pit of his stomach.

"You shouldn't drink, Dmitrii Pavlovich, you really shouldn't."

"I know I shouldn't," he said peaceably. "Only when everything looks gloomy and hopeless you have a drink, and your eyes are opened. The birds are singing, and there are all sorts of good smells in the trees and the grass, and life seems worthwhile." In his eagerness he raised himself on his elbows. "Makes you wish you never had to sober up at all."

"Lie down, Dmitrii Pavlovich, don't get uncovered."

"I'm frightened, Vadya, old pal, I'm frightened of dying." Mityai fell sideways across the bed and buried his tousled head in Vadim's lap. "It only seems like a second, as though I hadn't had any life at all yet . . . Sends shivers down my spine; I'm so frightened . . . I was going to stop wandering. Nyura and I had decided to get together when I left here. I mean legally, not the way it is now . . . I'm going to make it, aren't I, Vadya? It isn't fair!"

Telegin suddenly fell backward and lapsed into exhausted silence. Mercifully, he had fallen asleep, but his dreams were troubled. His lips moved restlessly, as though at the last moment he had failed to tell Vadim something supremely important, something vital.

VII

Bochkarev woke Vadim up in the middle of the night, whispering in his ear.

"Comrade Lashkov, Comrade Lashkov! Comrade Telegin is calling for you." In the half-dark of the dimly lit ward, Bochkarev's yellow eyeballs shone with terrifying earnestness. "Only please hurry. He seems to be in a bad way . . ."

He found himself standing at his friend's bedside while his heart thumped wildly, but Mityai had no more need of anyone. His jaw had sagged lifelessly onto his shoulder, his skinny figure was rigid under the blanket, and the crumpled sheet was growing chilly in his cold fingers.

This was the second time in his life that Vadim had seen death so close at hand, so intimately, and now, as had happened on that first encounter, he was not frightened, but fascinated by its utter peace. It was as if man crossed the border of death to be initiated into a secret which set him at rest with everyone and everything.

On that first occasion, after a winter spent at the Khantai staging post, doubling as ledger clerk and laborer, Vadim had decided in early spring to risk the journey on foot to Igarka. Undeterred by warnings that even experienced hunters were chary of going out into the taiga at that time of year, he threw some provisions and clothing into a rucksack and set off along the marshy river bank through the tundra in the direction of the Yenisei. Countless little streams which one could simply step over in summer had now swollen to the size of medium-sized rivers, and every one of them had to be tackled according to all the rules of military engineering.

When Vadim had managed to improvise something resembling a raft, using his underwear and his one and only spare shirt for ropes, and had somehow struggled over the first torrent, he realized that his walking tour was beginning to look like a doomed adventure. Threatening clouds hung so low that they seemed about to catch on the rust-colored treetops. The river was still dotted here and there with ice floes. The quagmire underfoot was so sticky and treacherous that every step became slower and more difficult than the last. But the most unbearable torture was the sensation of total isolation in this vast leaden silence.

Vadim managed to put yet another torrent behind him by walking almost to its source and fording it. But the return journey finally exhausted him, and when, after more than three hours of punishing travel, another belt of water appeared like a mirage before him, there was no fight left in him. He fell face down on the pebbles by the river, and wept aloud, giving vent to his helplessness in the face of this rivulet, this ribbon of muddy, dirty water no more than ten to twelve yards wide. But suddenly, when he was almost hysterical, he had an overpowering sensation that some form of human habitation was close by. When the will to survive is at issue, man can often instinctively distinguish between what is real and what is mere hallucination: This capacity suddenly gave him confidence that he was going to survive.

With a final, almost superhuman effort of will, Vadim forced himself back on his feet, and he went to the very brink of the river. With a sigh of relief, he saw that his faith had been justified; there to his left, fifty meters downstream, an enormous slab of ice, obviously thrown up by the first flood, was blocking the spring torrent. He used it as a bridge to the other bank, where, on the brow of a nearby slope, he suddenly saw a winter hut which seemed to be uninhabited, judging by the neglected state of its surroundings.

But as soon as he pulled open the door to the hut, which was dimly lit by a tiny window, a very bass voice, hoarse with illness, filled the room.

"Shut it quick. It's cold. Wind."

Even before his eyes had adjusted to the prevailing gloom, Vadim recognized the trapper Caspar Silis, a resettled Latvian; his accent was well-known to the whole Khantai shore. Caspar had been exiled to these parts in 'forty-five, and with his dogged peasant shrewdness had made himself so much at home in a strange and forbidding place that the natives were soon reduced to despairing incredulity when they compared his earnings with theirs. His catches of fish and game excited general envy, and in the polar fox season, when practiced old hands thought they'd struck it rich if they took ten pelts in a week, Silis generally picked up as many as five in a day's rounds. Vadim had often tried to trail the cunning Latvian, to glean some insight into his methods, but Caspar had always eluded his tracker without difficulty, even making a game of it. When he came back to the base with a rich haul, ready for a rest and the warmth, he would only laugh at Vadim.

"You'll never catch a fox, Vadya. He won't go into your trap . . . He wants mine . . . He likes mine better . . ."

Now Caspar lay before Vadim on his old sheepskin coat, perspiring heavily; beside him there was a boot slit from top to toe. His right foot had been roughly swathed in a piece of old rag.

"Light the stove, Vadya, we'll warm ourselves." His fever had not dulled the usual ironic twinkle in his eyes, but on the contrary seemed to have intensified it, made it more defiant. "I trapped foxes, and now I fall into a trap myself."

When a fire was roaring cheerfully in the long unused stove, Vadim literally tore off Caspar's sock, stiff with dried blood, and examined the foot which had been crushed by the teeth of a wolf trap. He realized the utter hopelessness of the situation. The bruised skin, with its scaly crust, was already erupting in blotchy dark brown spots. One didn't have to be much of a specialist to identify the symptoms of gangrene. Between themselves and the nearest Nenets settlement, Plakhino, lay a distance of at least forty kilometers, intersected at frequent intervals by streams raging in full spate of spring floodwater. Alone, Vadim had managed half that distance with the greatest difficulty. There could be no question of going on further with the helpless Caspar.

There was only one thing to do: sit and wait. Wait for death to complete its business. Doomed to witness its slow but inexorable progress, Vadim felt desperate.

"Warm yourself, Vadya." Caspar must have guessed that Vadim was afraid, and his usual sardonic mockery melted into indulgent kindness. "The water will last for a long time. There is fish and meal; sit down and keep warm . . . It's too late for it to heal now . . . Pity it's not Latvia . . . You been to Latvia, Vadya? Dear, dear, dear, Vadya, you not been to Latvia! Village of Aurumtsies . . . all fishermen . . . you can see the sea through the window . . ."

For five interminable days and nights Silis lapsed repeatedly into delirium and then regained consciousness, while his powerful system, toughened by suffering and Siberian frosts, fought for its life against the deadly poison that was creeping toward his heart. On the sixth day, when the June sun that never set had barely touched the horizon and started its slow ascent again, flooding the hut with reflections of red light, Caspar's haggard face with its brown stubble suddenly brightened and softened, and he looked over at Vadim in his old mischievous way.

"Put it on the ski track, put the trap on the ski track, Vadya. The fox is running on the snow. Running. The snow is soft . . . the ski track is hard. So the fox runs on the track. It's hard, and good. He won't leave the track. Put the trap on the track, Vadya. You will have many, many foxes. You will have a lot of money, you will go to Latvia. You will see Aurumtsies . . . the sea . . ."

The parched lips went on moving soundlessly for a while, but Silis's bulky body gradually relaxed and at last he was perfectly still; a ray of sun which flashed through the window and touched his forehead at that moment only served to highlight the shriveled features frozen in death. There he lay under Vadim's gaze, awkwardly stretched out on his sheepskin coat, the old Latvian who had been expelled from his native home to the outermost ends of the most inhospitable spot on earth. Yet not even death could wipe from his face the calm assurance of a man who has lived his life with dignity.

Now as Vadim stood rooted to the spot staring at Mityai's cold flesh, and his limp, outflung arms, he felt for the first time in his life the final stab of despair.

"Is this what I shall become? Is this how it will be?"

VIII

Kreps ranged up and down the deserted smoking hall trailing a blue cloud. Just lately insomnia had often brought them together here at night and the former producer passed the time away by giving Vadim an exposition of his vision of the world repertoire. Tonight it was Hamlet who had him in thrall.

"You see, everybody else makes the Dane an accuser. In my version he will accuse, too, but he will be aware at the same time that since he is morally superior to those around him, he has no right to blame them, let alone to stoop to vengeance. Hamlet is, so to speak, a being from another planet. And the more delicately this interplanetary visitor is constructed, the warier he must be of interfering in earthly justice. If he interferes, nonetheless, he must pay the price, which is to be tortured by compassion. The key line in my version is not 'To be or not to be?' but 'I must be cruel only to be kind.' Let him ask forgiveness for his intolerance, and let him have foreknowledge that blood spilled in the name of justice can bring nothing but more blood. He will not be crucified by his enemies, but by his own wounded conscience . . . Look . . ."

He deftly slung the dressing gown over his shoulder like a cloak, and struck a pose in the middle of the hall. "Alone at last . . ." And a miracle happened. The figure dying before Vadim's eyes on the concrete floor of a hospital lavatory, weeping with anger and pity, wearing a bedraggled dressing gown of cheap flannelette, was a true child of his century. It was not the Prince of Denmark who interrogated the darkness outside—"To be or not to be?" It was not the heir to a kingdom who leaned wearily against the battered doorpost, beseeching the world at large, but most of all himself, to decide—"Whether 'twere nobler in the mind . . ." It was Vadim's neighbor—his fellow patient, his fellow countryman, fellow human being—burying himself alive. Now he raised his arms shoulder-high, as though throwing himself on the mercy of a conqueror, and came toward Vadim with outstretched hands from the far end of the lavatory. "Look here upon this picture and on this . . ." His emotion was contagious, magical: It caught Vadim and made him shiver. And when the Prince, almost burned out with pity, cowered at his murderess mother's feet, moaning like a stricken creature—"I must be cruel only to be kind"— Vadim, choking back his sobs, cursed Kreps's power to disturb him so profoundly.

Kreps played all the final scene from "Heaven make thee free of it," when Hamlet feels that the end is near, clinging to imaginary crossed swords on the wall. He died like a crucified bird, between the door and the first lavatory bowl.

Mark sat down and flashed him an eager look out of his yellow eye.

"Well, do you think it's good?"

"It's good, all right." Vadim nudged his shoulder. "First-class."

"D'you know something?" Mark looked at him fixedly. "I would take you on now."

"Why've you changed your mind? My training is completely different."

"All of a sudden I can see something in you that I always look for in an actor. You've started listening."

"Too late, Mark, I want to pack this business in."

"When did you make up your mind?"

"A long time ago. Only I didn't have the willpower."

There was pure envy in Mark's searching stare. "You know, you're a bigger man than I thought."

"Thank you."

On the day of his return to Moscow, before going home, he had called at headquarters firmly intending to finish with the variety stage once and for all. His decision was still at a formative stage, but he was already obsessed with a notion of imminent upheaval in his life and to help events along he made straight for the booking department.

After the noise and bustle of the corridor, Vilkov's office might have struck the uninitiated as a haven of peace and quiet. But Vadim was well aware that it was right here and not somewhere higher up that all the tangled threads of what at first sight was the craziest institution in the world came together. With the meticulous precision of a calculating machine Ilya Nikolaevich Vilkov sorted his personnel into teams which traveled the length and breadth of the Union, sometimes even to its remotest corners. The occupant of the office kept hundreds of names in his balding head, along with a full dossier on every one of them. People with top billing, the category which included Vadim Lashkov, received special treatment, which was not a part of official instructions. So when Vadim silently placed his letter of resignation in front of Vilkov, the latter merely frowned contemptuously and pushed the paper away without reading it.

"Want to go to the Baltic?"

"No."

"The Caucasus?"

"No, again."

"Are your accommodations all right?"

"All right."

"Did you get your back pay?"

"In full."

A hint of surprise and curiosity crept into Vilkov's cold stare; he had bold, almost bulging eyes.

"So, what do you want?"

"To go away."

"Into repertory?"

"No, altogether."

"How d'you mean, altogether?"

"I want to change my profession."

"Don't be funny."

"I'm not trying to be."

"Can you explain a little?"

"I don't think I'm in the right job."

"Come on, if everybody thought that way . . ."

"Someone has to be first."

"Listen, Lashkov, I'm your friend . . ."

"I'm my friend, too."

"Let's be serious."

"I'm not joking."

"What's suddenly come over you?"

"I want to begin all over again."

"Begin what?"

"Living."

"You're thirty-five."

"It's never too late to begin."

Vilkov's normally impassive, blue-jowled face lost its arrogance and composure; his muscular shoulders slumped.

"Have you any idea what it's like, starting all over again?"

Vadim was familiar with Vilkov's story, as were most variety artists. While working in a very important organization, he had refused to testify against an army friend of his youth. The trial was rigged, but brief. Vilkov had to change his general's uniform for much more modest clothing. Many years went by before they allowed the ex-general to return from banishment; then, recalling that the work of the department which he had previously headed involved some contact with cultural matters, they put him in charge of recruiting and administering variety artists. Vadim rather disliked Vilkov, along with exaggeratedly correct people in general; he thought him a dry stick and a pedant, and turned to him only when it was unavoidable. He felt that the conversation had gone on too long and hastened to end it.

"To have any idea of it, I'd have to do it first. I'm not a schoolboy."

Staring absently through the window, Vilkov seemed to be thinking aloud.

"They made me live in Ryazan. There was nobody for me to go to. My own family were all dead before the war. My wife had remarried long ago, you know how it is. I don't blame her, it was the only way out for her. I didn't want to risk getting my friends in trouble by visiting them. So I arrived wearing the only clothes I had, my old uniform, that is, with the braid removed. I rented a room from an old woman and in the morning I went looking for a job in a warehouse. I was strong in those days. They took me on. As a loader. I remember getting back from my first shift, half-dead, aching all over because I wasn't used to work like that. But how I slept!—like a newborn baby. I ate my morning bread with yesterday's cabbage soup—and it tasted so good, you couldn't have dragged me out of it by my ears . . . I thought I was beginning life all over again . . . but my friends wouldn't leave me alone . . . They tracked me down, set me back on my feet, rehabilitated me. So off I went again, one office after another."

He sighed wistfully and looked enquiringly at Vadim.

"Where will you go?"

"I don't know, yet."

"Won't you change your mind?"

"No."

"Right." Vilkov touched a button. A guardian angel instantly appeared on the threshold in full warpaint.

"Draw up a 'Released at own Request' form for Lashkov. And tell everyone that I'm not in for the rest of the day." She vanished noiselessly through the door. "Want some tea?"

"Don't drink it."

"I know, I know . . . I've had my eye on you for some time. There have been complaints. Moderation, Vadim Viktorovich, you must practice moderation. Still, that's your affair. A wise man sleeps it off . . . Look"—he drew a photograph from under the glass table top and held it out to Vadim—"this is my new family."

Two little girls with light brown hair gazed out at the world, trustful and smiling, having no idea as yet that their very existence gave meaning and value to the lives of other people.

Vadim suddenly felt that he could trust Vilkov.

"So it is possible to begin again."

"Yes, but it's difficult."

"I shall try, then."

"Good luck to you."

Outside, the September poplars were slowly shedding their golden leaves. Through the trees, the city was sharply silhouetted against the unbroken pallor of the distant sky, and somewhere beyond the agglomeration of little boxes, each with its many windows, Vadim daydreamed that he saw a ship with its prow facing out to sea, riding at anchor and waiting for him, tantalizing him with its snow-white sides. This fleeting vision fired him with impatience, and he hurriedly took his leave.

"Perhaps I'd better be going."

Surprisingly, Vilkov wasn't offended by his guest's unceremonious haste. He rose, drew himself up to his full height—he was well over six feet tall—and looking athletically trim and erect once more, came around his desk, gave Vadim a quick hug, and pushed him gently away.

"This conversation is strictly between ourselves. So come back if you can't manage it . . . So long."

For Vadim, that memorable conversation had marked the end of his whole life up until that point; now, as he confided in Kreps in the hall that night, he was only confirming himself in his decision. He came out with an admission that surprised even himself.

"You see, I'm in the wrong business. I'm always doing things wrong. Something important is missing from my makeup. I'm no worse than a lot of others, of course, but no better either. Just a useful mediocrity. I want to try everything all over again, turn a fresh page, as they say. There's no way back for me now. I want to discover my own nature. What it is, I don't know, but unless I find out I can't go on living . . ."

Vadim broke off, startled. The figure of the doctor-in-charge had suddenly appeared in the doorway, as though there had been an abrupt cut in a film.

"It's you I want, Mark." His close-set eyelids fluttered anxiously in Vadim's direction. "What I have to say concerns you personally."

Vadim was somewhat dismayed by Pyotr Petrovich's unusual nocturnal visit, to the smoking hall of all places, and by the familiar way in which he addressed Mark. Half-guessing what it meant, he turned meekly toward the exit, but Kreps pulled him up short.

"Don't go away, Vadya." His cheeks were hollow with distress. "You can speak in his presence. Carry on."

The doctor did not take his eyes off Kreps as he spoke, and he obviously had difficulty in putting his words together.

"I've had instructions to send you to Kazan."

"Just me?"

"The parson as well."

"Not 'parson,' Petya—priest."

"Bah, what's the difference?" said the doctor with a weary wave of the hand.

Kreps flared up. "A big difference, Pyotr Petrovich, a very big one, Petya! Haven't you understood anything, after all this time? I thought that after that business . . . after those Hungarian boys you and I had to gun down, something had been awakened in you . . . Or is it still not enough for you, what's going on all around? Take your blinkers off, Petya, it's high time! I haven't written any underground protests, and Yegor Nikolaevich certainly hasn't, nor have we demonstrated in Red Square, nor tried to solve awkward questions in officially licensed magazines for the edification of intellectual deadheads, but all the same it's us they're packing off to Kazan. Us, not the so-called champions of liberalism who get paid by the state. What are we?—merely the bearers of the Light and the Word of God. Yet we frighten them more. We frighten them much more than all the dissident physicists and semiunderground poets. Because once a man has received the Light and the Word, he can never again be bought or broken. It's a waste of time for them to try! We'll be just the same in Kazan. We can no longer be separated from the kingdom. There are people in Kazan too, and so there is also the grace of the Savior."

Vadim had already heard quite a bit about the criminal asylum at Kazan. Incurable homicidal maniacs and all those whom higher authority deemed best forgotten were sent there. There was no way back. Leaders and governments changed, wars raged and quiet revolutions occurred: Only the laws of the Kazan maximum security hospital remained unchanged. Once a man crossed its threshold he was effaced from the memory of man. So as soon as he heard the name Kazan, Vadim knew that Kreps had nothing more to lose.

"Calm down, Mark." The doctor's face looked gaunter than ever. "You can leave if you want to."

"How?"

"Just like that. What happens afterward doesn't interest me."

"It interests me, though."

"I'd lose my diploma. And that's all. Nothing else would happen, I swear."

"Run away, you mean. With no passport and no means of support. In other words, I still go to Kazan sooner or later, but you have no hand in it, is that it? No, Petya, I won't contribute to your spiritual comfort. Kindly pay your own debts. Maybe you'll get sick of it someday and come to your senses. Anyway, I wouldn't leave the old man, not for any money. So let's forget it—you've made no offer, and I've sacrificed nothing. And we owe each other nothing at all. Sleep soundly, dear comrade."

"Is that all you have to say to me?"

"Yes. Not another word."

"Well, it's up to you."

He stood there a little longer, rocking onto his toes in his squared-off brogues, eyes shut and teeth convulsively clenched as though he were in a trance. Then he turned without a sound and vanished.

After a short silence, Kreps spoke to his friend with cheerful desperation. "Well, there we are, Vadya, it's my turn now."

"I would have run away."

"Where to, Vadya?"

"Who cares where. I would have run."

Kreps came up beside him and put a hand on his shoulder.

"That's not for me. I couldn't stand that sort of life for long. Anyway, I'm no good at anything except the nonsense they taught me at the Institute . . . And just remember, Vadya, if ever you think of trying to escape, the search will be thorough, very thorough. And they'll find you. They have to. Not because you are dangerous in yourself. Not at all! Simply because by now you've found out a little more than ordinary mortals are supposed to know. So think it over carefully before you do anything." He squinted satirically at the door and added an explanatory footnote.

"We went through cadet school together, and then we were in the same unit . . . He knows which side his bread is buttered on . . . one of the moderns . . ."

They didn't say any more to each other that night. Words were powerless to convey the stark thoughts and feelings which united the two friends in eloquent silence. One lone star shone through the upper pane of the frost-coated window, lighting their silent vigil with a fateful glow.

IX

One person Vadim would never have expected to see at that time was his grandfather. After their last meeting in Uzlovsk he could not imagine that they would ever see each other again. As he listened to the old man, he couldn't suppress a feeling of guilt, so every word came as a reproach or an innuendo.

"They won't release you into my care. They think I'm too old. But I'll go and knock on a few more doors, Vadya. Just be patient, hang on a little longer."

His grandfather didn't look at Vadim as he spoke, but gazed off into space. The parchment hands resting on the table had age spots on them, and as usual he was sitting with them well out in front of him. This was how Vadim had remembered his grandfather through all the years of his wanderings, ever since the first but irreparable crack had appeared in the notorious Lashkov monolith which Uzlovsk had expected to last forever.

Vadim would never forget that almost incredibly clear morning in Uzlovsk when Grandpa Pyotr's doors were flung wide and all his sons and daughters, together with their marital partners and first offspring, assembled in his cottage.

Grandpa himself sat at the head of the table, in a new satin overblouse, with the top button elegantly undone, and looked around with pride and satisfaction at his clan dominated by his first-born, Victor.

Victor—and this had left a vivid impression on Vadim's mind—was obviously conscious that all eyes were on him, and kept laughing and laughing to conceal his confusion, stroking his son's shaven head with one hand, and chopping the air with the other, as though lopping off his sentences.

"There you are, you see, the worker's eaten his fill now." He slipped the back of his hand under his tie and flicked it carelessly. "He's even pinned a ribbon on his silk shirt, as you see. But what comes next? They've driven the best peasants off the land, sent them over the Urals, and they keep up a song and dance to block their ears against what the world is saying. 'All along the village street, from one hut to another . . .' But what's actually going on in the kolkhozes doesn't seem to concern us at all. What are you looking so sulky about, Dad? Have I said something that doesn't fit in with your official line?"

His grandfather had indeed looked black as soon as Victor began to speak, but before he could open his mouth, Barbara's husband, Anatolii Tikhonovich, a thin rake of a quartermaster with a captain's tabs, stood up and hissed at Victor almost without moving his lips.

"The bird who sings in the morning is liable to get eaten."

Victor interrupted mockingly.

"Are you playing the cat? D'you think your claws are long enough?"

Red spots appeared on the captain's sharp cheekbones. "We didn't waste words on people like you at Lake Hasan."

Vadim's father jeered openly. "What were you doing at Hasan, counting rations in the baggage train?"

The embarrassment which had fallen on the company at first gave way to general uproar, especially among the women.

"We only get together once in a blue moon!"

"What a time to start!"

"Men are incurable! As soon as they get together, it's nothing but politics."

"They can't sit still and behave themselves."

They all talked at once, with everybody trying to get in the last word, so that the conversation grew steadily more heated; menacing notes were heard up and down the table, and it might well have ended in a free-for-all if Granddad Pyotr hadn't stood up and banged the table with his fist.

"Right then, Victor, my boy, let's be thankful for small favors. I appreciate your frankness and respect you for it. So let me repay you in the same coin. You may be my own son, but just remember: if the party requires it of me I shan't hesitate. Now take your things and get out . . ."

The wall clock over the chest of drawers measured out the silence that followed. Mitek, the youngest brother, who was as frail and shy as a girl, stared at them all with pathetically shortsighted eyes, and started to plead.

"For God's sake, what d'you think you're doing? . . . Everything was going so well . . ."

But Vadim's mother would tolerate no challenge to Victor's authority, especially from such an open enemy of their marriage as his father, and she cut short her brother-in-law's outpourings. Her slanted, gray Kalmyk eyes flashed with undisguised fury.

"Listen, dear Father, we thank you kindly for your hospitality, but don't start ordering Victor around, you aren't man enough for that. Who d'you think you are, Lashkov? You spend half your life waving a revolver at people, and now it's 'tickets, citizens, please!' Victor's a craftsman, a first-class template-maker, so he's a cut above you. You've talked a lot in your time, but you've never learned to do a thing yourself. You're always shouting for 'the people' . . . instead of learning a proper trade and doing some work. That would be more use to 'the people.' There's a glut of commanders like you around nowadays, and nobody to do the work. As for you Polynins"—she turned toward the quartermaster and her face lengthened and hardened with scorn—"I've known you since I was so high. Your little brother expropriated our property after we'd fed him so long, he expropriated us. And where's your little brother now? He thought he'd get to Heaven on somebody else's back. But what he got was ten years, from his own kind. I've been getting up at daybreak since I was twelve, and going to bed as soon as it's dark, and all our family's the same. You Polynins never set foot outside Mokeich's pub and now we're dirt under your feet. I've got one last thing to say to you. If you wipe us out, our children will still be left. If you destroy them, there'll be grandchildren after that. One way or another we'll outlive you, you parasites. We've had worse to put up with, and we'll put up with you. Anyway, I expect you'll eat each other before too long . . . Come on, Victor . . . get the boy."

"There you are—that's your real kulak mentality!" yelled Polynin, pulling away from Barbara, who was clinging to him silently. "I told you, Pyotr Vasilievich, I warned you . . . Where's your class instinct, your Bolshevik vigilance, let me ask you? You saved this snake from deportation, and now she stings us wherever she can."

"Who are you to talk about class instinct, quartermaster? Have you ever raised a single blister in your whole lousy life? Zhen'ka"—Vadim's father appealed to his younger brother—"why don't you say something; don't turn away, you're a craftsman, have your say!"

But Zhen'ka had hidden his head in the crook of his sister's arm, and was weeping quietly. All they heard from him was a feverish, incoherent mutter. "Why have they done this to us . . . why, oh why . . . We can't get along together even in the family . . ." Fedosya gently stroked his head, and looked around at all of them with bewildered, tear-filled eyes.

Maria, Vadim's grandmother, had sat through the general uproar without a word, huddled by the stove, and might have escaped notice entirely, but when Vadim's father snatched him up, and, followed by his wife, made for the door, she sprang forward and went down on her knees to him.

"Victor, my dear . . . Forgive them all, for the sake of our Lord and Savior." Grandma's voice was quiet and clear, and her thin face, which already bore the marks of fatal disease, was lit up by some secret knowledge accessible only to the newborn and the dying. "I shall never see you again, my life's over. Don't be angry, stay with me. You will be rewarded, my son."

For the first time ever Vadim saw his father's lips tremble as he choked back a sob.

"Mama, Mama, don't think of it . . . it was just a squabble . . . You know how brothers are . . . It's over now."

Grandma's frail body sank in his arms and the relatives stood aside to let him carry her into the next room, where he put her down on a long chest which had belonged to Great-Grandfather, carefully covered with his best jacket, and sat by her side for a long time while they whispered together.

Some of the gathering may have felt a temporary relief, but Grandpa Pyotr was not among them. He sat there, leaning back against the wicker chair, his fists thrust out before him on the table, upright and imperious, with not a drop of blood in his face, and it was obvious from the look on his face that nothing counted with him except what he himself had said. This was how he had always remained in Vadim's mind until their recent, only too memorable meeting.

On the surface, Grandpa was the same harsh, overbearing, self-righteous old man as ever. But Vadim did not fail to notice the tremor in his weakened hands, nor the way his voice, which used to ring as true as a bass bell, broke occasionally as though he were riding over bumps, nor in particular the weariness, so unlike his old self, which showed in every word and movement. Vadim felt a rush of love and pity for this old man who was closer to him than anyone on earth. A sigh escaped him.

"Don't upset yourself needlessly. They won't keep me here forever."

At last Grandpa looked at him cautiously but directly.

"Not forever, maybe, but they won't let you out in a hurry."

"You think so?"

"I know."

Grandpa was incapable of saying anything he didn't mean, and Vadim realized that his position was worse than he had supposed. Choking down a lump in his throat, he glanced involuntarily at the corner where Father Georgii had settled himself, away from the rest of them, and was exchanging affectionate whispers with his daughter. She was stroking his wrist tenderly, gazing at him with utter devotion. It was easy enough to guess what they were talking about. She had already been told. So as she listened to her father, the girl seemed to strain towards him, as though with every word and gesture he could absorb something of her, to keep forever. Vadim's surreptitious glances drew his grandfather's attention to them.

"Who are they?"

"He's a priest . . . that's his daughter." He was surprised to hear himself adding: "Her name's Natasha."

"Natalya, eh?" Grandpa was not noted for tact. "Nice name. Nice face, too. No kidding! She's rather different from that baby doll of yours."

"You needn't have reminded me!"

The pair in the corner noticed them looking. The girl flushed red, and the old man, rising slightly from his chair, smiled and bowed. Grandpa replied just as formally: They were now acquainted. And so, when everyone was making for the exit, the old men found themselves in conversation, and left the young people face to face.

"My name is Vadim." He could scarcely get his breath to speak. "Hello."

"Hello." Confusion made her somehow vulnerable. "Mine is Natasha."

"I know."

"Are you one of Daddy's friends?"

"More or less."

"What do you mean?"

"I haven't been here long. I haven't got used to it yet."

"Don't."

"Don't what?"

"Get used to it."

"All right, I won't."

A nervous silence followed, broken only by the leisurely conversation of the two old men behind them.

"Yes, yes, that is so." Father Georgii's voice seemed full of suffering. "All the same, one must not be in too much of a hurry to make such decisions. Divine Providence is at work in all things, you know. I too in my old age have abjured all the things I used to pay homage to. But it's harder for you, you're an atheist. You have no spiritual refuge. You are going against your own nature. It is much easier for me, no one can deprive me of that which is within me and beside me. What grieves me most is that I have been unable to convince them."

"Of what?"

"I tried to prove to them that the mystical life of the Church, though it has an enormous intrinsic significance for the believer, is nonetheless vain and senseless unless it is reinforced by the active participation of the pastor in everyday life. People are weary of words, they long for an example. The Russian Church has been sapped, not by any secular power, but by its own hollowness, by the dominion of its worldly vanity and foolishness. I was accused of pride. And here I am."

"Do they want to frighten you?"

"Hardly."

"Then what?"

"To get rid of me."

"How d'you mean?"

"To get rid of me altogether. Remove me from the face of the earth."

"But what right have they got?" Grandpa was obviously getting excited. As always, his morbid sensitivity to injustice sought relief in anger. "What right have they got?"

"The class concept of justice must be close to your heart." He said it without a trace of sarcasm, and, indeed, with compassion for the other man. "You are looking at an obvious target. So how can I possibly protest?"

In the corridor the stream of humanity divided: Some went toward the exit, the others with their orderlies toward the inner rooms. Before they parted, Vadim hesitantly touched the girl's fingers. She did not shy away, but gave him an inquiring look, then moved on very quickly without looking around.

At this point Grandpa's bulky frame finally screened her from his gaze. "Don't go to pieces," he said mechanically, his mind obviously elsewhere. Some new concern was gnawing at him and he was completely absorbed in it.

"I'm not old enough to give up at the first attempt. I'll find the right door in the end."

Grandpa gave Vadim a slight hug, pushed himself rather than his grandson away, and made for the exit. His bent figure could be seen for some time wandering in the depths of the corridor, and if Vadim hadn't known his grandfather he might have thought that he was drunk.

Father Georgii fell in beside Vadim, watched the elder Lashkov's departure, and remarked quite casually: "There goes a man who will not be able to live with himself unless he finds faith. Only faith can save him."

X

It was the first bright morning of the winter. The brilliantly sunlit wards were full of life and excitement. Traffic in the corridor was busier and more cheerful. The whole appearance of the section had changed. New faces, whose existence had somehow previously gone unsuspected, turned up in its darkest corners. Goremykin, a former schoolteacher, looked in on Vadim and stood blinking shortsightedly through the window, rubbing his hands in satisfaction.

"Just imagine what it's like in England now. In the county of Kent, for instance! Everything springlike, the heather in bloom."

He was so happy for the county of Kent that he burst out laughing. Some three years ago, Goremykin had been teaching English in a school just outside Moscow. He was so much in love with his subject, and had made such a meticulous study of everything to do with England, that he could probably have closed his eyes and taken any Englishman by the shortest route possible from the docks to the British Museum. The end of it all was that when he applied for permission to visit the country so dear to his heart he overlooked a slight discrepancy in the legal systems of the two states concerned, and, direct from the waiting room of the All-Union Ministry of Foreign Affairs, had fetched up in the Troitskaya, with no hope whatsoever of getting out again.

He continued to smile and rub his hands. "Do you know, Vadim Viktorovich," he said, "that spring to a great extent purifies the air over London? Because that smog of theirs, you know, is a real curse . . ."

Kreps, who had been lying quietly with the blanket pulled up to his chin, suddenly went tense, and a hunted look came into his damp eyes as they slid toward something behind Goremykin's back. Vadim immediately followed his gaze and saw Pyotr Petrovich turn into the ward from the corridor. The doctor gently pushed the teacher out of his way with the tips of his fingers, went up close to Mark's bed, and murmured.

"It's today, Mark." The next word was a mere whisper as he retreated from Mark's look of tortured entreaty. "Immediately."

Vadim would have given anything not to see Kreps's horrified eyes. But it only lasted a moment. Immediately afterward, Mark's lips set in an obstinate line as he stuck out his jaw more sharply than ever, nimbly swung his sturdy body into a sitting position, put his feet on the floor, and said, "Let's go."

As he went out, his eyes invited Vadim to follow him; then he strode into the corridor without looking back. Pyotr Petrovich, walking behind him, shot Vadim a warning glance from his birdlike eye. But nothing on earth could deter him. He would follow Kreps until the last moment, until they reached the boundary line at the door which would separate them forever.

Father Georgii was already sitting in the entrance hall to the lavatories with their two bundles of belongings, under the surveillance of the wet-lipped orderly from the reception room. Mark came in, the old man rose to meet him, they embraced silently, and stood like that for some time. Then, without saying a word, they made the sign of the cross over each other and busied themselves with their bundles.

They got dressed, each of them in character. Father Georgii, who had already served a sentence somewhere in the Pot'ma region, equipped himself with careful thoroughness, lengthily and ceremoniously donning each item of clothing, even drawing on a felt boot as though performing some solemn rite.

When he was finally ready, anyone would have known at once that here was a man with a long and difficult journey ahead of him. Whereas Kreps was wearing a haphazard assortment of garments: a flowery shirt, a flannel jacket over it, drainpipe trousers, an imported mackintosh that didn't reach his knees. At the old man's side he looked like a stray canary beside a wise and tough old bird. They discovered that he had no cap, either, and old "Doormat" had him issued a hospital cap on her own responsibility. You would have to hate the people they were intended for to make caps like that: lop-eared, of no known color, with peaks that hung as loosely as dog's tongues. Anybody wearing one might be taken for a pilgrim, an escaped convict, or both at once.

When their preparations were complete, Kreps absently surveyed the ring of curious onlookers, went up to Vadim, hesitated for a moment, then spoke quietly but clearly.

"Life will go on, Vadya." He did not hold out his hand. He obviously wanted to leave words, not gestures, to be remembered by. "Wherever we are, life will go on. Life must go on."

Then Father Georgii came up to Vadim, kissed him three times, and made the sign of the cross over him.

"God keep you! Somebody will visit you from me. Don't be surprised."

Nobody tried to hurry them. Not even the orderly from reception. Everyone seemed to sense, consciously or unconsciously, that something was happening which it would be wrong, indeed impossible, to interrupt.

Kreps and Father Georgii moved toward the exit together, without being told, and without apparently exchanging a sign. It was another manifestation of their perhaps short-lived but genuine dominance over their fellow men.

Old Vasya, the duty orderly, a coarse shaven-headed local employee, was positively respectful, and averted his eyes as he opened the door wide for them. They went out, and the semicircle of watchers slowly closed around the exit.

Just when old Vasya had his hand on the knob to slam the door, Bochkarev popped into the section like a jack-in-the-box wearing a bright smile which would have been even wider except for his ears. Flourishing a batch of fresh newspapers over his head, the wretched enemy of the Lord raised a rapturous cry.

"Thrilling news, comrades! The toilers of the Korenovo district of the Kuban have completed the spring sowing of cereals three days ahead of schedule . . ."

He stopped short as the half-circle closed in on him, realizing that he had gone too far. He turned a terrified eye on old Vasya, who went crimson in the face and looked away. Anything might have happened if one of the department's oldest inhabitants, Pal Palich Shutov, a chronic alcoholic, had not stepped out of the circle and defused their rage before it could explode.

"You're a bastard, Bochkarev, a lousy bastard, there's no other word for you. How the earth can bear to have your feet on it beats me, Bochkarev. Think of the people who turn into ashes while you hang around, using up precious space, getting in other people's light. Have some shame, take yourself off the earth, do at least one decent thing in your life."

Pal Palich spat—the great juicy gob of a virtuoso. One could see at once that here was a man who all his life had thought eating between drinks a waste of time. Then he shook a hand in rage and set off home to the far corner of Ward Number Four. The rest also went their various ways. And no amount of sunshine could draw them from under their blankets that day.

XI

That very evening, old "Doormat" brought Vadim's new neighbor into the yard.

"Here you are," she said, unsmilingly pushing him in front of her, "best I could find. Hasn't got much brains, but he's quiet. Works hard, too. Say hallo to him. Name's Gorshkov. He'll tell you all the rest himself."

The man was thin, gray, and disheveled, but everything about him—his prominent eyes, his mass of wrinkles, the random patches of soft hair on his face—gave him a good-natured, likeable air. He talked to himself in a singsong as he made his bed.

"New bed space is like a new fellow: Treat it right and it'll keep you warm at night. If he stays by me, even a fly won't notice that it's winter. The law of the sea: What's yours is mine and what's mine is my own. We'll manage fine here, there's nowhere else to go. I'm a master hand, you name it, I can do it. I can make boots out of rags and make holes out of nothing. And how!"

Gorshkov worked with the businesslike determination of a man accustomed to finding a special satisfaction, known to him alone, in each particular task. It was pleasant to watch the sheet stretching smooth under his hand, the blanket hugging the length of the mattress according to all the rules of barracks room training, the lumpy hospital pillow plumped up like a white swan. In the end, Vadim couldn't resist a bit of good-natured sarcasm. "Anyone would think you'd been doing that all your life."

Gorshkov turned around, eager for conversation. "Well, that's just about it, pal," he said. "Ever since 1930, you might say, when they pushed me off my land, and I started to do contract jobs. Then there was the

war—so it was a plank bed again. Then I was in a prisoner-war camp"
—that was how he pronounced it—"and of course I was in a hut there.
Then I landed in one of our camps, and you know for yourself how the
brass there likes everything done according to regulations. Now here I
am, this is my eighth year in the hospital. A hospital bed's like a mother
to you if you fix it properly."

After this he vanished abruptly and reappeared carrying a mop, and a
few minutes later the linoleum-covered floor of the ward steamed in the
sunlight as it dried in the draft from the half-open top windows. The
rickety locker between their beds was fit only for the scrapheap, but as
soon as he put his hand to it, it recovered its stability. And there was always some little story, some catch phrase, as if every movement for
Gorshkov had to have its counterpart in sound or in words, lest it be
meaningless and incomplete.

"Mother, oh mother of mine, if you'd thrown me away like a stone
in an open field, I wouldn't be here to moan and groan. . . . Like our
sergeant-major used to say in the war—your magazine hasn't been
cleaned, your barrel's dirty, that's how we get lice . . . Keep clean and
you'll keep fit . . . My feet would be cold if my hands weren't colder."

"What keeps such people going?" Vadim wondered as he watched
Gorshkov busily darting about. "How do they manage not to crack up
after all they've been through? He must have the strength of three men
to be able to stand it all."

There was a mystery here, some deep enigma which he would solve
someday, but not yet. One thing he could be sure of even now: If Gorshkov were to go through three times as much, he would still be himself,
and no power on earth could damage that innermost self.

Old "Doormat" looked into the ward, and grunted with satisfaction.

"Told you you'd be pleased. He's doing more work in here than
three orderlies. If only he had the brains to go with his hands!"

"Hold on, my love," Gorshkov cheerfully retorted. "There's brains
and brains. One brain's good at thinking things over, and the other's good
at doing them. Figure that one out!"

She good-naturedly waved him away and turned to Vadim. "I've got
to take you to Pyotr Petrovich. He wants to see you." Then, more
brusquely, "let's go, now."

Inmates were rarely summoned in this way, and it was usually for
some urgent reason, so Vadim didn't need to be told twice. The next
minute he was almost running along the corridor to the door with the
famous nameplate. The most fantastic conjectures chased through his
mind.

"They've given Grandpa custody? Or has my wife taken pity on me? Or perhaps? . . ." He didn't even want to think about that "perhaps," which seemed so frightening and remote.

Old "Doormat" caught up with him on the way and panted heavily at his shoulder.

"Be careful with him today . . . He's a bit upset . . . You never know what he'll be like . . . If he starts acting up, there's no stopping him . . ." She unlocked the door and let him in. "Go on, and good luck."

The doctor didn't even look around as he came in, but waved at him vaguely, which was probably meant as some sort of invitation to sit down. The scribbling pad which the whole section knew so well lay beside him, but it was shut. His exquisite fountain pen, tightly capped, lay decorative but useless in the pencil jar. None of these were good signs, and as Vadim sank down on a chair near the door he prepared himself for the worst.

"Listen." The director started talking but still wouldn't look him in the face. "You too regard me as a bastard, I suppose? I probably am, but perhaps you can tell me"—he abruptly swung his whole body around to face his guest, and only then did it occur to Vadim that the doctor was blind drunk—"perhaps you can tell me, my dear Vadim Viktorovich, what I could have done for him? I'm no fighter on the barricades, thank you! In Budapest, incidentally, he and I were side by side, sweeping those same barricades off the face of the earth . . . His conscience didn't torment him then, and he never mentioned the Savior . . . We killed the wounded on the spot . . . including little boys . . . some of them were hardly fifteen . . . And now I'm the only rotten bastard. He's a lamb with a crown of thorns on his head. He's adopted the ascetic way of life but he fears the judgment of this world. He wants to bear the cross and draw state rations at the same time, and he doesn't want to do it by himself but in a gang with all the others. Martyrdom in comfort is his goal. Right." He jerked open his desk drawer, took out a file, awkwardly thumbed through it, and removed a packet of documents. "All your stuff is here: passport, draft card, employment book, identity certificate. From tomorrow I'm putting your name down for a pass to see people outside whenever you like. I don't care when you run away, or where you run to. I only want to warn you that they'll look for you. And they'll be thorough."

"What about you?"

"That's not your concern, Vadim Viktorovich." There was a momentary flash of sober anger in his owlish eyes. "I'll look after myself." He pushed the documents to the very edge of the desk. "Pick up your playthings. Or maybe you're hankering after sainthood too?"

"No, that isn't it, but you must admit that buying one's freedom at somebody else's expense . . ."

"Oh, God, I am sick of these creative personalities! They can't say the least little thing simply. Don't let your conscience trouble you. Or, as Mark Frantsevich would put it, sleep soundly, dear comrade . . . Come on, pick them up."

The sardonic grin on the doctor's narrow face became more and more provocative. A minute ago Vadim was on the point of refusing, shunning the temptation, but that grin changed his intentions in a flash. He'd try it, come what may. It was too soon to pin all his hopes on the tender mercies of some unknown benefactor. They would have to drag Vadim Lashkov kicking and screaming to the judicial slaughter. A furious indignation made him rise from his chair, and impelled him toward the desk. And as soon as the documents were in his pocket he realized that he had made his choice, that there was no way back, that this was his one and only chance of ever getting out.

Pyotr Petrovich guffawed drunkenly in his ear as he escorted him to the door.

"I may escape myself soon . . . into space."

Vadim had no need to answer, because the door slammed behind him and he found himself face to face with old "Doormat," who raised her puffy eyes in a questioning look.

"Don't talk too much . . . It can happen to anybody."

"I'm not a kid."

He felt an urge to smoke, and went off to the lavatory where Gorshkov was already in action, painstakingly scraping the dirty bowls. Vadim's appearance increased his activity and his flow of words.

"We'll put such a sparkle on the crystal that it'll be a pleasure to piss in it . . . We'll turn the shithouse into a consulting room . . . It'll be a treat to sit in it."

"Haven't you had enough yet?"

"When there's nothing to do you start thinking things, and if you think too much you get lice. Working's like drink—makes you love the lousiest sods more than your own mother."

"A born hewer of wood and drawer of water!"

"Well, I daresay you're right. But I'm never short of warmth and a drink myself!"

Vadim inhaled deeply and blew out the smoke with enjoyment. But his thoughts were not particularly cheerful. "I wonder how many crackpots like that there are in Russia; there must be millions!"

XII

The rooks over the exercise yard were raucously proclaiming the arrival of spring. The end of April was usually cloudless and warm. The buds on the gnarled poplars along the fences soundlessly exploded into tiny tongues of green flame. Dirty wet patches spread in all directions from gray islands of porous snow.

Pyotr Petrovich did not go back on his word. The day Tatyana arrived, Vadim was allowed out for the first time without surveillance. They went out into the exercise yard and were silent for quite a time, not knowing where to begin. Too much had happened since they last met.

And so, although Vadim had planned the whole course of this final discussion with his wife in advance, their conversation began a lot more unpleasantly than he had anticipated. What all his arguments amounted to, as Tatyana saw it, was that they should get a divorce, and she behaved accordingly. She assumed an air of injured innocence and went over onto the offensive.

"Well, this is something I didn't expect. We all know about the life you lead . . . drinking bouts, casual affairs . . . Ruining a person's life is just your style. But here I am, still waiting for you!" She had a remarkable capacity for believing whatever she happened to be saying. "I've sacrificed my best years, my youth, to you. I've lived like a nun. But I shan't give in as easily as all that. You won't get the apartment. You have no right to anything at all. You are legally incompetent, my love. No court will find in your favor."

"Will you please listen."

"No, not to you."

"Please, I beg you."

"You want me to put up with your drunkenness again, and your crazy antics in the apartment, but I want a bit more of an orderly life."

Vadim hastily tried to avert the outburst of hysterical weeping.

"Don't upset yourself. Nobody wants to turn you out. If you will help me to get out of here, all I'll take will be a set of underwear and a shirt."

"Oh, it's love in a hovel, is it?" She tried in vain to hide her dismay with a pathetic little smile. "Isn't it a bit late for that, Vadim Viktorovich? What's she like, young and beautiful?" Her wet lips set in a thin vengeful line: That he should prefer someone else was more than she could understand. "She has a dowry, no doubt?" She had this habit of speaking in questions when she reached the point of exasperation. "A villa? A car?"

In the past, speeches of this sort had always reduced Vadim to wild rage, but as he listened to her now he remained wearily indifferent, and merely wondered helplessly how he had managed to endure ten years with this woman, reconciling himself to all the pettiness and the falsity which had grown like a canker in her since the day she was born. Everything about her was false: her voice, her walk, her way of talking. It seemed that if she made one single natural movement, she would vanish, evaporate, perish in it—any manifestation of simple humanity was so alien to her.

"Spare me the amateur dramatics just for today."

"Well, of course, I can't compete with a professional like you."

"You are incorrigible."

"Influence of my nearest and dearest, perhaps?"

"I gave you part of myself, and not the worst part, either."

"Whoever would have thought it!"

"You and I lived together for several years." He stuck calmly to the point, and did his best to get through to her. "All right, it was several years too long. But now that it's all coming to an end, we could treat each other like human beings."

"Well, tell me sensibly, without all this fancy talk, what you are up to."

"I'm speaking quite seriously. I want to begin a new life. I'm going to try again . . ."

"With another woman?"

"Tanya!" He had given up hope of arousing the merest glimmer of understanding, but his determination to leave nothing unsaid finally prevailed. "Be human for once in your life. I daresay that I was often in the wrong, but you didn't always behave as you should either. So let's forget all these grudges and part in a civilized way. I swear to you that this is no silly whim. Surely it isn't so hard to understand?"

The bitterness and suspicion in her startlingly golden brown eyes melted and gave way to bewilderment.

"You *are* mad." She slowly came close to him, and examined him carefully as if she were seeing him properly for the first time. "Yes, I see it now. You really are mad . . . How could I fail to notice it all this time! Whatever has got into you, Vadim? What's the matter with you?"

"In my opinion I'm beautifully sick, as the saying goes. Please, please help me."

"I never could understand you."

"You never had the time."

"Not the way you lived."

"Lord, Tanya, whatever their way of life, people should have time to get to know each other in ten years."

"Words are your profession."

"Other men's words, Tanya, not my own."

"All right," she promised hesitantly, "I'll see what Mama thinks."

Vadim immediately lost all desire to continue the conversation. She hadn't understood a thing. She no longer even irritated him. If anything, he pitied her, as people pity cripples and paupers. They lived in different worlds and could not understand one another. His mother-in-law would quickly curb any half-hearted impulse to help. Must he accept that there was no way out? He remembered the people he had met once out by Lake Baikal, and wondered whether he was destined to be like them.

That autumn, fate had landed him with a team from the Irkutsk Philharmonic, in a godforsaken lakeside village. They arrived at noon, and there was a lot of time in hand before the concert, so the chairman of the village council conducted the visiting artists through his spacious but far from rich domain. A chilly little breeze was blowing in from Baikal, and the gray sky hung low and heavy on the village, making the houses and farm buildings on the treeless streets look squashed against the earth.

They made a lightning tour of the fish cannery, which was half-empty at that time of year, and were heading for the tearoom, but on their way, through a gap in outlying houses, they glimpsed the walls of an abandoned monastery eroded by the passage of time, standing on top of a little hill by the shore. The chairman, a sluggish little man with a greenish powder burn on his face, realized his guests were showing an interest in this unscheduled item and started to fuss anxiously.

"That's nothing worth bothering about! We've had a mental colony there since last year. Nothing interesting, just idiots." He abruptly changed the subject, and hurried them away, "In the tearoom now, we've got freshly caught Baikal salmon. Try it—it's first-class."

The band of actors drifted behind the chairman toward the tearoom. Something he couldn't define—a presentiment, a distant voice—held Vadim back. He broke away from the rest and turned resolutely toward the monastery. They called out to him, but he waved them irritably away and then ignored their shouts.

He went through a breach in the wall, which served simultaneously as lodge and main drive, into the monastery courtyard, enclosed by rusty wire. Faint, narrow paths connected the church, which had been lopped down to its capitals and covered with old sheet iron, with two gloomy-looking residential buildings and a chapel by the entrance. A big-nosed bearded man, obviously drunk, with an old leather raglan coat slung over his shoulders, came out of the chapel to meet him, and without any further preliminaries declared in a way that left no room for denial: "You're the reporter. I'm the bursar, Babiichuk. Come on."

The former cells, each of which held four beds, bore traces of recent repair. But a damp, chilly draft blew up through the hefty cracks in the crudely painted floor, and the gimcrack window frames rattled noisily in the wind. Vadim could easily imagine what sort of time the inhabitants would have in the cruel Baikal winter.

Babiichuk meanwhile, puffing and blowing drunkenly, explained everything to him, offhandedly but at length, like a practiced guide in a local museum.

"Our concern for the welfare of our people is constant. We have carried out repairs, and laid in stocks of fuel. The calorie content of the food is according to prescribed norms. We are fully and completely prepared for the winter. Please come and inspect the feeding block."

There were only a few people having dinner in the church, which had been converted into a canteen.

The bursar hastened to satisfy his startled curiosity. "We are still recruiting. We expect another consignment soon. By winter we shall be up to strength."

The diners were too busy with their food to spare them a glance. Eating absorbed all the attention of these involuntary companions. Vadim stared into their faces, looking in vain for some glimmer of awareness or understanding. They swam before his eyes, one after another—obtuse, aloof, and seemingly hollow. When nature had fashioned them, she had breathed nothing but instinct into the clay.

But when he turned to leave, in the space between the door and a side window, he suddenly saw the profile of a face that was marked by prolonged and desperate sadness. The man looked straight at Vadim, but obviously did not see him. It was as though he were gazing into the distant depths within himself that were visible to him alone, and finding them infinitely dreary and tragic.

Vadim felt an immediate liking for him, and stopped to speak. "Hallo. Have you been here long?"

The man flashed him a helpless, childlike smile, and said nothing. Bubiichuk hurried up and grunted laughingly. "It's no use. He's literally a dummy. He's been silent for five years, according to his case sheet."

Out in the yard the bursar got down to brass tacks.

"Well, Mr. Reporter, shall we warm ourselves up? I've got something. And there'll be a bit of salmon, too."

Vadim disillusioned him brusquely. "I'm not a reporter, I'm an actor."

Babiichuk immediately lost all interest, and made for the chapel, muttering contemptuously into his beard.

"You had no business coming here. This is a clinical institution, not a fairground. Actor, you say!"

As he left the monastery courtyard, Vadim carried with him a reflection of the strange smile which the silent inhabitant of this godforsaken, abandoned place had bestowed on him. Now that life had the same fate in store for him, he realized that like the dummy in the church he had nothing to say to any representative of what was now the other world, and least of all to his wife. Quite simply, they could no longer hear each other's voices.

"Good-bye."

"Good-bye."

Without conscious effort, they found their hostility of a moment ago dissolving in the silence that followed, and when Vadim hesitated in the doorway on his way back into the section she impulsively squeezed him and whispered sorrowfully, "I did love you once, all the same. You're an easy man . . ."

Tatyana even seemed to be trying to follow him over the threshold, and in this instinctive movement of hers Vadim observed something that had been characteristic of all his recent encounters. The people he had met lately—the doctor, Kreps, Father Georgii, Moroz, all seemed to be envying him when they said good-bye, as though their own unrealized hopes of changing their lives were being buried in his own quiet certitude about his fate. "No, we haven't the courage to break the charmed circle."

As though agreeing with him, the rooks over the exercise yard were suddenly quiet. Only when he had gone a step further did he realize that the birds had done nothing: it was simply that the door had slammed behind him.

XIII

The panic among the staff developed slowly, and went unnoticed at first. Orderlies were always dashing about for a variety of reasons: They would be tying down a patient who had become violent, or else brute strength was needed to perform a puncture, or yet another terminal case had to be spirited away from the section in a hurry. The excitement would have left them unmoved on this occasion, too, if Tulchinsky, the medical superintendent of the hospital, had not appeared in person with a large retinue of administrative personnel. These VIP's bypassed the wards and went straight through to the head of department's office. Their grave haste warned the patients that something was wrong.

The department buzzed with excitement.

"It's a commission of inquiry."

"They're going to report on somebody."

"No, they're having a conference, they'll want somebody as an exhibit."

"Maybe someone escaped?"

"No, everyone seems to be here."

"It's an emergency of some sort, that's for certain."

"Why else would a mob like that be on the move?"

Bochkarev rose to the occasion once more. He jumped up on a bench in the corridor, and trumpeted a proclamation.

"Comrades, there is no need for panic! Everyone remain in your places! The enemies of socialism throughout the world never rest! Let us close our ranks. Our strength lies in unity! Let the warmongers over the ocean remember that for every blow received we shall give two in return! Retribution . . ."

He could probably have continued in this vein till kingdom come, but old "Doormat's" sharp voice interrupted his outpourings, with an unexpected quaver.

"Right, back to your wards! Everybody back to your wards! I don't want anyone in the corridor! Uncle Vasya, get them in! Vasilievna, keep an eye on your contingent."

When the orderlies had succeeded in clearing the corridors a stretcher was carried out of the office. A pair of shoes, polished till you could see your face in them, stuck out from under a sheet, and there was also a motionless birdlike profile underneath, making it easy to recognize Pyotr Petrovich. The skirt of his white coat trailed over the edge of the stretcher, and halfway to the exit the notebook with which he never parted fell out onto the floor with a barely audible plop. Nobody noticed it in the general confusion. Vadim, however, had been observing the cortege with heightened attention, and didn't miss the slightest detail; he did not take his eyes off the book for a moment.

When the procession, with the stretcher at its head, had filtered through the door, and the inmates came flooding out of all the wards excitedly discussing what had happened, the doctor's scribbling pad instantly found its way into Vadim's pocket.

The corridor was full of noise and confusion. One conjecture followed another.

"Looks as if his heart gave out."

"They say he drank."

"Overdid it this time."

"That's Pyotr Petrovich for you. Some doctor!"

"Just because he's a doctor, d'you expect him to be a saint?"

"Wonder who we'll have on our backs next?"

"A temple is never long without a priest."

"That's true enough."

Thanks to his friendship with the domestic staff, Gorshkov was the first to learn the precise facts. At a convenient moment, he beckoned Vadim over to his bed and reported to him in a rapid whisper.

"The doctor . . . Pyotr Petrovich . . . he . . . you know . . . killed himself . . . What a business . . . With some sort of powder."

He was transformed by a totally uncharacteristic distress. What Vadim saw in front of him, shifting from foot to foot and tormented with anguish, was an old man, crushed by life, with an ashen, gray face enmeshed in wrinkles.

"I shouldn't have thought it was your first time," said Vadim with genuine compassion.

"No, I've seen them before . . . more than one . . . Only it's more upsetting every time. If people like him do that, what am I to do? Might as well hang myself now."

With shoulders bowed, and hands behind his back, he shuffled slowly between the beds to the window and stood there motionless, as though shutting out all that was happening behind him.

In the lavatories, Vadim unexpectedly bumped into Tkachenko. He had never previously been seen smoking but now he was thoughtfully inhaling a cheap cigarette.

"Surprised?" To judge by the tone of his question, the old man also knew the whole story. "I used to smoke in the camp. It's a relief sometimes. Especially now that I think I've made up my mind." His sunken cheeks went in and out as he inhaled smoke. "You can't go on guessing forever. At least I shall have someone of my own at my side there. And who knows, maybe I can carry my homeland away on the soles of my shoes. There's not a lot left of it."

"I'm glad for you."

"You mean it?"

"Completely."

"Thank you. But will they still let me out?"

"They promised. Otherwise what sense would there be in forwarding the embassy document?"

"Young man, young man, you still don't know your government very well." The old man rose, carefully extinguished his cigarette butt, threw it into the litter bin, and strode through the door. "Promised! Think of their promises to all of you! To you yourself! And I certainly don't count for anything at all as far as they're concerned."

Old "Doormat" went past the smoking hall. She could scarcely lift her felt boots, and a pathetic weariness showed in every step.

A voice in the tobacco haze felt sorry for her. "She's taking it hard."

Voices from various other corners concurred. "She's gone to pieces, poor woman."

"It started when Telegin died."

"Now she's finished."

Late in the evening, Vadim hid himself away from curious eyes. Looking around furtively, he took the dead doctor's notebook out of his pocket and leafed through it. And something suddenly died in him and turned to ashes. All one hundred and twenty pages of small squared paper were virginally clean—not a single mark on them. "What a farewell present you had up your sleeve for me, Pyotr Petrovich!"

XIV

That Saturday morning Vadim woke up with a vivid impression that something important was about to happen. It remained with him all morning, so when his name was called out from the corridor after dinner he dashed for the exit without a moment's hesitation. Old "Doormat" herself let him out into the exercise yard, with a parting word of advice at the door:

"Don't go too far. It's getting late."

The frail poplar leaves, thrown into bright relief by the late afternoon sun, rustled very faintly beside the circular path, and their mournful whisper accompanied Vadim all the way from the door.

He saw Natasha at once, as soon as he went out into the exercise yard. She was standing with her back to him in the corner of the garden, and the wind, tugging at the skirts of her green coat, was shaping her into a weightless, flying figure. The latch of the garden gate clicked, and caused the girl to look around expectantly. Her eyes came to rest on him, and she seemed to cry out to him, though she did not move from where she stood, except to give a scarcely perceptible nod: "Here I am."

"I was expecting you, Natasha." He was almost too agitated to speak. "I knew that you would come."

"Did Daddy tell you so?"

"He didn't say who, but I felt sure that it would be you."

"He asked me to come."

"Thank you."

"I've come on business."

"Thanks all the same."

The sun, its brief stay over the yard nearly over, was drawing close to the budding silhouettes of the poplars. Natasha, shivering with cold, drew her thin neck down into the collar of her coat and yawned uncontrollably. Her whole appearance, from her cheap, high-heeled shoes to the flimsy headscarf above her heavy fringe, moved Vadim to such stabbing pity that he felt faint. But nothing in her glance encouraged him to show his feelings. He might not have been there at all. If he had gone away she would not have noticed, but would have gone on yawning and shivering and hunching her thin neck into the collar of her coat.

"Are you frozen?" He timidly touched her elbow. "Shall we walk for a bit?"

She obediently moved off beside him. After a short silence she spoke, as though she had long ago made up his mind for him.

"You must get away from here."

"Where to, Natasha?"

"Daddy's parents are still living. Both of them." There was something touching in her businesslike manner. "They live outside Moscow. Almost in the forest. You can hide out there till they stop looking for you."

"Was this your father's idea?"

"Yes."

"In this uniform I shan't get past the first person I meet."

"Nyura will help you. She has Daddy's summer clothes at home. You're almost the same size. Nyura . . ."

Old "Doormat"? He turned hot all over. "You mean old 'Doormat'?"

"Nyura," she repeated sternly, looking at him in reproach. "Nyura will let you out at night."

"I shall have to be careful not to get lost." He was already in a fever of excitement at the thought of escape. "It's a big village."

"Nyura's house is right by the turning onto the Moscow high road. The windows have green frames. Don't catch the train, hitch a ride. Only don't forget—Krivolkolenny Number Sixteen, Apartment Six."

As though afraid that he might detain her, she almost ran across the yard to the gate. Vadim mechanically took a few steps after her, then stood peering through the shrubbery by the fence watching the dimly discernible, quick little figure of the girl whom now—why try to disguise it?—he quietly and gratefully loved.

Time went by with agonizing slowness. It was no good thinking about sleep, even for a little while. Vadim forced himself to close his eyes, and lay eagerly listening to all that was going on around him. That was the duty orderly making his leisurely round of the ward, counting his charges. That was Gorshkov in the next bed groaning and tossing before he fell silent for the night. That was the scarcely audible click-click-click of the three switches. The opaque nightlights intensified the gloom. The silence was broken only by snoring, and by delirious muttering here and there in the ward.

"Lashkov!" The head nurse breathed his name as she shook him by the shoulder. "Come on." Old "Doormat" led Vadim past the orderly, now asleep on a bench, along the almost unlit corridor to the head of department's office. The window in the office was half-open. In the glare of the ceiling light Nyura's face looked longer and puffier than ever. But her big, dark, rather prominent eyes were bitterly, inconsolably sad, and, once he had seen them, Vadim admitted to himself that here again the Ryazan peasant Mityai Telegin had been more observant and perspicacious than himself.

Deeply moved, he reached out to her. "Goodbye, Nyura, and thank you, my dear."

"Don't get the wrong house," she answered impassively. "Mine's got a roof ornament, and the front gate doesn't shut. There's a light on in the hall. You're expected."

A stormy night swallowed him up as he moved off in the direction of the main ward, making for the light by which someone was waiting, keeping vigil for him, probably getting worried.

He knocked and an old woman holding a lighted paraffin lamp opened the door. Sharp, surprisingly youthful eyes looked him up and down severely, then stepped inside without speaking, letting the light fall on a stool in the corner, covered with a neat pile of clothes. She silently held the lamp while he changed his clothes, silently stuffed a five-ruble note into his jacket pocket, silently showed him to the door, and only when she was closing it after him did her toothless mouth utter a muffled "God go with you."

It didn't take him long to hitch a ride. With a sickening squeal of brakes a black Volga stopped dead in front of him. The dashboard light illuminated a tired face with eyes red from strain and lack of sleep.

"Get in . . . in the back, with the boss."

As soon as they started up, a dark mass at Vadim's side stirred restlessly and a powerful mixture of alcoholic fumes wafted toward him.

"Yes, friend, I'm a broad-minded, big-hearted sort of guy . . . I think to myself, there's someone standing there with his thumb in the air so why not give him a lift? . . . I was commandant in Berlin . . . and I'm still somebody . . . but I haven't lost the common touch . . . I keep in contact with the people . . . The common people love me. I've just been fishing down at the fish farm . . . They couldn't have treated their own father better . . . Everything the heart could desire . . . You know, I've been as close to Hess, many a time, as I am to you now . . . Four times a year . . . in the course of duty . . . He was a very simple man, too, I was quite sorry for him . . . He willed everything he had to the Party . . . He may be a son of a bitch, but he's quite a decent fellow . . ."

His speech became more and more incoherent until he finally sagged back into the corner and began to snore resoundingly. The driver was silent all the way to Moscow. These outpourings were evidently nothing new to him. They had crossed the city boundary before he half turned around and spoke.

"Where d'you want?"

"It doesn't matter. Somewhere near Trubnaya Square if possible."

"I'll take you there."

He didn't utter another word all the way to the square. He started up again without even looking at the money which Vadim held out.

"You may need it yourself."

The day was young, scarcely beginning, as Vadim strode the familiar streets, cutting corners as he went, half recognizing the city and half not, though he must have walked the length and breadth of it in his time. All the things that had previously seemed so ordinary and familiar now stood out in bold relief: shop signs, phone booths, traffic controllers' boxes. He had ceased to be part of all this, and stared around like a visiting stranger who tries before he goes home to memorize everything as fully and precisely as possible, so that he will have something to tell the uninitiated.

XV

She might have been waiting all that time by the door, she appeared so fast when he touched the bell. A burning constriction in his chest made it difficult for him to get a word out, and he hovered in the doorway looking lost and apologetic. The girl came to his aid and spoke first.

"Hallo, Vadim."

"Hallo, Natasha." He still found it hard to breathe. "Well . . . I made my decision . . . come what may."

Suddenly he felt hot and faint, his legs were like cotton wool, and the world was spinning before his eyes. Vadim had a vivid picture of himself as Yegor the ferryman, whose story he had so often told on stage. Perhaps it was only now that he sensed the full poignancy of the last words which Yegor's sweetheart whispered to him: "Yegor, my dearest. I love you, my darling, my precious." He so longed to be somewhere at the ends of the earth, on the banks of some little stream with this slender girl in the wide-sleeved cotton wrapper, that if she had taken just one step toward him he would have rushed forward, picked her up, and never put her down again as long as he lived.

But the girl said softly, "This way," and went on down the corridor.

She stood aside to let him enter a room that was dominated by icons and books. The carving of the icon cases looked expert, though not old. In all this kingdom of books, Vadim could not spot a single familiar spine, however hard he looked.

"This is Daddy's room. I left everything just as it was." The girl went on ahead, and he took it as an invitation to follow her. "I'm glad you've made up your mind. To tell the truth, I was a little bit afraid myself at first that it might make things worse . . . How stupid . . . as if they could be worse."

Her room was completely unlike her father's. A couch covered with a rug, a desk by the window that had seen better days, a chair by the desk, and an elderly armchair constituted all the furniture. There was no hint of ostentation in this austerity. Every one of her possessions satisfied some essential need, and that was all. As sometimes happens with impressionable people, when Vadim entered he had a startlingly detailed hallucination that he had been here before, in this casually furnished room, sometime in the past.

"Your room's like a nun's cell, Natalie." Making an effort to shake off the hallucination, he sank into the armchair. "There's nothing girlish about it."

She wrinkled her brow fastidiously. "I don't care for unnecessary clutter. It's too much trouble. Don't you like the room?"

"On the contrary. I myself have never had time to become attached to things. Always on the move."

"It'll all be different now."

"Will it work?"

"It has to work."

"I'm not like you—you have lots of time ahead of you."

"Everyone has his own time-scale."

There was something about her, her economical movements, her unsmiling look, her slow, almost laconic way of speaking, that made Vadim forget how much older he was and feel as awkward and nervous as a boy.

"I want to ask you a favor, Natalie." It was a sudden inspiration, but it seemed to him that he had been thinking about it since their first meeting. "I want you to be with me on the day I go away."

"I shall take you there myself."

"If only you knew how grateful I am."

"Of course, I shall take you. You would get lost without me."

In her cotton wrapper there in the twilight she looked like a butterfly at rest, with wearily folded wings. With a great effort, Vadim resisted the temptation to pick her up and carry her tenderly about the room until she fell asleep.

She sighed. "If only you could get settled!"

"I'll try. I'll try so hard."

"It is probably more important to me than it is to you."

"So I shall have to try twice as hard."

"I'm serious."

"So am I."

"Thank you."

"Natalie . . ."

They had still not said the most important words, but they sensed a communion of spirits that illuminated past and present, and filled them with recognition and hope.

"It may take a long time, a very long time, Natalie."

"Does that really matter?"

"Not to me."

"Nor to me."

"But what if they find me, after all?"

"That won't be the end of everything."

"How do you mean?"

"You can try again."

"It will be too late by then."

"Is it ever really too late?"

"You are like a precious gift. . . ."

"You may regret it."

"Never."

"Don't make rash promises."

"I feel like making them."

"Is it like that?"

"Yes." And still more emphatically, "Yes."

The night and its cold stars looked in through the windows; sensing its atmosphere, they were silent for a long time. But although not a word was spoken, they continued their lovers' communion, which is as old as time and which will last until the end of the world. In the darkness, Vadim cautiously brushed her shoulder, and she melted at his touch and came into his arms. His eyes were misty, and he was breathless with emotion as he drew the girl to him.

"My dearest . . ."

"What good am I to you?"

"You're my life . . ."

"I'm afraid."

"Of what?"

"It can't last forever."

"It'll last forever."

"That's what you think now."

"That's what I shall always think."

"Are you sure?"

"I love you."

"And I've loved you since I first saw you."

"Nata . . ."

When they awoke, the tender green of the May poplars was glowing in the bright dawn light outside and through the trees they could make out the contours of the city against a cloudless sky. Once again, Vadim had his vision of a ship, somewhere beyond the agglomeration of boxes with their little windows, a ship with its prow facing to the sea, riding at anchor and waiting for him, enticing him with its snowy white sides. And this fleeting vision disturbed him, fired him with such enthusiasm that he could wait no longer, but must hurry up and do something.

"Time to get up, Nata! Look what a lovely morning it is!"

She smiled and nodded without opening her eyes, slowly stretched toward him and hid her warm forehead against his shoulder.

"Just a bit longer. We have time."

In a little while she was rattling the crockery in the kitchen, preparing a hurried breakfast, while Vadim dressed, still dazed by the remarkable change which had occurred in his life. "Heaven knows, it's like a dream."

The chilly early morning sunlight lit their way along a deserted street with its first sprinkling of young poplar leaves waving above it; without further delay they walked to the first bus stop on the route to the three stations.

XVI

When they escaped from the crush in the station and boarded the suburban train they found themselves in facing seats, and as their eyes met they knew at last that they were united for all time. Their past lives seemed like a troubled dream, now vanished. A new life, still unknown, but alluring in its novelty, awaited them. They sat opposite each other, holding hands, and all that was happening around about—the jostling, the swearing, the laughter, the tears—ceased to exist for them. For the time being, they were all alone in the world. Just the two of them, and no one else.

Then they were walking through the forest. The intoxicating May scent of sticky buds made them dizzy, and wild grasses clung to their feet, scattering the first dew before them. They said whatever came into their heads, but every word was endowed with a meaning known only to the two of them.

"I haven't been in the forest for a long time," he said.

"Nor have I."

"Look at the growth on that birch tree! It looks like a lion's mane."

"More like a tortoise in its shell."

"You have a good eye."

"I'm quite talented."

"Aren't you modest!"

"Mmm."

A strip of river, its surface gleaming like a mirror, appeared through the dappled palisade of birch trees, and soon they saw the ferry station with a few apparently commercial buildings along the shore.

She gave a sigh of relief and hurried down the slope. "Here we are. Once we're across, it's quite near."

"I shall arrive like a bolt from the blue."

"They're used to it. In fact, they'll be pleased."

A thin little old man with merry, bloodshot eyes stopped them by the beer kiosk on the bank.

"I could see that you've just got married, so I thought, let's ask them for twenty kopecks." His cordial frankness was disarming. "Or to make it the right change," he said with a slow wink when he saw Vadim reaching for his pocket, "say twenty-two. Exactly enough for a whole bottle."

Vadim gave him a fifty-kopeck piece. The old man showed no surprise, but waved his hand to show that he understood: I can see you're having a good time, my boy, and you have my blessing. Then he touched his cap politely, and instantly bored his way through the noisy mob milling around the kiosk.

Their encounter with the old man brought them down to earth. The racketing crowd of people by the landing stage, every one of them fully loaded with bags and bundles, was suddenly only too evident. They could see that their crossing was not going to be simple, and that the first day's journey on the other side would be a decidedly hungry one. Vadim left Natasha in the line for the ferry and dashed to the one and only grocery stall on the river bank to buy some sort of food and drink. He lost at least half his coat buttons fighting his way to the counter. Face to face at last with the saleswoman, who was perspiring from the heat and the endless arguments, Vadim without stopping to think flung her a crumpled ten and a cryptic order. "Ten rubles' worth!"

Her reflexes were in perfect working order. In a moment, the counter was adorned with the "gentleman's selection, small size," in all its incomparable magnificence: two bottles of White Top vodka, two tins of sprats, and a slab of Gold Label chocolate. With this booty, he reached the bank to find the ferry already casting off.

Vadim immediately spotted her headscarf like a beacon amid the motley melee on the ferry and his heart quickened and faltered until he felt faint. "What have you done to deserve such a gift, you old devil?" When she noticed him she started waving good-bye. She obviously liked this game, so he joined in, sinking onto the grassy bank and waving in reply. They went on waving to each other, enjoying their childish fun till the very moment when someone, he didn't yet know who, sat down at his side. There was no obvious reason to do so, but he went cold and limp. The man next to him just sat there panting hard, not saying a word, but Vadim already felt, or, rather, knew for sure that this was the end. The end of all that had been waiting for him on the other bank. The end of everything. Kreps was right after all: There was no longer any escape from them. His ties with them became harder to break every day. Without even looking around he asked with deliberate rudeness: "Mind if I have a drink, chief?"

The answer was almost friendly, but it had a quality which for some reason set the fingertips tingling.

"Drink away, Lashkov."

Vadim knocked out the cork with a practiced hand, and gripped the neck of the bottle between his teeth. The harsh liquid scorched his throat, but brought neither oblivion nor relief. He was still watching Natasha out of the corner of his eye, and she was still waving to him, without the least suspicion that their game was now in deadly earnest. The bottle didn't make him drunk, but only increased his bitterness. So, with angry defiance, he asked again, "Mind if I kill the second one, chief?"

The answer sounded even more friendly than before.

"Go ahead, kill it, Lashkov."

He had drunk so much of it in his time, but never had it proved so ineffectual!

On the receding ferry, Natasha's yellowish headscarf still shone like a beacon over the multicolored blur of the crowd, and her hand was still waving good-bye. He couldn't help himself, and waved back. The burning in his chest became an unbearable stifling pain, so he rose and walked off without looking around. Heavy steps accompanied him, rhythmic and inexorable.

Politely but firmly installed in the van, Vadim had lost all hope, but his eyes were instinctively drawn toward the river. By now the ferry was docking on the opposite bank and at that distance it was probably impossible for him to make out whether she was still waving or not, but right then he wanted to believe it and he carried his belief away with him to last through all the bitter years ahead. Before the back door of the van slammed shut he had time to take a silent farewell of her: "Till we meet again, Natalie! Live your life, my darling. It must go on!"

They drove away from the river to the sound of a jarring tune on the accordion, and the shouts of a desperate, drunken tenor.

FRIDAY

The Labyrinth

Dearest Papa, whom I love and revere—How are you? Right at the start of my letter let me tell you that we are alive and well and wish you the same. Dearest Papa, how *are* you getting on there? Kolya and I have come to a new place. There is steppe all around, and it's very windy. Never mind, it's still a place you can live in. I miss you very much, Papa. I often get up in the morning and start to knock the wall out of habit. We're on a good team. The foreman is Jewish, but he's a nice man and kind. I've never seen one like him before. Our wages ought to be good this month. Of course, there's nowhere to go here. Bare steppe all around, not a bush or a blade of grass. I keep remembering when I was little and I was always trying to find fairy bread in the back garden and you used to laugh, as much as to say: just as long as it keeps her happy. I've started crying a lot lately, I don't know why. Must be my time of life. Dear Papa, I shall shortly present you with a grandson or granddaughter. Touch wood. Don't start worrying, I'm only working as much as I can manage. Kolya doesn't let me do any more and the rest of the team doesn't either. Please God, when I have it we'll all be able to live together in one spot so that I can bring up the baby and look after you as well in your old age. That would really be nice. Only when will it be? We're on a funny sort of site. We don't know what we're building, it looks like nothing but corridors and little tiny rooms. Still, it's none of our business, we don't count. As long as the pay's good, that's all that matters; let the bosses have the headaches, they can see better up there from where they are. I keep writing about myself all the time, I haven't said a word about you. Dearest Papa, drop us a line and let us know how you're getting on, if you're keeping well, how you're managing in the house. You must take care of yourself at your age, think of the grandchildren you're going to have. It will be awful for me here if you fall ill; I shall eat my heart out. I can't wait to hear from you, Papa. Please don't forget your Antonina, because I shall never forget you.

Your loving daughter Antonina and son-in-law Nikolai.

I

When Antonina followed Nikolai into the office, the Clerk of Works had somebody else with him, a thin young man of twenty-five, in overalls bespattered with mortar, who was new to them. The two men were too deep in conversation to look at them as they came in. The Clerk of Works, a shapeless lump of a man with a short, bulging neck, was penciling something on a sheet of paper and doing sums out loud.

"Let's say six kopecks, and I'll throw in three kopecks for the carrying. Plus keying—twenty. D'you realize what sort of money you can make?"

The thin man listened and shook his big-browed head dubiously; he was unimpressed as he watched the movement of the pencil point in the Clerk of Works' clumsy grip, and there was a suspicious gleam in his big dark eyes.

"You know how long keying takes, Nazar Stepanovich. While you're doing that, how much other work can you get done?"

"Don't be too keen. Go over it with a mallet, just for appearances, then cover it up. I'll pass it."

"I can't, Nazar Stepanich. A job's a job. I do it properly or not at all."

"Conscience won't butter your bread for you. I'm giving you a chance to earn real money and you start quoting the moral code."

"Anyhow, I haven't got enough people for that sort of work, Nazar Stepanich. We shan't meet the completion date."

"People are no problem. I'll give you people." He raised his heavy lids to look at the new arrivals. "What do you want?"

The Clerk of Works listened to Nikolai with half an ear, took the employment order from him and skimmed through it with a frown of dissatisfaction.

"Unskilled labor. Have they gone mad or something in personnel? There's no unskilled laboring here. You've just been released?"

"Six months ago."

"What did you do in the camp?"

"Building."

"What trade did you learn?"

"A bit of everything."

"Ever do any plastering?"

"That as well."

The Clerk of Works was surprisingly swift and nimble for a man of his build. Tucking the pencil into the side pocket of his overalls he jumped resolutely to his feet and made for the door. "Right, down to the site!"

His trailer stood on rising ground and the site could be surveyed in all its length and breadth from the door. The steppe, as smooth as a table, bluish in the heat haze, stretched as far as the eye could see on every side of the site. The building under construction was for the most part in a deep excavation. It rose only a few feet above ground level, so that from the door of the trailer the whole area looked like a conglomeration of squat, square-topped concrete boxes, with dusty tip-up trucks scurrying about among them. The work that was going on was inside these boxes, so that the site, considering its size, seemed almost deserted.

Antonina walked behind the men without listening to their conversation. What worried her right now was how long she and Nikolai would be staying here. Since leaving Uzlovsk they had already worked on a detachment in the Far North, and then they had been going to join up with a timber combine in Krasnoyarsk, but the usual agent with his lavish promises turned up to entice Nikolai with tales of big wages, and without a moment's thought he had dragged her off to Central Asia. In the past, Antonina had always been ready to move on without special regret. In fact, she herself felt a need to make up for what she'd missed in the forty years at home behind her. She was thrilled with all the variety and colorfulness which opened up before her, with their promise of still more alluring faraway places somewhere beyond the horizon. But one morning she felt a subtle transformation in herself. Another, secret life was stirring within her, and she kept a silent vigil over it with breathless delight. Since then Antonina had hankered after a settled, quiet life. All at once she passionately wanted a home of her own, her own four walls to protect the new life within her from the menacing uncertainties of the outside world. This was why she was now walking behind the men in genuine dread that Nikolai would not stay there long and that once again she would have to pack their humble belongings for another journey.

The Clerk of Works, who was walking in front, signaled to his companions to follow, and suddenly turned into the dark entrance of one of the concrete boxes. They went down wooden steps into the corridor of a semibasement, which had rather dim temporary lighting. From the infinite depths of the building came a smell of unset mortar and damp soil.

"All you've got to do is start here, and the rest will look after itself." The Clerk of Works hurried them on. "You'll have so much money rolling in you'll be able to get yourself gold-plated."

The corridor ran alongside a somewhat smaller inner box with several door openings in its front wall, each of which was the beginning of a transverse passage between the two sides of the building. To reach the way out on the opposite side, they went around exactly half of the concrete square. Before going out into the open, the Clerk of Works turned to the thin man.

"Anyone else would be grateful, but you make difficulties. You can start both sides, one lot at each end." Obviously considering the discussion closed, he pulled a notebook out of his side pocket, armed himself with the same old pencil, and scrawled something in huge letters. "Get these people fixed up in the hostel." As he handed over the page torn from his notebook, the Clerk of Works for some reason steadfastly refused to look the young man in the eye. "Arrange about the laborers and get on with it."

The Clerk of Works plunged through the door and vanished in the dazzling sunlight. The young man turned toward them, looking perplexed, and sighed in distress.

"Looks like a shotgun wedding." He twirled the paper in his hand and cleared his throat. "Right, let's go."

Antonina stole a glance at him as she walked along at his side. He was tall, thin, rather round-shouldered, with a clear-cut profile, and he screwed up his eyes thoughtfully as he went, as though he were scrutinizing some distant object that was invisible to the others. One would have taken him for thirty at least, if it hadn't been for the deep, almost boyish flush which showed through the soft fuzz on his hollow cheeks.

"We use the administrative block as a hostel," he explained on the way. "Married people live in the offices, single people in the storerooms. All the basic jobs have been done, so it's mainly plasterers, painters, and so on. I've got five in my team, you'll be the sixth. My name's Osip, surname Meckler. What's yours?"

"Nikolai."

"Antonina."

"We'll put Tonya in with the women who do our laboring."

"She needs something light for the present, foreman," said Nikolai, looking shyly away. "She mustn't do anything too heavy just now."

Osip immediately turned pink and glanced at her with a warm twinkle in his shortsighted dark eyes.

"All right, we'll add a seventh one to the team. It won't break us."
He stopped at a door adorned with a skull and crossbones in chalk. "Such
witty people! Come on in."

The only difference between the administrative block and the other
concrete boxes on the site was the large number of windows on each of
its four sides. Inside, identical doors stood in an endless row along a
corridor which ran around the building. Each one had a plastic number
plate screwed onto it. Without knocking, Osip pushed open the last
one, which had the inscription "House Manager" scrawled across it.

"I salute a superior officer. Some new lodgers for you, Khristoforich.
Issue them with ammunition and add them to the list for rations."

In a room heaped high with mattresses and folding beds, a hairy old
man was sitting at a sort of hospital bedside table. He was wearing the
shreds of an undervest, which exposed a tattoo on his chest representing
the arms of the Russian Empire framed with a garish inscription: "Shoot,
you bastards!" In front of the old man was a half-eaten tomato, and a pile
of papers on top of which stood a nearly full quarter-liter. He looked at
the newcomers with drunken eyes that oozed one-hundred-proof sadness.

"Another one? And a married man, too. What on earth have you
come here for, good people? It's God's afterthought. D'you think we've
got a larger size ruble? Well, you're mistaken. If anything, it's a lot
smaller. A lot smaller. Still, as they say in polite society, your wish is
my command." He gestured with his bony chin. "Pick what you like, and
move into Number Fifty-six. Here are the keys."

When they had finally settled in with Osip's help, and Antonina had
dusted and mopped the room, run down to the shop, and laid the table,
the house manager, who was already well loaded, invited himself in.

"You've only set the table for three. It isn't very nice to forget the
landlord! I may come in useful some time." He winked indulgently at
Antonina as she rose to correct her error. "Please don't disturb yourself,
dear lady, I've brought my own." A glass appeared in front of him as if
by magic. "Gentlemen, your health." His Adam's apple jumped just once
in his sinewy neck. "Yes, Osya, I can understand these people. They're
Russians. God himself decreed that they should dream and be disillusioned,
that's the nature of the beast. They're all forever trying to do less and
make more, to get rich quick. It's their Asiatic instincts coming out. But
you, Osya, are an educated man, a Jew. Surely your refined Old Testament
intellect could have thought of something a bit better for human consump-
tion than this place."

"Well, you've landed yourself here as well, Khristoforich." Only his
eyes were smiling. "Anyway, what have you got against the Jews?"

"What have I got against the Jews!" This was obviously a game they'd played before. The house manager came to life and advanced eagerly on his opponent. "You'd be better off asking what they've got against me. I'm an old man; I've got no reason to lie. I remember very well how it all started. There'd be a knock on the door. A knock with the butt of a gun, of course, it produces more of an effect that way. My old nurse, Anastasia Karpovna, God rest her, would open up, and there sure enough on the threshold would be some upstart in a leather coat with a revolver dangling by his side. And you could be sure it'd be either a Jew or a Latvian. The least little thing and you were up against the wall. You're a well-read man, Osya, so of course you'll start giving me all that stuff about the pale of settlement and the Jewish lumpenproletariat as a breeding ground for revolution. But you tell me, where did that cold-blooded taste for murder come from? A lumpenproletarian flares up and calms down just like that. His class anger lasts until the first good meal he gets. But your people killed methodically, killed as though they were fulfilling an obligatory vow. They didn't even spare children. The Romanov children, for example. They might have renounced the religion of their fathers, but they obviously hadn't got it out of their systems. Jehovah was there all the time, deep inside. So they crushed the goyim. It's all right to do it to a goy, goyim aren't people."

"There were the other kind, too, Khristoforich."

"I daresay there were," he lazily agreed, then filled his own glass and drank it off. "Only I never noticed them. I've traveled the world from Paris to Bugulma, and never noticed them. No, I did know one, it's true, in the camps around Igarka. Zyama Rabinovich, a real saint. He was a novelist, always scribbling stories. And then there's you; you must have been dropped on your head when you were little. Why the devil did you come here? It's quite different for me. I've been arrested three times. Can you understand what that means?" He carefully turned down his gnarled fingers one by one. "I came back from France in forty-six. What did they do? They arrested me. In forty-nine they let me go free for a week. Then what did they do? They arrested me. In fifty-two, a month after I was released, what d'you think they did again? Arrested me. I've had enough. God wanted me to go as far into the wilderness as I could. I just want them to forget me. I don't want to die behind barbed wire." He looked imploringly in Antonina's direction. "Don't begrudge an old man one for the road, dear lady." She poured, and he knocked it back in one gulp, pushed his glass into his pocket, sighed loudly, and stood up. "I'll go and get a bit of sleep."

After he had left they were silent for a while, then Osip spoke quietly without looking up. "He's all right, but he drinks too much.

He'll come and try to borrow from you tomorrow. Don't give him any money, he won't repay it. He'll always be given plenty to drink, there are lots of people here. When they can't buy bread, they'll still find money for vodka." He glanced briefly at Nikolai. "Do you go in for it yourself?"

"In moderation."

"Be careful. The boys here are so alike you'd think they'd been chosen for it. They'll drink anything, including the mixture in the fire extinguishers."

"It's all right, I know where to stop."

"Let's hope so."

Osip sat resting his cheek on his fist, gazing blindly in front of him. Antonina thought that she could read something in his sensitive face, the reflection of some special knowledge which she didn't yet share, but which shone out of this man whom she scarcely knew. What she saw was doubtless not only grief, or melancholy, or indifference, but a kind of prophetic wisdom which she would only sometime in the future come to understand.

As he left, Osip turned around in the doorway and said, "Tomorrow, come straight down to the place where we were today. We'll all get together and work out how to proceed. All the best."

A vague sense that something decisive had happened in her life stirred in Antonina and stayed with her all evening. As she was getting ready for bed, she caught herself singing. "You're in a bad way, Antonina Petrovna; you'll be dancing next!"

II

When she woke up the next morning, Antonina was flabbergasted. From outside there came an unwavering, monotonous howl. The window vibrated rhythmically, lashed by fine sand. But for the peremptory ringing of the alarm clock one might have thought it was still twilight outside. The overcast morning sky hardly lit the rectangle of their room. She flung a dressing gown over her shoulders and roused her husband.

"Look what's going on outside, Kolya . . . it's terrifying." She eyed him cautiously as she busied herself with the table. "Look where we've landed ourselves—we shall regret it!"

Nikolai tried to make a joke of it, although he was obviously not in the best of humor himself. "Up north we froze, now we'll be warm down south. We shall survive."

They were just ready to go when Osip looked in on them. He smiled understandingly and tried to cheer them up.

"Don't be downhearted, it'll be all right. This gale will go on roaring for three days or so and then stop. Anyway, we'll be working under cover." He gave them a conspiratorial wink from the corridor. "Don't drop behind."

The prickly wind stung their throats and almost swept them off their feet. Gritty dust from the steppe scratched their scalps, insinuated itself under their clothes, grated spine-chillingly against their teeth. The outlines of the buildings were barely visible through the unbroken curtain of dust. Osip, walking in front, called out from time to time.

"Come on! Keep moving! Just another last effort, as they say. You've got to get used to it!"

When they finally reached the site, Antonina felt as though she had been soaked in a dry, itchy drizzle. She was drained and depressed before she had even started work. The mere thought that this might last for several days plunged her into panicky dismay. "Why ever did we choose this inferno!"

As she climbed down, Antonina felt several pairs of eyes scrutinizing her suspiciously. Four young men in overalls were squatting by the wall, expectantly eyeing the newcomers. Two of them were as alike as peas in a pod: snub-nosed, with pale eyebrows over the startlingly green, shy eyes. Next to them a swarthy chap, like a gypsy, with a gaudy handkerchief tied around his short neck, was slowly smoking a cigarette. The sleepy face of the fourth man expressed nothing but wry boredom. Osip let his companions go first, then climbed down the ladder.

"Meet the others," he said with a nod. "These two matching ornaments are Syoma and Pasha. Brothers. The Lyubshins. The dark one is Sheludko. First name Sergei. And this sleeping beauty rejoices in the name of Alik. Otherwise, Albert, believe it or not, Guryanich. Tell them your names."

"Tonya."

"Nikolai."

"Right, the honorable parties to the contract are agreed." His voice changed immediately and became businesslike. "You know the conditions, boys. Make up your minds, shall we take it on or not?"

After a brief silence, the first response came from Albert Guryanich. "You know best, foreman," he said, yawning lazily. "But that Karasik, as you know yourself, is a double-crossing bastard. He'll swindle us as soon as look at us."

Sheludko shook his curly head. "It's no work for skilled men, foreman. It's a woman's job, daubing walls. More dirt than work in it. Still, it's up to you."

Syoma's answer to the foreman's inquiring look was a loyal "Whatever you say, Osya."

Pasha eagerly seconded his brother's "Whatever you say."

Osip's face softened with gratitude—he was obviously pleased by their faith in him.

"What I think is that if he cheats, Karasik stands to lose more than we do. It isn't work for skilled men, you're right; anyone can wave a trowel about. The Clerk of Works has promised to make allowance for the differences in rates. But there's just the right sort of working surface, and we've room to spread ourselves. We'll go at it from two sides at once. We'll divide ourselves like this: Syoma and Pasha, you go with the new ones, and we three will work together. Tonya's expecting, so she can help with the main job. We shan't ask more of her then she can manage. Anybody against?"

Albert Guryanich rose as though answering for all of them. "Let's stop messing around. Time is money."

The foreman turned to Nikolai. "You'll be in charge here. We'll go around the other side. We'll get the scaffolding done today." He moved on without looking around. "Follow me, milords."

The first job to be done was humdrum and menial. They had to sort out trestles stacked in the corner, make them firm, and lay plank walks on them. But anyone who saw the care and attention with which the twins set to work might have thought that an operation of major importance was under way. Every plank they picked up had to pass a thorough endurance test before it was put in place. When one of them knocked in a nail, any cabinet maker might have envied his precision. When Nikolai looked at them he only chuckled. "Busy as a pair of beavers. Look how they lick things into shape. Like template-makers. They ought to be working in a dispensary. No need to check up after them."

However hard Antonina tried to keep abreast of the others, and show that she didn't expect to get something for nothing, the thicker planks and heavier trestles kept slipping from her hands as soon as she touched them. "I can't keep up with them," she thought tearfully. "It's no good trying to compete with such people."

By dinnertime they had erected enough scaffolding, between them, for an uninterrupted three days or so. But while Nikolai, to judge by his sweat-soaked back, was thoroughly worn out, the brothers looked as though they hadn't even begun their working day yet. Pasha carefully inspected his handiwork, and announced briefly:

"We can start giving it a key after dinner."

Syoma nodded. "And how!"

The wind was raising a dense unbroken wall of sand over the site. They walked to the canteen in single file, each trying not to lose sight of the one ahead. "What do we care," thought Antonina, covering her face with the ends of her headscarf. "We'll work off our contract and say good-bye. But whoever's going to live here will have a terrible time of it."

The canteen was bursting with noisy chatter and laughter. A cloud of steam from the kitchen mixed with tobacco smoke swirled slowly over a sea of heads. The smells of lime, nitrous paint, cooking, and cigarettes came together in a harsh, throat-searing concoction. A plump blonde of about thirty-five, outlined against the serving hatch, radiated queenliness like a portrait in its frame as she calmed the passions that seethed around her with a word or a nod.

"Make my soup thicker, Musenka."

"If it's something thick you want . . ."

"Musya, this soup's salty. Are you in love?"

"Not with you, don't worry."

"I'm pining away for you, Musenka."

"You'll survive."

"Musya, will you let me have something on credit?"

"Who do I collect from when you drink yourself to death?"

She looked Antonina over searchingly with frank curiosity, evidently found the comparison favorable to herself, and broke into a stately smile.

"You aren't used to it, of course." Her black button-eyes beamed tolerantly. "This is nothing; when it starts blowing in the winter you'll want to creep up the chimney. Next!"

At the table everybody was waiting for Antonina. They instantly cleared a space, pushed over the bread basket, then left her to fend for herself and busied themselves with their food. But even while they ate the men could not stop worrying about the new job. It was written all over them, in their tense faces, their restless hands, their gloomy pre-occupation. Albert Guryanich chewed away methodically and was the first to speak.

"You'll never do it in a month, foreman. It'll take at least two. And that'll be a tight squeeze. You can only crawl along that wall. Just giving the damn thing a key will take two weeks."

"That's right," sighed Sheludko sorrowfully. "We'll all have a pain in the shoulder. We were their last hope, nobody else would do it. Not enough fools nowadays."

The Lyubshins simultaneously turned their faces toward the brigadier with confident curiosity, as much as to say, come on, give them their answer.

Osip went on imperturbably eating his soup. "In my opinion it can be done inside a month. If need be we can work off-days as well. You don't find wages like this lying around in the street. Don't panic, that's the main thing. The money's as good as in your pockets."

Albert Guryanich rose with a skeptical grunt. "All right, I'm just dumb." He nodded lazily at the serving hatch. "Watch out, foreman, she'll put a spell on you."

The expression on Musya's round face eloquently testified to her feelings. She accompanied Osip all the way to the door with a look of devotion and undisguised adoration. Osip's ears flushed an angry scarlet. He hurried out into the corridor as inconspicuously as possible. Sheludko, following him out, wagged his head in rapt admiration. "What a woman! She only has to look at a man and he's had it. She loves them to death."

The brothers also rose. "We'll be off," said Pasha thoughtfully. "There's no special hurry. You've got time."

Syoma seconded him. "A good half-hour."

As soon as they were alone, Nikolai ventured to touch her elbow.

"Tired?" he asked anxiously.

"A little bit."

"Don't try to keep up with them, there'll be time."

"I'll keep going as long as I can."

"If you strain yourself, it'll be too late."

"I'll take care."

"Please do."

"Be sure you don't kill yourself either."

His timid concern for her was moving; she stroked the back of his hand affectionately. "There's a limit to what you can earn."

While they were talking, the Clerk of Works sat down at their table.

"Well, how are you finding it?" There was something forced and unhealthy in all that nervous energy. "Of course, this breeze is no fun for any of us, and I don't suppose you feel at home here yet, after the north. Still, it's so warm that you don't need to go to the baths." He turned a searching stare on Nikolai. "Haven't you started keying the wall, yet?"

"We've begun, busy with the scaffolding."

"Yes, well. . . . The work is urgent, you know. The percentage for the whole job depends on speed. You must be on time."

"We shall try."

"I can see you've got a head on your shoulders, boy. You understand things. Osip is a hospital case. He'll go on fiddling and finicking like a watchmaker, and what's needed here is speed, understand?"

The clerk's little eyes were begging. "Just a couple of knocks with a mallet and then slap the plaster on. It isn't a palace after all—it'll do."

"I'm new here, Nazar Stepanich," said Nikolai uneasily, "I'll do what the rest do."

"Well, have a talk with the boys, they should know. I expect they'll see where the money is."

"I'll try."

"It's a deal." Karasik was immediately in a hurry to be off. "I'll look in tomorrow and see what sort of start you've made."

Back at the site, Nikolai told the Lyubshins about his conversation with the Clerk of Works, but they only sighed in unison.

"Say it again when Osya's around."

"Can't talk behind his back."

Nikolai was offended. "I'm only passing on what he said. If you work as if you're in a dispensary you won't earn much, that's all."

The brothers exchanged a glance and said nothing. But Antonina thought she saw a weakening, a tremor in their faces when wages were mentioned. She noted the change with angry regret. "Nothing like money for bringing out the worst in people!"

That night in her bedtime prayers she asked God's grace for herself, her husband, his comrades, all those on whom their welfare depended. Nor did she forget her father, but passionately wished him health and long life. Her last prayer was for Osip, an adherent of a different creed who was suffering for others.

She couldn't go to sleep. She lay staring into the darkness for a long time, then spoke aloud, more to herself than her husband.

"Perhaps we shouldn't?"

"What?" he answered drowsily. "Shouldn't what?"

"Do what the Clerk of Works wants us to."

"This isn't the time. Go to sleep."

Antonina dreamed of a mountain, with weird shrubs growing in its jagged stony crevices. She was heading upward, climbing toward a dazzling blue peak, sure that once she was there she would be able to see the sea beating against the other side of the mountain. Then the morning of another day woke her in the middle of her dream.

III

They got advances against their wages, and that evening the hostel livened up considerably. In the canteen there was a certain excitement in the air at suppertime. Afterward it gradually increased, spreading to the corridor and the rooms. By the time the onset of dusk revealed a sprinkling of early stars in the windows, the administrative block was ringing with oaths and laughter.

As the tide of drunkenness rolled nearer and nearer to their room, Antonina listened to its advance and was torn between hope and dread. Please, God, let it pass us by; please, God, let it miss us! Her hopes were to be disappointed. Around midnight, Albert Guryanich and the house manager, rolling drunk, burst into the room with bottles in their pockets. The house manager, trying to ingratiate himself with his hostess, bent his thin, stringy body in a low bow.

"We've brought our own, Antonina Petrovna, we've brought our own. We won't put you to any expense, but be gracious enough to permit us to drink to fellowship with your spouse."

"We won't eat you out of house and home, Tonya." Albert Guryanich could hardly stand up. "We're not fussy, we don't need any snacks . . . On your feet, get up, Nikolai . . . The three of us can down these two bottles of Whitetop."

While Antonina was getting the table ready, the guests resumed a conversation which had evidently been going on for some time. Steadying himself with a hairy hand against his companion's chest, the house manager bawled wisdom at him.

"You say the peasants are our breadwinners! They come and weep on your shoulder, telling you, 'There's famine in the kolkhoz, so we've come here to earn some money.' And you listen to them like donkeys. Look at me—I'm wearing Chinese trousers, a Romanian shirt, and Czech shoes; you and I eat Canadian bread, our sausage is made out of Australian meat, they improve our porridge with Danish butter. What's become of our breadwinner-through-the-ages? The poor soul is either sitting in the market, or in session in the Kremlin, covered in medals, or running around the shops. And then the idle bastard grudges us our bread—our own bread. We've ruined his life for him, he says. Workers and scientists feed themselves nowadays, they mine gold, extract oil, make medicine or books that go abroad for food and clothes. And your peasant has been sponging on them for a very long time. They even harvest his miserable wheat and potatoes for him. Anyhow, when Russia did live on peasant grain it was always starving. Because it isn't grain, it's a bad joke. He doesn't know how to grow it and he doesn't want to learn. Take the Germans, they get sixty a hectare on their sandy loam, and our miracle-working hero is still struggling toward an average fifteen on black earth. He's just ignorant and idle, the Russian peasant. We mustn't pity him, we must teach him. Teach him to work. Have you ever seen how he salts fat bacon? Throws lumps of it into a barrel and thinks he's smart. Just let anybody in the village try smoking or dry-curing it: They'll eat him alive, his life won't be worth living. The Russian peasant can't stand anybody doing something better. He lives like a pig, so everybody else has got to live that way, too. That's why he hates Europe and despises the whole world. They don't live right, or at least not the way he does. And that's why he's always bragging about being first in the world with everything. Have you read Leskov's story about the left-handed blacksmith? I saw a picture once— he's standing there, filthy, ragged, in rotten bast shoes. But he's managed to shoe the flea! But what's the point of shoeing?—just ask him that. He'd do better to wash, strip some bark, and make himself new shoes, then patch the holes in his caftan! They're lazy thieves, and you come here sniveling about the poor helpless creatures being oppressed and having to work for nothing. Just try and make him work a day for nothing. Blood out of a stone!"

But Albert Guryanich was obviously not in the mood for abstract discussions. He followed Antonina's hand with greedy thirst as she poured out the contents of the half-liter bottle.

"Oh, to hell with all that. You're an educated man. Supreme commander of blankets. We're ordinary people, we just want decent food and some dough."

The house manager took a drink and started off again. "That's just it, it's always been the same. So why blame anyone but yourselves? People like you are born to do the donkey work, there's no finer beast of burden. You can't get along without a nanny and a whip, and if you aren't flogged for a week you start pining. You stupid bastards!"

Antonina tolerated this men's talk but didn't pay much attention. Their preoccupation with the fortunes of football teams or incidents on the eastern frontier struck her as absurd. She was much more troubled by the latest price rises in the canteen, and still more by the frayed collar of her husband's best shirt. She forgave them their little weakness and, as a rule, when she was in male company she silently kept to her own thoughts. It was the same on this occasion. She poured drinks for the guests almost without hearing what they were saying, and only came back to earth when the house manager left.

"Is Ilya Khristoforich upset about something?" She had stopped being angry about their visit. "If there isn't enough I'll run and fetch some."

Nikolai covered her hand with his own. "Let him go. He knows how much he can take," he said, and turned to Albert Guryanich. "You were married once?"

"I'll say I was." He stared into space, suddenly sober. "I came home from the army, and didn't know where to go. I'd been trained as a driver in the forces . . . I read somewhere that drivers were wanted for taxi service. So I applied. Got taken on driving top brass. The work was steady, but the money went nowhere. A girl got in one time. Fairish hair. Pretty. Wearing trousers. Couldn't have been more than eighteen. We're on our way to the three stations. Suddenly she turns to me and says, 'Listen, kid,' she says, 'how'd you like to make some real money?' So I say, 'Depends where it comes from. If it's anything crooked,' I say, 'you can go somewhere else.' 'What d'you mean,' she says, 'it's a clean job. I'll find the clients and you just have to wait around for a bit.' I turned round and looked at her and my heart sank: there she sat facing me, smiling, just like one of those dolls in a foreign fashion magazine. 'What's the going price for youth and beauty nowadays?' I say, and my heart's bleeding. 'You'll get five a time,' she says, 'and the rest's mine.' 'All right,' I say, 'let's go.' From that day on we were in business together. You could say it was a whole firm. At first I felt dirty, but then I got more or less used to it. Besides, the money was good. I didn't need three jobs at once. I managed to collect some belongings, always had cash on me, wore a hat and a belted overcoat. I was better off than some engineers. She had more customers than she could handle. Sometimes we picked up three at a time. Well, she was something to look at, I can tell you: a dream. After work we often went out to the country. We took liquor, of course, and something to eat with it. There was never anything between us, we were just pals. If you get involved, it interferes with the work! Well, one day we're having a drink and she says to me, 'Alik, would you marry me, like I am now?' I was stunned. 'Why are you teasing me?' I say, 'What d'you want?' She bursts into tears. 'Because I love you; I've loved you for a long time, that's why.' That sobered me up fast. 'Have you gone crazy?' I say. 'How can you love me? Just take a good look. You could put me in the garden to frighten the birds, and that's about it.' 'You idiot,' she says, 'you don't know your own worth. Any girl would marry you unless she was blind.' Well, of course, I nearly went out of my mind, I wanted her so much; I was only young, just twenty-five . . . That's when it happened to us the first time. That's when she told me the story of her life . . . She came from an ordinary family herself. Her father was in shoemaking or something, and her mother was a cleaning lady. They lived in Kolomna, I think. When she was just a kid they used to tease her and called her 'the actress.' So when she left school she rushed off to Moscow, to try and get into the Theatrical Institute. Well, you know how it is, the place was swarming with girls like her, each one more beautiful than the next. She tried to make a place for herself but they wouldn't take her. Then she tried the roundabout way, but that was dirty. If she went home, she'd be laughed at. She was proud, she would rather have been dead than go back to Kolomna. Well, she saw an advertisement; hands wanted for garment factory, with residence permit. The factory is next to the three stations. She went to pick up her first wages, and found *she* was owing *them*. Enough to make you howl like a wolf. Then one of the girls in her team comes around, oh-so-friendly. 'You idiot,' she says, 'you've got good looks, and you don't know what to do. Come with me tonight, you won't regret it.' 'How can anyone bring themselves to do it?' she asks. 'You'll get a bit of pleasure and you'll have money. In our team,' she says, 'everybody with two eyes and a tooth is on the game.' So that's where the high living started. Restaurants every evening, or some place in the country; then the ones with more experience advised her to get a taxi driver. Increases the flow of production, as they say . . . To cut a long story short, I married her. All open and above board. We even went to the registry office. I took her to my bachelor's hovel at Cherkizovo. The neighbors had never treated me as a human being, but when they saw what a beauty I'd found, they suddenly became very respectful. We had a marvelous life. I used to come home from work and she'd be standing waiting by the gate and run to meet me. I've never had anything like it before, and I felt I could never manage to live without her. We hardly ever got out of bed at all. We just wanted to squeeze into each other and stay there. Then when she got pregnant I didn't know whether I was on my head or my heels. I couldn't bear the breeze to blow on her. The neighbors turned quiet. Touched their caps at a distance. Old Alik, the no-good, had set up as a solid citizen. I used to run home from work and I'd always be loaded with flowers or something sweet. I used to dream that once the child came, she would be rid of the past forever . . . But if you're made to eat shit, why go and buy bread?" At this point he even ground his teeth in despair. "I came home one day from work, and my Tanechka wasn't there, but there was a note lying on the table. 'So and so, and such and such,' it says, 'dear Alik, our life together won't work'—she says it's quite impossible for her to have a child at such a young age; she wants, it says, to see something of life, and, in all probability, to try the artistic world again . . . Well, after that my life was like a horror story, and it got worse as it went on. I drank everything I had, right down to my undershirt. They soon kicked me out of my job, of course, and took my driver's license away. The neighbors were practically wild with joy—why, Alik had taken a fall! I couldn't shake them off. To cut a long story short, when I came around, I was in a mental hospital; I'd landed there with the d.t.'s. After I was discharged, I hadn't got a kopeck or a stick of furniture, and the block sergeant was checking on me every day. So I said to hell with it all and went to the council to see the labor recruiting officer. Then I landed here. Give me the remains, Petrovna!"

The last shot was finally too much for Alik. Antonina and her husband together carefully lifted him to his feet and took him toward the dormitory, where he and the other single men had their beds. On the way he made repeated attempts to lie down, muttering drunkenly, "I'll just lie down for a minute, pals, that's all. And I'll be as straight as a die again afterward . . . Ready to work and defend my country. No, honestly, it's a law of all professional drivers. A minute or two of sleep at the wheel, then all the way to the airport if you like . . . I promise you!"

Antonina left her husband to undress him and put him to bed; she started back to their room, but on the way she changed her mind and went out of the building. The deserted site looked dead in the brilliant moonlight that shone over the sultry steppe. The occasional pools of light around the bases of the watchtowers picked out the bumpy, crumbling surface of the same landscape. The steady boom of a jet was boring through the starry depths of the night. Antonina had a glimpse of the mysterious and awesome world that lay beyond the confines of darkness.

When she had become accustomed to the silence that surrounded her, she suddenly heard two voices floating out of a dark basement opening nearby. For some reason, she felt hot. One of them, a low, throaty feminine voice, obviously belonged to the woman who served in the kitchen. In the other, a rich muffled bass, Antonina recognized her foreman.

"I'm not asking you for anything, Osya, don't be afraid." Musya sounded almost as if she were praying.

"That's not the point, Musya." Osip was embarrassed and evasive. "That's not the point."

"D'you think I'm too old for you? I'm not old at all. I'm only a little over thirty."

"What are you talking about, Musya?"

"Maybe you don't want me after I was with old Nazar? Do you think I wanted that? Did you know I've got a string of black marks as long as your arm in my labor book? If I didn't fall on my back I'd never get a job."

"You just don't understand, Musya. . . ."

"Osinka, my darling, I'll wash your feet and drink the water. Just as long as I'm with you. Whenever you want me. . . ."

"I can't, Musya. It isn't that simple, we aren't animals." His voice shook. "There must be love."

"I've got enough for two, Osya. You only have to call. I'll go through fire and water for you."

"You don't understand, Musya, you simply don't understand."

"Nobody will ever love you like I do, Osya . . . I'll shield you and protect you from everything."

"I can't, Musya." And, more firmly, "I can't."

"I'll wait, Osya, I'll wait. You have a good time, you're at that age. I'll wait."

"No, Musya. You mustn't."

"Osinka!"

"I'm going now, Musya."

"Os-ya-a-a."

Antonina tried to calm her racing heart as she turned back toward the block. Burning with something she had never known before, she hurried to her husband, afraid to admit even to herself that the emotion which possessed her at that moment was jealousy.

IV

Work the next day was a disaster. The men moved as slowly as flies in autumn. Tools fell out of their hands. Most of the mortar slopped under the level and onto the floor. Antonina tried to save the situation, patching up the rough bits as best she could, but she couldn't keep up from lack of practice, and in the end she too slowed down, and lost heart. As soon as the dinner bell in the timekeeper's office rang, the whole team collapsed where it was on the scaffolding to sleep off its hangovers.

Antonina also went to sleep in a corner. She dreamed that she was watering the flowerbeds in their little garden at Uzlovsk under the hot midday sun. Her father was watching her angrily through the window, and shaking his head in despair as if to say, "You're doing it all wrong, all wrong, all wrong." Tears of humiliation were choking her, and the water ran to waste out of her watering can—lots and lots of water. Moisture filled her eyes. Cold, icy moisture. . . .

"Excuse me." Osip's sad face appeared before her. "Be a pal and give me a hand."

She was embarrassed and upset. "The heat was too much . . . it's baking . . . Listen to them snoring!" Feverishly she tidied herself up. "What is it?"

"I want to put up a bit more scaffolding, and I can't handle it by myself." He asked so humbly that Antonina's embarrassment only increased. "You couldn't wake my lot with a cannon, either."

"The boys made a night of it last night . . . Lead the way, foreman."

Together they found some free trestles, set them up, and laid planks across them. Never before had Antonina worked with such pleasure. As she helped Osip, she watched every step he took, every movement he made; she was so delighted that she never took her eyes off him. When they began work he had stripped to the waist. His lean, muscular body gleamed with sweat, and every time he turned his flushed face towards her, Antonina's heart stood still.

Osip scrambled up on the scaffolding they had erected and winked down at her gratefully. "Thank you. Let them sleep a bit longer. I've got nothing else to do at present anyway. I can do quite a lot of keying in that time."

Sparks showered from under his mallet as he walked along the wall to the far end of the plank. Little by little the whole concrete surface of the wall was pitted with little indentations. The work was well done; nothing botched, nothing missed. She felt guilty and awkward in his presence. "People like him can't be bought. He has too much of a conscience."

Busy as he was, Osip let fall a friendly word from time to time.

"Do you get tired?"

"Only toward evening."

"The heat must take it out of you."

"I'm used to it now."

"D'you feel homesick?"

"Terribly."

"Will you go soon?"

"I'm not making any guesses."

"What d'you mean?"

"Anything can happen."

"Don't get any silly ideas." He looked down at her sternly. "Everything will be OK."

"Please God, it will!" she sighed, moved by his words. "I only hope you're right."

Then they sat under the scaffolding and took turns drinking from a bottle of kefir which Osip had conjured up from somewhere. After each mouthful he passed the kefir to Antonina and she drank her share, weak with affection and gratitude. The words he spoke, at first so ordinary and unassuming, struck her as the weightiest and most significant she had ever heard.

"My family, too, keeps writing to me and telling me to come back. It's a temptation, of course. I was born and brought up in Moscow. But I don't want to. It was probably not until I got here that I finally felt myself to be a man. From my childhood, for as long as I can remember, the cursed word 'Jew' has followed me around like a tail. Even people who liked me, friends and acquaintances, didn't forget to remind me occasionally, by way of a joke, what I was. But one day I ran away from home. I read a book about a Jewish tramp and I ran away. I remember arriving in Ashkhabad. It was winter and I was only wearing a light sweater. I'd sold nearly all the clothes off my back on the way down. I thought it was bound to be hot in the desert. But I discovered that the winter there isn't tropical. They turned me out of the station at night. I was sitting there in a little garden nearby with my teeth chattering. A woman comes up to me, rather drunk, nothing but bruises, and speaks to me. 'You've got the shivers, you poor boy, go down to the brickworks; you'll get warm there.' She showed me the way, and off I went. I found this brickworks on the edge of the town, next to the desert. I climbed up on top of a kiln, and there were lots of people up there already. Most of them were kids like me, but there were grown-ups as well. They made room for me; it was an enormous kiln. I lay down between two lads. There was a draft from above, the roof was like a sieve, but it was baking underneath. So we kept turning over, all together, all night long: You warmed one side, then turned over on the other . . . I lived that way for a month and a half, earning a bit doing some loading, stealing a little here and there. On the days when there was nothing, my neighbors on the kiln would give me a bite to eat. And during all that time, I never once remembered my origins. And nobody reminded me of it. There were Tatars, Uzbeks, Russians, Ukrainians, even Latvians, among us but nobody thought about it. They didn't even mention it in fights. My parents had me found and sent back before long, but I never forgot that blessed feeling of being as good as the next man. I realized then that what people hate isn't us, or our nationality, but our prosperity, our failure to share the general poverty, our professions which have no connection with manual labor. Our nationality is a label to attach to the hatred, an abbreviated name for outraged resentment. In Russia anyone who lives better than the rest is hated in his own way. So I decided there and then that when I left school I would deliberately fail my entrance exams so that I could go away and work with everybody else, on an equal footing, and the rougher the better. . . . Excuse me, I'll light a cigarette."

As he got out his cigarette and matches, Osip's elbow brushed Antonina and this accidental contact caused her heart to race wildly. His confidences had raised him still higher in her esteem, made him even more attractive. "He's had a hard time of it," she thought, damp-eyed with sympathy. "I wouldn't wish it on my worst enemy."

He inhaled deeply, and suddenly asked, "Have you got enough money?"

"Enough for the time being."

"And when you have the baby?"

"We shall have to see."

"You ought to give it some thought now."

"Thought or no thought, where would we find any?"

"Ask Nikolai if he wants a job—I'll find him one. I do part-time work in the town."

"But what about yourself?"

"I don't care about the money; it's interesting."

"What's the work?"

"Uh-huh. There's a sculptor from Moscow living there. I bring him earth from the depot, mix the clay for him, do various odd jobs. Five's the going rate. Look in on Sunday and we'll go there together."

"Thank you. I'll tell him. The money will come in handy."

"Right, that's settled." He rose and dusted off his knees. "Don't wake the boys, we shan't get any work out of them, anyway. . . . I'll go down and have a chat with Karasik about jobs."

Left alone, she said a long, silent prayer, asking the Lord not to judge her too harshly for the weakness in her heart and her sinful thoughts. When she had finished praying, her quiet joy was still with her. Her heart was singing, and there wasn't a cloud in the sky.

V

At one time the town had relied for its livelihood on the sea. Many of its adobe yards held the warped remains of boats, or fishing gear which had been adapted to shore use. Every year the sea retreated farther from the town until it was just a knife-edge gleam on the horizon. The town went into a decline and slowly began to die. Young people grew up and left to seek their fortunes elsewhere and the old stayed on to live out their days, scraping a living around the bazaar and the station with its decrepit freight yard.

But one sultry summer day, an army truck pulled up in the town square. A group of officers in field uniform got out. They stood there for a while, marked time around the platform erected for ceremonial occasions, then got back into the vehicle and drove off. Shortly afterwards, soldiers began arriving in the town. They set up camp on its outermost edge. Before a month had passed, a settlement of small prefabricated houses had sprung up beyond the town limits, and it gradually acquired auxiliary buildings.

The town came back to life. Not that there was any immediate, drastic change. It remained as it had been, a town of one-story adobe houses, with the mosque and the Orthodox church towering like twin lighthouses at opposite ends. But there was more bustle in the streets, louder conversation, more varied dress. This probably explains why the local authorities were fired with the ambition to immortalize the town's renaissance in monuments, on the ancient Roman model. Their first site was the municipal garden which had served up to now as a pasture for the goats of local old-age pensioners. Here they decided to erect a triumphal arch, decorated with sculptures that recounted the glorious deeds of their compatriots. For this purpose a well-known sculptor was summoned from Moscow, and the two best stonemasons in the province were hired on a piecework basis. The arch had already been under construction for more than a year when Osip took his friends to the visiting sculptor's workshop, and there was no end in sight.

The workshop itself was a long shed, which had once served as a harbor warehouse, divided into two equal parts by a wooden partition. While she was waiting for the men, who had gone to fetch plaster of paris and earth for the casting boxes, Antonina wandered slowly around the room, inspecting statues of various sizes and substances that were ranged on stands along the walls. None of them resembled anything she had ever seen before. In the past, it had always been so easy to understand: a man looked like a man, the kind of person she was used to seeing every day in the newspaper or at meetings. Here every figure looked entirely different. Statues reared up in silent agony, with gaping wounds in the breast or the solar plexus, seeming to cry for compassion and help. She was particularly struck by a crucifixion standing in a corner: a beautiful and powerful male torso, nailed to a cross, and topped by a child's head at a dislocated angle. If anyone had asked her why this crucifixion was so disturbing, she could not have found the words to express the vague and troubled memories it aroused in her.

The men she had lived with, the men she was accustomed to meeting —her father, uncle, nephew, husband—were strong and unafraid, but their essentially childlike nature put them at the mercy of circumstance. Thus the life of each of them was like the cry of a condemned man.

Her slow progress past the statues was accompanied by a stormy conversation on the other side of the partition; from time to time it suddenly subsided, only to flare up again with new intensity.

Two voices interrupted each other continuously, one a muffled burr, the other steely with defiance.

"Once again you're looking for a God to take care of things while you evade your responsibilities. Can't you foist the blame for your slavery onto somebody else?"

"I detest that kind of intolerance. It's straight out of a seminary. History has taught you nothing, my dear Yurochka. You hate everyone! Orthodox Christians, the petty bourgeois, block sergeants. And your confreres who have come from the camps hate criminals. I can just imagine what a cozy little regime you'll establish for your political opponents if you come to power. Surely it isn't so hard to understand, Yura, that if it's always 'an eye for an eye' there'll never be an end to bloodshed. Try to be forgiving just once—you'll feel better yourself."

"We've heard all that before. Vladimir jail is crammed with prisoners and you go driveling on about Providence." His voice sank almost to a whisper. "Have you heard? They've taken Kreps off to Kazan."

"There you are, you see." There was bitter grief in the voice beyond the wall. "They didn't take you, or one of your people, but an inoffensive preacher like him. Obviously Mark's words must carry more weight than yours."

"But who will follow them? No more than the odd individual. Their philosophy is so degraded that a century of prayer wouldn't clean it up."

The conversation was resumed after a short pause.

"Did you notice the boy who looked in here? The younger one?"

"Well?"

"He's from a good family, they say. He left school with top marks. But instead of a higher education he chose the remotest building site imaginable. Can you call that labor enthusiasm? It doesn't enter into it. The boy is too clear-headed for such cheap idealism. A crazy whim? Wrong breed for that. So tell me, if you can, what *is* the answer?"

"It certainly can't be religion!"

"Who knows. It's more likely to have been a premonition of belief. The incompatibility of a pure soul and the falsity of the life in which it finds itself may mean that it reaches for more primitive ways of life. But such people certainly won't follow you, I can assure you."

"We are not asking them to."

"Because you're afraid of them. Their whiteness would contrast too sharply with your darkness. Your appeal is to the social and spiritual lumpenproletariat. Riffraff who are longing to found their empires on blood. Other people's blood. And yours too, incidentally."

"History doesn't repeat itself. We shall remember past experience."

"Perhaps. But since your new experiments will cost Russia a further ransom in blood, I'm against it." His voice hardened and became unexpectedly harsh. "So if you start anything I shall get down behind a machine gun and defend the social order to the last bullet, although I have nothing in common with it. I will defend boys like that against yet another, still more hideous peasant uprising. Better to stick with what we have than get you . . . You are darkness. God preserve Russia from both you and it."

"At least you are honest. This virtuous conservatism serves to protect your source of income. Naturally! Where else would people of your sort find so many idiots stuffed with public money, and ready to build Parthenons to commemorate the opening of a Sorting Station."

"You should be ashamed. You know that I can't exhibit, and have nothing to live on. Anyway, you're in no position to talk . . ."

"So, you grudge me my bread . . . and you're a Christian." His voice rose to a shout. "I'll never set foot in your house again. To think that I dragged myself all those hundreds of miles so that you could tell me where you stand. I'll send you your money back . . . So long!"

"Yura!" And still more imploringly, "Yura!"

As the man rushed out, Antonina saw nothing but a little, rather colorless beard—the kind worn by scientists doing fieldwork—and coal-black eyes burning with anger in a broad, irregular face. He slammed the door with such force that it went on shaking. When she recovered from her surprise, Antonina heard a now familiar voice challenging her from nearby.

"Do you like it?"

The man who stood in front of her, legs wide apart and hands behind his back, was dark-haired, broad-shouldered, of medium height, and roughly her own age. He wore an open-necked cowboy shirt, the ends of which were knotted over his already well-defined paunch, and velveteen trousers bespattered with plaster of paris. His chest was hairy and muscular under his shirt; he was clearly a fanatically hard worker. An almost childlike hint of mischief lurked in his brown eyes.

"D'you like it?" he asked again, and without waiting for an answer started a flood of excited words. "The man who just went out doesn't like it at all. He only wants to adapt my work to his own purposes. But it refuses to be adapted. My work and his have quite different aims. You see, my dear"—this innocent lapse into familiarity won her over immediately—"I don't put my ideas into my material, I draw them out of it. It is all there to begin with, in the stone or the metal or the clay; one only has to find the form in which it can express itself. Tell me, what do you think I need for this cross?"

Antonina was flustered by such an abrupt question, but she suddenly felt weighed down by the agony which the sculptor had imparted to the crucified body, and whispered almost inaudibly, "Something very heavy."

He looked at her for a full minute in silent surprise, as though he had not noticed her before, then said slowly and quietly, "Yes, my girl, God hasn't forgotten you. He has given you his grace. Enough to last you for some time."

Evidently he was about to continue, but at that moment there was a noise outside and the men burst into the room, laden with sacks of earth and plaster. The sculptor rushed to give them a hand and between the three of them they had no trouble maneuvering the load deftly into place before finally allowing themselves to sit down and have a cigarette in peace.

Watching the men resting and smoking by the window, Antonina found herself envying their lot. Muscular strength, or knowledge of a craft, ensured them their place in the sun. They had never known the practice of the thousand little things without which a woman's existence is impossible. For her there was something more essential than either health or work. She could justify her life only if she remained constantly aware of her ties with the world about her and hence of her obligations to it. "What does a man care? He gets up and fastens his belt—and look what the woman's left with!"

Their host was the first to rise and speak. "Well friends, the day's over—let's go to my room and make a foursome. There's a bottle of some poison or other; we'll split it."

In the other half of the warehouse, which the sculptor had converted into living quarters, the triumphal arch reigned supreme in every imaginable and unimaginable form: mockups, papier-mâché models, details, photographs of it were everywhere, no matter where they looked. Figures of pensive maidens holding sheaves of grain, and others of helmeted machine-gunners besieged their host's bed on every side. The only thing that seemed to be deterring them from the final assault was the marble bust of a little girl, which was placed on a stand at the head of the bed. Its lines were all calm and serenity.

"You're judging me," their host commented mournfully when they had finished off the bottle. "You are right, but I have to do something to fill my stomach. They don't want my real work. What they want for their money is every possible gratification at the level of a cheap film by Pyryov. I can understand it. Why should they pay just to please my taste? It's better for them to please themselves." He fixed his eyes on Meckler. "I envy you, Osip. You have managed to avoid getting involved. But, of course, you couldn't have done it without a clear view of the world. But who gave your generation this clarity of vision? I did! We all did, we who spent decades inventing the bicycle and discovering America all over again instead of doing something worthwhile. We wasted years like that, but we gave you your perceptions ready-made at the very outset of your journey. And that is why you can start from the present, without wasting any effort on things which it took us so many years to learn. And what years they were! What a school to learn in! We paid dearly for our education. We were clearing the mine field for you, so to speak. We have no strength left for anything further. The little job we did cost too much blood. That's why all I think about now is being allowed to work at my sculpture. I've caught up with the present and I have no time for anything else. These are the only conditions that make life worth living for me." His tiredness suddenly betrayed itself: All at once he was limp and gray. "Right, boys, it's time you went." His gaze shifted to Nikolai. "You're lucky to have such a wife, pal . . . Take care of her. You won't get presents like that every day . . . Well, see you soon." He fumbled in his trouser pocket, brought out a handful of crumpled notes and handed them to Osip. "Here you are . . . should be enough there . . . That's for all of you."

Antonina looked back as she left the room. The master of the house was sitting with his eyes closed, resting the back of his head on the windowsill; approaching sleep cast shadows on his sturdy body and his striking face which suddenly gave him an air of childlike helplessness.

VI
Musya Tells Her Own Story

"Yes, dear, I've seen things you couldn't make a story out of or write about in a book. You don't even know you're born, but I've been through it all and come out alive.

"My mother, God rest her soul, was a nice woman, but she drank like a fish. She'd have a few and then start raising hell with the first person who crossed her. She used to hit my father and she shouldn't have, because he was quiet and never answered back, only he was a drinker, too. She'd hit him, and he'd lie there without moving, but he'd keep begging her. 'Sonya,' he'd say, 'Sonya, my darling, why do you hit me in the balls? Have some pity!' And she'd say to him, 'I'm hitting you there to teach you not to bring any more sons-of-whores into the world.' That's the way they lived, till he got drunk one day and hanged himself. Ma and I left on our own, just like in the song: 'Two little blades of grass in the field were standing.' So I was passed around from one man to another from the time I was twelve. I slept with anyone who had the energy. My ma broke any number of rolling pins over my head. I didn't care, as soon as I saw another pair of trousers I was out on the street. That's how I earned my clothes and I earned my food. I thought the man would never be born who'd put a harness on me. I'd go with whoever I liked whenever I liked. Well, it happened. A fellow turned up on our street with a bit of a limp; he had a little peaked cap. He was no beauty, but he could look right through you and he was tough; he'd done time once already. I took one look at his eyes, black as the ace of spades, and my heart went into a spin: This was it—my bad luck. I ran after him like a little dog. Conscience, pride—I lost the lot. When I was with him I went crazy. If I saw a skirt anywhere near him I thought the world had come to an end. It's like in the song: 'If beauty you'd love, then 'tis wealth you must have.' He stole everything he could lay his hands on, this man of mine. I used to take it all down to the market to sell. It caught up with us in the end. We went up in smoke. He wouldn't squeal on his mates, he took all the blame, so they gave him the full treatment and I got five years without deprivation of rights for being stupid. After that, it was all like the song: 'The warder's a bastard, a swine and a whore, he never even lets you lie in clean straw.'

"They took me to the camp and made me do timbering; five cubic yards a day was the norm. I worked two shifts and I thought no, this is no good. So I went to sick bay and said give me a bed. And he said to me, 'We could build a dam with all the phony cases we've got in here. Get out of here before you earn ten days in the cooler.' So off I went, thinking I'll be damned if I'm going out logging any more. I bumped into a sergeant-major from the prison service outside the guardroom. He's sodden drunk. Come on, Musya, I think to myself, we were born to make fable reality. My heart was going like an engine. I fixed my face in a hurry and went up to him. 'Citizen officer,' I said, 'I'm being murdered, have pity on me.' He looked at me with a drunken eye and said, 'Come with me, then, and let's see whether you're worth anything.' He took me into the boiler room and when we came out I had him trotting behind me like a calf. I worked for a bit as a cleaner, then went in the kitchens. And I was lording it there till the amnesty. When I got out I had nowhere to go. My mother was dead, the room was gone. I pushed my way into the council office, and they said sign up for a job in one of the new territories. Only I wasn't as crazy as they thought. I looked down the corridor, and there's a sign hanging up, 'Retail Trade Department.' I'd got nothing to lose, so I went straight in to the boss. 'Experienced catering operator,' I told him. I looked at him, and he was laughing. 'When did you get out?' he said. I nearly wet my pants. 'Don't be bashful, I need people who've felt the stick; they know better than to get caught.' He gave me a vegetable stall standing on its own, and I sold stuff. I soon found my feet. I was young, not bad-looking, the men were like flies around a jam pot. They gave me the best goods and the easiest sales target, and there was always free drink. Money sticks to your hands when you're selling. Sometimes you switch price tags around, another time you unload hot goods; the kopecks soon mount up. Altogether, life looked brighter every day. And the boss kept up the handouts: prizes, bonuses, personal attentions. True, he was getting weak on his legs, but what did I care: I was none the poorer for what I gave him. Everything would have been all right if this cop from the embezzlement and illegal trading department hadn't taken a fancy to me. If I hadn't been a fool, I'd just have got on my back and been done with it. But no, I had to be awkward. I wouldn't and that was that. He was so horribly ugly, that cop! Small, mean-looking, baldish, with a squint in his left eye. He tried all ways, but I wouldn't have him at any price. So he planted some hot goods on me. They picked me up and stuck me in jail. He came to see me in my cell and said: 'Just one little word and I'll drop it.' But he'd picked the wrong one. Sometimes I thought I'll just screw my eyes up and to hell with it, I shan't miss it, shall I? But then I saw him, and I just couldn't, it made me sick, I'd die if I had to give it to him. So then, they made an honest woman of me for another five years; I landed on a building job. What I didn't do there! Never got my trousers on, as they say, lay down for everybody, only I wasn't such quality goods as I used to be, and there were a lot of young girls, all begging. So I stayed on general laboring. I just don't know what would have become of me if our Nazar, old Karasik, hadn't turned up. He was Clerk of Works on that job as well. I don't know what he saw in me, because I was as dry as kindling wood—you could have used me for an ironing board. But it's like in the song—'Her dark brown eyes, her little yellow headscarf, lit a fiercely blazing flame in his heart.' He fixed me up with a job running errands for him. I had such an easy life. I can't tell you. I ate and I slept, and then I ate some more.

I got a bit more like my old self, and little old Nazar started agitating to get me remission, making the rounds of the brass, writing applications. As soon as I'd gone before the board he got himself a transfer here. Only I wouldn't live with him in any case. I rented myself a temporary room from a widow in the town so that I could have a place of my own. The takings in that canteen are rotten, but still I don't need a lot nowadays, I've done all my big spending. You can charge twenty kopecks extra for a vodka on credit, then there's the money on the empties, the pennies mount up, it's a living, and the future will look after itself. I've had offers in the town, but it isn't really what I'm looking for, and there would be too many temptations. Anyway, to tell the truth, all I live for now is right here. It's my last fling, that's for sure. I can't remember anything like it ever happening to me before. You wouldn't think there was anything special about him, he's all calluses and big eyes, but when he walks past, my heart's in my boots. It's just as if I was fifteen again and hadn't really had anybody yet. Like in that song. Yet there isn't a clean spot on me anywhere. When I was in the camp I had it with guard dogs, I poked myself, I caught a dose. Osya is like a red-letter day to make up for all my sufferings. The Lord saw his little handmaiden and took pity on her and endowed her beyond measure. When I was young I didn't believe in religion—how could there be a God when life was like it was? But fate has taught me better. Once in the camp old Nazar brought a dozen painted eggs down to the working zone for me—it was somewhere around Easter-time. Easter's all very well, but I was hungry. I gave the other girls one each and kept one for myself. Waiting for a free moment, I sat down in a shady spot, and I was just starting on my present when I saw an old terminal case looking at me, staring away, and her face was all screwed up with greed. I flared up in a rage: they wouldn't let me eat my own scrap of food in peace. 'Here you are, you rotten bitch,' I said, 'take the egg and I hope it chokes you, you cunt . . .' She grabbed the egg and went off with it, and all of a sudden I felt so light-hearted, so peaceful, as if I'd been born all over again. There were birds singing everywhere, and the leaves smelled nice, and the sun was shining right into you. It came to me then—this was how God rewards us! Before, if I gave a beggar five kopecks I used to expect a ruble for myself, like in a lottery. Ever since then I've believed. I go to church. I'm going tomorrow, in fact . . . it's the feast of Our Lady of Kazan. If you like, we can go together. You can be my guest and come and see how I live. . . . Ooh . . . the dough's risen too far."

VII

Musya lived not far from the town center, in an old house that looked like an adobe barn from the outside. A tall, bony old woman in a faded cotton sarafan looked around from the summer stove that stood under an awning and came to meet them. She screwed up her eyes shortsightedly and spoke in a voice that was surprisingly melodious for her age.

"Hallo . . . Happy Holiday."

"God bless you, Fyodorovna." Musya was already busy with the lock on the door of her lodging. "Nobody asking for me?"

"Nazar Stepanich was here early on." The old woman could hardly move her legs, which were swollen with varicose veins. "And the woman next door looked in to ask if you were coming."

Musya's tiny room was almost entirely taken up by the bed. It was a wide bed, gleaming with nickel, and on it was an imposing structure of feather mattresses, blankets, and sheets, crowned by a pyramid of lacy pillows. The rest of the furniture consisted of a table and two chairs by the window. An icon of the Savior, framed with paper roses, in the top righthand corner of the room only emphasized how bare and uninhabited it seemed.

"This is how I live," said Musya, hastily changing her clothes in the entrance hall. "What do I need marble halls for? I only come here on my day off, really. At one time, whenever I had a free hour I used to get a lift and come here, but now wild horses couldn't drag me out of the kitchen. I'm simply glued to that hole in the wall . . . How's it going back there, will you be knocking off work soon?"

"It's not going too badly, we're making progress," said Antonina cautiously. "The foreman's bunch are a bit behind."

Musya snorted sarcastically. "Shockworkers, eh? So you think you can go faster than Osip. You haven't got the legs for it. I knew all about your deal with old Nazar to start with. He bullied Sheludko till he knuckled under as well. As soon as the foreman looks the other way they slap it off regardless. If I wasn't sorry for you, you parasites, I'd have told Osip long ago!"

Antonina defended herself falteringly. "It was the boys who thought of it. We don't come into it. If we'd known . . ."

"The boys! We know those 'boys' of yours. The twins will crawl on their hands and knees, and they're all expecting something. Sheludko is saving hard, to go searching all around the Union for his father who was deported. And Guryanich would pawn his mother for a bottle . . . You must be crazy. If you did the work honestly, d'you think you'd ever catch up with Osip? The work does itself for him . . . All right, then, let's go."

Antonina was struck to see how puffy and pale Musya's face looked without its usual makeup when it was framed by a black shawl. It was as though the health and lifeblood had been drained from it, slowly and thoroughly, drop by drop, leaving nothing but an expression of hidden suffering and exhaustion.

"Let's go," Musya repeated. "We shan't be able to get through the crowd if we don't, we're a bit late already."

A procession of women, singly or in pairs, and all hurrying toward the same place, stretched along the town's sun-baked mud walls. The stream of people was swollen by more and more new arrivals as it approached a dazzling blaze of light that soared over the neighboring roofs: the church cupola. On the path to the church door the crowd was so dense that, once caught up in it, one lost control of one's movements: It pressed forward in a single solid bloc, never pausing or slackening its pace.

It was desperately stuffy in the church and the candles flickered with a feeble bluish flame. The tight-packed mass of perspiring humanity was breathing in short gasps. The priest, a youngish man with a sparse, fair beard surrounding a red face, wore full vestments. It was obviously costing him an effort to surmount his weariness and discomfort.

"Great is their pride. They think that they alone are invited to be guests at the Lord's feast. But it is not for them, the invited, that the heart of the Lord yearns, but for the uninvited. To the uninvited His grace is revealed, to the uninvited His love and goodwill are given today . . ."

Antonina felt faint and giddy, but as soon as the choir intoned, "I believe," she, like all the rest, joined in singing the creed, as though she had discovered a new way of breathing: her sense of unity, of being fused with those around her, bore her up and filled her heart with ecstasy and an inexpressible peace. All the fears and doubts which had tormented

Antonina receded beyond the bounds of the known world. At that moment she felt herself to be infinite and invulnerable to all the disasters and misfortunes which threatened or might threaten herself and her loved ones. Tears of joy welled up in her. "What have we to fear, O Lord. Who can do anything to harm us?"

When she struggled out to the street after the service, she had lost sight of Musya. She did not feel like looking for the house among hundreds of monotonous carbon copies, and, without really thinking about it, she set out for the workshop on the shore, secretly hoping to find Osip there.

As she approached the old warehouse, she heard voices, one of which made her heart pound. When she went in, Osip was pouring earth into a mold. From time to time he stared keenly at his companion, a hook-nosed little old man with a black cap on his thick, unruly hair. The old man stopped in the middle of a sentence; his pitch-black eyes fidgeted angrily over Antonina and he turned to the young man for an explanation. Osip reassured him with a nod, and greeted Antonina with a warm smile.

"Oh, Tonya! Come in, come in . . . Meet Izrail Samuilich. Carry on, Izrail Samuilich, Tonya won't bother us."

The old man relaxed, gave an approving shake of his sharp chin, and started talking again in a fierce falsetto.

"They are children. They don't understand what they are doing. All right, so they obtain permission to emigrate, but what will become of the others? The newspapers will start an outcry, 'The Jews do not love our homeland!' And we shall have a pogrom."

"Everyone must choose for himself."

"The Russian Jew cannot cut himself off. He must unite with all the others. They can't all leave the country! Leaving is not as simple as all that. The graves will remain here, graves of those who believed in us and hoped. Jewish boys must not forget that the Jews also contributed to everything they now hate. And that it was no small contribution. Why should the Russians be the only ones who are expected to pay their debts?"

"Each man pays his own personal debt."

"Not for bloodshed—everybody pays for that. So we Jews must share the burden of our national responsibility and not try to shift it onto other people's shoulders. To stay here and share the suffering with everybody else—that is our destiny." Suddenly the fire went out of him, and he ended lamely, almost pleading, "You know a lot of them. Tell them from me that if they do get their way, things will be very difficult for all of us . . . very difficult . . . Shalom. Be well."

The old man bowed silently to Antonina and moved towards the door. She knew then, watching his cautious, tottering steps, that he was mortally weary; his withered body had almost completed its earthly pilgrimage.

"Have you eaten?" Osip asked quietly when the old man had gone.

"Yes, at Musya's," she said untruthfully. She could not think of food while she was with him.

"Let's go home, then."

"Yes, let's."

Osip locked up with his own key, and tucked a note under the door handle; then they walked through the already sleepy town to where the lonely road led away from its outskirts and disappeared into the naked steppe that stretched away flat as far as the eye could see.

Antonina walked at his side, really close to him for the first time; she felt neither the airless heat nor her tiredness. Passionately, with her whole being, she prayed for one thing, and one thing only: that the road they were following would never end.

VIII

Late one evening when she was looking for the Lyubshins in the hostel, Antonina ran into Sheludko loitering in the corridor.

"Seen the twins?"

"Why, you missing them?"

"I've got their laundry here to give them."

"So they've got you in harness, already?" he said with a mocking grin. "They never fail, the crafty devils."

"Why should I begrudge them?" She sounded hurt. "You couldn't call their few things work anyway."

"I know you don't begrudge them, but where's their conscience? You aren't a dead weight around your husband's neck. You work the shift with the rest of us." Forestalling her objections, he raised one shoulder and shrugged deprecatingly. "All right, it's your business . . . I'll tell you what I wanted to ask you about." His prominent eyes were dark and strained. "The Far North."

"What about it?"

"Are there many deportees there?"

"Enough."

"What sort are they mainly? Where from?"

"All sorts. Mostly from the Baltic states. Germans as well."

"Any from the Ukraine?"

"Not many."

"I was born there, you know. My mother brought me out when I was little. But my father stayed there, he wasn't allowed to leave. He's a Carpathian, Mother said, from the Western Ukraine. I buried my mother when I was only in the fifth class, then I went to trade school. I started asking about my father, and they told me there was nobody of that name, he had left the district for places unknown. But where could he have been going when he was forbidden to leave? He hadn't even got a passport. He wasn't entitled. So if we do get through the contract this month, I've got a bit saved up as well, and I'll go and look for him myself, or maybe I'll sign on for a job up there and get free travel. He can't have vanished. I'll find him. It's no good, living alone. There's nothing to latch on to, no interest in life. There isn't even anywhere to go on leave. If you get a big pay envelope sometime, who is there to boast to?" He shook his big head mournfully and moved on. "Tell the twins to find another fool in town, there's plenty there."

Antonina was puzzled by this sudden talkativeness on the part of Sheludko, who was usually so quiet and slow. What did it mean? The only times she met him were at work and in the canteen, and never once in all that time had he made any attempt to talk to her. Their acquaintance was confined to the regulation "hallos" and "good-byes." At first she had imagined that he was displeased by her presence in the team. Who wants to work overtime for somebody else, after all! But it soon got through to her that what he felt was total indifference. So she felt a certain satisfaction as she walked away from him and made a mental note to ask for his father's full name so that she could remember him in her prayers.

She found the Lyubshins in the reading room. They had pushed aside the heaps of old magazine folders and sat face to face across a reader's table, each with a thumb-marked exercise book open in front of him.

"Three for old Polya." Pasha wet his pencil and wrinkled his nose in concentration. "And we'd better give Lyudka a five, she's got two kids."

Syoma made businesslike jottings in his exercise book and said, "Don't forget old Tisha, he's been more help than anyone else. He gets a five, or maybe even seven."

"Right."

"Who've we forgotten?"

"That looks like the lot."

"Think so? Oh . . ." Pasha noticed Antonina standing by the door and was flustered. "Tonya . . . can you wait till payday?"

"Expecting a big pay packet?" She put the pile of washing in front of them and sighed. "I had a job finding you, been all over the hostel."

Syoma beamed gratefully. "We'd have come for it ourselves." He hastily stuffed the exercise book into his pocket. "You can name your price. Me and my brother will pay our debts."

Pasha cleared his throat importantly, and confirmed this. "Not the slightest . . . !"

"We'll settle up later." As she went out she felt their eyes following her with affectionate goodwill and she warmed to them. "There's plenty of time."

On the way back Antonina passed the house manager's room, the door to which was wide open. Out of the corner of her eye she caught sight of Osip's face in profile, looking worried, and heard his voice.

"Do you know that for sure, Khristoforich?"

"Can't you see for yourself? It's all on the cameral pattern. Identical little rooms, all the same size."

"Perhaps they're laboratories?"

"With no communications? No water, no heating? You're joking! Only a sucker would believe that."

Antonina walked slowly, trying to catch what they were saying. After a short but oppressive pause Osip's voice was scarcely audible.

"So there's no getting away from them. They're everywhere . . . even if you buried yourself they'd be there."

"That's what I keep saying." The house manager sighed noisily. "Lot of good it was, your ancestors starting all that commotion just for a change of overseers."

"Maybe you're right."

With Osip's last words heavy on her heart she went back home. The anxiety which had suddenly stirred in her bit deeper. She had so far refused to ask herself what seemed to her a pointless and boring question, but now it insisted on asking itself. What was it they were building? Who needed these squat boxes that looked from inside like honeycombs, and for what? True, there were vague rumors among the workers that the structure had a secret scientific significance, and they even hinted at some military use. If this were so, why had Osip been so obviously distressed in his conversation with the house manager? She could come up with no answer. She suddenly remembered how Nikolai had asked the Clerk of Works about it when she had been there, and his only answer had been a nasty laugh and a shrug. It was quite obvious that he knew, but didn't want to say, or was afraid to. A chill of fear ran down her spine. "What a life—you weave the rope for your own neck without knowing it."

As she got into bed beside Nikolai, Antonina leaned close to his ear and whispered anxiously.

"Kolya, you awake?"

"What?"

"What are we building here?"

"We don't have to worry about that, Tonya."

"I'm terrified, Kolya."

"Forget it and go to sleep."

"I want to know."

"Go to sleep, Tonya, we'll be better off if we don't think about it. Go to sleep."

Nikolai turned to the wall and was soon asleep. She didn't close her eyes all night long, but lay awake thinking, thinking, thinking.

IX

The men were finishing off the last few yards when the Clerk of Works appeared in the doorway accompanied by a short man with glasses and a straw hat.

"Knocking off?" Karasik's eyes strayed absently around the walls.

"Well done. The others still have three days' work left."

The man in glasses hovered by the lime tub, twitching his duck's nose, and said hesitantly, "Well, Nazar Stepanich, shall we carry out our test here? While the trail is fresh, so to speak."

"This comrade is from our client," said Karasik, swiveling his head without looking at anyone in particular. "He's going to check your work."

The twins, as if in concert, turned the same look of startled inquiry on Nikolai. He in turn looked expectantly at the Clerk of Works. Karasik's answer was a helpless shrug—nothing he could do about it!

Without waiting for an answer, the visitor armed himself with a mallet, walked down the corridor, and with a few strokes knocked off a fair-sized piece of scarcely dried plaster. Then he went on farther, and did the same thing again, after which he stood by the exposed wall ominously biting his lip, and then spoke in an exaggeratedly loud drawl. "The covering will come away at the first touch of damp, Nazar Stepanich. You're plastering without giving the wall a key. That's not the way to do things."

Antonina went cold. If keying wasn't allowed for in the wage bill, they would be left with exactly nothing when they settled up. They'd be lucky to cover the advances they had received. But there was something which distressed her much more. She was worried about Osip. How would he take it? After all, the men had put their trust in him, not in the Clerk of Works. Put their trust in him and followed him blindly. What could he say to them now? Knowing his nature, she could imagine what this dirty trick would cost him. She looked at the face of the Clerk of Works and suddenly hated him. Her burning anger at Nikolai was almost intolerable —he had made the deal with him. Tears of rage filled her eyes. "How could he! How could he! Anyone could see that man's a crook from a mile off. We should have known all along that he'd screw us."

Karasik was on tenterhooks. He shuffled his feet uneasily and made incoherent excuses.

"It happens . . . The boys leave thin patches sometimes . . . Two places don't prove anything . . . You ought to try the other end."

But the other man had the bit between his teeth. "No, Nazar Stepanich, my dear comrade Karasik! That will do nicely. We can't pay for work like that. It'll be entered as a straight plastering job, without keying."

"Mikhail Mikhailich!"

"I can't do it, my dear fellow. I can't. I should lose my head. I wish I could oblige, but I can't. Don't hold it against me."

Karasik spread his hands, enlisting Nikolai as a witness to his helplessness. "Let's go and see what the foreman has to say."

He went first, nodding to Nikolai and the visitor to follow him. In a moment the sound of their footsteps had died away down the corridor. Syoma, neatly packing his tools, summed it all up.

"We've worked for nothing!"

Pasha sighed in agreement. "It happens."

In condemning her husband, Antonina did not absolve herself of blame. She should have prevented him from taking such a rash step. It was her duty. How could they have thought of making a deal with Karasik behind Osip's back? Who could possibly have guaranteed that the Clerk of Works would keep his word? Whether she liked it or not she had to admit that she, too, if only indirectly, was involved in the deception. So, now that she was left alone with the twins, the strain was too much for her, and she exploded.

"He didn't do it on purpose! He thought it would be for the best. He hadn't known that wretched Karasik five minutes, but you ought to have been aware of what might happen. Nikolai was taking his cue from you, he thought if you didn't say anything it must be all right. And now, of course, Nikolai is responsible for the whole thing. It isn't fair . . ."

She broke off. Syoma, whom she was addressing, was looking at her pityingly. With a disarming smile of apology, he reassured her.

"Why are you shouting? We aren't children. We've made our beds and now we must lie on them. Where does Nikolai come in? He's got nothing to do with it. I'm sorry for Osip. We've let him down. And the others."

Pasha agreed sadly. "We've let them down all right. And we've punished ourselves."

"We should have listened to Osip."

"Yes, we should have." The silence that followed was broken as Nikolai emerged from the depths of the corridor.

"Knock off now." His voice sounded muffled and flat. "That's enough for today. There's no hurry now, anyway." He turned to Antonina. "Wash the tools and put them away." He nodded to the twins. "Come on."

Left alone, Antonina could not get down to work for some time. What would hurt Osip most, she knew, was that they had tried to cheat by skimping on the work. His attitude to any job for which he was responsible was one of jealous perfectionism. He suffered agonies of self-reproach if the slightest fault went uncorrected. She tried to imagine for a moment how he would look at her when they met. She burned and choked with shame, and her heart stood still in alarm.

She had seen to the tools and was about to go home, when something she couldn't explain impelled her to go in the opposite direction, along the corridor. Guided by her instincts, she moved almost stealthily, as if she were feeling her way. She had never been here alone before. The silence of the corridor with its row of gaping doors, each one a terrifying temptation, seemed to Antonina to be full of watchful menace. They had been working so hard that it had somehow never occurred to her to wonder what was beyond those doors. Now she peeped into the first one from the end, and held her breath: Along each side of the transverse passage was another row of gaping doorways, just like those in the corridor, only smaller, and through the nearest of these she saw a cell lit by a square aperture in the ceiling. She wound her way around passage after passage and simply could not understand what it all meant, what use it could be. On her way through the last one she glanced mechanically into the end room, and felt the ground give way under her: There on the floor in the far corner, his arms clasped around his knees, sat Osip. There was a weary hopelessness in every line of his body. Silent tears ran unhindered down the sunken face with its curly beard. A stab of pity shot through her, and her throat was tight.

"Osya . . . what are you doing here?"

He raised his eyes, but did not stir.

"Nothing," he said.

Only once before had Antonina seen a man cry. She had got up one night after her mother's death, and come face to face with her father in the hallway. The moonlight shining through the wide open door had revealed that his beloved face was soaked with tears. Overwhelmed, she had sunk to the floor, impetuously pressing her head to her father's knees.

"I'll never leave you, Daddy! I'll stay with you forever."

Her father squeezed her shoulders gratefully.

"What are you doing, Antonina? Don't upset yourself. It's nothing, old age, that's all."

"You'll see, Daddy . . . you'll see."

That night had settled Antonina's future for many years ahead.

Now too nervous to approach Osip, she leaned her shoulder weakly against the doorpost.

"Aren't you feeling well, Osip?"

"It's all right."

"Let's go, shall we?"

"I'll sit here a bit, Tonya, I'm tired."

"Shall I be in your way, Osip?"

"No, I don't suppose so . . . stay where you are . . . What does it matter now? Ring down the curtain, as they say, life's a flop. D'you know, Tonya, my parents wanted to make a dentist out of me. 'In times like these a dentist will never be out of work,' my father used to say. 'War after war, famine after famine, interrogation after interrogation.' And my mamma simply thought that teeth were the most important thing in life. We hadn't got much space, so father used to receive his patients in the living room behind a muslin curtain. I remember the groans, the blood, the hum the drill. Ever since I was a child the mere sight of a dentist's chair has driven me wild. So I went along to the law school. When I got there the first thing they asked was, 'Do you have a recommendation from some social organization?' 'No,' I said, 'but I really want to become a lawyer.' 'That's not enough,' they said. 'First you must show your devotion to the common cause.' I was curious. 'How?' I asked. 'What cause?' 'You must display vigilance.' 'I've never had a chance to,' I said. 'Well, you must make one.' 'You mean . . .?' 'Right, yes, you've got it!' they said encouragingly. The way they saw it, before I could defend anybody I must first have somebody put in jail. That didn't appeal to me. So we parted company. And a bit later I ended up here. I thought I'd succeeded in getting away from it, I thought that out here nobody would try to involve me in dirty games. But I haven't got ahead of them after all—it's the other way around."

"What d'you mean?" She leaned towards him. "What are you talking about?"

He was calmer now, and even smiled through his tears. "What do I mean? You must know what's being built here?"

"How should I know? You hear all sorts of different things."

"A prison, of course, Tonya."

She gave a frightened gasp. "Lord! What d'you mean?"

"Just what I say, Tonya." He rose slowly and took a step toward the door. "And then we cheat each other into the bargain. People like Karasik know very well how to break a man. First buy him, then break him. He imbibed that with his mother's milk. I don't bear Nikolai any grudge, I'm just sorry for him. If you give way once, it's hard to hold out afterward."

Osip stood still, facing her, and she could not resist the temptation to touch him. As she did so she laid her burning cheek on his shoulder.

"Osya . . . one heart isn't big enough to suffer for everyone . . . You'll burn yourself out."

"Mine wasn't big enough." He gently stroked her head. "There isn't enough air. I can't get my breath, Tonya."

"Take my share."

"Don't, Tonya, you mustn't."

"I don't care about anything."

"Pull yourself together, Tonya, this is no good."

"Be quiet."

"You're like a child." He was trembling with her. "You'll feel bad about it afterward. You're just sorry for me . . . Tonya."

"Be quiet . . . be quiet . . ."

"I've never . . ."

"Shh. . . ."

If ever Antonina was fated to squander the full measure of love and tenderness which nature had granted her, it was now, as she humbly submitted to his timid advances.

"Osya, forgive me . . . I'm old and foolish."

"Don't, Tonya, you mustn't, you mustn't."

Afterward Osip got up, stubbornly avoiding her anxious look, and was at the door before he almost whispered, "Forgive me."

Antonina was not offended by this sudden departure. She lay there on the floor which was sprinkled with flakes of cement, unconscious of her body, staring up through the aperture in the ceiling at a sky that was flat, without depth or a single cloud. An eager feeling that her existence had sense and purpose was ripening and gaining strength within her. Perhaps for the first time since she had become aware of herself as a woman, she had a flash of insight into her own strength and what it could mean to someone living at her side. Now she knew for sure that, whatever happened, this could never be taken away from her. "Come what may, it is my sin, and I will answer for it."

X

When Antonina arrived in the hostel, the men were already finishing supper. Despondency reigned at their table. The Lyubshins buried their faces in their plates and tried not to look at anybody. Albert Guryanich finished eating his bun with an air which seemed to say he had foreseen it all and saw no sense in getting excited about it. Sheludko sipped his tea mechanically, looking bewildered and utterly defeated. Nikolai never for a minute stopped surveying his companions with sullen, haunted eyes. Her appearance seemed to give him determination, and he burst out:

"I'll go and talk to him again, he swore it was on the level. I won't let him off the hook. I've seen bigger fish than him. Nobody's making a fool of me. I've got my own way of dealing with him. He'll pay up. To the last kopeck."

Albert Guryanich grinned half-heartedly. "That's the stuff," he said. "He'll be giving us a bonus before we know it."

Sheludko flapped his hand hopelessly. "It's no use. If Karasik doesn't want to pay, he won't. Karasik knows his business."

The twins remained silent, but their spoons suddenly began working with new vigor, making it clear that Nikolai's promises had implanted a certain hope in them.

Musya, serving Antonina's first course, nodded conspiratorially in the direction of the men.

"Graveyard conversation! Go and eat. I'll come over in a minute. All stations transmitting. Urgent communiqué. They make themselves out to be God knows what, and they get taken in like a lot of simpletons."

Musya appeared at the table in all her painted glory. She bestowed on each of them a dazzling smile, and said teasingly, "You gentlemen might make room for a lady. Not one of them has a clue, how can they expect to get on in the world?" She self-confidently made space for her opulent body, sat down, and rested her plump elbows on the table. "Where were your brains when you were making your bargain with Karasik? Didn't you know who you were dealing with? Had you got your eyes stopped up?"

"It isn't Karasik who's the real trouble," Sheludko replied gloomily. "The client's agent dropped on us like a bolt from the blue. You can't go against the client. Whichever way you look at it, we've only ourselves to blame."

Musya's red face sharpened vengefully. "Client's agent! If he's the client's agent I'm a cosmonaut. He's a buddy of old Nazar's from Admin. I know him inside out. They arranged it specially. In front of me. Nazar can't get the books straight so he decided to save a bit on you. You call yourselves workers—nobody can teach you a thing. Fancy trusting somebody like that. Since when did clients go down into cellars to take over a job? You never been a bride before, or something?"

Contrary to her expectations, Musya's news made no great impression. The fact remained that nobody could get their wages back for them. They depended on Karasik, and if they went against him they could give up all hope of finding a way out of their difficulties. For that matter, he needn't have resorted to his trick with the "client." He could simply have refused to pay. And that would have been that.

"You'd do better to give us a bottle on credit," muttered Albert Guryanich, with his eyes on the table. "Can't make things any worse."

Musya rose without a word, went behind her counter, and came back with half a liter and a plate of salted gherkins. She set all this before them and sat down again. "Go on, drink. If you need it, I'll let you have more. We'll settle up later." She pushed her glass over to Albert Guryanich. "I'll have just a spot myself."

He silently knocked the stopper out, put the glasses together, and poured the vodka into them in a single, leisurely movement. He drank off his share without looking at anybody, then gave Musya a curt nod of command. "Wheel some more in."

Even the second bottle loosened nobody's tongue except his. He began grumbling in an indistinct mutter that was addressed to no one in particular.

"If your luck's out you can catch a dose from your own sister. Why was I doomed from the day I was born to eat shit all my life instead of bread? Is there a curse on me?" He swore vilely. "I remember when I was a kid we were always playing 'parcels.' You wrapped up some rubbish in a sheet of white paper, tied it up all neat and proper with a bright ribbon, dropped it on the pavement, sat yourself down behind a fence, and looked through a crack to see who'd pick it up. Some old woman comes along, grabs it, and nips around the corner. You nearly split your sides laughing: silly old bird. The laugh's on me now! I've been fooled a dozen times, and I still jump on these gift parcels done up in ribbon like any stupid station whore. To think I'd fall for a cheap trick like that!"

At this they all gave vent to their rage. Sheludko's normally impassive face shook with anger. "What a swine Karasik is." He banged his fist on the table. "Where's his conscience, the rotten bastard!"

"We ought to complain about him," Pasha blurted out. Syoma seconded his brother: "To the general manager."

Antonina listened with half an ear to a debate from which it emerged that there was no point in complaining, that they had only themselves to blame, and that they had better try to reach a friendly understanding with the Clerk of Works. She had no thought for anything except her last meeting with Osip. She still did not know where it would lead for either of them, but, however it ended, one thing was obvious to her: Sooner or later she and Nikolai must part. From now on they had nothing in common except the roof over their heads.

Nikolai interpreted her silence in his own way.

"Are you feeling ill?" he asked quietly.

She turned toward him automatically. "Why d'you ask? No, I'm all right, just tired."

"Shall we go home?"

"It doesn't look very polite."

"They don't need us."

"We need them."

"Whatever you want . . ."

"Let's sit a bit longer . . ."

"Don't overdo it . . ."

The men might have been expected to turn the main force of indignation against Nikolai, the ringleader in the whole business, but they talked without even mentioning him, and Antonina was grateful to them for their tact.

Albert Guryanich brought their discussion to a close. "Right, I daresay we shall get over it. We shall be wiser next time. And I'll put one over on old Nazar that he won't forget in a hurry." He glanced at Antonina, and said as though it had suddenly occurred to him, "Where's Osip got to? Eh?"

Musya, who had been dozing off on Sheludko's shoulder, started at the mention of Osip's name, and looked anxiously around the company. "You're right. He hasn't even been in for supper. If you don't remind him, he forgets to eat."

Pasha tried to reassure her. "He must have gone off to town." But he gave himself away by adding "—but he wasn't supposed to."

"No, he wasn't," Sheludko emphatically confirmed.

At this Antonina found herself rising from her chair. Her memory made her see the events of the past day in a new light; already expecting the worst, she felt herself choking with terrible intolerable anxiety. She dashed for the door, but it opened as she reached it and Ilya Khristoforich appeared.

"Osya . . . in there . . ." He looked awful. He could hardly control the trembling of his lips sufficiently to speak. "In the lavatories . . ."

A strange lucidity, such as she had never experienced in the past, came over Antonina. The causes and connections of all that had happened around her recently were laid bare. She saw plainly how step by step Osip's destruction had inevitably drawn slowly closer. The unexpected deception was the last drop which filled the cup of his suffering to the brim, but the drop which had made it overflow was their lovemaking a little while ago. The real world had proved too different from the one that Osip had created in his heart. The real world had simply evicted him. "If you pray for a lifetime, Antonina, you won't atone for it."

Osip was still lying in a storeroom next to the house manager's quarters, covered with a new sheet. Antonina, whose eyes were registering everything with unnatural clarity, examined every discernible detail of his appearance: the sharp line of his nose under the taut material, the bump made by a fountain pen in one of his breast pockets, even the ticket with a lucky number sticking to the sole of his left sandal.

The crowd which had gathered at the door of the storeroom kept a strained silence. But it was a silence that held no feeling of fright or dismay. They were numbed by the chill breath of a storm which might break at any moment. Just when the explosion seemed inevitable, the silence was shattered by Musya's long, despairing wail.

"Os-ya-a-a-a."

That night, for the first time since their marriage, Antonina slept apart from her husband, on the floor. He had evidently guessed a great deal of the truth, and merely asked her, almost inaudibly:

"Will you go away?"

"I don't know."

"Do you condemn me?"

"No."

"I'll wait."

"As you like."

Antonina didn't close her eyes all night long. She looked through the window, without thought or desire, to where the distant stars trembled in the pitch-black sky, and for one heart-stopping moment she fancied that every one of them was a living being, gazing down upon her from its dizzy height with gentle understanding. She was euphorically aware that she was not all alone in this world, but part of the unity of all things, and tears of gratitude for this gift from on high, this sense of kinship with everything and in everything, gave her heart ease. "Hallowed Be Thy Name!"

XI

The following evening, the Clerk of Works apprehensively put his head around their door.

"You won't throw me out, will you?" He came in, scuffed his feet on the doormat with demonstrative thoroughness, stepped resolutely up to the table, and produced a bottle from behind his back. "Up you get, Kolya, this business needs to be chewed on, as they say."

Karasik was trying his hardest to look as self-assured and authoritative as ever, but he could not avoid showing a certain strain and embarrassment. The haste with which he undid the half-liter as soon as he was installed at the table betrayed his fear that his hosts might refuse. Antonina had a sickening foreboding that something irreparable was about to happen. But, after glancing quickly at her husband, she sighed with relief. He rose to receive his guest not just pacifically, but, it seemed to her, with more than his ordinary good nature.

"Come in, Stepanich, come in." He nodded to his wife. "See to it." Then, to his guest again, "She'll soon get us something to go with it."

And at that moment, Antonina almost hated her husband. "Some friend he's found himself!" she complained to herself bitterly as she laid the table. "They've driven a man to his death and now they're having a drink on it. They should be ashamed!" After all that had happened, her attitude to Nikolai was, she thought, determined once and for all. Gratitude and respect had given place to a hostility which she could hardly conceal and which she herself found painful. Osip's sudden and senseless tragedy like a brilliant flare in the darkness marked out for her the light and shade, black and white, night and day of the world about her. Now she knew beforehand how she would behave in this or that event, what she would say, whose side she would take. Since that evening she had seen quite clearly that she would not come back to Nikolai from the maternity hospital.

Karasik obligingly kept his host's glass topped up, and Nikolai drank, nibbled thoughtfully, and listened to his guest's effusions without interrupting.

"What d'you think I am, a wild beast? I'm sorry for the boy. If I'd known, I'd have made the money up out of my own pocket. The devil must have sent the agent. It didn't work out this time, but I'd have made it up to him in the third quarter. Wouldn't be the first time, would it? Why has everybody turned so vicious? I hardly dare show my face on the site. Everybody is trying to take a bite out of me. I'm not a kid of twenty, I've lived my life. I've been through the mill. I've been knocked around and cheated and screwed in my time. Why should they want my blood now? How did I know what he'd be like, that client's agent!"

The Clerk of Works inclined his whole body toward his companion, staring into his face like a beseeching dog, but when their heads came close together something happened which took Antonina completely by surprise: Nikolai's hand seized his guest's open collar in an iron grip.

"Didn't know, eh?" Nikolai smiled serenely as he hissed out his words, but it was a smile which filled Antonina with sudden dread. "The devil must have sent him, eh?"

"Kolya," he croaked, "I'm talking to you like a son. . . ."

"Like a son, eh? Right, dad, I'm asking you: If you didn't know, why did you bring him to my part of the job? Maybe you accidentally got mixed up? Or did somebody force you to do it?"

"This is all wrong, Kolya," Karasik panted, "I come to you thinking you're a human being. . . ."

Without letting go of his collar Nikolai rose from the table, lifted his guest to his feet, struck him a swinging blow on the cheek with his free hand, and began steadily beating him.

"Human being, you say? Take that, you filthy swine, for what you did before, and that for what you've just done, and that for three years in advance. My long lost dad! Here's something from your little boy, dad! A present from someone who loves you."

With vengeful satisfaction Antonina watched the Clerk of Works' face turning into a bloody mask. Only once in her life had she seen anything like it.

After a day's travel on a narrow-gauge line, which slithered on sweating permafrost, a decrepit "tin kettle" of an engine had finally hauled the flat-car on which they were traveling as far as Yermakovo, their base. The road from the station went up a steep hill, and no sooner had Antonina and her husband set foot on it than a young man in a prisoner's cape, with a horror-stricken face, came rushing downhill toward them from the direction of the settlement, passed them, and flung himself into the copse by the railway line. Before either of them could guess what was happening, several half-dressed camp guards suddenly poured over the crest of the hill. Brandishing straps and sticks, they hurled themselves down, shouting and whistling, in pursuit of the fugitive.

Digging her nails into her husband's sleeve, Antonina spoke his name in a terrified whisper.

"Be quiet, Tonya, be quiet." He felt her trembling, and went tense and pale with anxiety. "It's none of our business. Let's go." There was something demeaning in his haste. "Come on, let's go . . ."

The main wave had rolled by, but soldiers still trickled down the hill one by one, and the looks of fanatical triumph on their faces made it easy to judge what awaited the fugitive if he were caught. Nikolai almost dragged his wife along, coaxing her in a whisper: "You don't know anything about these things, Tonya . . . They aren't human . . . not human. . . . Killing a man here and now means no more to them than spitting. They'll say it was just a mistake. In fact, they'll probably get a reward . . . for vigilance."

"I'm frightened, Kolya."

"Be quiet, be quiet."

"I'm frightened."

"Be quiet."

But the worst trial was awaiting them further on. On the outskirts of the settlement which was their goal, in the churned-up mud of a marshy patch by the roadside, surrounded by camp guards, sat a shaven-headed man in a cape like that of the fugitive, except that it hung in ribbons. There was an enormous bruise where his face should have been, a half torn-off ear swung like a dark curl at the side of his head, and his mangled arms dangled brokenly at his side. The man was not really breathing, but simply twitching, with an occasional violent hiccup.

An incongruously neatly turned-out lieutenant hovered before him, pistol in hand, defending the poor wretch from the soldiers pressing in on him and thirsting for summary justice. Conspicuous among them by his determined manner was a sergeant-major with a mustache, wearing a sleeveless fur coat over an officer's service jacket. The sergeant-major kept trying to get behind the lieutenant's back. The lieutenant in turn kept a sharp eye on every movement he made, and wouldn't let him get nearer his victim. But the ring around the lieutenant tightened all the time, and the murmuring became almost menacing.

"Ought to trample the lot of them to death."

"He's going to croak anyway."

"Move away, lieutenant, before you get hurt."

"If we don't finish him off now, we'll do it in camp."

"Move away, lieutenant."

"Mind you don't get in the way yourself."

In the end, the lieutenant couldn't stand the strain. He stepped aside, and turned away, as if he was trying to make out something at the vanishing point down the road. This was taken as a signal for the execution. The sergeant-major instantly seized the first slab of wood which came to hand from a pile of road metalling, swung it in the air and brought it crashing down on the squatting man, whose skull immediately split in two.

Colored lights danced before Antonina's eyes. The low gray sky closed in on her, and she howled aloud, crazed with anguish and her own impotence.

She came to in a strange room, with a single window which was blocked by carved shutters. The dim light of the eternal northern sun filtered through the openings in the carving. A woman was talking in an unhurried whisper beyond the half-closed door to the next room.

"Around here, when they're set free, they live on their own till the boats can get through again. They're given money for the steamer. In the winter, you can only get to the mainland by plane. So they live in tents down by the shore. They work on the loading to get money for food . . . They'd had a drink, of course. And they got into a fight with one of the escort troops they knew. They answered back—and then it came to blows. Well, they stuck a knife in his side. He sets up a yell. The barracks are right next door. Our lot, of course, went wild. It's lucky for you my man was there or they might not have spared you either."

Nikolai's voice could scarcely be heard as he thanked her.

It all flooded to the surface of Antonina's memory. Including the cry she had uttered. Then she closed her eyes again and retreated into merciful oblivion.

This time Antonina didn't shout. No longer realizing what she was saying, she formed the same words over and over again with lips that were parched with anger.

"More . . . more . . . more . . ."

Although Antonina realized that her frenzy was a grave sin, she took the sin upon her soul in an ecstasy of self-abnegation. It seemed to her that her loss was so irreparable that it could not go unavenged. And for that she would willingly accept any punishment, however heavy. Just so long as the one responsible for what had happened received his due in full.

When she came to, the room was already full of people, and the men from the dormitory next door were carrying Karasik out into the corridor half-dead. Nikolai stood leaning against the wall, with the same forced smile, and nothing could be detected in his sudden gray and sunken face except weariness and disgust. Antonina tried to make him look at her, but as soon as their eyes met he either turned away or lowered his head. Her feelings for her husband were now almost maternal.

She was overcome by a burning desire to shield Nikolai from the danger that threatened him, to hide him behind herself. So when the two internal security men started twisting his arms, she rushed to his defense with a fury that surprised her.

"Don't dare touch him! You great bullies! He'll go quietly."

The Labyrinth · 349

Nikolai looked at her with stricken gratitude, and moved with heavy steps toward the door. The security men hurried after him. The crowd drifted behind, swirling through the door as if it were a funnel. This was the order of procession all the way across the site to the main gate, where a three-ton dump truck was waiting to take him into town.

Antonina felt neither anxiety nor regret as she walked along behind the security men. On the contrary, she was proud of her husband, if anything, and with every step her reborn respect for him grew stronger. This was her Nikolai, as she wanted to see him, and as she wanted him to look in the eyes of others. What lay before him seemed to her no more than a tiresome but necessary delay before they were permanently reunited. Osip's death had brought them together once and for all.

Before he climbed into the back of the truck, Nikolai looked around at her for the last time, and his farewell nod seemed to seal their unspoken pact. The security men planted themselves on either side of him, the vehicle started up, and its vague outline soon dissolved in the rapidly encroaching twilight of the steppes. But Antonina stood there at the gate for a long time, listening to the silence around and within her, or rather to the strong and exultant pulse that beat under her heart.

Then it was night.

Greetings, Dear Lev Lvovich! I've sat down to write, and I don't know where to start. I don't know what I've done to rouse the Lord's wrath, but my life is in ruins again, and how it will end I can't say. My Nikolai has been put in prison again. But now I shall be waiting for him. For as long as it takes. Till I die. Now I am his wife in the eyes of men and of God and his loyal slave. I have given birth to my first-born as a grasswidow. I am sorry, for Papa's sake—when he finds out he will be upset. But I have nowhere else to go now, wherever else I turn there's no home for me. Perhaps you could go and see him. I know I can rely on your help. If he will have me, I will come and help him in his old age and bring up the child. If he is too angry, it's my own fault, and I shall manage just the same, there are kind people in the world. The saddest thing is that the man I wrote to you about is dead, the one who was Jewish, his name was Osip. When we see each other, Reverend Father, I will confess my grievous sins to you and my worst sin of being angry with people. I left the maternity hospital with just the clothes on my back, and had to think where to go and who to ask for bread. But the Lord did not withdraw his mercies from me. Before I was through the gate, I looked and there was Musya from our canteen in a taxi and she'd even thought of bringing flowers. "Congratulations," she said, "let's go to my place, you can live with me." It makes me sorry to think how I used to look down on her. What a sin it was. So I am staying with her and living on whatever God provides. I've stopped getting the maternity grant long ago, so Musya feeds me. She's a wonderful woman and she's completely reformed. There's a man here who comes to see her, Nazar Stepanich, the Clerk of Works at the site, he's ready to marry her anytime, but she won't have it at any price. He's the one to blame for Osip, and she loved Osip. So she won't marry him. I keep seeing things these days. I saw my mother the other day. She came into my room in the early morning and stood by the door, as quiet as can be, and said, "Weep for me, my little girl, and I will take your tears to Osip. It will comfort him." You are a righteous man, Lev Lvovich. Tell me, is it possible by prayer to save the soul of a servant of God who has taken his own life? If need be, I will gladly take the veil, just say the word. I remain your devoted friend, God's servant Antonina, and I humbly greet your wife Kapitolina Grigorievna.

SATURDAY

*The Evening and Night
of the Sixth Day*

I

His meeting with his grandson threw Pyotr Vasilievich off balance again. His efforts to obtain custody of Vadim were unavailing. Everywhere he went, even at the highest levels, officialdom met his request with sympathetic head-wagging, but flatly refused to assist him. Yet, although his conversation with Father Georgii at the hospital had shed some light on these matters for him, he did not give up hope. Waiving his normal rule, Pyotr Vasilievich wrote a tearful letter to an old acquaintance from the far-off time of troubles, now among the great ones of the land. He had been waiting, uneasily and impatiently, for over a week now for an answer which did not come, and his anxious expectancy was changing day by day into certainty of yet another failure. Probably for the first time in his life he felt the presence in the world about him of a dark and ineluctable force as soundless and deadening as cotton wool, smothering all resistance. For Pyotr Vasilievich the hardest thing to bear was the realization that he was powerless against it.

For some time now, he had seldom left the house. He went out only to buy food, and returned immediately. The rest of the day he spent sitting motionless at the window, looking into himself rather than at what was in front of him. Pyotr Vasilievich was painfully trying to find in his past life the day and the hour for which he and those dear to him had been so cruelly and inescapably compelled to pay, and were paying still.

However much he pondered, his thoughts invariably returned from their wanderings through the labyrinth of his memory to that echoing morning on the market square when he had found himself by the broken shop window, staring at the crudely painted dummy ham. "Surely it can't all have started from a stupid thing like that?"

For a long time after Antonina left, Pyotr Vasilievich could not adjust to the new rhythm of his domestic life. There was nobody now to wake him up in the morning and cook his breakfast. Dirty underwear and shirts lay in a pile under the bed for weeks on end, and he never got around to taking them to the laundry. Now that he was alone, he realized at last how much Antonina meant to him and how much he owed her.

The letters which she wrote with exemplary regularity he put away carefully in his wallet, and took out to reread from time to time. She and Nikolai were living somewhere in the Central Asian steppe, working on a building site. His daughter described their present existence for him in detail, and inquired anxiously about him, his health, and his affairs. All the signs were that Antonina was satisfied with her married life. He was glad for her, but deep down he felt jealous of Nikolai, who had gradually replaced her father in his daughter's heart. "You're a back number, Lashkov. Soon nobody will want you."

As he was returning from the shop one day, Pyotr Vasilievich suddenly felt a dizziness, and a burning weakness in his legs. He barely managed to stagger to the nearest bench in the public garden. When he had recovered his breath, he heard a series of slight coughs at his side, alternating with the rustle of a newspaper. Suddenly uneasy, he glanced sideways at this unexpected neighbor and his heart skipped faster. Sitting at the opposite end of the bench, casually leafing through the current number of a weekly paper, was Gupak. Pyotr Vasilievich's scrutiny did not escape him. He instantly folded the paper in four, and bowed a courteous challenge.

"Hallo, Pyotr Vasilievich. I hope you're in perfect health?"

"Can't grumble so far."

"God be praised."

"Yes, he hasn't been hard on me." He meant to answer his unwanted companion as rudely and provocatively as he could, but his voice sounded so timid and inoffensive that he didn't recognize it himself. "Thanks to your prayers, as they say."

"We do pray, Pyotr Vasilievich, we do pray," said Gupak in eager gratitude. "We don't forget those who have gone astray."

"And you are the one who decides who's gone astray?"

"No, whatever makes you think that, Pyotr Vasilievich? We don't take the sin of pride upon our souls. We pray for everybody. For ourselves as well."

"So you're not free from sin, either?"

"No, Pyotr Vasilievich, it's not for us to cast a stone. With sins like ours, we can only repent."

"That must be why people don't stick with you very long. Your holiness isn't up to standard?"

"You aren't thinking of your daughter, Antonina Petrovna, are you?"

"She'll do, if you like."

"Your daughter Antonina Petrovna is an angelic creature," Gupak said warmly, trying to please. "People like her never retreat from a decision once taken." He lowered his eyes. "Every letter she writes to me only goes to confirm that."

"So she writes to you?" Pyotr Vasilievich felt hot and stupid, but for some reason he was neither angry with Gupak nor jealous of him. "That's how much respect she has for her father!"

"Don't judge her too harshly"—Gupak moved a little closer to him —"for a believer, a father in the flesh and a father in the spirit are equal. You don't tell your own father, especially if he's an atheist, things which only a spiritual director will understand."

"Depends who the director is." He tried to adopt an implacable tone, but his words lost all force as he uttered them. "Anyway, all that business of yours is crank stuff, idiocy."

"You think so?"

"I know so."

"How can you be so sure about anything so soon, my dear Pyotr Vasilievich? Every human life is God's world created anew. How is it possible, with one's own profoundly personal knowledge of things, to comprehend another human being, and compel him to live like oneself into the bargain? Man must first change himself for the better, and not his conditions. But you were determined to begin with his conditions. You have changed those, but the human soul remains as much of a mystery to you as it always was. What we do is try to find a key that fits."

"How? With your fairy tales?"

"With words. With kind words."

"Does it work?"

"It is a lengthy process, Pyotr Vasilievich. Sometimes a lifetime is not enough. The soul requires constant attention. Take your daughter Antonina Petrovna, for example . . ."

"She'll simmer down, now she's married, and forget it all."

"It's all in the hands of God," Gupak meekly agreed. He rose, putting the newspaper in his jacket pocket, flashed his gold spectacle frames at Pyotr Vasilievich, and hurriedly took his leave. "I enjoyed our talk. Do drop in sometime. Company is good for people of our age. It often helps you to see things clearer. Good-bye."

In spite of himself, Pyotr Vasilievich succumbed to this disarming piece of cajolery, and heard himself humoring Gupak. "I'll drop in," he promised.

A minute later, Gupak was swallowed up in the rapidly gathering dusk, and Pyotr Vasilievich wondered at his own pliability as he rose to go. "You're cracking up, Lashkov; some devil's got into you."

The town in which he had been born and brought up, with which everything memorable and significant in his life was connected, now seemed alien and forbidding. And the people he happened to meet bore no resemblance to those he had been used to seeing in the past. There was a strange, jerky restlessness in their walk and their unseeing glances. It was as if they were hiding from pursuers they could not have named themselves. Pyotr Vasilievich reached home without in fact seeing a single familiar face, or an unworried one. "The town's growing—you can't keep up with it!"

The corner of an envelope was sticking out from the crack between the lock and the doorpost. Pyotr Vasilievich felt a sour sickness in the pit of his stomach. It took him a long time to find the keyhole, but when he finally went in and switched the light on he sighed with relief. "He's answered after all."

His comrade from the time of troubles on the Syzran-Vyazma line, after a friendly rebuke to Pyotr Vasilievich for his long silence, informed him that steps had already been taken in a certain direction, that events were developing favorably, and that an answer satisfactory to both of them might shortly be expected.

"There are some decent people in the world," he thought. His mental equilibrium, which had been somewhat disturbed by his conversation with Gupak, was restored, and, when he had settled down once more by the window, he quietly and contentedly dozed off.

He dreamed that he was walking through interminable narrow corridors; many, many doors were banging resoundingly, one after another, behind him. The corridors led Pyotr Vasilievich further and further, and with every step he took, he was pursued by a terror of the emptiness and silence. Suddenly, from around the next bend, Father Georgii came toward him, and, in lieu of greeting, addressed him with pitying reproof.

"No one can take away from me that which is within me and with me. It is harder for you—you are an atheist. You are going against your nature."

And—who would have thought it?—Pyotr Vasilievich had no retort for his hospital acquaintance. He was choked by a bitter spasm of distress such as he had never known.

When he woke up, Pyotr Vasilievich commiserated with himself ironically. "Even your dreams have gone crazy, Lashkov. You're getting old, should have gone on the scrap heap long ago."

II

Moscow greeted Pyotr Vasilievich with pouring rain. The first downpour of summer sent wave after wave sweeping over the platform and the station square, forming treacherous whirlpools over the gratings of the drains. The town shook off the sweltering haze of the last few days; details reemerged from the featureless blur and the place reasserted itself in scenes and moods which could belong nowhere else. Monumentally cumbersome buildings alternated with barrack-like two-story boxes, and they in turn rubbed shoulders amicably with decrepit family houses dating from the last century. On either side of the windshield, Pyotr Vasilievich saw streets branching off, revealing distant vistas of foliage in green suburbs, glittering with raindrops.

During the journey, while the silent, shifty-looking driver recklessly wound through innumerable backstreets, on the way to the street in Sokolniki he had visited before, Pyotr Vasilievich could not control his breathless palpitations. "It all went wrong last time. We didn't behave as we should."

The news of his brother's death had taken Pyotr Vasilievich aback. Not that he found it in any way surprising—it could happen to anybody of their age and at any moment. He simply hadn't thought, especially after all that had passed between them, that he would ever have news of Vasilii again. "He must have kept the address, didn't want to lose sight of me. Or maybe somebody just had a kind thought? That's the most likely thing."

Outside the familiar house, Pyotr Vasilievich loitered for a while in the slackening rain before he could bring himself to enter. The silent and watchful yard still bore the traces of what had just happened. All the windows were open wide, the doors were ajar, and a babble of voices was coming from the entrance hall of the wooden outbuilding.

As soon as he crossed the threshold, the howl of a single keening voice floated out to him from the open door of his brother's room, where he gradually distinguished the faces of several people gathered around the funeral meal. The faces turned in unison toward the new arrival, and one of them, large and pale, with a spark of humor in the deepset cornflower-blue eyes, separated itself from the rest and appeared in the diffused half-light of the hallway.

"Welcome, Pyotr Vasilievich. They have already taken Vasya away. I realize it's not nice. But it was very, very hot. We were waiting for you. My name is Otto. Otto Stabel." He went behind Pyotr Vasilievich's back and pushed him forward in a friendly way. "We all loved Vasya. Vasya was my good friend."

When Pyotr Vasilievich appeared in the room, the keening, in which nobody else had joined, was choked off as suddenly as it had begun. There was some movement at the table, and the faces drew still closer together, to make room for the guest. He sat down and all eyes were fixed on him with the same expression: So you really are Vasilii's brother! While the guest and his hosts sat inspecting each other, waiting in an agony of embarrassment for something to draw them into conversation, an old woman in a shabby dress of unidentifiable color which hung about her like a sack noiselessly waited on Pyotr Vasilievich. As she fenced him in with a lavish array of plates, her voice crackled faintly in his ear.

"Here you are, have some cheese . . . This is herring, do have some. . . . Try the galantine . . . Please take some bread."

There was something feline and predatory in the old woman's insidious attentions, which no doubt was why Pyotr Vasilievich involuntarily shuddered whenever he took food from her and their hands happened to meet.

"Thank you . . . I'm not hungry . . . Thank you . . . That will be too much for me . . . I'm most grateful . . ."

Before the third round, a short, elderly man with one shoulder higher than the other stood up at the end of the table, and with his eyes glued on Pyotr Vasilievich began speaking in a brisk recitative.

"I must begin by declaring as a matter of principle that the late Vasilii and I disagreed on many questions of home and foreign policy." Here he gave a significant little cough, obviously to show that he took for granted the mutual comprehension of people as important as himself and the guest.

"However, as a tenant I can vouch for his complete conscientiousness on other questions. As for instance: repairs to the plumbing, cleaning of the yard, and other miscellaneous works. In this regard, I have no complaints against the deceased. Vasilii knew his work inside out. But, citizens, we must never forget the need for vigilance. You know what times we live in. We must give no quarter to the foe! Revolutions are not made in kid gloves!" He realized that his tongue had run away with him, and his eyes roamed the room distractedly. "So I raise my glass. In a toast, so to speak . . . May the earth lie lightly . . . and so on, and so forth . . . To his eternal memory, citizens."

He sat down, and the padded shoulders of his shabby tunic, thickly powdered with dandruff, lifted defiantly: he had spoken his piece, and the rest was up to them. Looking at him, Pyotr Vasilievich could not rid himself of a persistent impression; he had seen that resolute face, those hard, dull eyes, and heard that uncompromising manner of speech somewhere before. And all at once, as often happens in moments of extreme tension, when an essential link is suddenly restored in the broken chain of time, he had a startlingly clear recollection of a winter morning and a station, where he had driven the operations squad after the crash in Petushki. This recollection was so vivid that he even seemed to feel the same ache in his teeth. And through the intervening layers of years and events the face—like a profile on a coin—of Avanesyan, chairman of the district Cheka, stood out clearly. "That rifle isn't an ornament; you were given it to fire, and fire without mercy." This extreme resemblance between two completely different people struck Pyotr Vasilievich as being full of significance. The grim fury of the one, and the shabby self-importance of the other, carried an acrid whiff of the same disease which was tormenting and consuming them both.

After the fourth drink, the conversation became general. The guests interrupted each other impatiently, each hurrying to speak his piece first, presumably supposing it to be uniquely important and appropriate to the occasion.

"Let us remember God's servant, Vasilii."

"He was a wonderful man, may he rest in peace."

"You'd come to him, and say 'Vasya, do so and so,' and there was never a refusal."

"Nobody ever heard a bad word from him."

"He was a good man: nobody can deny it."

A full-bosomed woman with a heavily rouged, flabby face, who had sat quietly till now at the other end of the table, bobbed up eagerly. "I remember . . ." But that was as far as she got. Her unwieldy body sagged helplessly, and her eyes, fixed on the door, went glassy and then dead. "Sima!" she cried.

A woman stood in the doorway, shifting irresolutely from foot to foot. A red plastic raincoat clung flimsily to her fragile, almost girlish figure, and a bunch of flowers touched by the recent rain trembled in her hands. Agitation had drained the blood from her wan face and emphasized the fine web of permanent lines it bore. But for these wrinkles she could indeed have been taken for an adolescent, so angular and immature was her whole appearance. The deep gray eyes, shining mistily, looked around the gathering; she smiled pathetically, lowered her head, and said, "Hallo."

The talk in the room ceased immediately. Faces lengthened, frozen and tense but within a moment bewilderment gave way to soundless weeping, which made Pyotr Vasilievich shudder. The guests sat without moving, weeping into empty space; somewhere out there in the dizzying depths of the past, a woman like a young girl still lingered wearing a red plastic raincoat and carrying a bunch of rain-drenched flowers. It suddenly dawned on Pyotr Vasilievich that his companions at the table were mourning for much more than his brother.

Stabel touched him on the shoulder. "We go, Pyotr Vasilievich. Crying is woman's work."

They went out into the yard, which was deserted and wet after the rain. Lightened clouds sailed by over the roofs. In the few clear patches between them, the first stars could be seen against the darkening sky. A damp wind filtering through the poplar leaves scattered the sounds of engine hooting, amplified by the wet air, and the clank of couplings from the freight yard across the street.

At the gate, the old woman who had waited on Pyotr Vasilievich caught up with them. "Don't go too far away," she coaxed in a whisper, "it's embarrassing when there are guests."

Stabel, heading for the park, tossed a good-humored reply over his shoulder. "All right. We'll walk a little." On the way he explained to his companion: "That's Lyuba, Lyovushkin's wife . . . Vanya himself vanished long ago . . . she's getting very old."

And there, to the rustle of the dripping poplars in the park, Stabel told Pyotr Vasilievich the story of the yard in which his brother Vasilii had spent a large part of his joyless life. Together with Otto he relived the brief love of Sima Tsygankova and Lyova Khramov. The Austrian told him all there was to know about Nikishkin, who, it turned out, had made the speech at the table. The fate of the Gorev family was mentioned in passing, but from the cautious way in which Stabel pronounced the names of its members, and especially that of Grusha, Pyotr Vasilievich could see what an effort it cost him.

"I finished my banishment. I don't like Moscow. My family is in Siberia. My children are grown up . . . I have a house, good work . . . I am old now, soon be in the grave . . . Time to go home, Pyotr Vasilievich . . . Guests there."

Near the house they came face to face with a tiny old woman with a dark straw hat pulled right down over her eyes. She was standing at the gate, staring at the ground and mumbling something to herself. Her heavily lined face spoke of an acute preoccupation which obviously gnawed at her ceaselessly.

Stabel bowed and spoke as he went around her. "How do you do, Maria Nikolaevna? I hope you are well."

She didn't turn a hair but continued her private conversation with herself.

When they were in the yard, the Austrian, looking around warily, explained to Pyotr Vasilievich. "The former mistress of the house. Shokolinist's her name. She must be a hundred years old. And still alive. Healthy woman. Very healthy." Stabel wagged his head enthusiastically as though marveling at the former householder's vitality and longevity. "What people there are! Where does she get such health!"

Lyuba put them both up for the night in Vasilii's room. Quickly and noiselessly she made up two beds on the white scrubbed floor, made the sign of the cross over them, and gave Pyotr Vasilievich final instructions as she left. "If you want anything, knock at Number Five. I'll pop down and see to it."

At once, the room was filled with darkness and the rustling of leaves in the yard, beyond which the starry sky was dimly visible. A voice emerged clearly in the silence of the night; it was Nikishkin maundering drunkenly on the second floor of the house nearby.

"Do you have any conception of who it is you live with, you old shit? Do you fully realize it, eh? I'll teach you love of freedom, you hag! What's that? . . . D'you want ten days solitary, with deprivation of exercise and parcels? Silence! I don't waste words on socially dangerous prisoners. A bullet in the head and that's the end of you. Silence! Look how you're standing! Who d'you think you're talking to, you cunt!"

With this in his ears, Pyotr Vasilievich fell asleep. And he dreamed.

III

The Vision of Pyotr Vasilievich . . .

Avanesyan was sitting with his back to the fiercely heated stove bench, leaning so hard against it that he might have been trying to lose himself in its warmth and reassuring solidity. But the stove was obviously not warming him. His bony shoulders shivered and a spasm from time to time distorted his big-nosed face. The chairman of the district Cheka was shaking with a raging fever he had brought with him all the way from his homeland.

"Don't write me any more of these little notes." His dark eyes, tinged with an unhealthy yellow, stared past Pyotr Vasilievich out through the snow-caked window, into the depths of the night beyond. "Just think— what a tragedy! A bourgeois specialist gets his teeth knocked out! He won't die. They never had pity on us. There's too much of the chief conductor in you, Lashkov, the aristocrat of the rail, the legalist. Riding about in passenger coaches has shaken the proletarian consciousness out of you. You're beginning to reek of political degeneracy."

Pyotr Vasilievich tried to argue with him. "If it was in a fit of rage I could understand it—the man might have lost control." Something about his guest, he wasn't yet sure what, had awakened his irritation and hostility. "But it wasn't, it was out of greed, his object was robbery. He had his greedy eyes on the gold. What gold there was in those teeth isn't worth mentioning. But it's caused any amount of gossip all along the line. And most of them aren't on our side."

"What the hell do we care what they say? A dog barks and the wind blows it away." Frank sarcasm and something like disgust could be detected in Avanesyan's tone, and it helped Pyotr Vasilievich to understand his aversion to the man: He was sickened by the Cheka chairman's habit of talking to others as though he knew something which they were not entitled or competent to know. "I've got ways enough of shutting up loud mouths." He didn't even try to conceal his feeling of superiority to his host. "I know Paramoshin, he's a proletarian to the marrow of his bones. It's people like Paramoshin who are the driving force of the revolution. And I won't let anybody touch him."

"You're new here, Leon Arshakovich, and you know people mostly by hearsay." He felt his anger running away with him, but made no effort to restrain himself. "Ask anyone you want what Paramoshin is like. He's a drunk and a layabout, and that's it. And a loud mouth into the bargain. And a coward. Anybody in Uzlovsk who could be bothered has thrashed him. Making a revolution with people like him is a scandal."

"Then, whom are you going to make it with, Lashkov?" Avanesyan's tone was becoming more and more sarcastic all the time. "With school-boys, maybe? Or with those émigré types in glasses who did their training in foreign libraries and scribbled nice little articles over their coffee? If so, pal, you're crazy. Those intellectuals are only interesting at tea-time. They're mighty good at chewing the rag. Give them their head and they'll talk any bit of work out of existence. We can't be bothered with philo-sophical fairy tales just now. Who beats whom—that's the extent of philosophy. We shall make the revolution with the Paramoshins, Lashkov. While the people in glasses are wondering what is permitted and what is prohibited, the Paramoshins do the job. Do it without whining, without unnecessary talk. And if he looks after himself while he's at it, that's his proletarian right. He's taking what he has an age-old right to. At least I know in advance what to expect from him. He's crystal-clear to me, Paramoshin. But you, Lashkov, you're not clear."

"But aren't you frightened?"

"What of?"

"Paramoshin."

"Why should I be?"

"He'll swallow you up, you and all of us."

"Well, we shall have to see who's quicker." His jaw muscles bunched angrily. "We'll wring his neck if we have to. And if we can't wring it, it means we've bitten off more than we can chew. In that case, he'll call us all to account. For everything."

"Nobody has ever owed Paramoshin a thing. He's the one who's in debt, to everybody in the town."

"He'll be making demands for his class, not himself. He has a his-torical responsibility, yet you measure everything in the world by what happens in your own little district, Lashkov."

Pyotr Vasilievich lost all desire to continue the discussion. He felt that in any case he could not reach his guest, could not break through that incomprehensible barrier of disgust for everything connected with the recent past. And although he did not regret sending his report to the district Cheka, he could see quite clearly that it had been futile.

The case itself was truly astonishing. While escorting Savin, the former manager of the Uzlovsk rail depot, to Tula, Tikhon Paramoshin, well known in the town as a drunken brawler and layabout, had knocked his prisoner's gold-filled teeth out with the butt of his revolver. The conductor of the coach in which the bourgeois expert was tied up and under Paramoshin's surveillance, reported what had happened to Pyotr Vasilievich. His authority did not extend to personnel from the district center, and all he could do was to write a report to Avanesyan. No action was taken on his message, but Avanesyan, as he now saw, had not forgotten the business, but put it by for future use.

"Still, that isn't what brought me here to see you." His guest relaxed and reached for his tobacco pouch. "I just happened to be passing—we had a roundup in this area, and I thought, let's drop in and see how commissars live nowadays." He unhurriedly packed his pipe, lit up, inhaled deeply, and, through the smoke, looked straight at his host for the first time that evening. "You live rather poorly, Lashkov, rather poorly."

"Like everybody else. Times are hard."

"Like everybody else, you say?" The old sarcastic tone was back again. "We didn't take power so that we could live like everybody else. It's our own property we're taking, not somebody else's. We are taking what belongs to us by right. The right of the victor. Let's leave asceticism to the Geneva idealists. Let them swallow their eighth of a loaf, we swallowed enough of those in Tsarist jails. We're people of flesh and blood and we don't propose to play at naive communist utopias. I can see the only thing of value in this house is the commissar's wife."

Maria, busy with the oven tongs, responded almost inaudibly. "I married a good man, not a commissar."

"Some people have all the luck," grinned Avanesyan, shivering again with cold. "What a queen you picked up. Now me, I've never had any luck in that line. Face isn't my fortune, as they say. This nose is quite enough by itself! I've tried so hard, though. I heard for instance that priests live well, so I enrolled in a seminary. I thought if I started getting a lot of money any woman would marry me."

Maria spoke up again by the stove. "Well, did you find happiness?"

"They expelled me before long."

"But what if they hadn't?"

"No, I expect it would have been the same. Nobody would have taken a fancy to me. Money is nothing. It's power that gives you the right to everything. Why, nowadays they volunteer. One girl turned up here not long ago . . ."

"Don't," Maria implored faintly. "Please don't . . . it isn't right."

"Very well." Avanesyan rose resolutely, and moved toward the door, carefully avoiding her eyes. There was something pathetic in his haste. "Mustn't overdo a good thing. I've warmed up, and I mustn't disturb you anymore." He nodded a command to Pyotr Vasilievich from the doorway. "Come and see me off."

Snow was falling in big, slow flakes over the town. The acrid smell of cooling clinker reached them from the station. The silence, broken occasionally by train whistles and the barking of dogs, seemed unruffled, soothingly secure.

"So long, Lashkov." Avanesyan turned up the collar of his excellent winter coat. "My advice to you is, don't write any more reports. I shan't read them, anyway. Paramoshin has already slapped three contradictory ones on top of yours. And any one of them's more than enough to get you shot. Your widow will find plenty of takers." He barked with laughter. "Better watch out, Lashkov."

The curtain of snow came between them, and Pyotr Vasilievich peered after his guest, conscious both of relief and pity. "You haven't come into much happiness since you've been in power, chairman, you certainly haven't! You're just bragging."

From the hallway, as he was shaking off the sparkling snowflakes, he heard his wife's low murmur from the parlor. "Blessed are they that keep the laws He hath revealed, and that seek Him with all their hearts . . . they do nothing that is unlawful, but walk in His ways . . . I seek Thee with all my heart, let me not stray from Thy commandments."

For the first time in their brief but eventful life together, Pyotr Vasilievich hadn't the heart to interrupt his wife at this occupation of hers. "To each his own, let her unburden herself."

IV

One midday as Lashkov was on his way to the canteen he was hailed by a familiar voice.

"How are you, Pyotr Vasilievich! Come in! Why don't a couple of old men like us sit here in the shade for a bit?"

Gupak, dressed in old working clothes, was beaming at him hospitably over the fence of the house he happened to be passing. Since their chance conversation in the public garden, a vague idea that Gupak was deliberately seeking him out, for motives still unclear, had been gaining strength in Pyotr Vasilievich's mind. So he nodded in reply, resolved as always on such occasions to confront the unknown. "Why shouldn't I? I'll go in for a bit."

It turned out that Gupak was not alone in the little garden attached to the house. There was also a thin, spruce old man with a straw hat, and sandals on his bare feet, busy at work on a spreading gooseberry bush. The old man put his fingertips to his hat brim in a crisp salute, then buried himself in his occupation again.

"Vladimir Anisimovich," said Gupak, introducing him. "Great enthusiast for everything that grows. He's one of us—old-age pensioner." He courteously steered his guest towards an awning in the corner of the yard. "We putter about a bit. Grafts, cuttings, and all that stuff . . . Come over here, please, it's cooler . . . I'll get you some kvass in just a minute . . . I'm doing my own housekeeping, you know. My wife's away."

Gupak disappeared into the house and came out in a little while holding a plastic container and a mug.

"Help yourself . . . it's homemade . . . straight from the cellar." He sank into a chair facing Pyotr Vasilievich. "It's hot . . ."

"Thank you . . . Yes, it's thirsty weather."

"Good for the garden. But everything's drying up in the fields. They say it's going to be a very poor harvest."

"We've had worse. We'll sweat it out."

The other old man came up to the table, sat down, put his shears down in front of him, took off his hat, and fanned himself with it.

"Sweating it out is something you do in circumstances beyond your control. But our crop failures nowadays are the result of negligence and laziness. There are no objective reasons for them. With world agriculture at its present level, we ought to be ashamed of pleading disasters of nature. Especially in a country with so many different climatic zones." It was as though at some time in his life he had lost his temper, never to recover it: He was exasperation incarnate. "We consider ourselves a European power, yet our farming is on the African level. If you listen to our politicians you'd think the elements persecute us and us alone. What's even odder, they're very selective about it. Volcanic eruptions, earthquakes, tidal waves, traffic accidents happen elsewhere. All we have is droughts or unseasonable rains. A handy consolation for windbags. Or take the war if you like. You'd think nobody but us did any fighting! The French sell us meat! With all the resources, all the potential, we have! It's shameful, my dear sirs."

"Yes, but half the country was in ruins," Pyotr Vasilievich protested cautiously, although he was stunned by the old man's sudden vehemence. "Whatever you say, there's a big difference between us and other countries."

"Well, whose fault is it?" The old man shot out of his chair in his rage. "Whose fault is it that the Russian state has lost one war after another during the last two centuries? If two of them were won, it's only thanks to our docile peasants. We can say that it was in spite of the state machine and the regular army. A people two hundred million strong couldn't hold its own in the very first battle with a country many times smaller! Because of political blindness at the summit, the bombastic conceit of the military and their stupidity, their utter and endless stupidity!" The old man was breathless with anger. "They occupied the western borderlands without firing a shot, won mock victories in maneuvers, but when it came to real fighting, the war minister and his staff were out of there so fast that the motorized units only just managed to pick them up at Smolensk. His deputy fought his way into a common soldier's cape, buried all his regalia and documents somewhere in the Rostov steppe, and bolted without a look back. While the Big Brain spent a full week drinking himself stupid and waiting for world revolution to break out to the rear of the enemy. What a self-infatuated moron you'd have to be to count on any such thing! And remember, all that time the land was ablaze. Blood was being spilled, and it wasn't the 'small quantity' they'd budgeted for, either. We have the peasant to thank for saving us yet again. We were victorious! Six-to-one, we were victorious! For victories of that sort the people should have monuments erected to them and the generals should be court-martialed. Instead of which they have the gall to write memoirs. 'Left flanking movement,' 'right flanking movement,' 'pincers.' They put on airs and graces like rival ballerinas. Strategists—the sons of bitches. They just hurled masses of people against machine guns. And what's more, stationed security troops behind them to block their retreat. They put twenty million in their graves. Enough to repeople Germany. And still they've learned nothing! They're at it again, hanging their bits of tin all over themselves, strutting about at parades: 'We will shatter,' 'we will crush,' 'we will repulse.' They occupy the backyard of Europe without a shot and brag away: 'a superb operation.' They've forgotten how they nearly broke their necks running away from that very same western Ukraine when it came to fighting there, instead of picnicking. Gold-braided blockheads! And it's the peasant who'll have to pay for their despicable stupidity again. Pay in blood. And what a price!"

"We're all armchair Napoleons," Pyotr Vasilievich answered uncertainly, after a short pause. "It's not quite so easy in practice."

Not a muscle twitched in the thin face which age had pared to the bone. He only surveyed the speaker with a pitying look in his keen eyes, rose, tugged on his hat, and took the shears from the table. But before he went away he declared in a surprisingly calm voice, "I commanded a corps during the war, my dear sir. An infantry corps, let me tell you. When I condemn other people, I condemn myself too."

With this he went away, leaving Pyotr Vasilievich alone with Gupak and his consternation. His host hastened to his rescue.

"His feelings are understandable, Pyotr Vasilievich. Vladimir Anisimovich's family all died during the siege. He was at the Academy lecturing on tactics at the time. He volunteered for the front. Spent practically the whole war in the trenches. His wife was a native of these parts, so he's come to spend his old age here."

"Does he live alone then?"

"There's a woman with him a bit younger than himself. Used to be a nursing sister in his unit. She looks after him."

"He was really angry, wasn't he?"

"No, no, Pyotr Vasilievich. It's only when he gets on his high horse. As a rule, he's the nicest of men. His home is like a hotel. Open house to all comers. He'd give the shirt off his back to a total stranger. You won't find such a good heart in a hurry."

Pyotr Vasilievich couldn't resist a dig at his host. "So, even an atheist can live according to his conscience? He's an example of it."

"You're wrong, Pyotr Vasilievich." His apologetic tone did not conceal the calm surety of a man for whom every word he speaks means exactly what it says. "Nothing can perturb a true atheist. Is there a God or isn't there? No such problem exists for him. The atheist vegetates, never troubling his mind about anything, feeling no emotions. As soon as he starts asking himself questions he is well on the way to the Lord. A man may consider himself an unbeliever and still live in God. There is such a thing as prayer in action. If without realizing it yourself you live according to the laws of the Gospel, your soul is already in communion. Only the final breakthrough is necessary for you to become aware of yourself in God. Incidentally, you were jumping to conclusions. Vladimir Anisimovich is a believer."

"Whatever for?"

Dismayed by the news, he glanced involuntarily towards the spot where the retired general was absorbed in pruning the shrubbery. "What more does he want? He seems to have achieved it all."

"People come to the Lord by different paths, Pyotr Vasilievich. Not from poverty, or from wealth, but from purity of heart. Your daughter Antonina Petrovna, for instance."

"That's all over, thank God!" His sharp interruption revealed the jealousy which had been festering in him for so long. "It was just out of boredom. Having no husband was driving her crazy. When she's lived away from here for a bit she'll forget all about it. Right." He rose and started to hurry away. "Thanks for the kvass."

Gupak, as cordial and willing as ever, escorted his guest past the old man who nodded good-bye to him, and on to the gate where he squeezed his hand and urged him in parting to come again.

"Why spend your days on your own? You go past here every day. If you start Vladimir Anisimovich talking, you can listen to him forever. I have other callers, too. Just as interesting."

Pyotr Vasilievich, relieved to be moving off homeward, hastily thanked him as he went. "I'll look in sometime."

That night he lay awake for a long time tossing and turning, recalling the details of his call on Gupak. A feeling that Gupak was constantly hinting at more than he said haunted Pyotr Vasilievich and forced him to go over their conversation again and again. "He's got something up his sleeve, I'm sure he has."

In this state of restless perplexity, Pyotr Vasilievich went to sleep. He dreamed of a strange building, unlike anything he'd seen, with a ceiling that receded into a dark abyss. He kept finding door after door and opening them in search of a way out, but behind every one loomed a blank wall. Then somewhere ahead there was a glimmer of light and Lashkov ran toward it with relief and hope. As he ran he heard behind him the thunder of many feet. The light got nearer and nearer, but the footsteps grew louder and louder. The fear of pursuit made his body weightless, and he soared above a forest of hands reaching out toward him. At the very moment when there seemed to be no hope left, and greedy fingers were about to touch his body which had suddenly become subject to gravity again, the light received him into itself. He found himself on a huge, deserted square in the middle of which sat a legless beggar woman holding out her hand to him for alms. Suddenly her face came nearer, looming larger and larger until it shut out everything else. In agonized bewilderment Pyotr Vasilievich recognized in it the well-remembered features of his Maria. But as soon as he moved toward it the face instantly blurred and vanished, revealing the same strange building with its ceiling receding into a dark abyss. He struggled to cry out, to summon someone who might help him to find his way out again, but his mouth fell open soundlessly in dumb frenzy.

Pyotr Vasilievich was awakened by a knock from a messenger, who wanted him to sign for an express telegram from his brother: "Getting married. Come. Andrei."

Pyotr Vasilievich's dream vanished as though it had never been. "Imagine doing a thing like that at his age, bald-headed old sinner!"

V

Rain-soaked pine trees marched out of the night to meet Pyotr Vasilievich as soon as he left the station. He had no intention of spending the night there and although there were some five kilometers of road ahead, lit only by the stars, he set out at a leisurely pace along the verge of the slushy track. But he had only just plunged into the forest when he heard behind him the tortured creaking of wheels and the faint snort of a plodding horse. Shortly afterward, a cart caught up with him, and he was immediately hailed by a sleepy voice.

"You real or a ghost?"

"Real enough."

"Which way you going?"

"To the warden's place."

"What d'you want there?"

"I'm going to see Lashkov—Andrei Vasilievich."

"You wouldn't be his brother, by any chance?"

"Near enough."

"Well I'll be . . . I must have watched five trains go through waiting for you." The shapeless silhouette on the front of the cart shifted. "Sit here, then . . . Let me stick a bit of straw under you, the road's bumpy. . . . I was wondering who could be making for the warden's place at this time of night. . . . You settled? . . . Let's go . . . Gee up, there."

Jouncing from wheel to wheel the cart staggered slowly through the damp night. A moist breeze played on their faces, and every now and then they were sprinkled with a fine shower of drops from the branches overhanging the way. The driver urged the horse on lazily, as though he didn't really mean it, and found time to ask Pyotr Vasilievich whether he smoked.

"I don't go in for it."

"Well, I'll be . . . And I was thinking I'd indulge in a city cigarette for free. I shall have to roll one of my 'eye-gougers.' " He busied himself in the dark, struck a match, and inhaled. "Andrei Vasilich was expecting you yesterday. He kept dashing to the station himself all day and now he's put me on the job . . . Sasha doesn't know whether she's coming or going either. She's a tigress, but she's mighty scared of you. He's a party man, she says. What of it, you can be a party man and still not bite, can't you? When her man died she was left with five kids . . . Andrei Vasilievich has been chasing her since he was a boy, from what they say. And she's always been sweet on him, it seems. She ought to have chucked that man of hers long ago. He called himself a husband and that was all. He was always dead drunk, and well, you know, he was a war cripple. But that's the sort of woman Sasha is, she wouldn't go against her conscience. It's a funny time of life for it now, of course, but still it's a good thing they've got together. . . . Get on, there!"

The warden's headquarters greeted them with empty silence. Light showed in only one window, and that was in the office end, not the living quarters. The driver condescended to put Pyotr Vasilievich's mind at rest as he pulled up by the veranda. "They went to the village to make a night of it. I expect they'll be back soon. If not, I'll slip over and give them a shout. It's only a stone's throw. They must have left Valentina to look out for us."

Sure enough, they found a hunchbacked girl of fifteen peacefully dozing at the desk in the office with a man's coat thrown over her shoulders. She had rested her freckled cheek on her folded hands and was snuffling contentedly in her sleep. Her awkward posture—one shoulder against the desk, the other thrust sharply forward—emphasized the delicate childishness which would probably stay with her for some time.

"Valentina!" In the light, the driver turned out to be a sturdy, short-legged man. Every feature in the unshaven face with its mockingly down-turned lips seemed to bear the mark of devil-may-care humor. "Valentina!"

He touched her carefully, and she started, opened her eyes and jumped up, letting the jacket fall from her shoulders; in some confusion she began straightening her dress.

"They're all in the village. . . . Aunt Alexandra left me here specially. . . . She told me to run down there if she was wanted. . . . You wait here with Yegor Ivanich . . . I'll be quick."

However, she didn't have to run down to the village. Outside somewhere in the depths of the night they heard a long drawn-out tune on an accordion, and it gradually came nearer until it filled the silence. Raucous voices interrupted each other's attempts to sing "If I Only Had Mountains of Gold," but the song wouldn't come right and in the end the singers fell silent and left the accordionist a clear field.

Yegor gave Pyotr Vasilievich a satisfied wink. "They're coming! They've swallowed a skinful . . . Just listen to it! Savelich must have served his own stuff—the extra strong."

Yegor was sitting on a bench by the door examining the guest with the frank curiosity of a man from whom nothing can be concealed and who knows it all in advance anyway. His provocatively ironical air was getting on Pyotr Vasilievich's nerves. To keep his growing hostility under control, he asked him a question.

"Do you work here, for Andrei?"

"I do a bit all over the place," he said with a cheeky grin. "Here and on the kolkhoz as well. It just depends."

"So you work by the day?"

"By the day as well."

"Do you make enough?"

"It's all right sometimes. Some days you eat, others it's not worth getting up."

The accordion, inside the enclosure by now, gave one last squeal and was silent. Then they heard the voices of people moving about under the window.

"Open the door, Mother."

"See if Yegor's here."

"Andrei, my love, the horse is back!"

"You all go on in, I'll be right with you."

The voices passed into the house, and were soon in full cry beyond the office wall.

"Sit down . . . sit down, my friends . . . Take your places . . . You're welcome to whatever we have."

"You don't have to ask a drunken man twice!"

"You're high already—why can't you just sit quietly? You can't drink it all, you know!"

"Stop nagging, Natalya, how often do folks like us go to a wedding? I know this'll be the last I'll get."

"Masha, pull the tablecloth your way a bit."

Andrei beamed happily as he emerged from the dark entrance to the office and advanced drunkenly on his brother with arms outstretched.

"You've really made my day . . . really made my day, Petyok. I'll never forget it! Come on . . . let's go to table . . ." Andrei hugged Pyotr Vasilievich and drew him toward the door, but before they went out he called back over his shoulder: "Yegor, unharness and then come on in . . . Go and help Aunt Sasha, Valentina dear."

Pyotr Vasilievich's appearance at the festive board caused some embarrassment among the guests. They froze, and stared at him expectantly. Andrei pushed him forward with encouraging little noises. "Come in, Petyok, come in, we're all friends . . . Come in, don't be shy . . . Make yourself at home."

In the dead silence which followed, someone rose from the table and advanced—almost glided towards the guest—a woman who was beginning to thicken with an air of assurance and authority and whom he immediately recognized as Alexandra. She stopped short of him, respectfully bowed down to the ground, and as she straightened up, spoke without a trace of confusion or embarrassment. "Welcome to our table, Pyotr Vasilievich. We are glad to have you as our guest."

She evidently didn't lack aplomb; her self-possession was genuine. But in the stubborn set of her full lips after she had spoken, Pyotr Vasilievich sensed a challenge and a warning: she was letting him know that he was not the only strong character here. Her show of independence met with his approval. "Better not put your hand in her jaws. She'd know how to stand up for herself. And her husband." He sat down, and the gathering exploded into life. They all spoke at once, trying to forget their embarrassment in speech.

"Pyotr Vasilievich is a long way behind—give him a stiff one."

"No, he'll choke if he doesn't get some practice—give him some red wine for a start. That's the stuff."

"Drink up, drink up, drink up."

"All gone!"

"Now have something to eat."

They made him repeat the dose. He drank it and then, without thinking, knocked back one after another, to the approving murmurs of the company. He didn't feel himself getting drunk, but a dull crushing ache at the back of his neck slowly pervaded his consciousness. Shapes gradually blurred and warped. Pyotr Vasilievich grew friendlier all the time, took a maudlin pleasure in every face, every word. The hunchbacked Valentina peeked at him gaily from behind the bride's shapely shoulder, and her gentle willingness must somehow have reminded him of his daughter Antonina, or even Maria long ago when she was young. He smiled back at her, to show that he appreciated her thought for him, and that he was just as well disposed toward her. Even Yegor, who was busy dancing up a storm right then, seemed a splendid fellow, and Pyotr Vasilievich couldn't wait to embrace him like a brother and drink some more. Indeed, everybody at the table, no matter whom he was looking at, had some uniquely attractive quality.

When the merriment was at its height, Alexandra seized an opportunity to come and sit by him and began to defend herself in a swift undertone. "Don't think that I've forced myself on Andrei Vasilievich. I can manage my five without him. My husband was like an extra child: It was no easier with him than without him. I got by on my own. I never had to borrow. I'll go away any day he wants me to. Still, it's no bed of roses for him, by myself. Nobody to wash or cook for him. Living on bread and lard all his life. I'm really sorry for him. Fine man like him deserves the best woman in the world. He's worth his weight in gold, the poor sucker." After a moment's silence she burst out passionately: "We were so unlucky . . . him and me, so unlucky! Thirty years now, we've been stumbling around each other, and we finally get together when it's time to think about dying. The best years of our lives we frittered away." On a sudden impulse she jumped up from her chair and joined the dance. "Come on, Vasya, don't grudge me a tune."

> "I have loved you long, my dearest one,
>   I'll love you ever more.
> While birds still sing their song, my love,
>   While waves break on the shore."

Alexandra floated around the room with half-closed eyes, and her splendid body, still supple after so many years, quivered under the vivid flaring dress. She laughed and cried as she sang, and her tears and laughter spoke of her desperate hope of wresting her share of belated happiness from fate at long last.

> "Down the path across the field I run,
>   Down to the river shore.
>   Drink my blood, drop by drop, my dear one,
>   I'll never chide you more."

"Look at her, Pyotr!" Andrei breathed in his brother's ear with feverish delight. "Would you ever guess how old she is? She's a queen! The sun's shining for me in my old age."

"I wish you all the luck in the world, Andrei." Andrei had put a hand on his brother's shoulder, and Pyotr Vasilievich, smiling beautifully, tenderly stroked his arm. "All the luck in the world."

Wet leaves rustled stealthily in the night outside, and a scattering of freshly washed stars peeped through them into the room.

> "People say my looks are homely,
>   And you're all pockmarked, too.
>   Like a thread pulled by a needle,
>   I'll always follow you."

Pyotr Vasilievich couldn't take his drowsy eyes off Alexandra, and in her he began to see someone else's features, from another time, now almost forgotten . . .

VI
Yet Another of Pyotr Vasilievich's Visions

That morning Pyotr Vasilievich woke up drenched in sweat, his head gripped by hot pincers of pain. There could be no doubt about it: his travels along a route jammed with typhus-ridden trains had taught him long ago to identify the first symptoms. "You couldn't have picked a worse time for it, Lashkov," he told himself ruefully.

A blizzard was raging outside. It had been scouring the countryside for three days already, and there was no reason to think that it would soon let up. For three days, Lashkov's special coach had been stranded all by itself out in open country, somewhere between Skopin and Ryazhsk. The sleeping car housed two of them: himself and his assistant, Venya Kryukov. The thought that Venya, snoring sweetly in the next bunk, would have to look after him now, and that they might both collapse as a result, distressed Pyotr Vasilievich. "I shall have to pack him off somewhere, he's a bit young for the last rites . . ." He called him quietly. "Venya! Venya!"

Venya had got used to sudden awakenings on the journey, and he answered at once, as though he hadn't been asleep at all. "What d'you want, Pyotr Vasilievich?"

"It looks as if I've—er—caught something."

"Maybe it's a chill?" Venya was tense and anxious. "I'll fix some hot water right away."

"No, Venya, this'll take more than hot water . . . You'd better move out of here and join the footplate men . . . It's safer there."

"Is it typhus, d'you think?"

"It is . . . just like in the book . . . I've got a fever . . and a head like a lump of iron . . . Fix something up . . . You've got to look out for yourself."

"Where am I going to do that then, Vasilich?" Venya grunted condescendingly. "D'you want me to go and sleep out on the steppe? You can't take much care of yourself on the train. The lice will find you whatever you do. Better get ready to move instead."

"Where to, Venya?"

"You'll go where I take you." He was already dressing. "We'll get to the first trackman we can find, and then we'll see. I'll just dash over to the footplate men, and fetch somebody to give me a hand. I can't handle you by myself, Vasilich, you're too big and strong. And there's such a wind out there . . ."

Kryukov came back shortly with the young stoker Timosha Samsonov, thought of in Uzlovsk as the most solitary and timid of men. Timosha gave Pyotr Vasilievich a hangdog look, blinked sleepily, and quietly said, "You'll be all right."

The two of them quickly and carefully equipped Pyotr Vasilievich for the march ahead. Timosha's hands were unexpectedly deft and strong; his stoker's training made itself felt. He skillfully inserted his shoulder under Pyotr Vasilievich's armpit and moved steadily toward the door, dragging him along behind. At the same time, he made little encouraging noises. "You're all right then, come on now . . . you're all right, Pyotr Vasilievich."

The blizzard seemed to have turned to madness. A solid howling wall of sleet joined earth and sky. The track was half-buried under drifts, and as soon as they had taken a few steps along it the train vanished from sight. Each step was more difficult that the last. Pyotr Vasilievich felt that his legs had ceased to obey him. More and more often he hung helplessly on Timosha's shoulder, unable to move, and in the end his legs gave out altogether. Then the men carried him on their backs, relieving each other at intervals of fifty to a hundred yards. Pyotr Vasilievich fainted from time to time, and in his semi-delirious state he clearly distinguished the outlines of a building with smoking chimneys not far ahead. Consciousness brought him back to the impenetrable whirl of the blizzard, and his feverish lips struggled to form the same few words. "We shall get lost . . . Better go back."

The stoker turned his frostbitten face around to him and said hoarsely, "It's all right—it's all right."

They probably wouldn't have noticed the keeper's hut if Timosha hadn't tripped over the boards on the crossing and fallen with Pyotr Vasilievich on top of him. As he helped him up, Venya shouted excitedly.

"We've done it! Wait a little bit. I'll have a look. If there's anybody on duty I'll shout. You follow the sound of my voice."

A few weary minutes that seemed endless to Pyotr Vasilievich went by. The whole route was in such a state of chaos that the hut might very well be deserted and in ruins. In that case he was done for: The men wouldn't be up to making the return journey with him.

"This way a bit." Venya's voice seemed to come to him through a pillow stuffed with cotton wool. "Pull him this way . . . over here . . . I've got him . . . Come on . . . come on . . . over here."

As soon as Pyotr Vasilievich felt the firm support of a floor under his head, his mind succumbed to the fever and he passed out. Of all the faces and voices which hovered in his imagination in the days that followed, one face fixed itself in his memory, one voice left an imprint. When he really came to for the first time, after three weeks of delirium with only brief intervals of lucidity, that face was bending over him, and the voice which by now he knew well sounded relieved as it asked if he would like some tea.

In the light of a dull winter morning the face of the woman standing by his pillow looked blurred and tired. At a glance, you would have taken her for a little over thirty, but her compact, supple figure, with its girlishly high, quivering breasts, indicated that she was a lot younger.

"Have I been here long?" he asked.

"It'll be a month soon."

"You must be sick of me."

"Sick and tired. But where could we put you when you were in such a bad way?"

"I'll get up now."

"You lie there, or the wind will blow you away."

"You live by yourself?"

"Where d'you think I'd get a man from? They're scattered over the face of the earth fighting the good fight, bare-arsed bullies."

"They'll be back."

"But what good will they be to anybody. All they know how to do is hold meetings. They think their pricks are just to go down to the yard and piss with!"

"You're hard on them, girl."

She couldn't resist a bit of coquetry. "Girl! I've got one foot in the grave. Soon be three times ten. Some girl."

"What do they call you?"

"They used to call me Sofia."

"Did they now! Like a queen's name."

"So what—aren't I good enough?" Her head with its heavy braids tossed provocatively and she was completely transformed: her rather harsh features relaxed, her voice softened and became more womanly.

While she was talking to him Sofia had found time to light the stove, fill an iron pot with water, put it on the cooking plate, sweep the floor, and air the stuffy room all at once. She did it all effortlessly, in a knockabout mannish fashion, as though she were enjoying a change from real work. Every time the woman looked at him a glow he had never known before stole through him and flared up into burning desire. At the back of his mind he was aware that his feelings went far beyond mere gratitude.

In the evening, after she and her guest had lingered over their tea, Sofia started making up a bed for herself by the stove. Then, without the slightest shyness of him, she pulled off her shoddy bombazine dress, and spoke to him as she was reaching out to turn the lamp off.

"If you should want anything, call—don't be shy. I'm a light sleeper."

"Thank you."

"You can thank me later on when you're more yourself."

"You've made me better already."

"Made yourself better, you mean. You're strong as a bull."

"I just look that way."

"You all just look that way . . . Go to sleep."

"Uh-huh."

But go to sleep was just what he couldn't do. Pyotr Vasilievich was conscious of her every pore in his reborn flesh. The heat and the silence which reigned in the hut gradually became unbearable. He was half-stifling, and almost deafened by his own heartbeat. In the end he could stand it no longer and called out, "Water."

His teeth rattled feverishly against the rim of the mug she held for him. As he flopped back on his pillow, he instinctively grabbed her hand, and she came to him without resistance.

"Look at your hands, like cotton wool."

"Don't go away."

"How can you . . ."

"Sonyushka."

"Wait a bit."

In a minute Sofia slid under the blanket, rested her cheek on his shoulder, enveloped him in the warmth and fragrance of her restless body. His head was spinning but, exhausted by the excitement he had gone through, he suddenly went weak and limp. Her lips trembled sympathetically by his ear.

"There you are! I told you to lie quiet. Getting all worked up like that!"

"I'm sorry."

"What d'you take me for, your ma or something?"

"Sonyushka . . ."

"Go to sleep . . . I'll be here for a bit."

That was how their first night together began. There were many nights afterward when morning seemed an unavoidable nuisance to be followed in time by the eagerly awaited evening. Everything he had left beyond the threshold of the hut—family, home, job—now struck Pyotr Vasilievich as an inexplicable misunderstanding. Then one day, about noon, Maria's slight figure appeared on the threshold. One look was enough to tell her everything. But, unused to fighting for her rights, she shrank back and submitted. All she said, in a faint whisper, was: "I've brought you a present. The children are well. They send their greetings. They miss you."

She put the little bundle of food on a stool by the water bucket and went out silently, leaving them to decide between themselves what they were bound to decide.

Swallowing the bitter lump in his throat, Pyotr Vasilievich hung his head.

"It's up to you."

"Go. You've got children."

"If you say the word, I'll stay."

"What do I want you for?"

"Sonya!"

"We've had our fun and that's that."

"Why d'you talk like that?"

"You can have too much of a good thing."

"Be nice . . ."

"I've been nice, now go away."

"Sonya . . ."

"Go on, go on. I don't want you. Wouldn't have you as a present. You can't be sorry for everybody. Go on, your wife's out there waiting."

Sofia looked straight at him with the calm hostility of someone who has reached a decision and is quite determined not to be swayed from it. Only the uncontrollable trembling of her small chin showed what it had cost her. For a long time afterward whenever he remembered that day, he had an immediate glimpse of Sofia's face, staring at him dry-eyed with anger and scorn.

VII

The January dawn had scarcely touched the inky blackness outside, when an irregular staccato knocking reached him from the front door. "Who's come to carry me off at this early hour?" When he got up, he groped for a slipper with his foot, but couldn't find it. "There's not much light."

Hunching himself up against the cold, he shuffled heavily to the door and stood stock-still, listening.

"Who is it?"

"It's me, Granddad, open up."

Pyotr Vasilievich's legs went weak. He released the catch with trembling fingers, and mumbled through the open door without knowing what he was saying. "Coming, Vadya . . . coming . . . Not as young as I used to be . . . Hands won't do what I want. Come on in."

In the parlor, carefully scrutinizing his grandson in the light, Pyotr Vasilievich found no great changes in him, but couldn't help noticing his still more painful thinness, the first gray flecks in his bristly hair, and the sensitive wariness of every movement and look, so unlike his old self. Vadim sat facing his grandfather, sipping tea, and gazed stubbornly into his glass as he spoke with unhurried deliberation.

"So, as you see, she did take me back after all. Of course, on condition that I should clear off immediately and never come back."

"To hell with her."

"That's what I said. Only I've been released into her custody, because I'm legally incompetent. I haven't any papers. Freedom on those terms is a pain in the arse. I'll stay with you and get fit if you'll let me, of course. Then I'll take myself down south. I'll remind myself of my days as a vagabond and then we'll see. No good worrying, it may never happen. I have a plan in mind."

"Never mind your plans." Pyotr Vasilievich was tense, and determined. "There's no reason for you to go anywhere."

Now that Vadim was there and in need of protection, there was no obstacle on earth which Pyotr Vasilievich could not have overcome to help him. He would wangle papers for him, even if it meant groveling at the feet of the local powers-that-be. After that, if he didn't change his mind in the meantime, he could go wherever he thought fit.

Pyotr Vasilievich was concentrating on this one overriding aim with every ounce of his being. He was so certain of his eventual success that without further thought he declared it out loud. "You'll get your papers."

Vadim grinned skeptically.

"I hope you're right, Granddad, but I doubt it."

Pyotr Vasilievich was upset and didn't conceal it. "It's only in that Moscow of yours that you can never get anywhere. In this place even I amount to something. We'll see which of us is right."

"Don't be angry, Granddad, I didn't mean to upset you." He stood up, left the table, and began rubbing his temples and pacing the room. "It's simply that I've seen all sorts just recently . . . My eyes have been opened to a lot of things. Once they"—he nodded upwards—"get their hands on somebody they don't let go until it's all over. They have a death grip. If nothing else, they've learned how to keep watch on people. They have a lot of experience in that line . . . Lord, what an extraordinary part of the world it is! Like a proving ground for all the world's outrages. Why, what sort of spell are we under? It isn't enough for us to be sinking in the mire ourselves—we have to shove our dirty servile snouts into Europe and teach them sense and wisdom." His eyes slowly filled with bitter tears. "I want to get away, escape, hide from all that! So that I don't have to see it or hear it or react to it! What do I want their passport for? So that I can put my head in the noose again? It's better to die like a homeless dog under a fence than to join in their nasty little games. I won't!"

Pyotr Vasilievich was scarcely listening to Vadim, or at any rate he barely heard him. Instead, he was staring at him, eagerly noting each resemblance to someone long forgotten. "It's my Victor, the spitting image of my Victor, only still angrier!" He recognized his son in every detail of Vadim's appearance and manner: the same urge to get right to the bottom of things, the same sudden twists in the conversation, unrelated to what had gone before.

A painfully vivid picture swam into his mind of that memorable morning before the war when he and Victor had met for the last time. "Why, oh why, need we have quarreled like that? Oh, God, what a life it is."

Never before had he felt with such a stab of anguish the loss of that one among his kin whom he had needed perhaps most of all. Once it had started working, his memory would not stop, and Pyotr Vasilievich felt sure that all of them—his children and relations—would now reemerge, one after another, from oblivion and each demand his due. He reconciled himself to the thought that he would have to go through this ordeal, however cruel it might be. It seemed to Pyotr Vasilievich that only when he had paid his debts to the past could he find in his heart the illumination which he had lacked all his life. He felt Vadim's present torment as though it were his own and he was full of sympathetic understanding.

"You'll come to grief, Vadya."

"That's one way out."

"What good would it do anybody?"

"Why should I care what good it does."

"When I die, there'll be no male Lashkovs left, only you." He was choked with grief. "Antonina's a woman, we can't make demands on her. You must live, Vadya. To put everything right for us."

"Why put it right?" was Vadya's muffled retort. He was standing now with his back to his grandfather, pressing his brow to the window-pane with its icy tracery. "Maybe there's no need at all to do so. Maybe that's the destiny of us Lashkovs, to disappear from this earth altogether, so that others won't be so eager to amuse themselves by shedding blood?"

"Is that what you think?" gasped Pyotr Vasilievich, almost too weak to speak. "Is that how you see it?"

"I'm asking you."

"We've always paid for our own mistakes."

"But you made others pay for them as well."

"You're not involved in that. Everybody must answer for himself."

"You're trying to get out of it too easily, Granddad."

"I'm too old for double-talk. A whole clan can't be held responsible for what one man does." He was getting more heated with every word. "It wouldn't be fair. D'you think our intentions weren't good when we started?"

"That's of merely historical interest. It doesn't make things easier for anybody now. You should have thought about what you were doing."

"There was no time for thinking." He was almost shouting. "We had to keep count of every minute. It was us or them!"

"Only 'them' meant each other, often enough."

"We couldn't always tell the difference."

"And afterward?"

"Afterward it was too late. Then what remained was the hope that it would all come right in the end. D'you think we alone were to blame or something?"

"Who else was?"

"Not just us."

"But the bigger share of guilt is yours."

"Maybe it is." His hurt feelings got the better of him. "So we pay more than others do, too. What did I, for instance, make out of being a commissar? Look for yourself how spacious my halls are, how rich I am. I'm wearing out my last pair of trousers. I kept nothing for myself—no property, not even my own children. I thought it would be better for everybody that way. You can punish people for greed, by all means, but d'you think I did it out of greed? D'you think it was easy for me to punish my own flesh and blood? Is it easy for me now, living all alone in my old age? They've all gone away, all abandoned me." He suddenly looked weak and helpless. "Now you're disowning me, too."

Vadim was obviously affected by his grandfather's state of mind. He turned quickly away from the window, and went back to the table with a conciliatory laugh. "All right, Granddad, do what you think best. If it comes off, good, if it doesn't come off, still better. Just as long as there's an end to it somewhere."

In the dim light of the new day, Vadim's face took on a muddy tinge. The dark hollows around his eyes were more pronounced. The gray in his short-cropped hair stood out more conspicuously. A haggard, almost inhuman tiredness showed in the hunched figure at the table. Looking at his grandson, Pyotr Vasilievich saw that he had been wrong to speak so heatedly. Vadim couldn't be bothered with him or with anything else on earth, Vadim simply wanted to sleep.

"Want to lie down?" Pyotr Vasilievich rushed to make up a bed for his grandson without waiting for an answer. "Come on, lie down."

"Maybe I will."

Vadim went to sleep at once, as soon as his head touched the pillow. In his sleep he looked much younger and gentler. Pyotr Vasilievich found it very hard not to stroke his grandson's stubborn crew cut, as he used to when Vadim was a child.

"There . . ."

This light word, like the sound of a lonely raindrop on a roof, brought back to mind every line and every color of a day washed out by time. It rose before his eyes with such almost palpable vividness and detail that it might in fact have been only yesterday.

VIII
And Yet Another . . .

Pyotr Vasilievich's carriage had been standing in a siding at Penza freight station for five days. Five days of pulsing heat and din in the train-choked station. And all that time not a wisp of cloud in the bleached August sky. The still air was dry, stifling, hot as a furnace. Gasping for breath, Pyotr Vasilievich waited restlessly by the open window while his mate kicked his heels in the station offices, pleading for a quick release. A train carrying a circus menagerie stretched out along the neighboring sideline. Right opposite Pyotr Vasilievich, in the middle of a four-axled flatcar, reclined a mangy lion, boxed in with iron gratings, and his round mad eyes glared steadily at Lashkov with misery and hunger.

A squat round individual wearing a string vest, and with a handkerchief on his shaven head, was leaning against the footboard of the flatcar and grumbling to a handsome man wearing leggings and a checkered shirt tucked into elegant riding breeches.

"To hell with this tour. Why on earth did we let ourselves in for this sort of slow torture? I'm so worried about Diamond! I don't have to tell you, Artur Polikarpich. Twenty pounds of luncheon sausage to him is like a peanut to an elephant. He hasn't had a bowel movement for two days. It's a catastrophe. At this rate we won't even make it to Moscow."

His companion heaved a doleful sigh, and his sharp features twitched violently.

"Don't I know it," he said. "My lot are pining away as well. They're used to a strictly scientific diet, and it's no joke trying to feed them on mush. Nothing but mush all the time, can you imagine! Corn mush!"

"Corn," as he said it, sounded like "poison."

"A circus dog is a lot more fussy than a man, you know. And I've got them working on the act of the century—'Mayakovsky's "Left March" with Orchestral Accompaniment.' No, you just can't imagine!"

On the other side of the flatcar, puffing hard, an engine inched in, drawing red passenger carriages. Their window spaces were untidily crisscrossed with barbed wire. Children's faces, hundreds of them, looked out through the spiky grid. When the lion loomed in sight, the youngsters inspected him with awe and reverence.

"Must be sick."

"He's just sleeping, it's hot."

"It's hot in Africa, isn't it?"

"In Africa he'd be lying under a tree in the shade."

"He's starving, look how thin he is!"

"Don't lions get rations, too?"

"Of course. A sheep every day!"

"And gingerbread. Sacks of it."

"Sacks of it! Lions are lucky."

"A lion needs more than anybody. D'you know what an enormous eater he is? He'll take whatever you give him."

"He's the king of the beasts!"

The two men by the flatcar looked around at the passenger train in speechless dismay. The fat man's tiny eyes opened wide in anger, his weak chin wobbled, his solid bulk suddenly went slack. Clutching his friend's sleeve he whispered in distress:

"What's this, Artur Polikarpich?"

The other man glanced away to hide the look in his eyes.

"Children. Evacuees, I expect."

The fat man wouldn't be fobbed off.

"Why the barbed wire, then?" he asked. "They're only children, Artur Polikarpich!"

At that moment Leskov arrived, sized up the situation in a flash, and said with a self-satisfied wink to Pyotr Vasilievich:

"R.E.P.'s—they're being transferred east."

The fat man turned on him eagerly.

"Eh? What's that mean, R.E.P.'s?"

Leskov gave a contemptuous guffaw.

"Relatives of Enemies of the People. Time you knew that, Pop! And you call yourself an artist!"

When the circus performer finally took it in, he seemed to age and shrivel on the spot. He stood there for a minute, clinging to his friend's sleeve and painfully debating with himself. Suddenly, as though inspired, he pushed Artur Polikarpich away and rushed to his living quarters, next to the flatcar. The handsome man in breeches looked after him in consternation and threw up his hands in defeat. "He's hopeless."

The fat man shortly reappeared on the flatcar, but now he was in costume, lightly made up, and with a miniature balalaika slung over his shoulder. In two incongruously youthful bounds he sprang onto the brake platform, and suddenly appeared in front of the lion's cage, facing the children behind the wire. A clownish smile on his face, he twanged a jaunty chord, and struck up a hoarse recitative:

"Have you ever heard of an animal by the name of Cham-ber-lain?
 Well, listen first, just listen first, to my little refrain.
 'The twinkling lights, the twinkling lights, they burn and burn and burn.
 But what they've seen and what they've heard we never learn.' "

The tempo was plainly too much for him, but he wouldn't give in.

" 'While he's wondering where he's at—while the sleep's still in his eyes,
 we'll spit in his face with an ul-ti-ma-tum, not once, not twice, but thrice.
 The twinkling lamps, you merry scamps, they burn and burn and burn.
 But what they've seen and what they've heard we never never learn.' "

Gasping for breath he called down to the man with the mustache:

"Bim! You hear me, Bim! Can't you hear the children calling you? Oh what a cowardly custard you are, Bim!"

But his friend ignored him, looked miserably around for sympathy, and kept appealing to Leskov, who stood there grinning with delight.

"What's he think he's doing? Just look at him—what on earth is he doing? He won't get any thanks for this. Anyway, he had to give up clowning long ago. He's had one heart attack. He isn't up to it! Stop him, why don't you?"

Leskov waved him off, and danced in time to the balalaika.

"Look at the old boy go! Just look at him go! Give them the treatment, Pop! Show the kids all you've got!"

The man with the mustache went on blinking and circling around Leskov for a bit, but, getting no support from him, suddenly braced himself, gripped the rail of the brake platform, and piped up in a startling falsetto, "I'm here, Bom."

In a twinkling he was at his partner's side. "Hallo, children, it's me, Bim!"

As though obeying orders, dozens of child voices chorused from the train. "Hallo, Bim!"

The friends did their damnedest. They sang, danced, walked on their hands, even beat each other. And, of course, wept while they were at it. There was a sort of ecstatic desperation in their actions. By now a menacing voice of command was thundering along the grim train, growing louder as it approached.

"Cut it out! Cut it out, I say! Get away from the convoy! I'm warning you for the last time, cut it out!"

The two men on the flatcar pretended not to hear his shouting and went on with what they were doing. The clatter of hobnailed boots drawing nearer and nearer only seemed to spur them on.

The fat man, drenched in sweat, let out a heart-rending wail.

"Bim, are you a good runner?"

"Yes, Bom," replied his partner in the same voice, "but I can't run as fast as that man who's running this way."

The fat man kept it up.

"I should say not," he said. "You've got to be a good runner to run away from the war. That man knows how it's done."

Over the edge of the flatcar, on the far side, appeared a service cap with a blue band, followed by a perspiring pockmarked face.

"Didn't I tell you to cut it out! Under the regulations of the prison guard and escort service, I've got the right to shoot. Understand?"

The man with the mustache stuck out his chest and advanced on the service cap.

"Don't interfere with our rehearsal. We're under government orders. We're rehearsing the act of the century. Leave the premises forthwith!"

The face over the edge of the flatcar vanished, but reappeared immediately, this time over the brake platform.

"I've got an act for you, you dirty Yid. You'll spit blood for the rest of your days . . ."

It would probably have ended badly for the circus people if the carriage full of silent and frightened children had not started moving at that very moment. The train, gradually picking up speed, glided past the flatcar. The service cap immediately vanished, but the voice of its retreating owner was heard from below in a parting threat.

"Lucky for you, you vermin. I'd have made you look like such a clown you'd have died laughing."

Now that he felt quite safe, nothing could check the fat man's inspired foolery.

"Bim, are you frightened of him?"

His friend played up to him.

"Yes, Bom, but not as much as he is of the fascists . . . No, I'm not that frightened."

When the train with an armed guard in the brake van had passed the flatcar, the fat man sank back helplessly against the cage. Then he turned around, pressed his wet, hectically flushed face against the steel bars and sighed deeply.

"Hot, are you, my little Diamond? That's life, Mr. Lion, sir, there's nothing to be done about it, you must just put up with it."

The man with the mustache laid a hand on his shoulder, gently but firmly drew away from the cage, helped him carefully down the steps, and soon both of them disappeared through the door of their wagon.

Leskov, scrambling into the top bunk, came out with some of his usual tiresome nonsense.

"We ask but little here below—just lashings of grub and plenty of dough. Am I right, Vasilich?"

Lashkov didn't answer. He had no time for his mate right then. Try as he might, he couldn't make sense of what had happened. "Why," he asked himself, "why those children? What have they done to deserve it?"

The answer was obvious, but Pyotr Vasilievich was reluctant or simply not brave enough to accept it. His mind rebelled, and he resisted the temptation of doubt.

"It can't be all a mistake . . . all I ever lived for. The cause is a just one. It'll all come right in the end."

As he fell asleep, this comforting delusion hardened into certainty.

IX

This time the secretary did not dazzle Pyotr Vasilievich with the full glory of her welcoming smile as she came back from Vorobushkin's office. The *amour-propre* of the council's leading lady, injured by his previous visit, had found full satisfaction at last.

"He's receiving from three." Undisguisedly triumphant, she spoke in a dry clipped voice. "Wait in the corridor."

Lashkov saw that things were bad. Kostya Vorobushkin hadn't forgiven him for remembering too much. But this only deepened his resolve still more. He had no more squeamish doubts as to what could or could not be talked about. If the former engine driver found forgetfulness so easy, Pyotr Vasilievich would remind him of two or three items from his far from immaculate biography. He would go on threatening, begging, demanding, until he extorted from Vorobushkin his agreement to provide Vadim with documents.

A sizable line of people waiting to be seen was already languishing on the pull-down seats which dismally lined the corridor walls. Next to Pyotr Vasilievich was a heavily-built woman in a plush jacket and an expensive-looking checkered shawl over a black headscarf pulled down to her eyebrows. Her tiny eyes fixed on the woman next to her tearfully pleaded for sympathy.

"Well, of course, an iron's nothing much, not a big article of property. Only to me that iron is a souvenir of my departed mother. I let them take Mamma's lampshade, and some overshoes she practically hadn't worn, and with never a word. What good were they to me? The style was wrong and so was the fit. But what I got from them, my sisters, I mean, instead of gratitude, was two broken ribs on account of this iron. And I don't hear so well anymore with my right ear. I'm just not letting them get away with it. I'm a member of a shock team where I work, and I'm well known in the housing association as well. It isn't the iron that matters, it's the principle . . ."

Her neighbor, a colorless girl—with a quilted nylon jacket and a skimpy beehive hairdo around her timid bloodless face—looked about in embarrassment and mechanically assented. "Yes, yes, of course! How could they . . . I should just think so! I know what you mean. Yes, yes, of course."

On Pyotr Vasilievich's other side a young man with high cheekbones and a square jaw, a taxi driver to judge by his peaked cap, was droning complaints into the ear of the pregnant woman next to him. "Don't be backward in coming forward, that's the main thing. Tell them just how it is. Where can you and me turn to? Where do they think we earn enough to go joining housing coops? Just because I'm a taxi driver, does that mean I'm a millionaire or something? Every kopeck you make you have to pay out all around. Maintenance men have to be paid, don't they? The car washer has to be paid. Then you've got to pay every time you check in. I should have more fingers to count them all. Don't budge an inch till he signs. Just refuse to go, and that's that!"

She maintained a brooding silence but from the agitated trembling of the arms folded over her swollen belly, you could feel that her husband's words awakened the most profound and anxious response in her.

An agonizingly long time went by, and Pyotr Vasilievich, sick of waiting, was just off to the yard of the council building to stretch his legs, when his favorite leading lady sailed importantly out of the waiting room.

"Which of you is Comrade Lashkov?" Her deliberately casual gaze slid past Pyotr Vasilievich. "Please come into Konstantin Vasilievich's office."

Followed by a murmur of indignation, he went through the waiting room, and with a certain relief—he was being seen out of turn, after all—found himself in Vorobushkin's office. His host did not raise his heavy head in greeting, but nodded at the chair before the desk.

"Sit down, Pyotr Vasilievich. Sorry to keep you waiting. That's the sort of job I've got. Everybody after me for something. I'm listening!"

Pyotr Vasilievich gave him the gist of his petition, trying to be brief. His host listened without interruption, occasionally stealing a glance through the window at children chasing a ball in the next yard. From time to time he grinned at some thought of his own, then grunted ambiguously and lowered his head still further. When Pyotr Vasilievich had finished, Vorobushkin stood up and unsteadily took himself over to the safe in the corner. He pulled the heavy door open and took out a partly consumed bottle of cognac and a small plate with two wine glasses and a halved lemon on it.

He filled one glass to the brim and pushed it over to his guest. "Lower it down, Vasilich. Here's to us."

They drank two more rounds in perfect silence, then Vorobushkin finally found his tongue. "Lord, these children of ours! Who on earth do they take after nowadays? We imagine we've sacrificed everything for them and when they grow up there's no recognizing them. Nothing of us is left in them at all. Where are they headed, what is it they want?" His speech was fluent, weighty, coherent, but from the dry glare in his bleary eyes one could safely conclude that he had been gloriously drunk for some time. "If you ask them, they say nothing. They've always got something of their own on their minds. But what? That's the question. If it's their damn silly dances and parties and all that, it's understandable— youth having its fling. That sort are crystal-clear, it's easy to talk to them. But how do you deal with one of the quiet ones! He goes around being a strong silent man, and that's all he does—keep silent. But what's he silent about? That's the question. He's as meek as a lamb to look at, but what's going on inside him? What's he thinking about? What's he plan- ning? Just try and get close to him. He's always got everything up to date, your quiet one. Good marks under every section of the moral code— but all the same, any fool can see that he's waiting for his hour of destiny. And when his hour comes, don't expect any mercy from your quiet one then." He stopped talking, looked irresolutely at his unfinished glass for a whole minute, then raised it and slowly drained it to the bottom with apparent enjoyment. "Yes, my oldest has sprung a pleasant surprise on me, too. This is just between ourselves, Vasilich. For the time being. He's stationed in Germany, you see. Well, I've just been informed that he was caught trying to cross to the Western zone. He's under investigation now. He'll get what's coming to him, of course. And it's not going to do me any good, either. To think what a little teacher's pet he was! Never answered back, always got top marks at school, used to write poetry . . . How can you expect to find out what makes anybody else tick when you're completely in the dark about your own son's character? I can see that thanks to his kindness I shall soon be joining you and the other pensioners for a game of cards in the town garden." He forced a painful grin. "Will you have me for a partner, Vasilich?"

"I don't play." Pyotr Vasilievich felt himself in the grip of his old hos- tility. "I've got plenty to do without that."

"Haven't you quieted down yet?" Vorobushkin was patronizingly sympathetic. "Time you sobered up, Vasilich. Now I realized right then, after my trial, where the power lies. All those beautiful words are for the benefit of the poor. The man who knows how to submit to circumstances is always right. You should have more sense than to piss against the wind.

D'you think I needed you to tell me that what they hung on Kolya Leskov was out of all proportion? I wouldn't have minded seeing his unfortunate victim buried with full honors. But he had the power, so right was on his side. You very nearly got me jailed with that cretin of yours. I had a job to wriggle out of it."

"In that case, we've got nothing to complain about, Kostya." The explanation, stumbled upon so suddenly and accidentally, of all the misfortunes which had plagued his last years, filled him with quiet grief. "We're getting our own shit back again."

He waved it away languidly. "That smacks of superstition, Vasilich. You mean like the law of karma, or something?"

"Never heard of it."

"It's a religious law they've got in India. It says that every action is requited by fate with its equivalent: good actions with good fortune, bad ones with misfortune. Well, I should call that something else invented for the benefit of the poor . . . Right; we go on talking, you and me, and I've got all those people to see whether I like it or not. Why don't you call on me at home? We could sit and have a friendly chat without any hurry . . . So long."

"What about my business? Are you going to help me?"

Vorobushkin wrinkled his brow disdainfully. "Oh, yes. Tell him to come and see me with his birth certificate. And a declaration—you know— 'In connection with the loss of my papers' . . . So long."

Still full of his unexpectedly speedy success, Pyotr Vasilievich bumped into Vladimir Anisimovich in the courtyard. In his general's winter uniform—tall fur hat and knee-length overcoat—he looked frailer than ever.

"The devil only knows what it all means." He was simply shaking with indignation. "It's impossible to get a bit of roofing material for a war hero's mother. Served in my unit, as it happens. In the municipal works department they say there isn't any and tell you something about the great development projects. Incompetents! Then in the corridor some smart guy shoved a bit of paper into my hand with the address of a local jobber, someone called Gusev. So it seems that Gusev the jobber has roofing material in spite of the great projects, while the state has no roofing material at all. Where, you may ask, does the jobber get his roofing material from? Does it come to him by lend-lease? Or does he sign individual commercial contracts with foreign powers? Or does he get special direct supplies via the Council of Ministers? It's scandalous! I'm just on my way to make a row with the city fathers. Excuse me."

Hastily passing Pyotr Vasilievich, he ran lightly up the steps, like a boy disguised in a general's uniform, and vanished into the entrance hall.

How often recently life had thrown old acquaintances across Pyotr Vasilievich's path! Gupak, Vorobushkin, Gusev! As though events had described a sort of predetermined circle, and locked together again at the starting point. "As though none of it had ever happened. We find ourselves exactly where we were."

Vorobushkin kept his word. Vadim was given a temporary certificate and registered as a resident in living space provided by his grandfather. But he refused outright to stay in Uzlovsk, and it was only with difficulty that Pyotr Vasilievich persuaded him to visit Andrei and stay there a while, have a look around. While Pyotr Vasilievich was exchanging letters with his brother, and straightening out money problems caused by unforeseen expenses, his grandson was lost for days on end in the town library. The old man was secretly pleased by this: give the boy a chance to cool off and come to himself a bit! But the more attentively the old man examined his grandson the more firmly convinced he became that the sadness eating away at him was in fact gradually working its way deeper, losing nothing of its strength and its edge. On several occasions Pyotr Vasilievich woke up in the night and caught Vadim hovering sleeplessly by the window with the invariable cigarette between his teeth. On the surface, he became more restrained and gentler, but still, every now and then there would be an outburst of his old ungovernable rage. Lashkov grieved about it silently. "The boy's been hurt. He won't get over it in a hurry."

On the day of his grandson's departure, he finished his chores about the house and then called at a shop to pick up a few presents for his newly acquired nephews. His way to the counter was barred by a rough lanky chap wearing an antiquated rubberized raincoat fastened under his chin with a safety pin. "Want to make a threesome, Dad?

Round bloodshot eyes gazed at Pyotr Vasilievich from under the peak of a beaver lamb cap, at first inquiringly, then all at once appealingly. "Hallo, Pyotr Vasilievich! Sorry!"

There was something vaguely familiar in the frozen, beet-root-colored face. All the same, he was about to pass him without bothering to search his memory—a lot of people in town knew him, after all—but the man appealed to him again. "Don't you recognize me? I'm your relation. Lyovka . . . From Torbeevka . . . Gordei Stepanich's son."

Of course Pyotr Vasilievich knew him! Lyovka had stayed in his mind as an ungainly mechanic at the depot, with an eternally unkempt mop of hair over a face masked by every conceivable vice, famous all along the line as the most inventive of spongers. As he looked at him now, Lashkov saw, with belated humility, a reminder of his own age in Lyovka's faded body, and that no doubt was why he hadn't the heart to ignore family ties and walk on.

"It's my age. Stopped recognizing myself in the mirror. I remember you now. So you're trying to make a threesome?"

Lyovka's gratitude overflowed. "The Russian frost nips at you, Pyotr Vasilievich. My total capital's one ruble, so I'm looking for a volunteer. Maybe you'll give me your support?"

A reckless gaiety suddenly took hold of him. "Why not! I've got nothing to lose. Here's a three, we'll manage without another recruit. We've got work to do!"

Lyovka was so pleased and grateful that he even broke into a sweat. "Pyotr Vasilievich, now you see me, now you don't. We'll do the thing in style."

It all went off like a well-rehearsed ceremony. Lyovka, impervious to abuse from the line, wedged himself in at its head as though he owned the place, handed over an empty bottle and received a scaled half-liter, winked proudly at Pyotr Vasilievich as he came away from the counter— "What d'you think of that, then?"—and invited him with a nod to follow.

They went down into the public lavatory in the town garden. Lyovka vanished behind the door of the attendant's little room, and then beckoned to Pyotr Vasilievich through the inspection window.

Here, to the accompaniment of inarticulate grumbles from the old woman who cleaned the place, they split their bottle, nibbling between drinks on the Valadol tablets lavishly sprinkled on the table by Lyovka. The first one didn't loosen their tongues. Pyotr Vasilievich slapped down another three rubles, Lyovka nipped smartly there and back, and only after the second bottle was empty did the tipsy craving for mutual understanding come to a head in the pair of them.

Lyovka was the first to speak, mournfully shaking his balding head. "Oh well, life's gone by like in a fog. It's like I'm not really born yet and I'm getting ready to claim my pension. And I've got neither house nor home. I rent a corner to this day. I tried marrying, but we couldn't hit it off. I admit, I do drink a lot. But what can I do? Not a bright spot wherever I look, I don't even fancy women anymore. The only thing I enjoy is a bit of talk with somebody."

He stopped short, lowered his eyes, and started doodling with his finger on the oilcloth in front of him. "Don't take it amiss, Pyotr Vasilievich, I wasn't straight with you . . . I've got money . . . I'll pop over there again, we'll be square. I feel awful, drinking by myself, so I was looking for partners . . . You can earn money as easy as winking these days, there's a lot of building going on, everybody needs a bit of metalwork done. Only thing is keeping up with it: a tap wanted here, a bath there . . . But the money doesn't matter to me . . . What can I do with it? Nothing to buy with it, only drink . . . I want to get down to Derbent where it's warm. I know those parts well—I messed around there all through the war . . . Met your brother, Andrei Vasilievich, down there once . . . Is he still living?"

"Yes. He told me."

Lyovka brightened up. "He remembered, then? I remember it like it was now. We drank some beer in the bazaar together. He kept fretting about Sasha Agureeva, I remember."

"They're together now. He's at Kurkovo, in the forestry. They've been together since the summer."

"Love!" Lyovka's drunken grin faded instantly and he looked miserable again. "I don't have any luck, though. I've signed on the dotted line three times, but it never came to anything. Foul sort of females you get nowadays. It isn't the man they're after, it's the money. Andrei Vasilievich, though, his love was like iron. All the town knew. And that woman's worth it. You'd pay anything just to look at her . . . Well, well, that calls for another . . ."

Ignoring Pyotr Vasilievich's feeble protests, he dashed off to the shop yet again. And once more they drank, with the same old Valadol to follow. And again they were talking about something or other, impatiently waving away the old cleaning woman who was earnestly attempting to show them the door.

Pyotr Vasilievich now found his distant relative remarkably young and likable, and invited him to drop in any time, without warning, no need to stand on ceremony, needn't be shy. Lyovka, in turn, assured the old man of his eternal love and devotion, and kept trying to plant a kiss on his hand, which Pyotr Vasilievich half-heartedly resisted, but in the end, though not without a certain confusion, permitted. Then they clambered upstairs, urged on by the cleaning woman, to the little park, where they went on a good deal longer vowing not to be snobbish but to remember their mutual obligations of hospitality and kinship, until at last a fit of drunken distraction dispatched them in different directions.

Pyotr Vasilievich returned home in that blessed state of mind when everything in sight cheers and delights. He listened with pleasure to the wholesome crunch of snow underfoot. "Lovely spot of weather! Made to order. I couldn't feel lighter if I'd shed thirty years. Vadya won't know me when I get home. What about Lyovka then, eh? What a fellow! Not mean either. Have to teach him the way here, or I'll be all by myself like an owl in a tree, he's family after all."

Before going to his room he turned into his daughter's part of the house. He hadn't been there since Antonina went away, and had left her room just as it was so that she wouldn't feel any change when she came back. He opened the door and looked around, trying not to make a noise. Everything here was familiar, down to the last detail: the bed made up with a patchwork quilt, the sewing machine under a cover by the window, the kitchen things concealed by a muslin curtain in the space between the stove and the door. A worn jacket which had belonged to his dead wife hung on a nail knocked into the door frame. Pyotr Vasilievich was about to go farther into the room, when voices suddenly audible on the other side of the wall pulled him up short and made him listen.

"I want to find it all out for myself." Vadim's voice was uncompromisingly harsh. "To feel it all with my own hands."

"Only love for all creation can be the source of knowledge." Gupak was choosing his words with quiet care. "But you are setting out into the world with a heavy heart. You can attain the truth without moving from this spot. Restless curiosity brings no increase of knowledge. Think a while first. Why hurry?"

"That way, you can go on thinking till you die. We live in an existential time, a time of final choice. I have chosen. Why go on talking, troubling the air?"

"What we must choose is a position, not a destination. Perhaps the more important and responsible thing for you to do is to stay here. Don't you think so?"

"What's the point of it? Why?

"Doesn't the fate of your grandfather concern you at all? You and he must help each other now."

"To do what?"

"To see the light ahead."

"It's no use. His blindness will last him a lifetime. He eats three like me for breakfast."

"Your experience has embittered you. But you must draw conclusions from experience, not make a defensive weapon out of it."

"Drawing conclusions is just what I want to do. But for that, I need to make comparisons. When I see I shall compare."

"With those eyes you will see nothing. Random anger is shortsighted."

"On the contrary, anger sharpens vision."

"Rarely, and never for long."

"I daresay I shall manage to see a thing or two."

Gupak was silent for a while, and then replied sadly, "Your doubts, however, will remain with you. It is always easy to think that a better alternative has been neglected." He was obviously weakening. "I have walked the world in many guises, and when in my old age I was, as I thought, vouchsafed the truth, it turned out that this was not the only source of light. Perhaps, after all, it is best for you not to linger. If you go you will have no time for regrets, I suppose. I grumble from habit, from physical and spiritual decrepitude, but really I am glad for you. In our frivolous times few would have the courage to do what you want to do. How happily I would take to the road right now, and stride off wherever my feet take me—but there we are, these feet won't take me anywhere. My day is done."

"Forgive me . . ."

"For heaven's sake! Your persistence is a lesson to me. You can't measure one man's world against another's. Certainly not against mine."

"Will you share it with me?"

"If you're interested."

"I'm interested in everything now."

"Well, if you want me to . . . Your grandfather and I have known each other a long time. Ever since that other postwar period. My paternal surname is . . ."

Gupak told his story, and as he listened Pyotr Vasilievich pressed his face harder and harder against his dead wife's old jacket. And the old, barely detectable smell, which belonged only to her and was known only to him, took him back to the time, lost forever, when the silent presence of Maria at his side was enough to give his existence inspiration and purpose. "What am I without her?" he asked himself and felt the tears choking him. "A nought without a one in front, a blank space." This thought came to him with the suddenness of an electric shock. He let himself go and wept silently, unashamedly. And his belated tears enabled him to see the past as it truly had been.

X

Yet Another . . .

The meeting was already drawing to a close when Paramoshin asked permission to speak. He rolled like an overstuffed dumpling from the body of the hall to the platform, stowed his ample body behind the crude rostrum on the clubroom stage, cleared his throat importantly, and spoke up in orotund phrases.

"The international situation is fraught, comrades! World imperialism is sharpening its knives. The class enemy does not slumber. Enthusiasm is red-hot at the construction sites of our five year plans. Our task is to ensure iron discipline in transport and traffic free from stoppages. Our region can point to success in this respect. But there are, comrades, alarming facts. Our struggle with remnants of the old order is not what it might be. There are people who have their children christened. And some have icons as well. And that includes some from the ranks of the party. Present here tonight is chief conductor Comrade Lashkov. He is well known in the region. He is an old party member, and was commissar on the line in the civil war. But to this day he has a whole stand full of icons in his house, you could make an exhibition out of them. That sort of thing won't do, comrades. The foe lies in wait. Any weakness of ours is meat and drink to him."

The hall was abuzz with concern.

"Shame!"

"Let him answer to the meeting!"

"You're wasting your time slandering Lashkov. We know him better than that."

"Facts are facts."

"Demagogy."

"Come out here and tell us."

"All right, I will."

The orator called for silence with a practiced wave of his puffy hand and swept on. "The enemy is on the alert, comrades. Capital is trying to strike us a blow on the straight path of our development. We must put an end to rightward leaps and left deviations in the railwaymen's ranks . . ."

He talked like this for another half hour before rolling back into the body of the hall, well pleased with himself and confident of the result. He sat down and his clean-shaven skull was a challenge to the presidium: right, then, what have you got to say about that?

Their duel had gone on without a break ever since Paramoshin had found out about Pyotr Vasilievich's report to the district Cheka. In the meantime, the former member of the escort service had prospered, obtained himself an indigo service jacket, and a job; but he had never forgotten his old grievance, and tried to repay his debt a hundredfold whenever occasion offered. Pyotr Vasilievich had no wish to tangle with him just then. He knew only too well from his past work that public explanations only obscure the essentials, and give rise to more pointless discussion and wild talk. But dozens of pairs of eyes were turned on him at that moment and he could not, he had no right to, deny them an answer. At the same time, to answer the accusation meant finally putting himself in the power of Paramoshin and his crew. So that his only hope of salvation was to turn it all into a joke.

"I'll speak to my old woman," he grunted, squinting quizzically at his jubilant opponent. "I'll tell her to take them down. But if you ask me, people who're afraid of priests should stay at home where they're safe."

He sat down to the approving laughter of more than half the hall. He felt tolerant pity for his discomfited enemy. "Poor old Paramoshin, this nut's too tough for you to crack. I can swallow your sort whole, buttons and all."

Skripitsyn, the secretary of the party cell, a glum young man, lame from birth, and better known in the district for the little things he made out of wood than for his party rank, caught up with him at the door and asked with a show of casualness if he was going home.

"That's right."

"What are you going to do?"

"I've got to get some sleep. I'm off on a trip tomorrow."

"I don't mean that."

"Let Paramoshin worry."

"You joking?"

"You can't say bless you to every sneeze."

"Watch out."

"All right, you've frightened me."

They walked on silently for some time. Autumn was rustling in the little front gardens, scattering veined and crackling leaves from trees and bushes. The neighborhood was loud with the hoots of shunting engines echoing from the station. Sparse clouds blew wispily in the fading sky. Peasants were selling hay and poultry in the town market. Tumbler pigeons circled over the roofs of sheds on the outskirts, urged on by the piercing whistles of the pigeon fanciers. The town had withstood the long pressure of the troubled times and was now surreptitiously leading its old, indestructible, and stable life, intrinsically unchanged.

Skripitsyn began again. "Paramoshin is a demagogue and a loudmouth, of course. But you're not one to talk—all sorts of people come to your house, and you've got a religious display in the place of honor. That way you'll be handing your party card in before you know where you are. He won't give up so easily, he'll sound the alarm in the proper place. And thanks to you I shall get it in the neck, too. Do you follow me?"

"How do you make that out, secretary? I live a completely open life. Everybody in town knows what I live for. What I did for the revolution is also well known. I was one of the first to begin and the last to stop. Now it turns out that none of this matters a fart. They'll believe any lying bastard rather than me. Do you really think that's fair? Or don't you know Paramoshin? He's a grabber, an informer, a bootlicker. He's picked up a few big words and now he talks a load of rubbish at every meeting there is, trying to make himself important. If we did it all for people like him, it wasn't worth starting it."

His companion at once looked black. "Cut that out. You won't get thanked for it nowadays!"

"You scared, Skripitsyn?"

The other man stopped, felt in his pockets, brought out a crumpled cigarette and lit it, but forgot to smoke it. He turned away and spoke in a hurried whisper.

"I'm frightened of that Paramoshin, Petya. Frightened to death. I'm powerless against his endless speechmaking. As soon as he starts talking, I feel as if I'm drowning. You say to him, 'There's work to be done,' and he answers 'world imperialism.' Just try talking to him. If the least little thing doesn't suit him, he cooks something up, catches you out in opportunism, accuses you of covering up for people. It wouldn't be so bad if it was only him. But others are starting to model themselves on him. And they're all the kind who would sooner play the fool than work. Just try and shut them up. They'll have you on trial in a flash. God, how I should like to let it all go to hell. But they won't let me leave with no hard feelings now, it's too late . . . Well, so long. I've still got to go to the town committee."

Skripitsyn went down a side street and even the way he turned the corner showed his bewilderment and distress. When, many years later, the secretary shared the fate of so many others, Pyotr Vasilievich often remembered that long autumn and how they had parted at that crossroads in the suburbs.

As he approached the house, Pyotr Vasilievich was already living through the distressing scene with his wife which awaited him. From the very beginning of their life together, Maria, with her characteristic gentle firmness, had taken the little world of her interests outside the family and fenced them off from his authority. In any case, he had no spare time to concern himself with her affairs. That was the way they had lived, neither of them interfering with the other's beliefs. And now he had to break this tacit understanding with his wife. His heart was like lead, and everything in the world around him seemed suddenly hostile.

At home, Maria quickly and quietly set an array of plates before her husband, went to the oven to fetch an iron pot with the goulash she had kept specially for him, and as usual stood stock-still by the door, with her hands hidden under her apron, ready to rush to him at the first sign.

His youngest son, Zhen'ka, was monotonously memorizing some homework in the next room: "Oxygen is the most important constituent part of air . . . Oxygen is the most important constituent part of air . . . The two gases hydrogen and nitrogen are present in air . . . This was established by the French scientist Lou . . . Lavousier . . . Lavoisier." All through the silent meal, Pyotr Vasilievich painfully searched for words for the discussion ahead. He wanted to find the supreme arguments, which she could not possibly contest. But everything that came into his head was utterly trivial and unsuitable. He began to feel vexed with himself. "Why drag it out? Let's come straight out and be done with it."

As Maria repeatedly changed the plates before him, he ate mechanically, without noticing what the food looked or tasted like until at last he couldn't stand the silence around and within him.

"Where's Antonina?" he asked gruffly.

"Asleep."

"Make my bed up as well. I'm off on a trip first thing. Deyev's gone sick." As he rose from the table he spoke up with a suddenness that surprised him.

"Listen, Mother. You ought to put that junk"—with a nod at the corner—"where nobody can see it. It's embarrassing. I have people coming to see me—I'm a party member . . . Paramoshin's made it the talk of the town already, next thing you know . . ."

Pyotr Vasilievich looked up at his wife, choked, and was silent—he had never seen her like that. She stared at her husband, pale and trembling, with her head thrown back in defiance, as though she were seeing him in a new light. The towel in her angry hands was slowly twisted into a taut anxious skein.

"As you wish, Pyotr Vasilievich, you are master in this house. But if that is the way it is to be, let me depart in peace. You and I never had any agreement for me to lose my faith. Your way of doing things doesn't suit me, because it is not for me to judge others. All I want is to keep myself in the paths of the Lord. But if my faith doesn't suit you, don't be angry. I'll go away and take that icon-case with me."

Pyotr Vasilievich had not expected such a rebuff. Her forceful show of independence roused him to reluctant respect as well as annoyance. "There's more to you, Madam, than I thought, much more!"

"Always carrying on," he grunted in some embarrassment, not because he cared about getting his own way anymore but for form's sake, to have the last word.

"I never learned to pretend."

"We are getting willful, aren't we!"

"I will never go against your will, Pyotr Vasilievich." She sensed that she had got her own way, and softened. "But leave me my darkness."

Once convinced that his wife would not give way, Pyotr Vasilievich reconciled himself to the situation and mentally shrugged off the consequences. "Dogs bark, and the wind carries it away. They'll yap for a bit and then let me be."

Ever afterward, when things were difficult, he never lost the sense that there was a staunch and steady presence in his life, and that it would always make him feel secure. For this he was always grateful to Maria.

XI

Spring came to town suddenly and caught Pyotr Vasilievich unawares. He fell asleep one night to the furtive whine of a ground wind, and when the shrill tremolo of the alarm clock woke him in the morning he could not believe his eyes. The sound of snow melting and dripping reached him from the street: it seemed deafening.

He cheerfully teased himself. "You've been given one more spring, Lashkov. Rejoice, you old buzzard. Wonder if you'll live to see another."

What nature usually did gradually, unhurriedly, in the course of weeks, it accomplished during the next few days. The snow all melted, buds swelled and burst into green flame, ponds in the neighborhood were cleared of ice. The sky over the town was high and cloudless, steeped in a rich, almost tactile blue.

On one of these spring days that seemed to be made to order, Gupak called. He had looked in on Pyotr Vasilievich soon after Vadim's departure and taken to visiting him frequently since, on the most varied excuses: to find out whether there was any word from Vadim, to greet Pyotr Vasilievich on the occasion of a church feast, to pass on some piece of town news that couldn't wait. At the beginning, Pyotr Vasilievich was irked by his uninvited guest. They had so little in common. But without noticing it himself he became so used to Gupak's visitations that soon he could not do without them. His arguments with Gupak brightened up his lonely attitude to things. Now, after a short break in their meetings, he was frankly delighted by his guest's arrival. He welcomed him with unconcealed excitement.

"Thought you'd quite forgotten an old man, Lev Lvovich. Haven't shown your face for over a week now. I began to wonder if I'd offended you."

Gupak crossed himself, bowing toward the corner where the icon should have been, before offering his host a chilly hand. "What a thing to think! I've been a bit under the weather. As soon as I got up again, I came straight to you. How are you getting on? Some spring, eh? Like in a fairy tale." He walked about the room, rubbing his hands in satisfaction. "God's in his heaven! Wouldn't be a bad idea to take the window frames out, Pyotr Vasilievich. Maybe we could do it between us? Why put it off? It'll air the place and get rid of the damp in no time."

"It can wait. I'm hardly ever at home lately, I've got so many awkward little jobs on my mind. I just sleep here."

"You must have air all the same."

With a single skillful movement, Gupak tore a strip of gummed paper from the slot which held the winter frame. "It'll make you dream better. Help me, Pyotr Vasilievich."

Between them, in the space of half an hour or so, they gave all the windows in the house an appearance more appropriate to the time of year, carried the rubbish out, and, well satisfied with their handiwork, settled down to rest on the bench in the little front garden.

People walked past, vehicles rumbled by. A jet fighter was describing smoky figures-of-eight in a sky cluttered with high-tension cables and television aerials. A power saw was whining hysterically in the builder's yard nearby. Yet the world around them bore the seal of tranquillity, which was, no doubt, why their conversation began placidly and unhurriedly.

"What's the news from Vadim Viktorovich?" Gupak asked with an appearance of casualness. "Does he write?"

"He's fixed himself up as a forester. Working with his great-uncle Andrei. And living with him."

"Where there are seven mouths to feed, an eighth can eat for nothing. I only hope he settles down."

"His great-uncle isn't God Almighty, he can't feed the five thousand."

"Simplifying again, Pyotr Vasilievich. You mustn't reduce the Gospel to a simple collection of miraculous tales like the Greek myths. The Holy Fathers recounted the events of the first coming in a language accessible to the masses. Hence its apparent primitiveness. But the faith can never be overturned by the banalities of practical argument. The Savior shared with us not bread in the literal sense but the bread of truth for all mankind. There was enough of such bread for everyone. Including those five thousand. And for many many millions afterwards."

"Well, that food of his seems to be running out." The spirit of contradiction was taking control. "People are sobering up—and taking to drink. They seek the truth in raw liquor."

"Our people's age of faith, in reality, is only just beginning, Pyotr Vasilievich. To attain greater faith you must first pass through great doubt, and perhaps even through the unholy ordeal of bloodshed. What for many people used to begin in fear and boredom begins now in meekness and humility. People come to the faith with torment and in total self-surrender. Look carefully, Pyotr Vasilievich, there are proofs of it all around you." He was silent for a moment, then lowered his heavy lids, and his voice sank almost to a whisper. "Your daughter has written me a letter. She wants me to have a talk with you."

Pyotr Vasilievich was seized with jealousy and resentment. He had suspected often enough before that his daughter was keeping up her correspondence with Gupak: his familiarity with her life in Central Asia became more obvious every day, and he hardly tried to conceal it in their conversations. But it had never occurred to him that Antonina was capable of hiding things from him and writing about them freely to outsiders. This was something he couldn't understand, and he turned away without concealing his annoyance.

"What's the matter with her now?"

"You're wrong, my dear Pyotr Vasilievich, to take it so much to heart. You must have confessed things more than once to strangers. To a doctor, for instance. It's easier to confess to an outsider because you can always go away and forget him. What is more, my wife and I are not altogether outsiders to your daughter. We share the same faith. That is a detail of some importance in our conversation . . . Antonina had good reasons for turning to me, Pyotr Vasilievich. She loves you and is afraid of grieving you, so she asks my advice."

"Never thought I'd live to see the day!" He was still in the grip of his irritation, but gradually calmed down. "Let's have it, then, what's it all about?"

Gupak informed him in detail and in carefully chosen words what had happened to Nikolai. And—strange as it might seem—the more hopeless Antonina's present situation appeared to be, the more fully he sympathized with her.

"Antonina, Antonina, to think you wouldn't confide in your own father. What am I, a wild beast or something?" He could hardly sit still to the end of the story, and as soon as Gupak was silent he rushed impatiently into action.

"We must send a telegram." Life had acquired a real purpose again. "What is she doing down there all by herself with the child?"

Lev Lvovich had obviously not expected such a quick and definite reaction to his news, and seemed flustered.

"We must get things ready first."

"What do we need? We've got everything. Whatever we're short of, we'll buy."

"The apartment must be put right, Pyotr Vasilievich. A child will be living in it."

"How can we do it in time now? If we hire somebody they'll be messing about for a week. Or longer. We'd be sorry we ever started, so why bother?"

Gupak answered with bated breath. "It needn't take a week. If you call the Gusevs in, they'll manage it in two days."

"The Gusevs?" His old neighbor's name jarred on him, but it was too late to retreat. "If it must be the Gusevs, then it must. Will he take it on, though? He prefers a different sort of client."

Gupak jumped up like one inspired. "Not him! He'll consider it a particular honor." He was bursting with eagerness for immediate action. "No point in delaying, let's go right now."

"Perhaps it won't be convenient. All of a sudden . . . like a bolt from the blue."

"Nothing could be more convenient. He'll simply be pleased."

"Well, in that case . . ."

"Set your mind at rest . . ."

The few people in the street at that time of day looked around in surprise at the two old men, whom nobody in town would ever have expected to see walking along peacefully side by side. But they were oblivious to anyone else. Lost in animated discussion of the jobs to be done, they had crossed the town before they realized it from one end to the other, to where the carved roof ornament of Gusev's house loomed majestically over an outlying suburb.

They found the master of the house himself deepening a drainage ditch along the outer side of his fence. Wiry and strong-boned, he wielded the sharp-edged spade with the rhythmical dexterity of a man used to doing any job conscientiously and thoroughly. When he noticed his guests, Gusev pushed the spade firmly into the ground and wiped the sweat from his brow. His stubborn lips revealed a full set of teeth parted in a friendly but not at all ingratiating smile.

"Well, look who's here! Welcome, dear guests." He turned toward the house. "Mother!"

A woman in an oilcloth apron, not as old as all that, appeared on the high porch beyond the fence, as though she had been awaiting her husband's call. Rubbing her hands on a kitchen towel, she too beamed down at them hospitably.

"You are welcome! Why are you standing outside there? Please come in, dear guests!"

No, his former neighbor Xenia Fyodorovna had scarcely changed at all. Time had merely overlaid her youthful face with a fine web of barely perceptible wrinkles. As he sat at the table on the open veranda, Pyotr Vasilievich watched her surreptitiously; she waited on them swiftly and unobtrusively, taking care to offer him the best bits and the fullest glass, and in his heart he envied his host and his talent for getting the best out of life. "Born with a silver spoon in his mouth, lucky devil."

Slight tipsiness only heightened Gordei's expansive dignity. "Goes without saying! Of course we'll do it. We shan't let you down, Vasilich. I'm not the municipal repairs department when I work, I don't just hope for the best. And I'll give you an honest price. In fact, as a former neighbor, you get a discount anyway. I'll send my boy around first thing in the morning and I'll come along myself toward evening and help him. So that's all settled . . . How are you keeping then, Vasilich?"

"I creak along somehow."

"You're tough. All you Lashkovs have nearly reached the hundred mark. And you're made of the same stuff. You'll last quite a while yet!"

"Some hopes! I'll be lucky to struggle on to eighty. Sometimes when I tie my laces I haven't got the strength to straighten up again. The ground's pulling me down into it." He suddenly intercepted a significant look from Gordei to Gupak. "I'll soon be settling my account with the Almighty."

Gupak glanced at his watch and hurriedly prepared to be off. "Perhaps I'd better be going. They're expecting me."

"Sit down, Lvovich, they'll wait," said Gusev, but he got up to see his guest out.

"No, no, I mustn't set my flock a bad example . . . Thank you for your hospitality."

Pyotr Vasilievich did not fail to notice the look they exchanged, nor the haste with which Gupak took his leave, nor his host's relief when he had gone. The dim suspicion which had risen in his mind at the beginning of their meeting was at last confirmed. "They'd arranged it all in advance, the old devils!" He wasn't aggrieved at their conspiracy—in fact, if anything, he was pleased. The vague attraction exercised by Gusev and his kind was becoming almost irresistible as time went by. An inexplicable aura of strength and dependability which made life seem less worrying and puzzling emanated from these people. When you looked at them, at the strong, firm set of their jaws, you felt sure that life on earth was eternal. The urge to act, to work, pulsed so powerfully in their veins that they would never let it end.

"There's somebody who'll live a while yet." Pyotr Vasilievich nodded toward the door. "Not a single gray hair!"

"He has cancer, Vasilich." Sitting down opposite his guest, Gordei told him this news casually, as though it had no special significance. "He'll drag on for two or three months, no more. So there we are, Vasilich."

"Maybe he'll get over it?" He sighed, alarmed by his own lack of conviction. "It has happened."

"No, he won't get over it," said Gordei, still more calmly and firmly. "I roofed his doctor's house for him. There's no chance of him getting over it. And he knows it."

"He knows?"

"He knows." Gordei looked straight into his eyes, and his gaze made Pyotr Vasilievich realize how utterly blind he had been to the world around him. "So there we are then, Vasilich. If only we had his strength. And his inner light."

"Yes . . ."

Gordei raised his unfinished glass to his guest. "Why shouldn't we be open, Vasilich? I've been wanting to get close to you like this for a long time. It's time we had a heart-to-heart talk. Life's nearly over. All our quarrels are in the past."

"All right, then." His liking for Gusev was growing stronger by the minute. "I've never shammed deafness, you know that."

"That's the stuff." He drained the contents of his glass at a gulp, and fixed Pyotr Vasilievich with light, smiling eyes. "Drink, Vasilich, there's plenty of time. You and I are going to talk about all sorts of things. Nobody will ever tell you the whole truth, except me. They'd be afraid to."

They sat at the table far into the night. Gusev did most of the talking, and Pyotr Vasilievich listened. For the first time, hearing someone else talk about it, he could stand aside and see his life as it looked to those around him. Gordei did not spare his pride or his self-respect. Gordei reminded him of events which he had long forgotten. In his mind's eye, Pyotr Vasilievich saw his whole destiny in perspective, the totality of his successes and mistakes, his workdays and holidays. Summing it all up to himself, he was suddenly sober, devastated by the knowledge that he had lived his life in vain, in pursuit of some poor insubstantial phantom. And then Lashkov wept, wept silently and with relief, and this was the only answer he had for the man who sat in front of him.

XII

Next day Gusev arrived with a tall, thin, already balding young man, obviously another Gusev, whom he pushed gently forward to introduce. "My flesh and blood. He's obviously half-baked, but he knows his job. You won't feel let down. Come outside with me, Vasilich. Let him take a look around and size up the job. We'll have a smoke while we wait."

They settled down on the top step of the porch. The guest lit up, and Pyotr Vasilievich, fighting to overcome his embarrassment, said what he was thinking.

"You'd better name a price. I shouldn't like to die still owing you."

"We'll come to some agreement."

"I'll do my best to see you don't lose."

"I don't want any of your generosity, Vasilich." He sighed sadly. "You'll pay the going rate, and good luck to you. D'you think I'm a profiteer? D'you think I'm avoiding having to work in a factory? It isn't state-paid work I'm afraid of, Pyotr Vasilievich, it's state-paid idleness. Three bosses to every pair of working hands. What's the good of that? And everyone looking for ways to cheat on the job and speed it up. They're only interested in bonuses, not in the job itself. But I'm a craftsman, Vasilich." He almost groaned the word. "A craftsman! D'you know what that means, Vasilich? What's the good of talking!" He stubbed his cigarette on the sole of his shoe, put the butt in his pocket instead of throwing it away, and rose. "I'll be off, I'm up to my neck. I'll come around and keep an eye on things."

Pyotr Vasilievich watched Gusev's erect, youthful figure cross the street with a firm step, and he was frankly envious: "We're the same age, after all. Seems some people are born older than others."

The young Gusev was already moving the unpretentious Lashkov furniture out into the hallway. He worked briskly and almost noiselessly. Objects seemed to arrange themselves, one after another, and of their own volition, into a compact rectangle between the outer wall and the cellar door. Pyotr Vasilievich, helping to drag the sideboard with a plaintive tinkling of crockery through the door, affably asked his name.

The young man dissolved in embarrassed smiles. "Alexei. Didn't my father tell you?"

"He must have thought I knew."

He smiled still more broadly. "That's Dad all over. Thinks a lot of himself. Imagines everybody knows all about him without telling. The old man's tough, you'd have to be pretty smart to put anything past him."

Then between them they tore off the old bug-stained wallpaper and the layers of yellowed newspaper under it. This shared work soothed Pyotr Vasilievich and reassured him that all his recent tasks and anxieties would end well. Unconsciously he began to enjoy himself and to help Alexei with the rest of his job. With a businesslike word here and there they primed and whitened the ceilings in both parts of the house, and painted the window sashes. Then, satisfied with a good afternoon's work, they emptied a quarter-bottle along with a snack hastily prepared by Pyotr Vasilievich. Completely mellowed by now, he wanted to run to the shop for fresh supplies, but his guest resolutely turned his glass upside down.

"I pass, Dad."

"How's that?"

"The old man doesn't like it in the middle of a job."

"So he's strict?"

"I don't know if I'd say that. He isn't exactly strict, but he likes things to be proper. If he takes you down a peg, it's always for a good reason. I started work at the depot, you know. When your Nikolai had all that trouble, my old man fetched me out of there and took me on himself."

"You know Nikolai, then?"

"I should say so."

"I've never had it properly explained to me."

"Well, there was a panic at the depot one time. They always put the pressure on at the end of the month. We were slaving away with no days off, but the plan was going to hell just the same. The town bosses turned up when things were really hot. One of them, the most important one, started yelling and using bad language. Well, Kolya lost his temper and punched him between the eyes . . . He couldn't stand people being unfair. He was one of the best, real good company."

Pyotr Vasilievich had often tried to imagine what sort of man his son-in-law was. They had never really become close. The older man liked Nikolai's seriousness, but had no idea what his previous life had been like, who his friends had been. The younger Gusev's last words, like flashes of distant summer lightning, let Pyotr Vasilievich see the outlines of someone who was strong, a whole man.

"So what did you all do?" Tense and angry, he was reliving that distant moment. "What did you do?"

The young man looked glumly at the floor. "What did we do? You can't get anywhere against people with power."

For some reason Pyotr Vasilievich remembered the buffeting he had taken himself in Moscow offices, from which he had always emerged with a stifling feeling of helplessness and exhaustion. It went against the grain, but he gloomily agreed. "No, you can't get anywhere . . ."

They heard steps outside, then the click of the latch, and Gusev's vigorous tenor floated through the wide open door from the dark, cavernous hallway.

"Some workers! Couldn't leave a light on in the hall." He appeared on the threshold and appraised what they had done with a swift, searching glance. "It'll do. Color's a bit wishy-washy perhaps. Right then, Lekha"—with a brisk nod to his son—"let's have some paste ready. We'll paper it today as well. We can do it as quick as peeing."

Pyotr Vasilievich had watched many craftsmen at work in his time, but had never seen work like this. It wasn't work, it was a religious rite . . . Father and son seemed to compete in deftness and agility. Each harmoniously complemented the movements of the other, as though they were parts of a shuttling device. One after another, lengths of bright springlike wallpaper were aligned and flowed downward right to the baseboard without a single wrinkle. As they worked, they exchanged only the brief essential phrases.

"Straighten it just a bit."

"There you are."

"Bit more to the left."

"That do?"

"Just right."

"Let's have the border."

"One straight run?"

"That'll do."

By nightfall, both halves of the house were dazzlingly smart and new, exuding a pungent smell of paste and paint into the starry darkness. Carefully washing his hands under the tap, old Gusev chuckled proudly at his host.

"Gusev's hand hasn't lost its cunning yet. Look it all over, Vasilich. You won't be able to pick holes in it. I'll get you some bright linoleum by tomorrow. Your grandson will be able to crawl around in safety . . . Lekha, a towel!"

As he was seeing the craftsman off, Pyotr Vasilievich caught Gordei gently by the elbow, but he guessed what was coming and resolutely freed himself. "Forget it, Vasilich. I shan't take a thing from you, except the cost of the material. Not so much as a quarter-kopeck. Don't be offended—just remember that the Gusevs are human, too. So long."

He spoke, and vanished into the night. Pyotr Vasilievich, alone with himself and the measured echo of Gusev's retreating steps, took a long time to recover from his burning embarrassment. "That's Gusev for you! Rubbed my nose in my own mess as if I was a puppy! Well, I suppose I've asked for it."

XIII

He arrived at the station two hours before the train was due, and wandered aimlessly around the half-empty halls in the secret hope of meeting one of his former colleagues. But however hard he peered at the railwaymen he met, he didn't see a single familiar face. "Prewar generation's gradually dying off, be nobody left soon," he grumbled to himself. Until at last, down by the very end of the platform, at the open window of the hot water shed he saw a face he knew, though it was crumpled and somehow flattened by time. The old woman caught his look and smiled toothlessly.

"Hallo, Pyotr Vasilievich."

"Hallo, Tatyana."

He had known Tatyana Govorukhina since she was a little girl. She was the daughter of a trackman at the Bobrikovo halt, and had spent all her life around the railway. She had been a greaser, a train guard, and one of the first women on the footplate, although later on she had mostly killed time in the presidium of meetings large and small. At thirty-five, Govorukhina had married Mishka Zolotarev, an engine driver whose name was on everybody's lips, but the year after, with her first child in her arms, she was taking him parcels in Tula Prison. In those days, Pyotr Vasilievich had still had influence with the local authorities, and, with his usual concern for the fate of fellow railwaymen, he had helped her to find a home and a job. Ever since, Tatyana, who had remained a little girl in his eyes, was always overcome with gratitude on the rare occasions when they met.

"You meeting somebody?" She was still beaming affectionately at him. "Family?"

"Antonina."

"On a visit or for good?"

"For good."

"With Nikolai?"

"She's had a baby." In a town like Uzlovsk even the smallest event could not pass unnoticed, so he accepted it as her due to be well informed on his family affairs. "She's bringing me a grandson!"

"Good for Antonina!" Govorukhina's puffy face went pink with pleasure. "Well done, girl."

"She hasn't let me down." Grateful for her open-hearted friendliness, he found himself being even more forthcoming. "Pyotr they've called him."

"Didn't forget her father, then."

"No, they didn't forget me." He would have liked to add something warm and full of feeling, but at that moment the loudspeaker announced the approach of the Moscow express, and he moved toward the track with an absentminded farewell nod. "So long, Tatyana."

When the train emerged from among the coaches drawn up in the nearby freight station, his heart fluttered violently.

"Perhaps I shan't recognize her with these eyes of mine. I daresay she's had a rough time of it so far from home." His nervous misgivings stayed with him while the windows of coaches with faces pressed to them glided slowly past. He moved unthinkingly along with the train, working off his doubts and worries as he walked.

But as soon as the train shuddered to a stop, Pyotr Vasilievich immediately spotted among the assorted hats, caps, and shawls at the rear of the eighth coach, a dark-blue headscarf tied in the way he remembered. He felt breathless. Blindly pushing his way through the crowd he hurried toward the rear step. His daughter was already looking imploringly toward him, holding her flannelette bundle out in front of her, as though excusing herself and asking for mercy.

"Here you are." He took his grandson from her, forgetting to greet her in his feverish agitation. "Don't hurry . . . that's the way."

"Hallo, Papa," she stammered, pressing her head to his sleeve in relief and gratitude. "It's good to be here."

On the way home, Antonina from time to time glanced inquiringly at her father, to verify first impressions. He sensed her concealed anxiety, and did his best to cheer and reassure her. His grandson, snuffling almost inaudibly in his arms, awakened an aching tenderness. "Listen to you whistling there, Pyotr, son of Nikolai, you sound as if you could sleep forever." As they went through his native settlement he felt proud and gratified whenever he spotted a curtain pulled back in a neighbor's house, or a curious glance or nod from passersby. "The Lashkov breed isn't done for yet, my friends, it lives on!"

At home, Antonina looked around in delight and clapped her hands. "Papa!"

"Couldn't sit around in the muck forever." He was flattered by her approval, but tried to look as indifferent as he could. "And then there's the child."

"It's just like moving into a new house." With practiced ease she removed her first-born's diaper on her father's bed, and invited Pyotr Vasilievich to join in admiring him. "He weighed nearly eight pounds at birth. And he's never once been sick."

"He's a Lashkov." When he looked at the wriggling lump of live flesh he found his lips trembling. "Never any weaklings in our family."

"Please God."

"We shan't leave anything to chance."

"You know what they say about seven nurses forgetting the child."

"Don't worry, we'll keep an eye on him."

Absently exchanging these brief remarks with his daughter, he helped her to lay the table. They sat down and looked into each other's faces for the first time that day. All that they had left unsaid now said itself: life had begun all over again for them, and they tacitly agreed to leave the past out there beyond the threshold.

"I mustn't drink too much, I shall lose my milk." She resolutely checked the bottle which her father was holding out toward her glass. "Just a drop to drink to our meeting, Papa."

"You know best." He filled his own glass to the brim. "Well, here's all the best to both of us."

"Thank you, Papa."

Antonina drank off her share with thoughtful enjoyment, put the glass aside, and got up without touching the snacks.

"I'll feed him and go and lie down. It was a long journey. I've been rocked so much my legs will hardly hold me."

"We haven't had a talk yet."

"We shall do plenty of talking, Papa." She hesitated on the threshold, and there was a hint of sadness in her voice. "We shall have time now."

Pyotr Vasilievich had to recognize that something scarcely perceptible but important about her had changed. There was a new strength and assurance in her gestures, her walk, her speech; faced with it, he was overcome by an unaccountable timidity. This was an Antonina he did not know. "What's bred in the bone is finally coming out this time!"

Left alone, Pyotr Vasilievich was not afraid to admit to himself that he was concluding life where he should have begun it. The causes and connections in the world about him stood out sharply and in depth, like a developed print of something he had only seen in negative. He was amazed by their mysterious rightness, and saw himself for what he really was: a tiny particle of that harmonious organism, existing perhaps at the sorest spot on one of its extremities. The recognition that his "I" was part of an immense and meaningful whole gave Pyotr Vasilievich a feeling of inner peace and equilibrium. His thoughts flowed in easy tranquillity. "So you don't have to look for the truth in somebody else's back yard. It's in ourselves. What Gupak says is right: it wasn't bread He shared with us, but His soul, that's why there was enough for everybody. It's simple enough to give away what belongs to somebody else, but just try to give away what's yours. That must be a good deal harder. Now Gusev doesn't go around talking about justice, he's busy with his work, his craft. When he dies his work will remain. But what about me? What will remain of me when I die? A mere tremor in the air? Hurry up, Lashkov, be quick, before you give up the ghost. Every day's a birthday present, you're coming up to eighty, you know!"

It was the baby crying beyond the partition that brought him out of his half-doze. Through the window he could see a faint sliver of light already inserting itself between the edge of night and the horizon. Quietly, so as not to wake his daughter, he rose and went to her room. Antonina's face looked more youthful and relaxed in the soft glow of the nightlight. Even in sleep, she was still a mother. So that her pose—arm crooked uncomfortably right under her chin—was one of tense watchfulness.

Pyotr Vasilievich cautiously lifted his wailing grandson out of her arms, changed his diaper as best he could, swathed him in a big blanket, and took him out onto the porch. Dawn light was beginning to glow over the distant rooftops, the outlines of houses and trees were becoming clearer and sharper every minute. His grandson, evidently feeling himself secure within a protective embrace, stopped crying, and Pyotr Vasilievich unthinkingly drifted away from the house, to where the asphalt road ran glittering in the early morning light from the edge of the settlement to the horizon. He crossed the street, and walked along the road toward the new dawn.

Listening closely to his grandson's scarcely perceptible breathing, Pyotr Vasilievich felt more and more certain with every step that he himself, and the world about him, were one and infinite. It was no longer mere supposition! He knew that the ascending spiral, in which he would soon complete his part of the journey, would be continued by the next Lashkov, his grandson—Pyotr Nikolaevich—who would assume his alloted share of the burden in this mysterious and ennobling cycle.

Morning lit up the road in a single blaze to the far horizon, and Pyotr Vasilievich went down it with his grandson in his arms. He went, and he knew. He knew, and he believed.

AND THE SEVENTH DAY DAWNED—
THE DAY OF HOPE AND RESURRECTION . . .

A NOTE ABOUT THE AUTHOR

Vladimir Maximov was born in 1932. His parents perished either in the Stalinist purges of the thirties or during the war, and he was brought up in various orphanages. His first trade was that of a bricklayer, and he traveled to various remote parts of Russia as an apprentice worker. He began writing at the age of twenty. In 1956 he published his first collection of poems, and this was followed in 1961 by a long short story that appeared in a collection by K. Paustovsky. In 1964 Maximov published a play. His first novel, *Man Alive,* appeared in 1965, and in that year also he became a regular contributor to the conservative literary magazine *Oktyabr.* His association with this journal ended in 1967, when, without explanation, his name and his writing disappeared from its pages. In 1968 he was rebuked by Moscow's writers organization for having signed a declaration in protest against the trial of two Soviet dissidents, Galanskov and Ginzburg, and in November 1969 he protested the expulsion of Solzhenitsyn from the Writer's Union. In the fall of 1973 he himself was expelled from the Writers' Union, and in 1974 was exiled from his country.

A NOTE ON THE TYPE

The text of this book was set on the Linotype in Janson, a recutting made direct from type cast from matrices long thought to have been made by the Dutchman Anton Janson, who was a practicing type founder in Leipzig during the years 1668–87. However, it has been conclusively demonstrated that these types are actually the work of Nicholas Kis (1650–1702), a Hungarian, who most probably learned his trade from the master Dutch type founder Dirk Voskens. The type is an excellent example of the influential and sturdy Dutch types that prevailed in England up to the time William Caslon developed his own incomparable designs from these Dutch faces.

This book was composed, printed, and bound by The Book Press, Brattleboro, Vermont. The typography and binding design are by Christine Aulicino.